# SWORDS IN THE DESERT

## A NOVEL BASED ON THE BOOK OF LUKE
## DOUG PETERSON

Ó 'Shea Books

To Cornerstone Fellowship and Urbana Theological Seminary

**Swords in the Desert**

Copyright © 2025 by Doug Peterson

Cover illustration by DogEared Design

Map by Santiago Romero

ALL RIGHTS RESERVED. No part of this publication may be reproduced, stored in a retrieval system, or transmitted in any form or by any means—electronic, mechanical, photocopying, recording, or otherwise—without the prior written permission of the publisher and copyright owners.

Published by O'Shea Books

Champaign, IL 61821

www.bydougpeterson.com

ISBN: 978-1-7358151-3-8

# NOVELS BY DOUG PETERSON

### KINGDOM COME SERIES
### Book 1: *Thrones in the Desert*

The story of Jesus, seen through the eyes of five fictional characters—a slave, a guard in Herod's palace, a Pharisee, the daughter of a Zealot, and a tax collector. They all encounter Jesus, who overthrows the thrones in their lives.

### Book 2: *Swords in the Desert*

Book 2 follows Jesus's footsteps as He heads steadily toward Jerusalem. *Swords in the Desert* also continues to follow five fictional characters.

### NORTH-SOUTH SERIES
### Book 1: *The Vanishing Woman*

Ellen and William Craft escape when Ellen poses as a white man while her husband pretends to be her slave—a true story.

## Book 2: *The Disappearing Man*

Henry "Box" Brown mails himself to freedom. He ships himself in a box from Richmond to Philadelphia—a true story.

## Book 3: *The Tubman Train*

Harriet Tubman's name is legendary, but most people do not know her complete story. *The Tubman Train* is one of the first novels to tackle her remarkable life.

## Book 4: *The Lincoln League*

John Scobell, the first African-American spy for the U.S. intelligence service, operates deep within Confederate lines during the Civil War. Based on a true story.

## Book 5: *The Dixie Devil*

André Cailloux is the forgotten first black hero of the American Civil War. This is the story of André and his wife, Felicie, as they try to survive in the turbulent world of New Orleans.

## ANNIE O'SHEA MYSTERIES
### *The Puzzle People*

A suspense novel that spans the rise and fall of the Berlin Wall. Inspired by real events.

# HOLY LAND IN THE TIME OF JESUS

# CAST OF CHARACTERS

## Main Characters

**Eliana**—The daughter of a Zealot freedom fighter
**Asaph**—A tax collector
**Sveshtari**—A former bodyguard for Herod Antipas
**Keturah**—A woman who escaped slavery in the House of Herod
**Nekoda**—A priest and member of the Sadducee party

## Supporting Cast

**Chaim**—Nekoda's younger brother
**Malachi**—Asaph's assistant, a fellow tax collector
**Zuriel and Gershom**—Childhood rivals of Asaph
**Rufus**—A captain in the House of Herod Antipas
**Judah**—A Zealot freedom fighter and father of Eliana
**Lavi**—Eliana's dog
**Babette**—Keturah's daughter

## Figures from History

**Jesus**—The Messiah, the Son of God
**Mary**—The mother of Jesus
**Peter**—A fisherman and disciple of Jesus
**Joanna**—Wife of the head of Herod's household
**Herod Antipas**—Tetrarch (ruler) of Galilee and Perea
**Pontius Pilate**—Roman prefect (governor) of Judea

# 1

## Luke, Chapter 13

### Eliana: Magdala

Eliana slipped down the narrow, winding streets of Magdala on this dry, dusty day. The street ahead was empty of life, but as she turned a corner, a man darted out from behind a small, squat building. He stepped directly in front of Eliana, stopping her dead in her tracks.

It was Zuriel, a recent addition to the Zealot freedom fighters led by Eliana's father. He put his hands on his hips. "And where do you think you're going?"

Without a word, Eliana tried to slip around him, but Zuriel blocked her move. He put his hands on her shoulders, an audacious thing for a man to do to an unmarried woman. Eliana shook free and scuttled backward. She glared at Zuriel, a stocky man with thick, curly hair and a squared-off jawline. His black hair was tinged with glimmers of gray.

Eliana sighed. "Jesus is teaching at the synagogue. I am going to hear him speak if you must know."

"But your father does not approve of Jesus, the Nazarene."

"I am aware of that—and he knows that I follow Jesus." Eliana made another move to go around Zuriel, but he slid to the side, continuing to block her path. His smile sparked with menace.

"Step aside," Eliana said. "My father did not forbid me from attending synagogue."

"But he would if he knew Jesus was teaching."

"So, you can read his mind?"

"I know his wishes."

"You know nothing of my father. You joined the Zealots only recently, which surprised me. You were never one to fight for a cause other than yourself."

Zuriel took a step closer. "So, who's the mind reader now? You underestimate my motives, Eliana. I heard about what happened on the Cliffs of Arbel, so I decided to join the Zealots."

The Cliffs of Arbel looked down on Magdala, protruding like the bow of a great ship. On those cliffs, the Romans had lowered themselves in baskets, intending to wipe out a nest of Zealot freedom fighters, which included her father. Instead, the Zealots were ready for them, and the Romans were humiliated.

Zuriel stabbed the air, as if he were wielding an invisible knife. "I am good with a sling and a blade, and I thought I would add my talents to the freedom cause."

Eliana stared at him for a beat. "Yes. You were always good with a rock."

Zuriel smiled back. If he was angry that she brought up memories of their clash as children, he didn't show it. When she was ten years old, Zuriel and his friend Gershom had threatened to pelt her with rocks. But Asaph, her closest friend at the time, beat Zuriel to the ground. Now, all three men were Zealots under the leadership of her father.

"I have put my weapons to better uses since those days," Zuriel said. "I'm delivering blows against the Romans."

"Don't get ahead of yourself. You have not yet seen action."

Zuriel's smirk vanished instantly; he looked like he had swallowed a handful of sour grapes. "I willingly give my life to fight Rome for the cause of the Jewish people, and yet you mock me?"

"I do not mock you. I simply remind you that you are new to the Zealots and need to maintain a degree of humility. You have a lot to learn from my father—and from Asaph and Gershom."

Eliana glanced at Zuriel's hand, which curled into a clenched fist. Would he dare strike her? If he hit her, Eliana's father would have him severely punished and then banished from the Zealots.

Just then, a small dust devil rushed toward them from behind, picking up dirt from the dry ground and swirling it in a tight circle, as if the very earth were trying to rise up and attack them. As Eliana became immersed in the spiraling sand, she pressed an arm across her mouth. Briefly, Zuriel's body became a shadow in the whirlwind, so she took the opportunity to step around him, plunging from the dust's embrace and striding back into the sunlight.

When she looked over her shoulder, the dust devil had moved on, and Zuriel was glaring at her.

"Your father will not be pleased when I tell him you are listening to Jesus teach!"

"Tell my father he is welcome to join me!"

Before Zuriel could answer, Eliana hurried down the street and made a right turn toward the synagogue. She plunged into the stream of people flowing through the open door.

The synagogue in Magdala was stunning, with dark red frescoes framed in yellow. The central room featured six pillars with the same rich red color. Eliana found a spot on the stone benches that hugged the walls.

In the center of the room was a rectangular stone, beautifully engraved to represent the Temple in Jerusalem. It served as the base for a podium from which the Torah would be read. On the side of the stone facing south—in the direction of Jerusalem—were the seven lamps of the menorah. These seven lamps, according to the prophet Zechariah, represent the seven eyes of God, the seven spirits that search the entire world, peering into people's lives and drawing them toward Him. Eliana felt the eyes upon her, drawing her out of darkness and into the sevenfold, all-embracing light of the menorah.

The *hazzan* brought out the first scroll—the first reading of the Law. The readers were not allowed to speak more than one verse by heart. The rest had to be read from the scrolls—and the *hazzan* stood nearby to correct any mistakes. The words were precious, like jewels, and the *hazzan* was their guardian.

Jesus was the seventh and final reader of the day, the *maphtir*. As he read from the prophets, Eliana felt Jesus's eyes land on her; like the menorah eyes, she felt him drawing her toward him, seeking her, protecting her, filling her with light.

Jesus had just started talking about the Kingdom of God when there arose a sudden stir at the door. People parted to make way for an old woman who was bent over so severely that her only view of life was of her own feet. Eliana had seen this woman before, but she couldn't recall her name. People said the woman had been bent over for eighteen years. *Eighteen years staring at the ground!* Her body had forced her into the perpetual bow of a slave.

Eliana knew what it was like to be enslaved, for her mind had bowed down to the demon Cavel for many years—before Jesus and his disciples set her free. But even in the deepest pit, she could at least lift her head and raise her eyes to the mountains. There were no mountains in this woman's line of sight—only insects and other creatures of the dust and dirt.

Jesus paused in his teaching. He watched while a man stood to give up his space for the old woman to sit on the bench. The woman groaned as she lowered her distorted body onto the stone; but even seated, the poor woman's view was of the ground, as if she were in the process of leaning over to tighten her sandals. As Jesus moved toward her, people began to murmur. It was the Sabbath, and Eliana wondered whether Jesus would heal this woman on the day when all work—including healings—was forbidden. Would he dare?

Eliana hoped he would. She *prayed* he would. She closed her eyes and bowed her head. It occurred to her that by bowing in prayer, she put herself in the same position as this woman.

When Eliana looked back up, she saw Jesus come to a stop, an arm's length from the woman. The woman may not have been able to lift her head, but she seemed to sense agitation and anticipation on all sides; surely, she could also sense the presence of the teacher. She strained to lift her head, to look into Jesus's eyes, but it was fruitless.

Fragments from the prophet Isaiah sprinkled into Eliana's mind as she prayed. *Bind up the brokenhearted, bestow a crown of beauty on this woman, raise her up like an oak of righteousness, proclaim freedom for this captive!*

Finally, Jesus spoke: "Rise and come forward, woman."

As typical, Jesus asked the sufferer to become part of the process—to take a step forward in faith. The woman did not respond immediately. She seemed confused. Because she couldn't look up, was she uncertain whether Jesus spoke to her? The woman seated to her right whispered into her ear and then helped the old woman to her feet. Together, they shuffled forward, stopping before the teacher.

Eliana leaned forward in her seat, holding her breath.

Jesus placed both hands on the woman's shoulders as gently as two birds alighting. "Woman, you are set free from your infirmity."

*Set free.* Eliana pictured cords of taut rope snapping and springing loose as if cut by an axe.

The woman slowly adjusted her gaze, her back straightening, her bowed head tilting up, up, until she stared into the eyes of Jesus. Her back, which had been locked into place, broke free from its imprisoned pose—and a smile broke across her face.

She looked around in wonderment. "Praise God for His mercies abundant!"

People leaped to their feet, some shouting in shock, some celebrating, some protesting. A few men began to argue that healing on the Sabbath was a form of work. But Eliana, knowing what it was like to be freed from bondage, stretched her arms wide and proclaimed her praises, trying to drown out any bellows of anger.

"The righteous will flourish like a palm tree, they will grow like a cedar of Lebanon!" she shouted, drawing on the Psalms of David and emphasizing the image of a tall, straight, strong tree.

Two women sitting nearby cast judgmental eyes in her direction, but Eliana would not be seated—or silenced.

"Planted in the house of the Lord, they will flourish in the courts of our God! They will still bear fruit in old age, they will stay fresh and green, proclaiming, 'The Lord is upright'!"

"Silence, woman!" shouted a man, seated in her row.

"Sit down," growled another, this one at her side. "You are causing a scene."

"Jesus is the one creating the scene—and thank God he is."

Before the man could respond, their attention was drawn to the synagogue leader who shot to his feet and moved swiftly toward Jesus. His face was red, and perspiration beaded on his forehead. As he approached Jesus, he wouldn't look the teacher directly in the eyes. Instead, he turned to the people gawking from their seats.

"There are six days for work!" the synagogue leader shouted to the crowd. "So come and be healed on those days, not on the Sabbath!"

Although the synagogue leader still would not make eye contact, Jesus seemed determined to confront him. "You hypocrites! Doesn't each of you on the Sabbath untie your ox or donkey from the stall and lead it out to give it water?"

That was true. Releasing animals to give them water was one exception to the rule that forbids the tying and untying of knots on the Sabbath.

Jesus motioned toward the woman who continued to beam upward at the ceiling—a perspective she hadn't seen in a long, long time. "Then should not this woman, a daughter of Abraham, whom Satan has kept bound for eighteen long years, be set free on the Sabbath day from what bound her?"

The synagogue leader turned a deeper shade of red. He cast a quick glance at Jesus, but just as quickly looked away. He still would not make eye contact. He was at a loss for words.

Jesus was not done. "What is the Kingdom of God like? What shall I compare it to? It is like a mustard seed, which a man took and planted in his garden. It grew and became a tree, and the birds perched in its branches."

Once again, here was the image of a tree, standing tall and straight like this woman now did. She was a full member of the Kingdom of God, a branch that still bore fruit, even in her old age. The Kingdom, like all things, is born of seeds and small beginnings, and Eliana sensed that she was part of a miraculous movement, about to burst from the soil. It was happening right here, right now. The Kingdom of God, buried underground, was breaking out from the earth, stretching for the light of the Lord.

The service ended, and Eliana floated on a wave of hope as she exited the synagogue. She tried to get close to Jesus, but he was pressed on all sides by men, most of them challenging him about the miracle he had just performed. She would talk to him later.

"Eliana!" Her father's voice cracked the air.

She turned to see her father standing before her, with Zuriel on one side and Gershom on the other. Zuriel had made good on his threat to inform her father that she had gone to hear Jesus teach. Her father stood before her, his arms across his chest. His eyes were dark. Had he come to apprehend her like a common criminal?

"Yes, Abba?"

"It is time for you to come home."

"Yes, Abba." Eliana felt like a child again, despite being over forty years of age. She looked down at the ground, a posture of subservience, like the woman who had been bent over for eighteen years. But even with her eyes downcast, she felt her father's gaze boring into her, bending her to his will.

Zuriel, Gershom, and her father escorted her back to the lodging where many Zealots were staying in Magdala. But truth be told, it felt more like she was being hauled back to prison.

## Keturah

Keturah lowered her head as her heart began to race. Two men approached—unsavory sorts. One large, one small, both scarred on their faces. Where was Sveshtari? He told her to wait for him while he went to collect food, so she sat down on a flat stone in the fish-processing sector of Magdala. Directly behind her was a vat of salted fish.

"Greetings, woman," said the smaller man, who carried a fishy smell on his stained robe.

She kept her head down. "Shalom."

"I couldn't help but notice the ink on your forehead."

Keturah's hand flew to her forehead, confirming her fear. She had inadvertently let her headdress slide up, revealing some of the remaining dabs of ink on her skin. Although Sveshtari had been working hard to remove her tattoo, there were faint remnants of a couple of the words in the phrase that once blazed across her face: "Arrest me, for I have run away."

Keturah had once been a slave, but she escaped, only to be recaptured and tattooed for the crime of stealing herself from her master. Now, she was on the run for a second time—and the tattoo was not completely gone.

*Where was Sveshtari? Where was he when she needed him?*

Despite being believers in the gods, Keturah and Sveshtari had blended in with the followers of Jesus, hoping to lose themselves in the crowd as it passed through Magdala. She looked around, trying to catch the eyes of a sympathetic soul to rescue her from these two men. But the only person in sight was far down the street, busily placing fish in a layer of salt in another rectangular vat.

The tall man loomed over her, as silent as the stone that she sat on. The small man crouched beside her and reached his hand out, pushing her headdress even higher. "That certainly looks like a slave tattoo to me."

Keturah raised her head and glared. The man was missing most of his upper teeth. His breath was also fishy—the kind of fish that had been out in the sun too long.

"It is not a slave tattoo," she said, trying not to breathe through her nose.

The man smiled. "Do not be afraid to admit if you are an escaped slave. I will help you find freedom."

That was an obvious lie. The man was probably a *plagiarist*—one who specialized in stealing slaves from other masters and making them his own. *Plagiarists* pretended to help slaves escape, only to lure them into a trap.

"It is not a slave tattoo," she repeated.

"I think it is. Do you think it is?" the man asked, turning to his taller friend.

The other man was a giant. As he leaned down, it was like like a tree bending in the wind. "Looks like it to me."

"Then you need to do something about your eyesight," came a voice from behind.

Keturah shot a look over her shoulder and spotted Sveshtari approaching with several fish in his hands. She had never been happier to see him. Sveshtari, a former bodyguard in Herod's palace, struck a fierce figure, with intense eyes beneath growling eyebrows. His face was framed by a brown hood, tattered at the fringes.

"And who are you?" The small man rose to his feet.

"I am her husband, her stronghold. She belongs to me," Sveshtari lied, handing the fish to Keturah. She would never think of Sveshtari as her husband, never in a million years, but she was fine with the lie, given the circumstances.

"Then why does your wife have the signs of a slave tattoo on her forehead?"

"We are Thracians. Her tattoo is a mark of glory."

It was true that Sveshtari was a Thracian. For Thracians, tattoos were something to flaunt, a source of pride.

"If it's a mark of glory, then why are you trying to remove it?" The little man was unrelenting.

"We are following Jesus, and we no longer believe it is fitting to have the tattoo of a goddess on her forehead."

"The tattoo of a goddess?" The small man leaned over and peered down at Keturah. "Let me see it again."

"You want to see it?" Sveshtari asked. "Do you really want to see it?"

The small man paused before nodding.

"Then lean in closer."

The small man didn't move at first. He stared at Sveshtari for a few heartbeats before doing as he said. The man leaned closer to Keturah, putting him slightly off balance. Sveshtari worked with that forward momentum, grabbing a fistful of the man's hair and hurling him into the nearby vat of fish. Before the tall man could come to his partner's aid, Sveshtari sprang into a fighting position, avoiding the big fellow's clumsy swing and driving his fist into his throat. The giant buckled, clutching his airpipe and gasping for air.

Sveshtari drew out his knife and stuck it into one of the nostrils of the small man, who was slipping and sliding on the fish in the vat. With the knife in his nostril, he wisely tried to remain perfectly still.

"The next time you bother my wife, you're both dead men."

Lowering his blade and taking Keturah by the hand, he drew her away from the still-stunned slave catchers. Keturah ventured a backward look and saw the big man struggling for breath, while the small man tried to explain to a fish producer why he had been flopping around in the vat of salted fish.

With their own fresh fish in hand, she and Sveshtari vanished into the Magdala market.

The next day, there was still no sign of the slave catchers. Keturah prayed that the two men had moved on to easier prey. She stared into a silver plate and studied her distorted reflection. The morning sun glistened on her crown of long, black hair, and her brown eyes showed white pinpoints of reflected light. She smiled, for the tattoo on her forehead had almost vanished.

Sveshtari peered over her shoulder. "It looks good."

"Thank you," she said. Grudgingly.

"One or two more treatments, and it will be gone completely." Sveshtari drew Keturah's red headdress down to cover the faint ink marks on her forehead.

Sveshtari had been making regular applications of ointment over the past thirty days to remove the tattoo—and it seemed to have done the trick. She was indebted to him, for both removing the tattoo and providing protection. Still, how could anything make up for the pain he caused her? He had killed her father who had attempted to assassinate Herod Antipas. As a one-time bodyguard in Herod's palace, Sveshtari said he had no choice; it was his duty to protect the tetrarch.

"Climb on. It's time we made for Joanna's." Sveshtari extended a hand. He eased her up and onto the donkey. She loathed his touch. Keturah made it clear that they could never go back to being lovers because of what he had done. He argued that if he had preserved her father's life, Herod would have had him tortured and then killed slowly and agonizingly. At least her father's death was swift and relatively painless.

It all made logical sense, but Keturah could not, would not, ignore the bleak fact that Sveshtari was the one who slit her father's throat. Keturah had come to tolerate Sveshtari's presence only because she needed his protection.

Jesus was working his way down to Jerusalem, although so far it had been slow-going as the teacher stopped to preach in various towns and synagogues. They were expecting to leave soon for Scythopolis, a route that would continue to take them south, hugging the Jordan River.

Sveshtari took the reins of the donkey and walked in front, leading the animal along. They traveled in silence as they made their way to Joanna's lodging, where Keturah's former mistress greeted them with dinner.

Keturah had to remind Sveshtari to wash his hands before the meal—a Jewish custom that she found pleasing. When washing hands, they also had to make sure the water was pure—that nothing had fallen into it—and they had to use a quarter of a log of water, equal to about one and a half eggshells. For the Hebrews, even handwashing was layered with rules.

Joanna gave Sveshtari the place of honor at her table that evening as they all settled down on cushions. Joanna took a bite of a fig and swallowed. "My friends, do not be concerned about food and lodging along the way. I will meet all your needs."

Sveshtari waved off the offer. "That is not necessary. I can take care of myself and Keturah."

Keturah wished he would speak for himself. Sharing was what the followers of Jesus did, so why turn down Joanna's generosity? She was a wealthy woman.

"Everyone along the road needs help from others," Joanna reminded Sveshtari.

"And we thank you, *Domina*," said Keturah, still in the habit of addressing her as a slave would. She had once served Joanna in Herod's palace.

Sveshtari bowed to Joanna, a Jewess who now followed Jesus. "I too thank you for your kind offer, but we have resources. I have been hired by one of the disciples as a bodyguard."

This was news to Keturah. "A bodyguard? I cannot imagine that Jesus would ever seek a bodyguard."

"It's not for Jesus."

Joanna rubbed her forehead. "Then who are you protecting?"

Sveshtari paused as they watched a man being carried past the window on a stretcher. There was no shortage of sick people wherever Jesus went.

"I am protecting the disciple in charge of the money. He asked me to guard him and the treasury."

"Oh." Keturah wondered if Jesus knew about such an arrangement. "And which disciple is that?"

"The one they call Judas Iscariot."

## Eliana

Eliana rose before the sun to flee from her father.

Magdala was quiet, except for the occasional cries of distant jackals. With a bundle of clothes in her arms, she crept into the house's central courtyard, where several men slept on the floor on mats. All of them were Zealots, like her father. Enemies of Rome. Moonlight poured into the courtyard, giving the shadows a bluish-black tint.

Eliana looked down at her dog, Lavi, who followed at her heels, and she whispered the word "quiet." Levi was a medium-sized dog, but as strong as stone with a muscular neck, a short foreface, and a fierce bite.

She had trained him to respond to the word "quiet," and she was confident he would not bark. When her eyes had adjusted to the dark, she slunk across the courtyard, careful not to trip on any of the shadow-draped hulks of slumbering men. Lavi scurried after her, also careful to sidestep or hop over the men. Eliana knew that Asaph would be standing guard during the fourth watch, which was why she chose this time and day to leave. Asaph loved her, so surely he would let her go without sounding an alarm.

One of the sleeping men stirred, and Eliana paused, holding her breath. She was like a thief in the night, stealing her father's greatest possession—herself. Seeing Jesus heal that old woman, bent over for years, had sealed her decision. She would leave her father and join the Nazarene.

When the man ceased his murmuring and moving, Eliana resumed her escape. One of the Zealots, her old friend Gershom, was sprawled in front of the door on the opposite side of the courtyard. She stepped directly over him while Lavi hopped over his prone body.

The courtyard door creaked when she moved it, but Gershom didn't budge. Letting out a held breath, she slipped through the door and hurried across the room where the animals were kept—three donkeys and two goats.

Although a donkey would ease her travels, she had decided against taking one of the animals because it wouldn't be right. It was bad enough that she was stealing herself from her father; she wouldn't take one of his animals too. Besides, she was on her way to join Jesus, and most of his followers traveled by foot. She moved through the room quickly, before the animals could react to her dog's presence.

Jesus was the protector of her heart, and she was determined to be with him. But Jesus's words were often a puzzle. He spoke of love, but he also said he did not come to bring peace.

*I did not come to bring peace, but a sword. For I have come to turn a man against his father, a daughter against her mother, a daughter-in-law against her mother-in-law—a man's enemies will be the members of his own household.*

With Lavi at her heels, Eliana stepped outside, pulling her cloak tightly around her shoulders and shivering in the fresh morning breeze. Jesus's followers were camped just south of Magdala. She could reach them by sunrise.

As she took her first step toward a new life, Asaph strode out of the shadows, and she stifled a shout. Lavi snarled, baring his teeth; if Eliana hadn't held him back, Lavi might've sunk his teeth in Asaph's leg.

Asaph blocked her way. "Eliana, what do you think you are doing?"

"Quiet," she hissed. "You're going to wake my father."

"Perhaps he needs to be awakened."

Eliana had been certain he would let her go without a fuss, but his expression was severe. Not the look of an ally.

"I am going to Jesus's camp."

"Without saying goodbye to your father?"

"You know that if I did, he would not let me go. I must leave in the night."

Asaph put a hand on her arm. "You were snatched away from your father once. Don't do it again."

When Lavi let out a low growl, Asaph removed his hand.

If Eliana hadn't been so concerned about making noise, she would have slapped Asaph hard. How dare he compare what she was doing now with the last time she was separated from her father! She was just a child when brigands kidnapped her near Bethlehem and sold her into slavery. Today, she was leaving on her own free will.

Eliana glared. "If my father wants to be with me, he can follow Jesus too."

"A daughter doesn't dictate to a father."

"I am not dictating. He can *choose* to go with me using his own free will."

"But your behavior is rebellion against your own father."

"And my father knows that rebellion is sometimes necessary. He has spent most of his life subverting Rome."

"You're comparing your father to Rome? He loves you."

Eliana felt the tears of weariness building, but she was determined to hold them in check. Asaph was right. Her father was not Rome. He loved her, and she loved him.

Asaph stared at her with a growing softness in his eyes. He pushed back his loosely curled black hair, which draped down over his forehead. She could sense that Asaph wanted to put his arms around her, but he didn't dare. It would not be proper, and besides, Lavi would take a piece out of him if he tried. Asaph wanted to someday make her his wife, but so did Gershom and Chaim. At just over forty years old, she was ancient for a bride. But it still seemed as if everyone wanted to stake a claim on her.

She had made her choice. She would give her life to Jesus completely. She would lose her life in the rabbi. *Whoever finds their life will lose it, and whoever loses their life for my sake will find it.*

"Stay." Asaph moved closer, triggering another growl from Lavi.

Asaph backed up a step.

"I can't stay," she said.

"You mean you *won't* stay?"

"I can't and I won't. Don't tell my father you saw me. Just pretend this is all a dream."

"He will blame me for letting you go."

"It's your job to protect the men from a surprise attack. It's not your job to prevent people from leaving."

"I don't think your father will see it that way. Please. Just wait until the morning light before you leave. Tell your father goodbye. Don't break his heart a second time."

"I didn't break his heart the first time. The brigands who captured me did that." She injected as much anger into her voice as possible while still speaking in a whisper.

"I'm sorry, I didn't mean . . ."

"Shalom, Asaph." She made a move to go.

"Eliana..."

Before Asaph could say another word, two more figures appeared from the darkness—Zuriel and Gershom. Eliana was tempted to run, but she didn't dare. Zuriel brandished a sword, and he wouldn't hesitate to kill her dog.

"What's going on?" Gershom demanded.

Asaph stepped between Eliana and the other two men. "This is none of your business."

"It isn't proper for you two to secretly meet, especially when Asaph is on duty."

Asaph scoffed. "We're not secretly meeting. Eliana is planning to leave us to follow Jesus."

"She's going nowhere." Zuriel waved his sword in the moonlight.

"Put that thing away," Gershom growled, but Zuriel continued to brandish his weapon. Then Gershom turned to Eliana and tried to speak in soothing tones, but it came across as if he were talking to a child. "You cannot leave without your father's blessing. You know that."

She had been over all of this with Asaph, and she was in no mood for more argument.

When Zuriel grabbed her by the arm, Lavi lunged and nipped him in the leg. As Zuriel raised his sword to strike her dog, Eliana covered Lavi with her body. Asaph shoved Zuriel back two steps with a slam to the chest. Zuriel staggered, recovered, and pointed his sword at Asaph. Eliana was certain that blood was going to be spilled.

"Draw your weapon!" Zuriel spat at Asaph.

Asaph started to go for his sword, but Gershom stepped between the two men. "Stop it, both of you."

By this time, the household had been roused and torchlights were lit. Several other men staggered sleepily into the open air, and Eliana expected that her father would be confronting her next.

She slouched to the ground, drew Lavi into her lap, and wept. How could she have reached this point? How could she have ever foreseen that she would become a prisoner of her own father?

## Sveshtari

Sveshtari and Keturah made their way south amid the multitude, which seemed more like a large family than a large army. He and Keturah continued to put on their act, behaving as Jews, with Chaim serving as their instructor. Chaim was the brother of Nekoda, a Sadducee priest, but he had also become a follower of Jesus. Sveshtari had a difficult time understanding or even taking seriously some of the finer points of Jewish law that Chaim tried to teach him.

That evening, around a campfire, Sveshtari tossed a stick into the blaze and turned to Chaim. "Let me understand this. I cannot place an egg too close to a kettle because it might become slightly cooked, and cooking on the Sabbath is forbidden."

"Correct."

"But I can break an egg on a stone and allow the sun to cook it naturally because the heat of the sun is not under the same Sabbath laws as the heat started by a man."

"Exactly."

"I can also tie a bucket with a linen cord or belts, but I cannot use ordinary rope on the Sabbath."

"That's right. But judging by the smirk on your face, I suspect you do not appreciate these rules."

Sveshtari leaned back and grinned. "It's very difficult to be a Jew on the Sabbath. But what I'd most like to know, Chaim, is whether kissing is allowed on the Sabbath." He cast a knowing glance at Keturah.

Keturah rolled her eyes, while Chaim folded his arms across his chest. "Now I know you are making light of the Sabbath," he said.

"I am serious. Could I kiss Keturah, for example, if I wanted to on the Sabbath?"

"Yes, you could. The goal of the Sabbath is to make room for joy, rest, and holiness."

"Kissing Keturah would certainly bring joy."

"But would it bring holiness?" Chaim said, playing along.

"I don't know." Sveshtari turned to face Keturah. "Keturah, would it bring holiness if I kissed you on the Sabbath?"

Even in the firelight, he could see her grin. "Kindling a fire is one of the thirty-nine forbidden activities on the Sabbath," she said.

This triggered a blast of laughter from Sveshtari and Chaim.

Chaim tossed a stick of wood into the flames. "Wise response."

"Regardless, tonight is not the Sabbath," Sveshtari said. "So, nothing is stopping us from kindling a flame."

"That's not true. *I* am stopping us." Keturah stirred the flames with a stick, kicking up a cloud of sparks. "If you produce fruit in the next year, then maybe I will consider kissing you."

"And what kind of fruit do you expect me to produce?"

Keturah's smile slowly faded, and she stared into the fire. "I expect you to give me the fruit of atonement."

Sveshtari scowled. How many times did he have to seek atonement from Keturah? He had already risked his life to save her—twice. He looked at Keturah and tried to make light of her deadly serious words.

"So, you are telling me that there is hope for a kiss?" he asked, their eyes locking across the fire.

"There is always hope."

## Eliana

Eliana retreated to the corner of the room, pulling her chair against the wall. Lavi sat by her side, licking her hand furiously. Even though she was forty-three years old, she felt like a child again, forced to sit in the corner as punishment. When she was growing up, her father had used a stick to discipline her little brother, but he spared the rod when it came to his only daughter. She spent a lot of time sitting in corners as a young girl.

Just as in childhood, Eliana's father stood before her with his arms folded across his chest. His mouth was a tight line, his jaw clenching and unclenching. She could see his cheekbone pop.

Eliana bowed her head as she spoke. "Why should you stop me from following Jesus?"

"Because Jesus is not a true prophet," her father said. "No true Jewish prophet would tell you to turn your back on your father."

"I am not turning my back on you by following Jesus. You said yourself that I cannot continue living with you in the Zealot camp. It's too dangerous."

"And where do you think you'll be living if you follow Jesus? You'll be in camps much of the time! It is not proper or safe without a man's protection!"

Eliana scratched Lavi behind the ears. "Yours is an armed camp, stirring rebellion. It, too, is no place for a woman."

"So, an *unarmed* camp, stirring rebellion, is better? With Jesus, you will be in even more danger than if you stayed with us. I assumed you would live in a village, along with the other wives."

*The other wives.* It appeared that her father had already married her off. But to which man? Asaph, Gershom, or Chaim? Two of these men had just betrayed her, preventing her from escaping into the night.

On the other hand, her father might be right that she would be in even more danger in Jesus's camp. The crowds following Jesus had swollen to the thousands, and the prophet was marching them all in the direction of Jerusalem. Pilate and Herod will surely see them as a threat to their thrones. They might even decide to massacre them all and wash their hands of the Christ.

Eliana raised her head to look her father in the eyes. "Jesus is the Chosen One. I must follow him, whatever the cost." As if to reinforce her words, Lavi let out a low growl in her father's direction.

"What authority does Jesus have in your life? I am your father, and you are an unmarried woman! I am your covering, your protection!"

"Where were you when I was ten years old? Or eleven? Or twelve? Where were you when men started passing me around like a plate of food?"

The moment those words flew from her mouth, she knew she should not have said them. It wasn't fair to remind her father that she had been snatched right under his nose when they were on the run and hiding in caves near Bethlehem. It wasn't his fault. She knew that, but she wanted to hurt him.

She succeeded.

For a moment, she thought her father was going to slap her. But he had never raised a hand against her, and he held back. He stood over her, and he opened his mouth as if trying to clear his ears. No words came out, and she could see tears well up in his eyes.

She bowed her head again. "I am sorry, father. That was wrong of me to speak such a thing."

Her father pulled up a stool and dropped heavily onto the seat; suddenly, he looked so old and pitiful, and Eliana began to weep for him. She moved her chair out of the corner, positioning it closer to her father; then she laid her hands on his shoulders. His head was down, and she thought he, too, might be weeping. He hid his face in shame. She wished so badly that she could take back the words.

"It was not your fault, Abba. I didn't mean that."

"But it was my fault. If I had been a normal Jewish father . . . If I cared more about your freedom than the freedom of the Jewish nation . . ."

"The same thing could have happened to any father. Think of all those young children slaughtered by Herod; those were the children of 'normal' Jewish fathers. Herod had them all killed because he knew that a rival king had been born."

Eliana's father sat up straight and wiped his eyes with his sleeves. He looked weak and vulnerable. "Jesus is not a king. Kings lead armies."

"Jesus does have an army."

"An army without swords."

Eliana smiled. "At least we agree on something. He has an army without swords."

This drew a slight smile from her father. They sat in silence—a brief truce. Then her father spoke softly.

"I cannot allow you to follow Jesus. You are my only remaining child, and I cannot lose you again. Stay with me. Marry Asaph."

*Asaph*? The man who just spoiled her attempt to leave?

"I cannot," she whispered.

"Then marry Gershom."

"I will marry no man. I will follow Jesus."

"Then you leave me no choice, daughter."

As her father rose to his feet, he had a hard time standing up perfectly straight; it appeared that his back had stiffened, as it sometimes did. Her father was still strong, but at that moment, as he shuffled for the door, slightly bent, she wondered if she might be able to get past him and escape.

But she did nothing other than watch him walk to the door. When he left the room, she heard the bolt click into place.

## **Sveshtari**

The followers of Jesus pulled down their tents, packed their supplies, and renewed their trek toward Jerusalem—the City of David, the City of the Great King. Sveshtari helped Keturah onto the donkey, and they moved with the masses, pausing to break bread when the sun had reached its zenith. The days were becoming steadily hotter, as if they were walking into a furnace.

One afternoon, as they traveled just steps behind Jesus, Sveshtari overheard a couple of Pharisees warn the teacher of the dangers awaiting him in Jerusalem.

"Herod wants to kill you," one Pharisee said to Jesus.

"Go tell that fox, 'I will drive out demons and heal people today and tomorrow, and on the third day I will reach my goal,'" Jesus answered. "In any case, I must keep going today and tomorrow and the next day—for surely no prophet can die outside Jerusalem."

*No prophet can die outside Jerusalem?* Was he planning to die? Sveshtari sensed a sudden coldness sweep over him.

This springtime day was scenic and sunny. But no matter how pleasant the path, Sveshtari couldn't shake the growing awareness that he and everyone else were on a road hurtling in the direction of death. Like most people, he found ways to distract himself from reality and convince himself that the days would always be sunny, smooth, and spring-like. Those were the kinds of days that Sveshtari now experienced, for once in his life. But with every step closer to Jerusalem, it was more difficult to deny the inevitability of death and suffering. They were marching into battle.

Jesus must have sensed the same thing, because Sveshtari overheard him speaking to his disciples. "O Jerusalem, Jerusalem, you who kill the prophets and stone those sent to you, how often I have longed to gather your children together, as a hen gathers her chicks under her wings, but you were not willing! Look, your house is left to you desolate. I tell you, you will not see me again until you say, 'Blessed is he who comes in the name of the Lord.'"

*O Jerusalem, Jerusalem.*

It had been a long time since Sveshtari had last seen Jerusalem. Over the years, he had witnessed many Passovers in the Holy City, when the blood of thousands of lambs flowed through an intricate system designed to carry it all away. The springtime Passover was approaching once again, a time when Hebrews remembered how the Children of Israel were spared by the Angel of Death in Egypt. That same angel awaited them in Jerusalem, and he sensed it with increasing certainty every day. Someone was going to die in the City of David. Maybe it would be him—or Keturah. Maybe all of them. But someone was going to die.

*O Jerusalem, Jerusalem.*

Even Keturah seemed to notice Sveshtari's increasing gloom.

"You may kiss me if it will brighten your mood," she suddenly said one morning as he continued to lead her donkey.

Sveshtari brought the donkey to a halt and stared at her in utter shock.

"What did you just say?"

"You may kiss me if it will make you happier."

"Will it make *you* happier?" he asked.

"It might."

Keturah leaned down from her seat atop the donkey, and Sveshtari reached up and held her chin in his right hand. He noticed the scar under her right eye—a scar that had not been there the last time they kissed, a long time ago.

Their lips met, gently but for an extended time. He could taste the honey on her lips from their most recent meal. He pulled away and stroked his beard.

"Feel better?" she asked.

"Much better."

He gave her a bright smile, and they continued, adding their little cloud of dust to the whirl of dirt being kicked up by the masses following Jesus. There were hills to their eastern side, as the followers of Jesus streamed like a river through the valley that cut its way from the Sea of Galilee north of them toward the Dead Sea in the south.

Sveshtari savored the kiss—a welcome distraction as they headed into enemy territory where powerful people jockeyed for thrones. People with names like Pilate and Herod and Caiaphas.

He looked over his shoulder at Keturah, who smiled back.

As a bodyguard, it had always been his job to keep kings alive. But something told him that preventing what awaited Jesus in Jerusalem would be an impossible job for any bodyguard.

"O Jerusalem, Jerusalem, you who kill the prophets," Sveshtari said aloud.

"Blessed is he who comes in the name of the Lord," added Eliana.

They marched onward.

## Asaph

Asaph was almost afraid to open the door. He wasn't sure who would attack first—Eliana or her dog. He reached through the hole in the door to insert the long, cylindrical key into the wooden Egyptian lock, which was mounted on the inside of the door. He drew back the bolt and entered.

The door creaked on its hinges, and he found Eliana sitting on the floor in the corner with her knees pulled up to her chest. It was evening, and a single oil lamp flickered on a lone table. Beneath the layers of age, Asaph could see the girl he once ran alongside through the narrow streets of their hometown. Her face was round and inviting, marred only by a small scar on her cheek—but even that blemish added to her wounded beauty. Her olive skin was still smooth for someone in her forties, except for the laugh lines at the corners of her eyes.

As Lavi leaped to his feet and began barking like a demon, Asaph tried to dance away from the dog without spilling the bread and wine. But Lavi didn't bite, although he certainly looked like he might. His ears were back, his teeth bared.

Eliana smiled at Asaph's nervousness. "Lavi knows a traitor when he smells one."

Finally, Eliana called off her dog, and Lavi padded back to her side. But the animal remained standing, keeping an eye on Asaph as he ventured closer. The dog let out a low growl.

"I brought you food," he said.

"I would have preferred your loyalty."

Asaph set the food down, his anger rising. "Your father lost you once, and if he loses you again, he will die. Honor thy father."

Asaph could see that his words had an impact; her face was heavy with sorrow.

"You're right," she said quietly, resting her chin on her knees.

Asaph softened at her sadness. He took a seat cross-legged in front of her. "I spoke the truth when I said I would have escorted you to Jesus's camp. But I still think it is good that you talk this over with your father."

"There is no talking to my father. His mind is made up."

Asaph was wise enough not to point out that Eliana's mind was also made up. He rubbed the swollen fingers of his left hand. He had jammed a couple of fingers during the skirmish on Mount Arbel, and they still ached. "Your father knows he can't keep you locked up for long."

"I don't know about that. I was locked up for a long time once before. It can happen again."

Asaph didn't need to point out the obvious—that her father would never put her in shackles or threaten her with death—the kind of tactics that were used to keep her in slavery for so many years.

"I think your father simply wants to make sure you do not go anywhere for the time being . . . so he can protect you."

"So he can try to talk me out of doing what I know is right is more like it."

Asaph grinned, but Eliana didn't return the smile. "You really are Judah's daughter, aren't you? Both so stubborn."

"But we're also so different. That's the problem, isn't it?"

"I'm not sure you're that different. You both want a revolution."

Eliana nodded through her tears. Then she began to speak what seemed to be a memorized line.

"He has performed mighty deeds with his arm; he has scattered those who are proud in their inmost thoughts. He has brought down rulers from their thrones but has lifted up the humble. He has filled the hungry with good things but has sent the rich away empty."

"Sounds like a passage from the Torah, but I do not know where."

"You don't remember hearing those words?"

Asaph shook his head, feeling stupid. He was never studious as a boy.

"Mary, Jesus's mother, sang these words when she met her cousin Elizabeth."

"You mean that day when we were children? You still remember the words?"

"I asked Mary to teach me. I had never forgotten the essence of what she said, but now I say those words every day."

"And you think Jesus can do all of that? Bring down rulers from their thrones?"

"I do."

"Is that why he is going to Jerusalem? To overthrow Pilate and Herod?"

"I don't know. Jesus can be so confusing sometimes. But I must follow him."

Silence came down on them like darkness. Asaph glanced at Lavi, who still looked ready to bite. Then he said the words he had been burning to say since the day they reunited.

"Don't go, Eliana. I love you. I always have."

Eliana smiled. "I love you too. You're a brother to me."

Asaph smiled uncomfortably, trying to hide the sting of the word "brother."

"Eat some food. You'll need your strength." He took her hand and kissed the back of it. Then, to his complete shock, she kept hold of his hand, pulled him to her, and kissed him directly on the lips. It was not the kiss of a "sister."

His head spun as she pulled away and looked down. She seemed as confused by her behavior as he was.

"Please go," she said.

He nodded. Did she kiss him to bring him to her side of the argument with her father? Was it purely tactical and nothing more?

Asaph decided it didn't matter what her motivation might have been. He had already made up his mind about what he was going to do next, and he didn't need any additional encouragement.

As he walked to the door, he heard Lavi at his side, letting out a soft warning growl. Then Asaph went out the door, down the passageway, and into the Magdalen night.

He didn't lock the door on his way out.

## Eliana

Eliana noticed that Asaph did not slide the wooden bolt in place when he left the room. Had he left the door unlocked on purpose?

Rising, Eliana rushed across the room and put her ear to the wood. Hearing no movement, she cracked the door open, and it gave out a soft creak of moving wood. Then she stepped into the passageway, which ran past two doorways, leading to an exit that spilled into the night.

Crouching, she hissed the word "quiet" to Lavi. Then she eased out into the hallway with her dog close behind.

To escape, Eliana only had to slip past two adjacent rooms. She paused before passing in front of the first door, listening for any life within. The door to the room was slightly ajar, and she prayed there was no one inside as she scurried across.

No shouts rose up. No alarms.

The second door was wide open, and she heard voices from within. Her father's voice—plus another man's. It sounded like Barabbas the Zealot.

"She is your daughter, and she has no husband. Make her obey."

This gem of advice came from Barabbas.

"It is not as simple as that," her father said.

"Of course, it's as simple as that. Daughters obey their fathers until they are married, and then they obey their husbands. What can be simpler?"

She heard her father sigh.

"What was that sound?" Barabbas suddenly said, and Eliana flattened her back against the wall. She thought she had been as quiet as a stone.

"You are being paranoid. There is no one else around, except for my daughter, and she is going nowhere."

"It pays to be paranoid. It's kept me alive thus far."

Hearing the scuffing sound of sandaled feet, Eliana considered her options. She could duck back inside her prison and wait for another opportunity to sneak out. Or she could make a run for the exit, not far down the hall.

Too late. Barabbas was at the door.

The door suddenly slammed shut. Then she heard their muffled voices coming from behind it.

Eliana didn't hesitate. She slipped past the room and hurried to the exit. Opening the door with a gentle click, Eliana slipped outside and paused, taking one last moment to decide whether she should go through with this. Her father had given her no other choice. He forced her to choose between him and Jesus. She had come to the sad conclusion that she could never really be safe with her father. He had a way of bringing danger upon her head.

Then again, Jesus was marching toward Jerusalem, which was like walking into a snake pit. How safe was that?

When she heard movement coming from inside the house, she sprinted along the dusty path as darkness fell, hoping she could catch up with Jesus and his followers by dawn. Lavi was right beside her.

# 2
## Luke, Chapter 14

### Keturah

Keturah rose early to grind the grain for their daily bread. Joanna provided the quern, a portable millstone—two round stones, one on top of the other.

Keturah listened to the morning birds as she poured the grain into a hole in the center of the upper stone, and the grain tumbled down, filling the space between the two rocks. Taking hold of a handle, she cranked the upper stone around and around; it ground the grain trapped between the rocks, spinning and spitting out the final product to all sides. With this flour, she would make bread for Sveshtari and others before they woke.

A brisk western wind flapped her robe as she cranked the quern. The two rocks ground away like stone teeth, cracking the grain. As the morning light crept across the land, many other women and a few men began to stir in this village of tents. Keturah noticed a familiar figure marching in her direction. It was a woman with a dog by her side.

Keturah stopped her work and swiped away a wisp of hair from in front of her eyes. That could be only one person. Rising to her feet, she rushed toward the woman.

"Eliana!" she shouted, forgetting that she might be awakening people in nearby tents. She couldn't help herself.

The two women embraced.

"Eliana, it is a joy to see you. What brings you here?"

Eliana linked an arm with Keturah's, and they strode back toward Keturah's tent. "Jesus does."

"Oh." Keturah still didn't know what to make of this Jesus, even though she and Sveshtari were pretending to be Jewish followers of the Nazarene. "And your father gave his blessing to this?"

Eliana's smile melted away. "He did not. But I obey my Father in Heaven before my father on Earth, and He tells me to follow Jesus."

Keturah crouched to rub Lavi behind the ears. "And how is this little one doing?"

"He still protects me."

"Much the way he protected both of us so long ago?"

Eliana nodded. As the two women grew silent, Keturah recalled how Lavi had saved their lives when they traveled together along the King's Highway. Keturah still couldn't believe that Eliana was the same woman she had met on that road. Back then, Eliana was tormented by demons, spitting at people like a camel. Now, she was the sanest person Keturah knew.

"And how about you?" Eliana asked. "Are you and Sveshtari safe?"

Keturah proceeded to tell her all about their recent run-in with two slave catchers.

"Thank God for Sveshtari," Eliana said.

Keturah shrugged and looked aside.

Eliana put a hand on her arm. "I am sorry. I realize how difficult it is for you to be thankful for Sveshtari in any fashion."

Again, a shrug. "I appreciate his protection. But . . ."

When Keturah could not fight away the tears any longer, Eliana embraced her. "We will talk no more about slave catchers and possessive fathers and bodyguards. Let me help you with your daily bread."

"I assume you will be sharing a morning meal with us?"

"I would love to. There is nothing greater than making and breaking bread with my dearest friend."

The two women took turns pouring the grain into the millstone and cranking the handle. The shattered grain created a fine powder, ideal for making dough and baking bread on a hot griddle. Lavi lay by Eliana's side, his eyes following the women as they worked.

## Asaph

"Where are you going?" Asaph asked.

"To find my daughter."

It was morning, and Asaph found Eliana's father, Judah, angrily jamming a few supplies into a sack. Judah picked up a staff, which leaned against the wall, but he left his sword on a table. Judah never went anywhere unarmed.

"You're leaving the Zealots?" Asaph was astounded. Judah had been a Zealot leader for most of his life.

"My daughter comes first. If I had learned this lesson early in life, she might never have been taken from me as a child."

It had been two days since Eliana had slipped away. On the first day, Judah was crestfallen. But then he became angry, and most of his fury was directed at Asaph. He said he suspected that Asaph had left the door unlocked so Eliana could get away. Asaph did not deny it.

Asaph pleaded. "You can't go. You're needed here."

"I am too old for fighting. It's time someone younger took control."

"You mean Barabbas?"

"I have already talked to him. He knows I am leaving, and he is in charge."

Judah's eyes went to his sword on the table and remained fixed on the weapon, as if contemplating whether to take it with him.

"I can accompany you to find Eliana," Asaph said.

Judah whipped his head back in Asaph's direction. "You have done enough! You have torn my daughter away from me. Out of my way!"

Judah slammed his shoulder against Asaph's as he made for the door, the force of the collision knocking Asaph off balance.

Asaph followed him, rubbing his left shoulder. "You know that Jesus is not only taking Eliana away from you. He's also taking her away from *me*."

Turning to face him directly, Judah seemed to understand. The red fury drained from his face. "Don't try to follow me. Remain here with Barabbas. He can use someone like you."

Asaph would never admit it to Judah, but Barabbas terrified him. Barabbas was a wild wolf. Where Judah was calm and measured, Barabbas was impulsive and reckless. Where Judah was driven by passion and intellect, Barabbas seemed driven by blood lust.

Judah's eyes returned to his weapon on the table. "Also . . . take care of my sword."

"But you already gave me a sword."

"And now you have two. If I need it back, I will let you know."

Asaph hoped this was a good sign. Perhaps Judah's mission was only temporary. Perhaps he would return to the Zealot fold after he had a chance to talk with Eliana.

As the old man exited the building, Asaph followed him into the light of day. With the staff in his right hand, Judah looked like Moses or Elijah marching into the wasteland. Asaph shielded his eyes from the morning sun, low on the horizon, and watched until Judah disappeared into the brown haze.

Returning to the room, Asaph sat down and studied the sword. The blade was wasp-waisted, made of iron, and the sheath was gilded bronze. He turned the sword over, watching sunlight play on the silver blade. Like any Mainz *gladius* sword, the weapon was light and double-edged, tapering to a sharp point.

Technically, he was Barabbas's man now. But as long as he carried this sword, he would remain Judah's man. He slid the blade back into its sheath.

## Nekoda: Eight Months Later, the Month of Adar (Early March), 30 A.D., Jerusalem

Nekoda marveled at the grounds of Herod's palace, a structure second only to the Temple. He passed by a narrow canal that snaked through a grove of trees in the massive garden between the north and south wings of the white palace. The stones used to build Herod's stronghold were twenty cubits long, ten in breadth, and five in depth, and they were so closely fitted together that the palace towers looked to be made of a single stone.

At the northern end were three large towers, the most beautiful one named "Mariamne" in honor of Herod the Great's favorite wife. Nekoda twinged with trepidation at the thought that even Mariamne, the king's favorite, had been killed with poison when Herod began to suspect her of treason.

The latest Herod, Antipas, was no less suspicious—and dangerous—than his father, and Nekoda always tried to keep that in mind in his dealings with the tetrarch. He remained ever conscious that he was walking on poisoned ground. Herod Antipas governed Galilee and Perea—not Judea, where Jerusalem was found. But he had come to the palace in Jerusalem on business with Pontius Pilate, governor of Judea.

"Peace be with you," Nekoda said when he spotted Rufus approaching through the gardens. Rufus, a captain in Herod's guard, had agreed to meet and give him the full report about what had gone wrong with the attack on the Zealots at the Cliffs of Arbel. The Romans thought they had the Zealots trapped in the caves, but when they rappelled down the cliff, the Jewish freedom fighters had been waiting. Who had tipped them off? Nekoda had his suspicions.

He offered an ingratiating grin, but Rufus retained his emotionless expression. The captain's eyes drifted to Nekoda's head, which was mostly bald, except for some stubborn strands. Nekoda tried to make up for what he lacked on top with a moderately long beard.

Rufus let slip a slight grin, as if amused at Nekoda's retreating hairline. Then, as his eyes drifted back down to meet Nekoda's gaze, he hardened his expression.

"The tetrarch is not pleased." Rufus didn't even bother with preliminary niceties.

"I can understand he would be disappointed that the attack did not go as planned."

"But can you understand that he would be upset with *you*?" Rufus took a step closer, invading his space. "Herod put considerable effort into negotiating with Pontius Pilate to obtain his assistance in rooting out these rebels. And then Pilate's soldiers are caught unawares. It does not look good for you."

Suddenly, the palace grounds felt even more dangerous. Nekoda instinctively looked around for the nearest exit. Did Rufus ask to meet at the palace because he had set a trap for him? Will he be allowed to leave here alive?

"Why would the tetrarch be displeased with me, a priest?" Nekoda spoke with a smile, seeking to soothe Rufus's anger. Nekoda wasn't a soldier. He was a Sadducee priest, a member of the Sanhedrin, the Jewish ruling council. He hoped that gave him protection.

"Someone alerted the Zealots that the soldiers were coming." His cold words implied that Nekoda was the one.

"I told nobody." Nekoda stood up taller. But even as he made his defense, he realized that he did tell someone about the attack on the Cliffs of Arbel. He told his brother, Chaim. Nekoda had had a hard time containing his excitement and let the information spill. But surely his brother would not have been so stupid as to alert the Jewish freedom fighters.

Nekoda lowered his head. "I have always been a reliable source of information for Herod and Pilate. It was me who identified the Zealots in Jerusalem on the Day of Atonement."

That bit of information led to the slaughter of many Jews, a sin for which Nekoda made many sacrifices as atonement. But Pontius Pilate was pleased about the execution of Zealots that day. Nekoda had been elevated in his eyes.

"You have served faithfully as the eyes and ears for Herod," Rufus said, "but your mouth tends to run away with itself."

"I told no one. Someone must have spotted the soldiers' preparations on the mountain. That's the only explanation."

"Your friend's body was found at the bottom of the cliffs," Rufus said.

Nekoda braced himself for more bad news. "My friend? Who?"

"Jeremiel. The leper."

"He's not a friend of mine."

"But Jeremiel used to be a good friend. Do you think he could have been the one who sounded the alarm? Did he learn of the attack from you?"

"How could he? We have had no contact. He's a leper—*was* a leper—and I didn't even know he was living on the Cliffs of Arbel! The last I knew, he was on the other side of the lake, near Gergesa."

That too was a lie because Nekoda's brother had told him he had seen Jeremiel on the Cliffs of Arbel. Chaim must be the link in this disaster. Nekoda knew his brother had been upset about the blood spilled in the Temple on the Day of Atonement, but he never could have imagined . . .

"The tetrarch expects you to make up for this debacle."

This was good news of a sort. At least it meant that Nekoda would keep his head. It's difficult for a decapitated man to make amends.

"What does he want me to do?"

"We need information. Find out who alerted the Zealots, so we can have him killed."

Nekoda had always protected his brother, and now he was being asked to expose Chaim and throw him to the wolves? He nodded his agreement.

"The tetrarch would also like information on the whereabouts of a man named Sveshtari, a former bodyguard in the palace. Sveshtari feigned his death and fled his post, and it is believed that he was with the Zealots on the mountain."

"And what will I get in return for this information?"

"You will be allowed to keep breathing."

"The tetrarch is merciful."

"If you locate the Zealots, you will probably find Sveshtari. Some of them are likely mingled into the crowds following Jesus of Nazareth. Our sources say they are heading here to Jerusalem."

Rufus provided a description of Sveshtari and then turned and walked off through the gardens without another word. Nekoda found a small bench and sat, feeling the cold stone beneath him. Already, he was beginning to formulate a plan. He could offer his brother's head on a platter, or he could find a way to blame the debacle at Arbel on this Sveshtari.

Either way, someone's head was going to roll, and he was determined to keep it from being his. Nekoda stood and hurried from the beautiful palace grounds, not even pausing to admire the statuary.

### Sveshtari: On the Road to Jerusalem

The thief arrived in the night.

Sveshtari's eyes opened to see a shadow creep across the room of the inn. The moon cast just enough light through a window to throw the shadow into view. Could the figure be one of the disciples, returning to the house from answering nature's call in the middle of the night? Sveshtari didn't think so. He had been trained to sense intruders, and this man did not belong.

Lying on his side, Sveshtari watched calmly as the thief slinked his way across the room, where several disciples of Jesus slept. The thief was sneaking his way toward the man they called Judas Iscariot. This rogue obviously knew who was in charge of the moneybags among Jesus's disciples.

Sveshtari's eyes became accustomed to the dark, following the slinking shadow. Sveshtari was no Argus, the giant with 100 eyes that guarded a sacred white heifer. He had only two eyes, but years of training as a guard in Herod's palace had given him the ability to pop them open at the faintest breath of trouble.

The shadow reached the corner of the room where Judas slept with his body curled around two bags of coins. Still, Sveshtari didn't make his move. Not yet. He waited for the lurking man to incriminate himself. He wanted proof of the man's intentions before he drew his knife.

Judas had hired him as a bodyguard—an ideal cover for a man like Sveshtari. But until now, his job as guardian had been incident-free.

The shadow paused, as he seemed to be assessing the best way to lift the moneybags without waking Judas. The disciple was known to roll over onto the bags in his sleep, which would have made it impossible to steal them. But Sveshtari could see the two bags sitting there in the open, a handbreadth away from Judas's prone body.

Just as the shadow began to bend down toward the coins, Judas let out a snort and adjusted his body. The shadow straightened up and remained standing as if waiting to see if Judas would wake.

Sveshtari smiled. He could have told the thief that he had nothing to fear from Judas, who was difficult to rouse. Sveshtari could give Judas a kick in the ribs, and the slumbering disciple would probably just mutter and shift his body. Peter, the big disciple, sometimes awakened Judas in the morning by placing small lizards on his face while he slept. Even then, Judas would often keep sleeping, awkwardly slapping at the lizards while he slumbered. The last time Peter used this wake-up tactic, six of the disciples gathered around to watch and hoot at the entertainment.

Once again, the shadow bent over the sleeping figure, only this time Sveshtari saw him reach out with one hand, slowly, carefully. The man's fingers curled around the neck of the first moneybag; then he took hold of the second bag and slowly raised them into the air simultaneously. Sveshtari had to hand it to him. Not a single coin clinked together. The man was a practiced thief.

Sveshtari knew how to be equally quiet as his right hand slipped to the dagger strapped to his side. He held his breath and waited for the shadow to turn back toward the door.

Then he pounced.

Sveshtari moved with the speed of a leopard, pulling out his dagger with his right hand as he rose from the ground, then slapping his left hand over the thief's mouth while placing the blade against the skin of exposed neck. All of this was done before the thief could cry out.

"Not a sound," he whispered into the thief's ear. "We don't want to wake the sleepers. Wouldn't be polite."

The thief's eyes bulged as Sveshtari, positioned directly behind, forced him out the door and into the central courtyard of the inn where they were staying the night.

"What's stopping me from slitting your throat right here, right now?" Sveshtari hissed.

"I am stopping you, right here, right now," came a voice from behind.

Sveshtari cast a look over his shoulder and spotted one of the disciples of Jesus moving into view. It appeared to be Nathanael.

Sveshtari tightened his hold. "I caught this man stealing from the community. He is guilty of manifest theft. Caught in the act. He must die."

Nathanael stepped into the moonlight. "You speak like a Roman, Sveshtari."

Sveshtari's mouth went dry. Under Eliana's tutelage, he had been trying to pass himself off as a Hebrew. But in the heat of the moment, he had reverted to the ways of a Thracian soldier who worked within Roman law.

Nathanael reached out his right hand. "Please remove your knife from the man's throat."

Sveshtari felt the thief's body relax as he pulled the knife away. But he kept his left arm around the man's body, increasing the pressure to make it clear that this thief was going nowhere. As he did, he tried to recall the Jewish punishment for theft. Although Sveshtari had spent several years as a bodyguard in the palace, Herod Antipas was only part Jewish and didn't abide by Jewish law in matters such as this. If Sveshtari had caught a thief in the act in the palace, he would have killed the man on the spot, and Herod would not have blinked; the tetrarch didn't worry about the finer points of Jewish law.

But he was no longer in Herod's palace. He was in the presence of a Hebrew rabbi named Jesus—and in the presence of his followers, who had different ideas of justice.

"What is your name?" Nathanael asked the thief.

"Abel." The thief had the audacity to grin at the disciple. Sveshtari wanted to slap the smile from his face.

But Nathanael smiled back at Abel. Smiling at a man who just tried to rob you revealed weakness, even compassion. Sveshtari did not approve, but he could not say a word in protest. He had to think like a Hebrew, as humiliating as that might be.

Nathanael leaned in close. "Why did you attempt to steal from us?"

"To feed my family."

Sveshtari couldn't stifle his laugh.

Nathanael turned to Sveshtari. "You think he lies?"

"I *know* he lies."

"People do not despise a thief if he steals to satisfy his hunger when he is starving," Nathanael said. "Yet if he is caught, he must pay sevenfold, though it costs him all the wealth of his house."

It sounded as if Nathanael was quoting some Jewish law, but Sveshtari could not be certain. He bit his lip. He despised thieves, no matter what their motive.

"Release the thief," Nathanael said.

Sveshtari tightened his grip. "But he will run."

"I will not run. I promise," said Abel.

"Release him."

Sveshtari had no choice. He released his grip from around the man's chest. Immediately, the thief fell to his knees and bowed his head to the dust.

"I beseech your forgiveness. Be merciful, just as our Father is merciful."

Sveshtari nearly laughed out loud, but this time he controlled the urge. Nathanael would be a fool to believe that this man sincerely sought forgiveness. Nathanael was a scholar of the Law, so he had to know the danger of giving mercy to a thief. But he was also a gentle man—a weak man in Sveshtari's eyes. This thief was quoting the words of Jesus—an obvious play for sympathy.

"He speaks falsely," Sveshtari said, unable to control himself.

"I am not false!" The thief remained prostrate, his face still in the dirt. "I only want to feed my family."

"Then what are your children's names? Quickly now. Tell us," Sveshtari said, hoping to catch him in a lie.

"Ruth, Stephen, Sharon, and Noah, and my wife is Abigail." The man spoke quickly and confidently, not like someone pulling false names from thin air.

"Why did you not approach us and ask for money?" came another voice. All eyes turned to see Peter, the big fisherman, enter the courtyard. "That is what our money is for—to feed and clothe those in need. And you can rise to your feet. No need to grovel."

Abel rose from the ground, brushing the dust from his robe. Once again, the man smiled, this time at Peter. It made Sveshtari want to spit.

Abel glanced from face to face. "I've heard stories about the followers of Jesus and how they share freely among themselves. But I . . . I didn't believe the tales."

"If your family joins us, you can discover the truth for yourself," said Peter.

Sveshtari groaned inwardly. He didn't take Peter for such a fool. They had hooked this thief—caught him in the act—but Peter spoke like they were going to catch and release. What kind of fisherman does that?

Instantly, Abel was back on his knees, kissing the hem of Peter's robe. Peter raised him back up.

"None of that," Peter said.

"Come and follow Jesus," added Nathanael.

"Thank you. My family thanks you! May the Lord shine His face on you and bless you with peace and prosperity!"

Abel made a move to turn, but Nathanael grabbed him by the arm.

Good, Sveshtari thought. *He's not going to let him get away without a consequence.*

"Wait, my friend. Here. Take."

To Sveshtari's utter disbelief, Nathanael drew three coins from the moneybag and pressed them into Abel's hands. The thief stared at the money as if the disciple had spoken the coins into existence. Abel bowed over and over, before backing his way out of the courtyard and disappearing into the night.

*We'll never see him again*, Sveshtari thought.

Grunting, Sveshtari left the courtyard without saying a word to Peter and Nathanael. Back on his sleeping mat, he tried fruitlessly to get back to sleep, his mind buzzing with things he should've said and done.

Meanwhile, he heard Judas snoring from across the room. The roof could fall in, and that man would keep sleeping.

## Nekoda

Nekoda was shocked by the sheer number of people following Jesus. The last time he had encountered the man from Nazareth, Jesus had been surrounded by a handful of smelly fishermen and hundreds of people, mostly seeking healing. But now . . . the number was in the thousands.

Jesus was becoming more dangerous by the day.

Nekoda hunted for his brother, Chaim, amid the multitude, and when he finally tracked him down, he nearly didn't recognize him. Although Chaim had always been the chubbier of the two brothers, living on the road with Jesus and his followers must've changed his diet because he had trimmed down. Nekoda had always been naturally thin and tall, but he took pride in his growing gut. It was a sign of his elevated status in life.

After initially looking shocked to see him, Chaim broke into a forced smile and strode to meet him. "Shalom, brother!"

"Shalom, Chaim!" They exchanged brotherly kisses.

"What brings you from Jerusalem?" Chaim asked.

"I have come to assess the size and commitment of the crowds following Jesus. I see that the numbers have grown."

"Every day. You would not believe the number of healings that Jesus has performed."

*True. I would not believe it.*

"Do you remember when we witnessed Jesus heal the paralyzed man who was lowered through the roof?" Chaim seemed to be loosening up the more he talked of Jesus.

"Yes, I remember." Nekoda spoke with little emotion. He had to admit that the "healing" was dramatic, but he always suspected it could have been staged. Even still, that moment always nagged at him.

"I have seen dozens more like it." Chaim threw out his arms in exuberance.

"Oh." That was the only word Nekoda could muster.

"I am dining with a local Pharisee this evening, and Jesus will be present," Chaim continued with growing passion. "Would you join us? I am sure our host would be delighted to have a member of the Sanhedrin present!"

Nekoda agreed, realizing it would give him the perfect opportunity to size up Jesus from close range—to see how much he had changed since the last time he encountered the teacher in Capernaum.

But Nekoda had other business as well. "Brother, I'm also wondering if you know what happened to a man by the name of Sveshtari."

Chaim looked shocked. "Sveshtari? That is not a Jewish name."

"The man is Thracian, a former bodyguard in Herod's palace. You once told me about him—how he helped rescue a friend of yours who was drowning. I think Eliana was her name."

"Oh yes, yes, I remember now. That seems ages ago."

When Chaim was young, he was a pretty good liar. He had obviously lost the touch.

"I heard that Sveshtari is among Jesus's followers." Nekoda kept a close eye on every flinch from his brother. "Perhaps you have seen him."

Chaim seemed to be putting on an act, trying to recall. "No, no, I can't say I have seen this man. Why would a Thracian bodyguard be following a Jewish teacher like Jesus?"

"Why would *anyone* follow Jesus?" Nekoda asked pointedly.

"Because he heals."

"There. You've answered your own question. But I am very interested in finding this Sveshtari. Are you sure you haven't seen him?"

"I'm certain."

And Nekoda was certain his brother was lying.

"Why are you interested in finding Sveshtari?" Chaim asked.

"Herod is very interested. Not only did Sveshtari desert his position as a guard in Herod's house, but he may have tipped off the Zealots hiding in the caves of Mount Arbel."

"Yes, I heard about what happened." Chaim stroked his chin. Nekoda noticed he was sweating heavily. His brother was afraid. Clearly.

"Herod demands that someone pay for what happened on Mount Arbel," Nekoda said, piercing Chaim with his gaze. "Someone's head must roll, and I would prefer it to be Sveshtari's."

He hoped Chaim got the message. If it wasn't Sveshtari's head, it might be Chaim's.

"I will ask around." The sweat streamed down the side of Chaim's face.

"Thank you, brother!" Nekoda's eyes lit up, and he gave Chaim a warm embrace. "I look forward to dining tonight with Jesus."

Chaim tried his best to smile.

That evening, at the home of a Pharisee named Abner, Nekoda kept his eyes on Jesus. He watched with mild surprise as the teacher took a lower seat at the table. Nekoda fully expected that Jesus, like most would-be prophets, would insist on taking the seat of honor, reclining on the cushion directly to the left of the host. But Jesus seemed to go out of his way to flip conventions upside down.

Jesus's display of false humility was too blatant, too obvious. It was a game that Nekoda was not willing to play. So, he chose the seat of honor. As the only member of the Sanhedrin among these fourteen men, it was his rightful place—although he was beginning to regret the choice because the man on his other side turned out to be the table's greatest bore.

Chaim sat to the left of Jesus, so he too passed up the chance to take a seat of honor. It embarrassed Nekoda to see his brother fawn over Jesus, grinning like a fool. Nekoda watched as Jesus listened to Chaim babble for a spell before the teacher turned to the person on his right, a man named Hushim who clearly suffered from dropsy. The signs couldn't be missed. Hushim's legs and ankles were puffy, and when he reached down to massage his sore and swollen calf, he left a small indention in the skin.

Nekoda was shocked that Abner had even invited someone like Hushim who displayed such obvious disease. Visible ailments were often a sign of hidden sins, putting the sick person too far down the social ladder to warrant an invitation to a meal such as this. But Abner clearly didn't stick by the rules; in addition to inviting a man with dropsy, he had invited a controversial teacher.

"What do you make of Jesus?" asked the bore on Nekoda's left. Jeziah was his name. "Jesus says the door to salvation is narrow."

"I cannot argue with that." Nekoda's eyes locked on Jesus on the opposite side of the table. "But Jesus better be careful. The door may be too narrow for even him to pass through."

Jeziah leaned in closer and exhaled. His breath smelled of the honey and pepper used to spice the wine. "I heard Jesus say he desires to gather God's people together and protect them like a hen gathers her chicks beneath her wings."

Nekoda rolled his eyes. "Scripture says that God, not Jesus, gathers us beneath his wings. I see no wings on Jesus."

As if Jesus could hear what Nekoda said, the teacher placed his arm around the shoulder of the man with dropsy, like a bird's sheltering wings.

Jeziah noticed too. "Do you think Jesus would dare to heal that man?" he whispered excitedly—as if he were hoping for a little scandal with his meal.

"It is the Sabbath. He would not do such a thing." The moment the words left Nekoda's mouth, he realized he was sounding more and more like his old friend, Jeremiel, who would not even extinguish a fire on the Sabbath. When had he become such a hard-liner?

"The Sabbath never stopped Jesus before," Jeziah said. "Did you hear how he healed a woman bent over for almost twenty years?"

Nekoda grunted his response, as the bread passed from person to person. Nekoda took a piece, careful not to drop it, for that would bring shame. Then their host, Abner, said a blessing, and they broke the bread and ate. The meal was modest, with fish, fruit, and pickled olives. Several women cleared away each course, making sure they gathered all crumbs of bread. Some believed that demons could perch on wayward crumbs, but Nekoda hoped that none of the men here were so foolish as to believe such nonsense.

Following the meal came the *symposia*, a time for the men to conduct a dialogue about the Torah and other weighty matters. Jesus began, and he didn't waste any time tossing out a question guaranteed to provoke.

Jesus glanced around the table. "Is it lawful to heal on the Sabbath, or not?"

No one said a word. Most of the men just stared back at Jesus, while a couple of them exchanged awkward glances. Nekoda heard Jeziah emit a giddy giggle as if excited by the chance to witness a religious quarrel. Jeziah was not only a bore. He was also a fool.

Jesus's eyes drifted across the table, and Nekoda sensed that the teacher paused for an extra heartbeat when his gaze landed on him. Nekoda glared back but said nothing. He wasn't going to let this man draw him into a theological squabble. He would leave the nitpicking to the Pharisees.

Still, no one responded to Jesus's question. Not even Chaim, who just grinned at Jesus as if pleased that his hero would ask such a bold question.

When Jesus had finished glancing around the table, he turned back to face Hushim, the man with dropsy. Then Jesus placed his hand on Hushim's shoulder and closed his eyes.

"I think he's going to try to heal the man," Jeziah whispered over Nekoda's left shoulder. Nekoda waved his hand to quiet Jeziah, like flicking his fingers at an annoying fly.

But Jeziah wasn't going to be swatted away so easily. "I think he's praying for Hushim. Do you think we would even be able to notice if Hushim was healed of his dropsy? Can you get a good look at his ankles?"

"Sshhh." The last time that Nekoda had witnessed a healing by Jesus—when the paralyzed man had been lowered through the roof—he had felt excitement mixed with skepticism, even disdain. He had the same ambivalence now.

Jesus's eyes were open, and he stared directly into the face of Hushim. What's more, Jesus's lips were moving, but no sound was coming out of his mouth—at least nothing that Nekoda could hear from his end of the table. Hushim stared back into Jesus's eyes but kept glancing away as if embarrassed by Jesus's intense gaze. After what seemed like an uncomfortable amount of time to Nekoda, Hushim put both hands to his face, trying to hide his tears which flowed like a spring.

Nekoda heard the stirrings around the table. The men began to fidget. Two moved out of their reclining positions and sat up straight.

"What does he think he's doing?" one man finally said in a voice slightly above a whisper.

Another man cleared his throat, while the person beside him sighed heavily. It was as if people wanted to speak but could manage nothing more than inarticulate sounds. Nekoda smiled at this spectacle of awkwardness.

At last, the silence shattered. Hushim reached back to massage his ankles, a light flashing in his eyes. Hushim leaped to his feet.

"The pain . . . It's gone!"

Hushim lifted one leg, then another, raising his robe just a few inches from the floor and staring down at his ankles.

"My ankles . . . look . . . they're . . . they look normal!"

All around the table, men leaned forward and stared down their noses at Hushim's ankles. From a distance, his ankles did appear normal. No more swelling, as far as Nekoda could see. But how could he be sure? This was not as dramatic as a paralyzed man being told to rise and pick up his mat.

Then Jesus told Hushim to go—to show his wife his new legs—and then stroll around the village to test them out. Hushim's tears were flowing freely by this time, and he dropped to his knees and bowed his head to the ground.

"Get up!" one of the Pharisees exclaimed, clearly upset by this posture of devotion that only God deserved.

Jesus raised Hushim from the dust and planted a kiss on each cheek.

When Hushim had entered the house of Abner for this meal, he hobbled through the doorway. But as he left the house, he strode confidently, and he couldn't stop grinning. Jesus smiled as he watched the man exit.

From the awestruck look on Chaim's face, you'd think the skies had opened and God had spoken directly to him. Chaim glanced over at Nekoda and bobbed his head up and down, as if to say, "See? I told you so! Jesus heals!" But most of the other men around the table appeared irritated, some even furious. Yet no one spoke a word in protest.

Jesus set down his cup of wine, licking droplets from his moustache. He looked around the table and sighed before launching into yet another challenge. He seemed determined to create offense, Nekoda thought.

"When someone invites you to a wedding feast, do not take the place of honor, for a person more distinguished than you may have been invited.

If so, the host who invited both of you will come and say to you, 'Give this person your seat.' Then, humiliated, you will have to take the least important place."

Nekoda nearly choked on his drink, his cheeks flushing red like wine. Was Jesus openly challenging him? He had taken the seat of honor, but he had earned it. He *deserved* it.

Jesus continued. This time, he looked at Chaim.

"But when you are invited, take the lowest place, so that when your host comes, he will say to you, 'Friend, move up to a better place.' Then you will be honored in the presence of all the other guests. For all those who exalt themselves will be humbled, and those who humble themselves will be exalted."

After Jesus said this, his eyes returned to Nekoda, who held the rabbi's gaze. Jesus's eyes did not show open hostility—only pity. But Nekoda didn't want Jesus's pity. It made him feel as small as one of those breadcrumbs the women had cleaned up. Finally, Nekoda could hold the gaze no longer, and he turned his attention back to his wine cup. He was furious. He knew Jesus was brazenly comparing his brother with him—a rich Sadducee.

Next, Jesus directed his attention to the host, Abner. "When you give a luncheon or dinner, do not invite your friends, your brothers or sisters, your relatives, or your rich neighbors; if you do, they may invite you back and so you will be repaid. But when you give a banquet, invite the poor, the crippled, the lame, the blind, and you will be blessed. Although they cannot repay you, you will be repaid at the resurrection of the righteous."

Was Jesus commending Abner for inviting a man with dropsy to this meal? Or was he criticizing him for inviting the rich to his table—people like himself.

As if to change this awkward subject, Jeziah blurted out, "Blessed is the one who will eat at the feast in the Kingdom of God."

In response, Jesus launched into a ridiculous story about a man who prepared a great banquet, but all the guests responded with excuses for why they couldn't come.

"I have just bought a field, and I must go and see it.

"I have just bought five yoke of oxen, and I'm on my way to try them out.

"I just got married, so I can't come."

Jesus paused, glancing around the table before continuing. "Then the owner of the house became angry and ordered his servant, 'Go out quickly into the streets and alleys of the town and bring in the poor, the crippled, the blind, and the lame.'

"'Sir,' the servant said, 'what you ordered has been done, but there is still room.'

"Then the master told his servant, 'Go out to the roads and country lanes and compel them to come in, so that my house will be full. I tell you, not one of those who were invited will get a taste of my banquet.'"

Nekoda fumed, buffeted by every word. Sharing a table with a man with dropsy was one thing. At least that man was a law-abiding Pharisee. But now Jesus was saying that the Great Banquet at the end of all time would be made up almost entirely of the poor and crippled. The rabbi seemed determined to insult his host—and guests. More to the point, Jesus was determined to insult him.

Jeziah set a hand on Nekoda's shoulder and leaned in closer. "I think he's saying we are the ones who turned down his invitation. What do you make of that?"

Nekoda glared in Jesus's direction. "I think we all need to keep our eyes on this man."

Jeziah turned to look at Jesus. "I think you're right."

## Keturah

As the dust kicked up in swirls all around her, Keturah balanced the earthenware pitcher on her right shoulder and carried a leather bucket in her left hand. Eliana walked at her side, along with her dog, Lavi. It was late afternoon, and many women streamed toward the community well.

Keturah strained at the pitcher perched on her shoulder. "I'm not sure I'm ever going to get used to this." When she had been a servant in Herod's household, she had a variety of duties, but collecting water was not one of them.

"It is easier than trying to balance it on your head." Eliana nodded in the direction of a woman who was doing just that.

Eliana continued to teach Keturah the ways of a Jewish woman, and she was an eager student. Keturah was especially fascinated by the many Jewish celebrations throughout the year.

"I still do not understand your Feast of Booths," she said.

Eliana smiled. "As the rabbis say, 'He who has not seen Jerusalem during the Feast of Tabernacles does not know what rejoicing is.' It is a great harvest festival."

"That I understand. But why create booths?"

"The Lord said that all Israelite-born people shall dwell in booths for seven days. So, we build booths using branches for walls and thatch for roofs. Then we wave lulavs made from willow and palm branches that are tied with a golden thread. And we bring an ethrog offering, a fruit that symbolizes the fruit of the Promised Land."

Keturah stumbled and nearly lost control of her pitcher. When she steadied herself, she asked, "Why?"

"The festival is a remembrance of the forty years in the wilderness when God's people lived in tents. But it's also a picture of God's protection. He will give us shelter beneath His wings—under the wings of Shekinah glory. On the seventh day of the Feast of Booths, water is poured from the golden pitcher, horns are blasted, and people wave their palm branches while chanting Psalms. It is the Great Hosanna for the coming of the Messiah."

Keturah came to a stop and turned to face Eliana. "Many say Jesus is your people's Messiah. Do you believe it?"

"I think so, but Chaim does not. He believes the Messiah will come with a sword to conquer Rome and deliver his people. If he's right... then Jesus doesn't meet expectations."

Keturah nodded but said nothing more. Over the days and weeks, her feelings about Jesus had softened, but she still didn't know what to make of him.

As they stepped into a short line of other women with pitchers, Eliana suddenly gripped her arm. "Keep your face covered."

Immediately, Keturah drew a cloth across the lower portion of her face. "What's wrong?"

"Are those the men who are hunting you and Sveshtari?"

Keturah sneaked a peek, and her heart nearly stopped. There stood the two men who had tried to apprehend her in Magdala. Even worse, they were accompanied by Rufus, the man who had caught her after she fled slavery; he was the one who forced her to carry a beam of wood on her back as punishment. He was also the one who sought to kill her and Sveshtari.

Rufus seemed to be studying every woman who approached the well. Was he looking for a tattoo on the women's foreheads? Keturah nearly dropped her pitcher. She put her head down, then slipped out of line and headed back to the city where they were staying with Jesus's followers. Eliana followed and walked directly behind to block any view of her.

"Don't look back. Just keep going," Eliana said.

Keturah picked up her pace, afraid to go too fast and draw attention as they neared the edge of the city.

"The men are moving this way," Eliana whispered.

"You looked?"

"I did. Run!"

All at once, Keturah set down her pitcher and took off running, sprinting through the city gates, then making a sharp left turn down a narrow street lined with produce sellers and other tradesmen. Eliana was right behind her.

"We need to split up," Eliana called out. "Maybe they'll confuse us and follow me."

As Keturah turned to answer, she ran blindly into a finely woven rug hanging from a line. She batted away the rug and plunged headlong down the street. As soon as they reached a branch in the street, Keturah went right, and Eliana turned left.

Keturah had young legs, running faster than she ever had in her life. But she lost all sense of direction, turning at every street corner. First right, then left, then left again. These were unfamiliar streets, so she had no idea where she was going. People stepped aside and stared as she darted down side paths and alleyways. Fearing that she might be going in circles, she paused at a basket maker's booth to catch her breath and see if she was still being pursued.

She saw nothing but merchants and customers bartering until Rufus came running from a side street and stopped in the middle of the intersection. The man, breathing heavily, spun around in circles, hunting her with his eyes. Keturah slipped behind the wall of the seller's booth.

"You want to buy a basket?" An elderly man shoved his wares under her nose.

"Sshhh."

"Don't shush me! Are you running from someone?"

The merchant looked around for the source of Keturah's worry, and his eyes locked on Rufus. He was about to shout out to the soldier when Keturah grabbed the basket from his hands.

"I'll buy this. How much?"

As they bartered, Keturah kept an eye locked on Rufus, who seemed to be trying to decide which direction to go.

"That's my final price! No lower," said the merchant.

When Keturah saw Rufus run in the opposite direction, she shoved the basket back into the merchant's hands and took off running.

"Wait! That's not my final price! Come back!"

Up ahead, another gate led out of the city, and as she neared it, a foul odor swept over her, like a dead man's shroud. She was heading toward the city's garbage dump, located just outside the walls. She had a hunch that no man, least of all Rufus, would come near this filth, so she raced through the gate, running into an invisible wall of stench. Coughing, she breathed through her mouth and worked her way around the right side of the mound of decaying food and human waste. It was disgusting, but at least the city had the sense to pile it outside the city walls. Many other cities allowed people to toss their filth in the streets during the night.

She came to a stop and glanced around for her pursuer. No sign of him. Crouching, she decided to remain at the dump for the time being, protected by its uncleanliness. Flies buzzed everywhere, and she had to fight them away as they circled her head. The mound of garbage formed a small hill, and it appeared there had been some attempt to bury the refuse underneath a covering of soil to contain the odor.

Eventually, Keturah's legs ached from crouching, so she stood up straight and felt a growing sense of evil as she moved around the perimeter of this mound of refuse. She was taught as a little girl that evil spirits lurked at trash heaps and other unclean places.

So, it came as no surprise when the image of Orcus slipped into her mind.

One of the servant women from Herod's palace, Claudia, loved to scare her by telling stories of Orcus, the god of the underworld and punisher of broken oaths. Claudia would spin tales about Orcus, a monstrous man covered in hair, lunging at them from the dark if he suspected that Keturah had broken any oaths. Now, beside this mound of rotting refuse, she prayed to Isis for protection against Orcus, and then, for added security, she decided it couldn't hurt to pray to the Jewish God as well.

Keturah rounded the corner of the garbage dump, unable to stand the stench for a moment more when she suddenly heard a sound that seemed so out of place in this demon-drenched space. It was the sound of a baby crying. She tried not to breathe through her nose as she continued around the side of the steaming mound, where she saw the partial remains of a dead wolf stare back at her from the trash heap. She let out a muffled scream because half of the wolf's skull was still intact, and for a moment she thought the creature might be alive. The other half of the skull swarmed with worms and flies.

Again, the cry of a baby.

Her eyes searched the trash, and she wondered if her ears deceived her. Or maybe it was the trickery of Orcus, luring her into a trap.

Then she saw: A baby, without a shred of clothing, had been placed amid the garbage. The infant girl's ribs showed, and the skin was tight on her face. She had none of the newborn baby fat. She lay on the trash heap, kicking her legs and reaching out with her arms, like a bug stuck on its back, pawing at the air.

The baby had clearly been left to die.

For the Roman *pater familias*, it was the father's right to decide a baby's fate. A child was placed before the *pater familias*, and if the father picked up the baby, it would be welcomed into the house. But if he chose *not* to pick up the child, the baby could be sent into slavery or placed in a spot where someone could take the child and adopt it as her own. But to place a helpless baby outside a city in a trash heap? For that child, there was only one outcome.

Keturah felt an urge to take hold of the infant and rescue it from the garbage pile, but she was terrified. Surely, this trash heap swarmed with demons and spirits. If she leaned over to grab the child, it would be like leaning into a tangle of cobwebs weaved by spider-like spirits to keep mortals away.

Keturah backed up a few steps and sat down in the dust, unsure what to do. The baby, as if sensing her presence, mustered the strength to cry much louder. But hadn't the child been abandoned for a good reason? Was it a monster? She couldn't tell from this distance. But it was clearly a girl. For some Roman fathers, that was reason enough to dispose of a child.

She knew what Eliana would tell her to do. Eliana would insist they lift the child from this tomb and give her new life. Eliana would then start quoting Jesus. *See to it, then, that the light within you is not darkness.* Eliana constantly recited that line. *We think we are filled with light, but we easily fool ourselves,* Eliana would explain. *Our light is actually darkness. So, see to it, then, that the light within you is not darkness. If your whole body is full of light, and no part of it is dark, it will be completely lighted.*

If Keturah left this child on the trash heap for jackals to devour, would she be letting the darkness slip inside of her, like a viper slithering into a room at night? Keturah began to rock back and forth as panic rose within her—a feeling of unbearable fear. Orcus was nearby. He was approaching. He wanted to take this child back with him to the land of the dead, and if Keturah did not act soon, the baby would be swallowed up in smoke.

Keturah began to cry, thinking about her own needs, her own fears. How could she take care of a child? *See to it, then, that the light within you is not darkness*! She heard footsteps. Was it Orcus? Or was it Rufus, coming to drag her back to slavery?

Screaming in frustration, Keturah leaped to her feet and tried to reach for the baby, but it had been placed just out of reach. She would have to climb this mountain of death if she hoped to save the child. Hitching up her robe, she stepped onto the trash and climbed, slipping as she did. Bracing her fall with her hands, she touched human filth and dead animals. Impurity and evil clung to her like rags, but she kept going. On hands and knees, she crawled up to where she found the child, red-faced and screaming.

Gathering the child in her arms, Keturah began to weep. She glanced over her shoulder, fully expecting to see Orcus standing there with a sword to kill them both. Her heart thumped in her ears as she slid back down the mound of trash, the child wrapped in her arms. Then she took off running, sensing a fiend hotly pursuing her.

*See to it, then, that the light within you is not darkness.*

Keturah kept running, desperate to stay one step ahead of the darkness. And when she entered the city with the child in her arms, she collapsed in a heap on the ground, relieved to be within the safety of the walls.

## Asaph

Asaph knew something was wrong the moment he opened his eyes. It was the middle of the night, as dark as pitch, but a strange light flickered in the window on the opposite side of the room. Outside, people were shouting. The smell of smoke filled his nose.

Hurling aside his blanket, he roused the other two Zealots in the room, and all three of them tumbled outside. A house in Magdala, only five homes away, was engulfed in flames. Someone jammed a wooden bucket in his hands and shoved him from behind.

"Don't just gawk! Fight the fire!" bellowed Barabbas in his right ear.

Barabbas and others were trying to form a bucket line stretching from the well, but the out-of-control crowd was making this impossible. Panicked people blocked the way to the well, and many shouted and screamed at the flames as if words could put out fire.

"Out of the way! Clear a path! Clear a path!" Asaph pushed through the crowd, trying to reach the well. When someone tried to snatch the bucket from his hand, he flailed wildly, striking a man in the face. Ahead, he could see the beginnings of a disorganized bucket line taking shape. But amid the crowd, someone suddenly let out a powerful scream.

Then, in another part of the crowd, another scream. He saw a person collapse to the ground, while others reached out to help. Moments later, in yet another part of the crowd, a third scream.

"I've been stabbed!"

It was like an angel of death was snaking through the crowd, striking down people right and left, sowing seeds of chaos. As confusion and terror spread, so did the devouring fire. In disbelief, Asaph saw someone shove a man into the blaze. The Jewish man had been using a wet blanket to smother flames at the edge of the fire when a shadow bolted from the crowd and gave him a powerful push. The man with the blanket tumbled face-first into the flames. The poor man writhed, fire latching onto his robes and wrapping him in ribbons of flame. Screaming, the man got back to his feet and began to tear off his robes.

Then, yet another scream, only this one came immediately to Asaph's right. A woman collapsed at Asaph's feet. As she groaned, Asaph crouched to find out what was wrong.

"How are you hurt?" Under normal circumstances, putting his hands on a strange woman would be forbidden. But this was not normal circumstances.

"My back!" she shouted.

Asaph put a hand on her back and felt something moist. In the light of the fire, he could see blood spread across her back, soaking the fabric of her robes. She, too, had been stabbed.

"Murderers!" someone shouted.

There had to be more than one killer in this crowd to drop so many people in such a short time. That could mean only one thing. Roman soldiers, dressed as civilians, had coordinated the attacks. Most likely, they had started the fire, and when a crowd collected in the darkness, they began moving through their midst with hidden daggers, killing randomly and swiftly. The panic spread more rapidly than flames.

Since this woman had been standing next to him when she fell, he realized just how close he had come to the angel of death.

Asaph put his arms beneath the woman's body and raised her from the ground. By this time, the panic was so great that people were either fleeing the scene or throwing fists at each other, terrified that if they didn't fight back, they might be the next person struck down.

The woman in his arms began to pray, calling on God's mercy.

"Leave her and fight!" someone shouted from his left, but he ignored the command. In the darkness and the madness, how would he even know who to fight? Besides, he didn't have a sword or knife on him; he couldn't do anything to stop the Roman wolves in their flock. The best he could do was get this woman to safety, so she wouldn't be trampled to death.

Asaph found himself praying aloud. "I will not fear the terror of night, nor the pestilence that stalks in the darkness, nor the plague that destroys at midday. A thousand may fall at my side, ten thousand at my right hand, but it will not come near me!"

Asaph began to run, as best as he could with a bloody body in his arms. Let the house burn. If he could save this one woman, then he would have done so much more than put out a flaming building. As he kept running, the sounds of the chaos behind him began to fade, and he sputtered his prayer between heaving breaths.

"Because you love me, says the Lord, you will rescue me; you will protect me, for you acknowledge my name. You will call on me, and you will answer; you will be with me in trouble, you will deliver me and honor me. With long life you will satisfy me and show me your salvation."

When Asaph could run no more, he staggered to his knees. Then he lowered the woman to the dust and shook her. "Are you with me? Are you still with me?"

Drawing his arms from beneath her back, he could tell, even in the dark, that his hands and wrists were soaked in her blood. The woman didn't answer. Kneeling, he leaned over her face to listen for any sound of breath. Nothing. As his eyes adjusted to the dark, he could see that the woman was young, barely older than a girl. Her eyes were open but staring at space. He felt no breath, heard no sound coming from her lips.

Letting out a wail, Asaph scooped dirt and tossed it on his head, again and again and again.

"For he who avenges blood remembers, he does not ignore the cries of the afflicted! Lord, see how my enemies persecute me! Have mercy and lift me up from the gates of death!"

With his right hand, Asaph held up a handful of dirt and let it sprinkle slowly on his head. He felt the grains tumble across his face as he buried himself in grief and fury.

# 3
## Luke, Chapter 15

**Eliana**

Jesus continued to follow the road hugging the western side of the Jordan River as he passed through Perea, heading south toward Jerusalem, to be there in time for Passover. It was late morning, and Eliana felt especially jubilant walking amidst the multitudes.

*Though there are no sheep in the pen and no cattle in the stalls, yet I will rejoice in the Lord, I will be joyful in God my Savior. The Sovereign Lord is my strength; he makes my feet like the feet of a deer, he enables me to tread on the heights.*

Eliana was so bright and buoyant that she suddenly realized she was skipping like a girl.

"You are in good spirits," observed Keturah, trailing behind with the infant wrapped in her arms.

Eliana spun around and spread out her arms. "Why not? Rufus didn't find you. And now you have a baby girl! My heart is filled with greater joy than new wine!"

Eliana was as shocked as everyone when Keturah showed up holding a baby. But when Keturah explained how she had come upon the child, Eliana knew it was the hand of God.

The little girl, who had not yet been given a name, suddenly began to squall. Keturah did not get much sleep the night before, so her mood seemed considerably darker. Eliana hoped her friend wasn't regretting her choice to save the baby.

Keturah passed the child off to the Jewish wet nurse she had found, a woman named Ruth. As Ruth nursed the baby, Keturah paced back and forth, fretting. Eliana knew it was no use trying to soothe her friend, so she picked up a stick and hurled it ahead for Lavi to fetch. Her dog was filled with as much boundless energy as her, and she tossed the stick a half dozen more times before she told Lavi, "No more."

By early afternoon, the crowd had gathered on a dry spot not far from the Jordan. As Eliana leaned back on her right elbow, chewing on a reed, Lavi snuggled up to her. Then Jesus began to teach. His voice floated across the field like a song.

"Suppose one of you has a hundred sheep and loses one of them. Does he not leave the ninety-nine in the open country and go after the lost sheep until he finds it?" Jesus asked.

A very good question, she thought. Most shepherds work in teams, so a single shepherd could take off in search of the missing animal, while the others kept an eye on the ninety-nine. Made sense.

"And when he finds it, he joyfully puts it on his shoulders and goes home. Then he calls his friends and neighbors together and says, 'Rejoice with me; I have found my lost sheep.' I tell you that in the same way, there will be more rejoicing in heaven over one sinner who repents than over ninety-nine righteous persons who do not need to repent."

"I felt that way, you know," came a voice from behind Eliana, shocking her into a sitting position. She turned and looked. It was her father! Had he come to capture her, as Rufus tried to do with Keturah?

Eliana's first instinct was to leap up and flee, but as her father lowered himself beside her, it became obvious he had no plans of dragging her forcefully away. At least for now.

"Stay," he said, taking a seat beside her. He sighed as he stared at the teacher, who continued to move through the crowd. "You were my lost sheep, Eliana, and when you came back to me, I wanted to call together the entire world and tell them that I had found you."

Her father's tone was soft and sincere, much different than their last few encounters. Was it a trick to catch her off guard?

Eliana lowered her head and spoke softly. "I, too, wanted to sing to the world. I was back with my Abba."

"Then why did you leave me?"

"You know the answer, Abba. I must follow the Nazarene. He saved my life. I was that lost sheep, about to stumble over the ledge of a cliff, and he found me. He carried me to safety, like a shepherd carrying a sheep over his shoulders."

Her father's eyes misted with sadness at her words. "That's all I have ever wanted to do for you—to protect you, to rescue you. I wanted to be that shepherd, carrying my little lamb to safety."

She didn't mention the glaring difference. Her father wanted to keep her safe by locking her away. Jesus wanted to rescue her by freeing her, releasing her from the shackles of this world.

Her father drew circles in the dirt. "Do you love this teacher?"

Stunned, Eliana stared at him for several heartbeats. "Not in the way you mean. I do not seek to be his wife, but I do love him. He teaches us to love all people, even our bitterest enemies."

Her father shook his head. "That is wrong. He should never expect you to love the men who abducted you as a child."

Eliana felt a shadow drape her spirit. She was drawn to Jesus's teachings on love, but when her father put it that way, he made a strong point. She had been working so hard to distance herself from the child who was abducted that she never even considered that those men deserved to be loved. Her father had poked at a deep bruise.

Jesus moved in their direction. "Or suppose a woman has ten silver coins and loses one. Does she not light a lamp, sweep the house, and search carefully until she finds it? And when she finds it, she calls her friends and neighbors together and says, 'Rejoice with me; I have found my lost coin.' In the same way, I tell you there is rejoicing in the presence of the angels of God over one sinner who repents."

Eliana's father smiled at her. "So, the Nazarene has moved from losing one sheep out of one hundred to losing one coin out of ten. He's raising the stakes."

"Abba, we can be together. Travel with me. Follow Jesus. You've come this far. Please be by my side."

"You mean I am supposed to obey and follow my daughter? Daughters are expected to obey their fathers, not the other way around."

"I'm not asking you to follow *me*. I'm asking you to follow Jesus."

"The priests say this Jesus speaks dangerous words," her abba answered. "He is abducting you with smooth speech."

"He is not abducting me. I go willingly. I have never been happier."

"Weren't you happy in our family?" Her father sounded like a child whose feelings had been hurt.

When Eliana reached out and touched her father's hand, he flinched. "Of course, I was happy. I meant that I have never been happier since the day I was taken from you. I disappeared like a coin in a crack, and I was in darkness for many years. But God lit a lamp and never stopped searching for me."

Her father sighed once again. "I never stopped searching either."

Eliana squeezed his hand. "I know."

Her abba swiped at the tears that were springing up.

Then Jesus transitioned into yet another lost-and-found story, this one an elaborate tale of a young son who demanded that he receive his father's inheritance so he could travel to a far land and live freely and riotously. Eliana's father scowled at the story. She knew what he was thinking. A child who demanded his inheritance while his father lived was like telling the father he wished he was dead. But in this story, the father gave in to the youngest son's demands, allowing him to squander his wealth with raucous living.

"After he had spent everything, there was a severe famine in that whole country, and he began to be in need," Jesus continued. "So he went and hired himself out to a citizen of that country, who sent him to his fields to feed pigs. He longed to fill his stomach with the pods that the pigs were eating, but no one gave him anything."

Being knocked down to working with pigs—an unclean animal—was the ultimate humiliation for the youngest son. But to crave the food of pigs? That was even worse. Her father smiled because the son in the story had gotten his comeuppance.

The mention of pigs also made Eliana think of the night she was healed, when the demons inside the man in the cemetery were cast into a herd of swine. That night, she, too, was dragged down to the lowest level when the demon Calev tried to convince her to destroy herself. She became an unclean animal, no better than a pig . . . until she was healed.

Jesus's story continued. "When the son came to his senses, he said, 'How many of my father's hired servants have food to spare, and here I am starving to death! I will set out and go back to my father and say to him: Father, I have sinned against heaven and against you. I am no longer worthy to be called your son; make me like one of your hired servants.' So he got up and went to his father.

"But while he was still a long way off, his father saw him and was filled with compassion for him; he ran to his son, threw his arms around him, and kissed him."

*The father runs?* But a father never runs in public! It was shameful for a man to hitch up his robes and sprint in the sight of his neighbors. Eliana could see the puzzlement in her father's eyes as he, too, absorbed this bizarre image. Jesus paused to scan the crowd, his eyes alighting on her father. As he smiled and continued, Eliana noticed the intense connection between Jesus's eyes and her father's.

"But the father said to his servants, 'Quick! Bring the best robe and put it on him,'" Jesus said. "'Put a ring on his finger and sandals on his feet. Bring the fattened calf and kill it. Let's have a feast and celebrate. For this son of mine was dead and is alive again; he was lost and is found.' So they began to celebrate."

"I see that Jesus raised the stakes again," Abba whispered as Jesus turned and moved among the crowd. "One lost sheep out of one hundred. One lost coin out of ten. And then: One lost son out of two."

Eliana smiled. Her father had always been a sharp listener. But Jesus had one more twist to his story. The oldest son would not join the celebration because he was jealous and upset that his father had thrown such a big celebration for the youngest son, who had dishonored him. The irony was that the oldest son was heaping dishonor on his father by not agreeing to attend the party.

Jesus continued: "'My son,' the father said to his oldest boy, 'you are always with me, and everything I have is yours. But we had to celebrate and be glad, because this brother of yours was dead and is alive again; he was lost and is found.'"

"I was dead and am alive again," Eliana whispered, not even trying to hide her tears as her father was doing. "Please celebrate with me. Do not be like the older brother in the story."

Eliana's father came to attention. *"I am not the older brother of the story. I am the father of the story. I lost my child and then found her."*

"But why do you try to control me? The father in this story gave the youngest son the freedom to choose his path, however wrong it was."

"But you are not a son. You are my *daughter*. You belong in my household until you marry."

"I belong with Jesus."

At those words, Eliana could see her father shut down. He closed his eyes, and she sensed a hardening in his spirit. He was a fighter. She knew he wouldn't give in to her or to Jesus without a struggle.

"You belong to me—and to God." He rose to his feet, as if there were no arguing such a truth. Then he wandered off like a lost soul, disappearing into the crowd.

## Asaph

"An eye for an eye, a tooth for a tooth, and a Roman for a Jew," declared Barabbas.

"Agreed," said Asaph as the other Zealots around the campfire nodded their approval.

It had been two days since calamity struck Magdala, and the Zealots were on the move, seeking vengeance and blood. Two homes had been torched that night in Magdala, but much worse was the loss of life. Five men, four women, and two children. All knifed in the dark. Asaph and the other Zealots were sure it had been the work of Roman soldiers, sent in disguise by Pontius Pilate.

This was not the first time Pilate had used such deadly stealth. When Pilate spent sacred money from the Temple treasury to pay for the construction of new aqueducts, a pagan project, there were widespread protests among the Jews. Pilate responded by mixing his own soldiers, dressed as private men, into the midst of the multitude; then, on a signal, the soldiers suddenly produced staves and began beating people. Some of the Jews were so badly beaten that they died.

Now, Pilate had done it again. He had sent assassins in the dark as vengeance for the soldiers killed by the Zealots on Mount Arbel.

Barabbas pinned Asaph with a stare. "What do you think of your Jesus now? What do you make of his teaching to love our enemies? Shall we turn the other cheek after what they did to us?"

Asaph bristled. "Why are you looking at me? I never believed those words for a moment."

"But the woman you love believes them."

Barabbas never stopped reminding him that he had betrayed Judah by unlocking the door and letting Eliana go free. Asaph was tempted to remind Barabbas that the only reason he was now a leader of this group of Zealots was because Judah had gone off looking for his daughter. Barabbas should be thanking him, not mocking him, for freeing Eliana. It set the stage for his elevation to leadership.

But Asaph didn't dare speak those words. There was no telling how Barabbas would react.

"Tomorrow, we attack." Barabbas pulled out his sword and drove it into the ground.

"What's our target?" asked one of the men.

"The *vehiculatio*." Barabbas paused to take in the stunned looks on everyone's face.

"Good," said Asaph, trying to suppress his own surprise. He wanted to prove that he was more than willing to strike at the heart of Roman authority. They would attack the *vehiculatio*, the transit system set up by Augustus to carry communication and taxes from the provinces to Rome. Augustus had established a series of stations throughout the Empire, and a trail ran through the heart of Galilee.

Barabbas stared directly at Asaph. "We leave no one alive."

"Agreed. We leave no one alive," Asaph said, a tactic he enthusiastically embraced after what had happened in Magdala. He thought about the woman who died in his arms, young and innocent, and knew he would have no problem avenging her death by killing a Roman or two or three.

Asaph drew his sword—the one given to him by Judah—and he jammed it into the soil, next to Barabbas's blade. "An eye for an eye, a tooth for a tooth, and *two* Romans for a Jew!"

As Barabbas clapped him on the back, Asaph couldn't contain his laughter.

## Keturah

For such a small thing, this baby was beginning to weigh heavily in Keturah's arms as she trudged through Perea amidst a thousand people or more following in Jesus's wake. She had given up her spot on the donkey to the wet nurse, Ruth, who looked exhausted from night feedings. But now Keturah's arms were aching.

Even with the help of Ruth, Keturah was beginning to think she had made the biggest mistake of her life by rescuing this child. The baby girl spent half of her waking hours crying—and the other half defecating. Sveshtari didn't make things any easier.

"You don't have to keep this child," he said. "You've had her for only a week. You are not her mother."

"So, I should expose her to the elements as her father did?"

"If it is the will of the gods. Maybe the father decided it was the will of Vesta."

"Or maybe it was just the will of her selfish father. Romulus and Remus were abandoned by their father and raised by a she-wolf. If the she-wolf had not saved them, they would not have founded Rome. There would be no Eternal City."

"My point exactly," said Sveshtari. "If they had died and not founded Rome, perhaps the world would be a better place."

The baby, still unnamed, began to squawk until she let the baby girl suck on her finger. "I don't think you have to worry that this child will ever have the power to build an empire."

"No, she is a girl. But perhaps Vesta and the gods want her destroyed for other reasons. There might be great evil in her future."

Keturah could not believe she was hearing this nonsense. She started the day doubting her decision to rescue the child. But the more that Sveshtari hectored her, the more she wanted to keep the baby.

"What kind of god would want to destroy a baby?" she said. "Jesus would not kill a baby. Eliana tells me it was King Herod who slaughtered the innocents, trying to destroy the newborn Jesus."

"And who's to say Herod was wrong?"

"I say it! So would the thousand people you see here today. Herod was treacherous without excuse, and so is his son!"

"All right, I'll give you that one."

As the baby continued to suck on her finger, the wind began to whip, and Keturah could smell rain in the air. They were heading to Jerusalem for the Passover, the celebration that stretched back to the days of Moses—another child who had been plucked from death in the Nile River.

"We shall call her Babette," Keturah suddenly said. "Promise of God."

Sveshtari clicked his tongue. "But that is a Jewish name."

"We're supposed to be Hebrews. Remember?"

Sveshtari grunted. "Sometimes I wonder how many people really believe our act. Judas certainly suspects that I am not your typical Jew."

Keturah felt a flutter of fear. "That is not good. If word gets out... Authorities are looking for you."

"That is why we must not be burdened by a child. We may need to flee, and a child will only slow us down."

"*We*? Why do you speak of we? There is no we."

Keturah saw a wave of disappointment cross Sveshtari's face, but she was too tired to soothe his feelings. She already had her hands full trying to soothe Babette.

That's when it dawned on her. Maybe Sveshtari was jealous of the attention she was giving to the baby. Before Babette, they were just beginning to rekindle their relationship.

"Keturah..." Sveshtari said in a tone of reconciliation. But before he could say another word, Babette began to wail, flutter her arms, and turn red in the face.

Sveshtari quieted as Keturah stepped aside to comfort Babette. *Promise of God*. Keturah liked the name, but she had no idea what kind of promise this child held. She pushed away Sveshtari's ominous words about the evil in Babette's future. It was a ridiculous statement, born of jealousy.

Sveshtari kicked a rock as Keturah slipped away from his side and handed Babette to Ruth, who began to feed the baby girl. Sometimes, Keturah felt like she had two babies on her hands.

## Asaph

Asaph chose his rocks carefully before crouching in the brush, accompanied by a dozen other Zealots alongside a Roman road. He had become an expert at using the sling, even better than Gershom. In addition to the sling, he was armed with Judah's sword and a knife like the one that a Roman soldier had shown him when he was just a boy.

They were preparing to pounce on a small contingent of Roman soldiers. Four of the Zealots, Asaph included, carried slings and rocks, while the others were equipped with *pila*—javelins.

One of the Zealots, Tyrus, came running up to Barabbas, out of breath, to report.

"How many did you see?" Barabbas asked.

"One driver, five soldiers," Tyrus said between wheezes.

"Are you certain?"

Tyrus nodded.

"Five soldiers. That's good odds. Hit them swiftly, and this will be over in moments."

Although the attack might last only moments, the repercussions of what they were about to do would last much longer. Attacking a wagon carrying tax money was a serious offense. More than worthy of crucifixion.

"Let no one escape alive, and no one will identify us," Barabbas whispered. "No mercy. A life for a life."

*A life for a life.* Asaph closed his eyes and once again sent his thoughts back to the image of the woman who died in his arms. This attack would be for her—and for Eliana, whose family fled when the Romans descended on their village like vultures. This attack was not just about retrieving tax money pilfered from his people. It was personal. No mercy.

"You look nervous," Asaph taunted Zuriel, who crouched to his left. Zuriel's forehead gleamed with sweat.

"Shut up. Just worry about yourself."

Asaph grinned. "I'm concerned about your inexperience. You are a virgin in battle."

"And one battle makes you an expert?"

Asaph had struck a nerve. He hoped that if he got Zuriel distracted and angry, the man might make a mistake and become a casualty during this attack. If Zuriel didn't come through this alive, Asaph's life would certainly be much easier. Zuriel had spent the past month buttering up Barabbas and spreading his subtle poison.

"Do you even know how to hurl a spear properly?" Asaph asked.

"My *pila* will do more damage than your sling. A spear strikes a man's internal organs."

"David took down a giant with a sling."

"So, you're comparing yourself to King David? Barabbas will be interested to know that you fancy yourself as another David. I suppose that means you see Barabbas as the King Saul to your King David."

"I said nothing of the kind."

The sudden sound of rattling wheels along the Roman road interrupted their verbal duel, and Asaph tensed. His job was to strike one of the soldiers in the forward position, then reload and hit whoever might still be standing. The bushes were thick enough to conceal them, but low enough for them to fire over the top when they stood.

Next came the sound of voices. The chatter of soldiers meant the Romans would not be completely focused on their surroundings. The voices rose in volume, and so did the clank of wagon wheels. They were drawing closer. Asaph's heart began to race. He tried to steady his nerves by taking deep breaths. The sling was set, the rock studded with sharp edges.

Barabbas let out a war whoop and flung his javelin, which struck a soldier in the shoulder, knocking him from his horse. Asaph sprang to his feet, focused instantly on his target—another mounted soldier. He released a rock. The soldier had just been wheeling his horse around and turning toward the sound of the attack when Asaph's rock met him squarely in the face. Asaph quickly reloaded and flung a second rock, this one crushing the side of the head of a soldier trying to extract Barabbas's javelin embedded in his shoulder.

Only one Roman survived the initial onslaught. He raised his shield in time to deflect a javelin hurled by Zuriel. But a second javelin, thrown by Barabbas, took down his horse. The soldier was crushed beneath the weight of the falling animal.

Barabbas was right. It took only moments, and all five soldiers were on the ground, injured or dead. Several Zealots moved from body to body, driving swords through the soldiers' chests to finish off the living and make sure the dead remained that way.

They had focused their fury on the Roman soldiers, leaving the driver still alive—for now. He was a corpulent man who had initially drawn a sword, but he dropped it and put up his hands. "Mercy," he bleated. "Please. Let my wife and child go free."

*Wife and child?*

As Asaph pushed his way to the front, his stomach turned. Seated next to the driver were a plump young woman and a boy. He couldn't be more than ten years old.

"Mercy. Take me, but let my wife and boy go."

Sometimes, people took advantage of the Roman courier system and used it for their own personal transportation. For this driver, bringing along his wife and child for a free ride was a costly mistake.

"He's right. They are innocents," Asaph said, immediately regretting that he had spoken up.

Barabbas pulled out his knife and pointed it at Asaph's nose, a handbreadth away. "There are no innocents! They have seen our faces."

"We will tell no one," the man pleaded. "Take me as a hostage, and my wife and child will not tell a soul."

"We cannot be bothered by hostages!" Barabbas spun around and plunged his knife into the stomach of the driver. The woman screamed while the man looked down at the knife in disbelief. Barabbas twisted the blade, taking his pleasure. Then the driver stared at his wife, who would be the last person he laid eyes upon in this life.

"Do not harm the woman and boy," Asaph said. "God will judge us for shedding innocent blood."

Finally, Barabbas withdrew his knife from the man's belly and waved the bloody blade at Asaph.

"I do not take orders from you!"

Zuriel moved to Barabbas's side. "Asaph sees himself as another King David. And you are his King Saul."

"I said nothing of the kind! I am under your authority, Barabbas."

"Then perhaps you should order him to kill the child," Zuriel told Barabbas. "That would be the easiest way to test his submission to your authority."

This idea lit up Barabbas's eyes. He laughed and pointed his blade at Asaph.

"A fine idea! I order you to execute the boy!"

Asaph's mouth went dry as he gazed at the child. The boy had wet himself and was trembling and sobbing. "But he's only a boy. We are better than child killers."

"See! He thinks he's better than you," Zuriel told Barabbas.

"I said we are *all* better than child killers. We do not kill innocent children."

"How many children did the Romans kill the other night?" Barabbas said.

Asaph hung his head. "Two."

"Then we must kill four. This is only the first. I will have you kill three more before the month is up."

Asaph looked around for sympathy. He knew he wasn't alone in his reservations about Barabbas, but he found no allies. His eyes landed on Gershom.

"Gershom, you don't kill children. I know you."

"Leave me out of this," Gershom growled.

"I'm not ordering Gershom to kill this child. I'm ordering *you*." Barabbas stepped within an arm's length of him.

Suddenly, the boy shot from the wagon like he was catapulted from a sling and sprinted down the road, running for his life. The mother screamed, so Barabbas used his knife to shut her up for good. By the time the mother's death was complete, his eyes scanned the road for any sign of the boy.

"Spread out. Find the boy. He has seen too much."

Asaph could sense the reluctance in his fellow Zealots to hunt down a child, but no one else spoke up against Barabbas.

"You stay with me." Barabbas shoved Asaph from behind as if he were driving a prisoner forward. Did he intend to kill him too?

For a moment, Asaph thought about running off, just as the boy had done. But Barabbas had taken up his javelin, and he had a strong arm and eagle aim. Asaph wouldn't get far before being pinned in the back.

He did as Barabbas commanded.

# 4.
## Luke, Chapter 16

### Nekoda

Nekoda mixed in with the crowd following Jesus and flowing toward Jerusalem; he continued to keep his eyes and ears open for any sign of Sveshtari. Eyes also went in his direction because he was wearing his purple robe, a potent symbol of his station in life.

As Jesus and his followers neared the spot where the Jabbok River met the Jordan, Nekoda spotted his brother. Chaim sat on a rock, listening to Jesus teach, and next to him was a woman. He had seen Chaim with this woman before. Eliana was her name.

Chaim kept a proper distance from Eliana, as any unmarried man should, but it was obvious that his brother was smitten. At his age! Chaim had been married when he was young, but his wife and baby died in childbirth. Since then, grief followed at his side, and he always made it clear that he was not interested in taking another wife—although that may have changed from the looks of it.

Jesus began to teach, so Nekoda found a place to sit nearby, where he could keep an eye on Chaim and monitor the Nazarene's words. The rabbi addressed his disciples, who had gathered closest to him, but he spoke loudly enough for the Pharisees and others to hear. After telling a baffling story about a landowner and his dishonest manager, Jesus suddenly launched into a forceful lesson on trustworthiness and money.

Jesus picked out a few of the Pharisees in the crowd. "Whoever can be trusted with very little can also be trusted with much, and whoever is dishonest with very little will also be dishonest with much. So, if you have not been trustworthy in handling worldly wealth, who will trust you with true riches?

"No one can serve two masters. Either you will hate the one and love the other or you will be devoted to the one and despise the other. You cannot serve both God and money."

This caused a stir among the Pharisees, but Jesus didn't let up. He told the story of a beggar named Lazarus, covered in sores, who was taken to heaven after he died. Meanwhile, a rich man who dressed in purple and lived in luxury also died, but instead of going to heaven, he was tormented in Hades because he had neglected to help the poor man. When the rich man spotted Father Abraham in the distance, he begged Abraham to warn his brothers about the torments of Hades. But Abraham said his brothers already had received warnings from Moses. Let them listen to Moses.

The rich man continued to plead, saying that his brothers will surely repent if someone from the dead goes to them.

Father Abraham replied, "If they do not listen to Moses and the Prophets, they will not be convinced even if someone rises from the dead."

Several Pharisees left in a huff after this story was over, knowing the barbed words had been aimed at them. Nekoda understood their anger. He, too, felt like Jesus might've been talking about him. Was he the rich man in the story—the man dressed in purple? The only way you could get the color purple for a garment was to extract it from a sea snail. But because you can only obtain one small drop of color from each snail, it took 5,000 to 6,000 snails to make one garment. Only a rich man could afford such a rarity.

Nekoda suddenly felt conspicuous in his purple robe.

When Jesus was done speaking, Nekoda watched as Chaim followed Eliana like a puppy. No doubt about it. He was besotted. This gave Nekoda an idea. Eliana might provide leverage over his brother.

After Eliana parted from Chaim, Nekoda swooped in on his brother, approaching from behind. Chaim just stood there, staring at Eliana and looking heartsick. When Nekoda suddenly spoke, Chaim nearly jumped out of his sandals.

"Nekoda! You gave me a fright."

Nekoda nodded in the direction of Eliana. "You obviously had your mind on other matters. Looking for a wife? At your age?"

"Who said I'm looking for a wife?"

"Your eyes said it all. It was hard not to notice from where I was sitting."

"You were in the crowd? Since when do you listen to Jesus?"

"I found his teaching intriguing—although a bit puzzling. But tell me . . . do you love Eliana?"

Chaim hesitated before answering. "That's none of your business, brother. So, if you'll excuse me . . ."

Chaim turned and walked away, and Nekoda had to jog to catch up with him in the crowd. He slipped up beside him, but Chaim did not even give him a cursory glance.

"You told me earlier that you didn't know the man named Sveshtari, but I believe you do," Nekoda said.

"You believe wrong."

"He used to be a bodyguard in Herod's palace. I think he was among the Zealots who attacked a Roman contingent on the Cliffs of Arbel. But you already know that."

"Are the Romans paying you to track him down?" Chaim spit to the side. "I will have no more to do with your betrayals of our people."

"This is no betrayal. The Romans allow us to worship as we see fit, and the Zealots are forcing the Romans into a corner. Our freedom to worship is at risk because of the Zealots' antagonism toward Rome. You will do our people a favor if you help me rid the land of Sveshtari and his ilk."

"I will not aid Rome. I will not aid *you*."

Nekoda neared a breaking point. A surge of fury rose in his chest. The polite approach was not working, so he came at Chaim like a bull. "I *know* you were involved with the Zealots! You helped to ambush the Roman soldiers on the Cliffs of Arbel."

That stopped him in his tracks. Chaim turned, and the brothers came face to face.

"You know nothing. I follow Jesus, not the Zealots."

"But I think you tipped off the Zealots that the Romans were coming."

Nekoda studied his brother's face. Chaim looked away, his face turning a light tinge of red. Guilty as charged.

"You stand out like a peacock in your purple robe," Chaim said, trying to change the subject. "You have been paid well by Rome. But maybe you should've listened more closely to Jesus's story about the rich man in purple who was cast into Hades after he died."

"Are you warning me about Hades?"

"I am warning you to turn away from the wealth given to you by Rome."

"There is no sin in wearing fine clothes."

"But there is sin in taking Roman money to pay for those clothes."

Nekoda had to fight the urge to punch his brother in the face. He had only struck his brother in anger a few times in his life. Today might be another one of those days.

"I recall that you didn't turn away Roman money when you were supplying me with information, brother," said Nekoda.

"That was before I met Jesus."

"You're still the same Chaim. Like everyone, you need money to live. And I will pay you handsomely if you provide me information on Sveshtari. I know he is somewhere among this multitude."

Chaim shook his head. "Your money no longer tempts me."

"If money will not tempt you, then hear this. I am under pressure to deliver someone to the Romans who was responsible for the attack at the caves of Arbel. I prefer to hand them Sveshtari. But if I cannot give them Sveshtari, I will give them someone else."

Chaim stared long and hard into Nekoda's eyes. "Is that a threat?"

"I do not want to see you harmed, but you give me no choice. I must hand over someone. My life depends on it."

"What about *my life*?"

"Both of our lives can be preserved if we give them Sveshtari. He is a murderer. A brutal pagan bodyguard. Aren't our lives more valuable than his?"

Chaim said nothing. He continued to stare daggers at Nekoda.

"You wouldn't want to be implicated, would you?" Nekoda brought the threat into the open. "And you wouldn't want Eliana to be implicated along with you. She is the daughter of a Zealot."

Nekoda could tell that this last threat fell on Chaim like a stone the size of a house.

"Leave Eliana out of this."

"You leave me little choice."

"We all have choices."

"True, true. And my choice is to hand Sveshtari to Herod, but if not him, then maybe Eliana."

Chaim stormed off. But Nekoda knew . . . he had his brother cornered.

## Asaph

"Be reasonable," Asaph said to Barabbas, who trudged a few cubits behind him, carrying a javelin in his hand. Asaph could sense the tip of the weapon pointed directly between his shoulder blades. "Zealots despise Romans. But we do not murder children. Surely, you must understand that, Barabbas."

Barabbas scoffed. "That boy has eyes, doesn't he? He can report us to the Romans. We have no choice but to dispose of him."

"You're talking about *killing* a child, stealing forty years of life from him."

"Pah! Most children do not live that long. I'd be doing him a favor, removing him from this Roman world."

Asaph did not respond. He walked on, convinced that Barabbas was going to dispose of him with the same unrepentant ease. Barabbas had taken away his knife, sword, and sling, leaving him as defenseless as a lamb.

The Zealots were on the eastern side of the Jordan Valley—the long, narrow gouge in the land where the Jordan River stretched south like a ribbon connecting the Sea of Galilee to the Dead Sea. Asaph knew that Jesus and his followers were somewhere on the western side of the Jordan, passing through Perea and heading south toward Jerusalem. If Asaph could break away, he could cross to the other side of the river, find the Galilean and his followers, and lose himself in the multitude.

But that was a big "if" when you have a spear pointed at your back.

"Judah would never kill a child," Asaph said impulsively. He should have realized that any comparison to Eliana's father would rouse Barabbas.

*"Judah was weak!"*

"I thought he was your friend."

"Pah! He did not have the resolve to lead a real revolt against Rome. He attacked a few Romans here and there, but his efforts were little more than a mosquito nipping at an elephant. I have bigger plans, and greater plans require greater bloodshed."

Asaph wondered why Barabbas hadn't already killed him. Perhaps he was waiting to track down the child so he could still force Asaph to murder the boy. Then Barabbas would kill Asaph in turn.

The Zealots fanned out and scoured the riverbank for any sign of the child. The boy was fast, and Asaph prayed he had the sense to keep running until night fell. They passed through a cluster of oleanders—flourishing pinks and reds on both sides. Then they moved into brush and tamarisk trees, thick evergreens that can thrive in the most brutal, dry conditions—a bit like the Jewish people. Asaph, still walking ahead of Barabbas, noticed a shadow darting through the tamarisk trees off to his right. At first, he thought it might be an animal of some sort, but it was moving on two legs. It came to a stop and crouched.

It was the boy. Asaph's heart sank. Why did the boy stop and hide? Why wasn't he still running? The fool! Asaph had risked his life for a boy without brains!

If he didn't do something soon, Barabbas would surely spot the child. Asaph had to act, but not just to save the boy. He had to do something to save his own skin.

Running would distract Barabbas from the boy, but there was a good chance he would be killed in the process. Barabbas would sink his spear in his back before he sprinted a few cubits. However, if he didn't act, he would be killed regardless, so what did he have to lose? He should at least try to get away because the Zealots were closing in on the boy.

"Over there! I see the boy!" Asaph suddenly shouted, pointing to the left—the opposite direction from the boy. It wasn't the most sophisticated of tricks, but it was enough to take Barabbas's eyes off Asaph for just a moment.

When Barabbas turned to look left, Asaph took off running right—in the direction of the Jordan River. Asaph was thankful for the thick brush in this area, despite the sting of the branches whipping him in the face as he ran forward. He sensed something fly by his right shoulder; from the corner of his eye, he saw Barabbas's spear drive deep into a tree trunk. Barabbas had missed, but he lugged a sizable sword and several knives. He still had plenty of ways to skewer Asaph.

Asaph reached the edge of the Jordan River, where lush green bushes grew up on both sides. The river was narrow and not very deep, and it would take only moments to cross. The soil was muddy along the bank, making it difficult to run as his sandals caught in the suction of the muck. Struggling to run, he worked his way into shallow water, but he made a sloshing sound, which Barabbas could easily track. Asaph had no choice but to dive beneath the water and hope he would not be spotted swimming beneath the murky brown surface.

As he plunged beneath, water filled every pore of his garments, and he felt the weight of his clothing tugging him down. Asaph frantically began to swim through the shallow water, kicking his legs and trying to move with the current while staying only a foot above the river bottom.

When John the Baptist lowered people in the Jordan River, the action symbolized death as the people rose from the water to new life. But if Asaph dared to rise from the Jordan, he would face death, not life. This was unlike any baptism he had ever seen before.

## Keturah

Keturah was energized for a change because baby Babette had slept through the night. With the child in her arms, Keturah passed through a small village with Eliana and Sveshtari at her side and Eliana's dog, Lavi, by their feet. Keturah suspected that Sveshtari wanted to talk with her alone, probably to harass her again about whether to keep Babette or not. So, she made sure Eliana was with them as a buffer.

"What was all of that about John the Baptist?" Keturah asked, referring to the latest words of Jesus. "He makes it sound like history turned a corner when John preached and baptized."

"John opened wide the doors to the Kingdom of God, inviting all to enter," said Eliana.

Keturah nuzzled Babette in her arms. "It's an outrage that John was arrested and killed. But Eliana, who do you suppose led the contingent that arrested him?" Keturah felt the sudden urge to hurt Sveshtari, and what better way than by pointing out his culpability in John the Baptist's arrest.

"I was under orders from Herod," muttered Sveshtari, a few steps behind them.

"You did many things under orders from Herod." Another dart hit her mark. Keturah was pleased with herself until she saw judgment in Eliana's eyes.

"Do you really think Sveshtari is still the same man he was then?" Eliana asked.

Keturah's face reddened. "I don't know. You'll have to ask him."

Why was Eliana turning on her? Sveshtari was the one who had arrested John the Baptist. He was responsible for sending him to prison, where the whims of a spoiled girl led to his death.

"I should have fled from Herod's palace long before I did," Sveshtari said glumly, looking at Eliana.

Does he mean he should have fled the palace before he was ordered to arrest John—or before he killed her father? Keturah was tempted to ask him bluntly, but she was afraid Eliana would judge her again.

Sveshtari turned his gaze to the ground. "The gods have punished me for my sins. They continue to torture me."

Eliana put a hand on Sveshtari's arm—a brazen move. "We are all sinners, and the one God forgives all. Haven't you noticed that Jesus draws the greatest sinners to his side? People like us."

*Speak for yourself*, Keturah thought.

Keturah's parents were murdered in Herod's palace, she was nearly killed on more than one occasion, and she was sold into slavery! She had been constantly sinned against. *Where is my sin?* She was tempted to demand an answer from Eliana. But she held her tongue and gently bounced her sleeping baby in her arms.

They went quiet as they passed alongside the village's modest-sized synagogue, where Jesus had recently taught. But as they rounded the corner of the building, Sveshtari suddenly took Keturah by the arm and pulled her backward.

"Sveshtari! Let go of me!"

Sveshtari put a finger to his lips and led her around the corner of the synagogue. Eliana retreated with them.

"Didn't you see?" Sveshtari whispered. "Rufus and his men."

*Rufus again?* Almost instinctively, Keturah's hand went to her forehead, where her tattoo had once proclaimed that she was an escaped slave. "Will he ever stop looking for us?"

"Doubtful," Sveshtari said.

Eliana was a stranger to Rufus and wouldn't be recognized, so she peeked around the corner of the synagogue. "He's coming this way."

Keturah looked for any possible escape route. There was only one option. The synagogue.

Eliana must have been thinking the same thing because she took Babette from Keturah's arms and motioned toward the front door of the synagogue. "Inside, quickly."

Sveshtari threw open the synagogue door and pulled Keturah roughly into the building. Then they pressed their backs against the wall and waited.

## Eliana

Eliana sang to Babette and tried not to look at the four soldiers from Herod's guard who moved in her direction, all on foot. Babette stared at Eliana with wide, open eyes. The child had large, brown eyes, and they were transfixed by Eliana's face.

Eliana could sense the soldiers coming closer, could smell the pungent odor of their clothing, could hear the clink of the swords at their sides. When she heard them come to a halt, she finally looked up from Babette.

"Can I help you?" She gently jiggled Babette in her arms.

"You can step away from the synagogue door," commanded Rufus.

"I'm sorry. Have you come to pray in the synagogue?" Eliana spoke loudly in the hopes that Sveshtari and Keturah would hear that the soldiers were planning to enter.

"We're looking for two people—a man and a woman. I saw you speaking with them only moments ago."

"Those two people? I don't know their names, but they're headed back into town."

"If they were heading into town, they would've gone past us. Now kindly step aside."

"Certainly. I am sorry."

Taking her sweet time, Eliana began singing again to Babette and slowly stepped to her right. Rufus and one of the soldiers barreled by, barging into the synagogue, while the other two soldiers kept watch in front. Eliana sang even louder, praying for deliverance for her friends.

## Sveshtari

Sveshtari helped Keturah climb through the window on the opposite side of the synagogue. When he heard the front door beginning to open, he dove headfirst through the window, ending with a somersault and landing on his back. With the wind knocked out of him, he lay still in the dust for a moment, as Keturah rushed to his side. She helped him to his feet.

He was tempted to take Keturah by the hand and start running, but one direction led out of town and into wide open spaces where there was no place to hide. The other direction required them to pass in front of the synagogue, but he had a hunch that Rufus had left some of his men there to stand guard.

Keturah allowed him to take her by the hand. They moved to the corner of the synagogue, where they paused. He could hear the guards talking at the door.

"What if they're hiding behind the synagogue?" said one of the soldiers, as clear as day.

"You go around one side, and I'll go around the other."

Sveshtari glanced around for a place to hide. There was only one choice. On the side of the synagogue was a small structure that housed a *mikveh*, a ritual bath. During their many lessons on Jewish rituals, Eliana had explained the uses of a *mikveh* for ritual purification.

The rabbis would be outraged at the idea of a pagan immersing himself in these waters, but what choice did they have? Sveshtari opened the door and drew Keturah inside the dim interior. Before them was the *mikveh*, a small, stone pool with a set of steps leading into the water and a divider running down the middle. The idea, as Eliana once explained, was for a person to enter on one side of the steps as an unclean person. After total immersion, they exited up the other side of the steps completely purified.

Sveshtari didn't believe or understand any of this, but he instinctively did as the ritual ordained, leading Keturah down into the water using the right side of the steps. The water hit them with cold fury, and Keturah tightened her grip on his hand. But neither said a word as they slid into the water as silently as possible, trying not to stir a sound.

A *mikveh* was required to hold at least forty *se'ah* of water, enough for full immersion. Sveshtari and Keturah crouched low and let the water reach the tips of their chins, but they did not fully immerse. Keturah began to shake from the cold.

They had no idea what was happening outside, but they could hear muffled voices, including Eliana's. The sounds were coming from all directions outside the *mikveh*. Then the door began to squeak. Someone was entering.

Sveshtari and Keturah slowly lowered themselves until they were both fully immersed. He closed his eyes as the cold waters covered him like a shroud.

## Eliana

Eliana followed one of the soldiers as he made his way around the side of the synagogue. She spotted the *mikveh* and wondered if Sveshtari and Keturah could be hiding inside. They certainly weren't in the synagogue any longer or else Rufus would have discovered them by now. Where else could they be but the *mikveh*?

She leaned down and spoke a single word into Lavi's ears. Her dog took off, barking and nipping at the heels of the two soldiers who had just opened the door into the *mikveh*.

One of the soldiers kicked back at Lavi. "Get that mutt away from me, or I'll kill him!"

He would, too. But she needed Lavi to keep up the distraction. Her dog stood a cubit away, barking and snarling while the guards took a quick look inside the *mikveh*. Eliana, with the baby still in her arms, rushed up to Lavi and put on a show to keep him at bay. As she did, she glanced through the open door of the *mikveh*. The interior was dark, but she saw no sign of Sveshtari or Keturah.

She let Lavi take one more go at the soldiers' feet, and they cursed her dog as they exited the *mikveh*, leaving the door slightly ajar.

"I said keep your dog under control!"

With the soldiers away from the *mikveh* and Lavi's job of distraction done, she calmed her dog and drew him to her side. "My strongest apologies."

One of the guards snarled at Lavi while the other one backpedaled, as if this large, armed soldier was terrified of a small dog.

## **Keturah**

Keturah had to come up for air. She could not hold her breath for a moment longer. Even if the soldiers were still in the *mikveh*, she had to rise from the water, or she would pass out and drown. She took her chances, emerging from the water and gulping in a lungful of glorious air. As she did, she noticed that Sveshtari also had his head above water.

"You can hold your breath for an incredibly long time," he marveled. "I was about to raise you up, fearing you had gone unconscious."

Keturah noticed that the *mikveh* door was slightly ajar. "The soldiers? Where are they?"

"They've come and gone."

Keturah made a move to rise from the water, but Sveshtari stopped her. "Not just yet. Give the soldiers time to clear away from the synagogue."

Obediently, Keturah dipped back into the water, keeping her nose and eyes above the surface. The water was freezing, and her face had gone numb. She and Sveshtari didn't dare speak, so they simply stared into each other's eyes. She thought, once again, about Jesus's words; he said your eye is the lamp of the body. If your eyes are healthy, they will be full of light, but if your eyes are unhealthy, they will be full of darkness.

She looked deep into Sveshtari's eyes, trying to determine what lay behind them. Light or darkness? He stared back with equal concentration. She had never looked into someone's eyes and held the gaze for this long. His left eye was slightly bloodshot, with a cluster of tiny red rivers wriggling from the corner. His brown iris had widened in the dark, with the black hole at the center letting in as much light as possible.

She never thought before about how strange eyes were, these round white eggs, slick with moisture, taking in so much of the world, absorbing light and pictures, horrors and marvels. Sveshtari's eyes had watched her father die. His eyes had absorbed that horrific scene and planted it in his memory, deep behind his eyes. She also saw sadness. He said the gods had been torturing him, and she could see that. There was a weariness, and she noticed, for the first time, the lines beneath his eyes, a slight bagginess, with creases like elephant skin. What did Sveshtari see in her eyes? Did he see her anger, her bitterness, her suffering, her darkness?

*If the light within you is darkness, how great is that darkness!*

She sensed the darkness inside, filling her body like smoke from a burning building. A tear formed in the corner of her left eye. Sveshtari raised one hand from the water, reached out, and wiped it away. "I think they're gone now. We can rise."

Sveshtari stood and slogged up the right side of the *mikveh* stairs. As he did, he turned and reached out to take Keturah by the hand. She hesitated. If she declined to put her hand in his, that refusal would hurt him and give her pleasure. But didn't he have enough pain? Didn't she see it all displayed in his eyes? Hadn't he been tortured enough by the gods? Why should she add another crease to the weary folds beneath his eyes?

She took his hand, and together they rose from the water.

## Asaph

Immersed in the Jordan River, Asaph's lungs were about to burst, but he did not dare come up for air just yet. He was sure that the moment he raised his head above water, an arrow or javelin would pierce his skull. Instead, he kept swimming underwater until the moment his lungs burned and he was forced to surface for air.

But the moment he raised his head and opened his mouth, he spotted something black and long swimming along the surface of the water in a fast-moving S-shape, coming straight toward his face. In a defensive strike, the snake lunged for Asaph, nipping him on the lip before skimming away to safety.

Trying to ignore the pinching pain in his lip, Asaph dipped below the surface and swam, terrified that the snake had injected him with venom. Panic powered his strokes, and he kept going until once again his lungs began to ache. This time, when he came up for air, he saw that the river was constricting and becoming shallower.

Glancing around, Asaph saw no sign of his pursuers, so this was as good a place as any to exit. He rose from the river and felt his lip to gauge the damage, his hand coming away with traces of blood. He had no idea what kinds of serpents lived in these waters—or whether they were venomous.

Taking sluggish steps, he sloshed forward, clambered halfway onto the bank, and fell onto his stomach, his feet still mired in muck. Then he flipped over on his back and stared up at the sky. Only a few wisps of clouds interrupted the perfect blue.

Suddenly, a sword appeared directly overhead, followed by the face of a man staring down at him. A familiar face. It was Gershom, who kicked him in the ribs. "Get up."

As Asaph turned onto his stomach, he reached his right hand beneath the water, latching onto the largest rock he could find. He slid backward into the water and slipped the rock into the pocket of his garment.

Gershom kicked him again. "I said get up!"

Asaph got onto his knees and crawled, his long hair dangling and dripping into his face.

"Where are the others?" Asaph asked. Fortunately, he saw no sign of the other Zealots.

"And why would I tell you that?"

"Because we're friends, Gershom. I saved your life on Arbel, if you remember."

"You exaggerate your heroism."

"Exaggerate my heroism? I killed the soldier who was about to finish you! And what's my crime here—that I would not kill a child? I know you, too, would not have killed that boy if Barabbas had ordered you to do it."

"You have no idea what I'm capable of doing." Gershom smacked Asaph's shoulder with the flat side of his sword.

Clambering to his feet, Asaph stared into Gershom's eyes, trying to discern the man's intentions.

"What happened to your lip?" Gershom asked.

Asaph put a hand to his lip and felt the torn, swollen skin. "Snakebite. Please, Gershom. You know me. We traveled together; we found Eliana together. I know you are not a murderer. You will not kill me."

"Maybe not. But I intend to take you back to Barabbas and let him decide what to do with you."

"That's as good as killing me."

"I have no choice. You know that."

"Please, Gershom. Barabbas doesn't need to know that you found me. Just let me go. Do not end my life."

"Shut up and start marching back."

Asaph slipped his right hand into his pocket.

"And bring your hands out where I can see them."

Asaph drew out his hand, which clutched the rock, and he hurled the stone point-blank into the side of Gershom's face, from only an arm's length away. Gershom dropped instantly to the ground.

Then Asaph turned and ran for his life. He ran like Cain, heading south toward Jerusalem, where he would lose himself in the thousands of people flocking there for Passover. His legs strained to move through the thick grass, and his waterlogged clothing pulled him down like a millstone hanging from his neck.

# 5.

## Luke, Chapter 17

### Asaph

Asaph was light-headed, and his lip felt like it had swollen to the size of a beef bladder. He alternated running and walking for much of the afternoon, ever conscious that the Zealots were not far behind. By now, they had surely discovered Gershom's body and were seeking vengeance or justice or whatever they wanted to call it. Any way you looked at it, they wanted him dead.

Asaph was in much better physical shape since joining the Zealots, but he wasn't used to running this far, this fast. He thought he would've reached Jesus and his followers by this time, but they had moved much farther south than anticipated. By his estimates, he must be getting close to the boundary between Galilee and Samaria.

The image of Gershom flashed through his mind again and again. He saw the rock crashing into the side of his head, the blood bubbling out like a spring, and the wide-eyed look of betrayal before Gershom crumpled to the ground. Asaph was utterly ashamed of what he had done. They had lived and fought side by side, and even though they weren't friends by any stretch of the imagination, the intimacy of killing someone he knew weighed on him like a stone too heavy to bear.

*My spirit is broken. Save me from my bloodguilt! Give ear to my words, O Lord!*

Reaching a well, he came upon several women drawing water. He must've looked like a monster, with a swelling lip, sweat pouring down his face, and grime, dust, and blood on his garments. It was probably his own blood, but the women didn't know that. They fled from the well the moment they saw him approaching. With his back aching and his mind fogged by the heat, he staggered to the well, where he drew up the bucket and drank deeply until his belly felt like it would burst. Sick to his stomach, he sat on a stone, praying for the nausea to subside.

Casting a glance over his right shoulder, he saw—far down the winding road in the valley below—a male figure running. The man carried a spear. It was difficult to tell from this distance, but he would swear it was Zuriel.

Asaph was furious with himself because he had alternated too much walking with too little running, and now his enemy had tracked him down. Asaph paused to vomit before resuming his run. His head began to swim, and he prayed he wouldn't faint. If he lost consciousness, Zuriel would be upon him in short order and pin him to the ground with his spear.

Up ahead was an expanse of bushes and trees, as the barren, brown landscape finally gave way to cover. With increased hope, Asaph felt a lifting of the spirit that powered his feet. But when he plunged through an opening in the wall of bushes, he suddenly found himself in the presence of monsters.

*Lepers.*

Ten lepers hobbled along in a pack—like specters wrapped in rags. Their bodies were in different degrees of disintegration. Some were missing noses or ears or even a leg. They seemed equally surprised to see him suddenly appear in their midst.

After recovering from the initial shock, a brazen idea popped into Asaph's head. "May I travel with you?"

None of the lepers responded. They looked at each other as if trying to gauge whether Asaph was insane. Who asks to travel with a group of lepers, other than someone with leprosy—or a madman?

"You're not afraid?" one of them asked.

"Not at all," Asaph lied. Yes, he was terrified of lepers, but he was much more afraid of what would happen if Zuriel caught him. He didn't have the strength left to fight, and he no longer had a weapon. "Where are you headed?"

"To find Jesus. To find healing."

"That's where I am going too. I will accompany you."

A couple of the lepers looked at him and shrugged.

"Then we welcome you," said the one who seemed to be their leader. "My name is Abner."

"And I am Asaph. Thank you."

Quickly, Asaph tore several pieces of cloth from his robe. He used one piece to wrap around his mouth, as if to hide sores. He draped the other over his head to cover his face.

Several of the lepers stared at him as if he had lost his mind.

"Let's go!" he said, and the lepers resumed their trudge toward Jesus.

It wasn't long before Zuriel came crashing through the brush. From the corner of his eye, Asaph saw Zuriel come upon this platoon of living corpses. But just as quickly as he ran up, he changed course, clearly wanting to give the lepers a wide berth. Asaph's enemy raced past, not noticing an imposter amid the monsters.

When Zuriel was gone, Abner gave Asaph a sly smile and nodded. "Now I understand. You joined our death march to avoid death at the hands of that man."

"Thank you for your protection."

Several of the lepers laughed. "Imagine that! We have become your bodyguards, even though our own bodies are falling apart."

Asaph smiled uncomfortably as he moved among the lepers, making slow progress in the direction of Jesus. He looked around at the men who were wrapped in bandages that couldn't fully cover their oozing sores. He was certainly surrounded by death, but what else was new?

"What crime are you being sought for?" Abner asked.

"Who said I committed a crime?"

"Your eyes tell me." The leper stared at him with pity. A *leper* pitying him! "Maybe *we're* the ones who should be afraid of *you*."

## SVESHTARI

Sveshtari was humiliated. He sat cross-legged in the dust, keeping watch on a small flock of sheep as the day came to a close.

*Sheep!*

He had once been bodyguard for a tetrarch, and now he watched sheep.

It turned out that Judas never informed the other disciples that he had hired Sveshtari to be their bodyguard and help watch the money. The disciples had thought Sveshtari was just another follower of Jesus until the night when he nabbed the man trying to steal money.

The disciples were furious with Judas. You'd think they would be thankful that Sveshtari had prevented a robbery, but the disciples were against spending money to hire a guard, especially an *armed* guard. The disciples did not blame Sveshtari for Judas's misjudgment, and they said they would still share food and water with him freely. When Sveshtari said he didn't take charity, the disciples offered to pay him to watch the sheep being herded along with the crowds.

So here he was, watching animals. A job fit for the lowest of low. He hated this work, but the alternative was taking the disciples' money for nothing. He had some dignity left.

Torches went out across the camp, and the darkness became cold and complete. It drizzled earlier in the day, but the night was clear and swimming with stars. Sveshtari had seen no sign of Rufus and his men since their near capture earlier in the day. He prayed to Mars that their pursuers had left the village and were seeking him elsewhere.

Uncommonly bored, he sighed. When he had been a guard in Herod's palace, he fought boredom by making a game out of staring at various objects, and he found he could study a stone pillar for an hour, memorizing every nick and crack, or count the number of insects that wandered by. He would also try to concentrate his ears, picking up every single sound and making note of it. Tonight, he absorbed the sounds of crackling fire, murmuring voices, wolves in the distance, a nearby owl, frogs in the nearby pond . . .

And the sound of a pebble striking stone.

Sveshtari leaped to his feet and turned toward the noise.

"You're looking in the wrong direction," came a voice.

Drawing his knife, Sveshtari spun around and found a young man grinning at him.

"Easy with the knife, Sveshtari. I come as a friend."

"How do you know my name?"

"You don't remember me?"

"Should I?"

"I suppose it was dark when you caught me."

Sveshtari glared at the grinning man—about twenty years old, much shorter than him. Then it dawned on him. This was the thief whom he had caught trying to steal from Judas's money purse—the thief whom the disciples had so foolishly released.

Sveshtari scowled. "Have you come again to steal from the disciples?"

"Why should I steal? They give me money freely so I can feed my family."

"And they believe you have a family?"

"They do." Abel said this with a sly smile, confirming Sveshtari's suspicion that it was a lie.

Sveshtari jabbed the air with his knife. "So, what do you want?"

"I've come to say that the men who pursue you have left the village. They seek you elsewhere."

Sveshtari stared back at this young man with growing suspicion.

"Don't worry. I am here to offer you my services, not to turn you in. My name, if you have forgotten, is Abel."

"I don't need help from a thief."

"I have repented of my thievery. And I do think you need my help. Rufus and his men will not give up in their pursuit of you. They will be back."

"Why would you want to help me? Our first meeting was not the friendliest of encounters."

"That is true. You put a knife to my throat, and now you're poking a knife in my face."

"You snuck up on me. What else am I supposed to do?"

"You could be impressed by my ability to sneak up on people. That's what once made me a good thief. It also makes me a good spy, and you could use someone to keep an eye on your enemies."

"Someone like you?"

"I am offering you my services. You need a second set of eyes."

Sveshtari remained unconvinced of his sincerity. "What's in it for you?"

"I need your protection, especially as we near Jericho. I have many enemies in Jericho and Jerusalem. I can protect you with my eyes, and you can protect me with your muscle and sword."

"I don't need your help. I can deal with Rufus on my own."

"You barely escaped him today. He was almost upon you when you spotted him. I could have given you warning."

Sveshtari glowered. Was this all a ploy, a diversion so Abel could rob Judas and the disciples?

"I'm good at what I do," Abel said. "I've been watching you since the day we first met, and yet you don't seem to have noticed."

It was true. Sveshtari had never spotted Abel.

"I also watched you with that beautiful woman and the child. What's her name? Keturah? I am glad to see your treatments finally removed her tattoo."

Sveshtari bristled. He didn't like the idea that he had also been keeping watch on Keturah.

"How do you know her name?"

"I told you I'm good."

"If you're so good, then why didn't you warn me about Rufus before he almost caught us today?"

"That was my misjudgment. I saw Rufus, but I wanted to find out how perceptive you were. I wanted to see if you could detect him on your own. As I discovered, you aren't very good at it, and you were nearly caught. It convinced me that you need my services."

Again, where was Abel's proof that he had spotted Rufus before he did?

"I know the reason why the soldiers are looking for you," Abel continued. "You helped the Zealots fight the soldiers on the Cliffs of Arbel, and I like that about you. You are a rescuer. A protector. And I need a protector."

Abel bowed low before him. He stretched prostrate on the ground.

"Get up, you fool."

Slowly, Abel rose back to his feet and brushed the sand from his robe.

"My protection is all you ask? Not money?"

"I told you. The followers of Jesus provide all my needs—except my safety. That's all I ask from you. And all you need to do is make sure my enemies don't kill me." Abel's eyes flitted to the sheep. "Protecting a person is far more interesting than protecting sheep, wouldn't you say?"

Sveshtari couldn't deny it. "I will provide you my protection in exchange for your spying on my behalf. But protecting Keturah takes precedence over protecting you."

"As it should be." Abel sat on a large stone, picked up a handful of sand, and tossed it in his palm like sifting grain. "What are your sheep's names?"

Sveshtari shrugged. "How am I supposed to know?"

"A good shepherd knows his sheep by name."

"Then I'm not a very good shepherd. But I am a good bodyguard."

"I know." Abel patted one of the sheep on the back.

## Asaph

Asaph couldn't shake the sense that he was trapped in a living nightmare—surrounded by lepers. It couldn't have seemed stranger if he were part of a pack of walking skeletons. The road they traveled was dry and dusty, and the wind whipped the earth all around, stinging his eyes.

Abner lowered the cloth from his mouth to speak. "So, who did you murder?"

Asaph's stomach dropped. He was many things, but he had never seen himself as a murderer.

"I didn't murder anybody. Why would you say that?"

"Just a hunch."

"A poor hunch."

"If you say so. But my hunches are usually correct."

They continued in silence. Then Asaph let out a big sigh. "It was self-defense." It felt strangely liberating to speak the words.

"I'm glad to hear it was not a pre-meditated murder. I may be condemned to death by leprosy, but I have no desire to see my life shortened by the hands of a killer."

Although it seemed like Abner took him at his word, Asaph had the urge to further explain himself. "Men were hunting me down because they wanted me to kill a child. I refused, so they intended to kill me."

Abner shot him a sidelong glance, although it was difficult to tell where the man was looking. His eyes were partly concealed by bulges and bumps. The rest of his face was swollen, lined with nodules, and riddled with sores. Asaph diverted his eyes.

"Your story becomes stranger by the moment, Asaph. Why would anyone want you to kill a child?"

Asaph stared at the ground, afraid to make eye contact with a nightmare. "The child had witnessed something."

"Ah. It can be a dangerous thing to be a witness. What did the child see?"

Asaph paused, unsure how or whether to answer. "That is one question too many." He wasn't about to admit to being part of a band of Zealots who had robbed Rome of its taxes.

"Then I will pry no more. Thank you for your honesty."

"You weren't prying. You have a right to know about the man you are protecting in your midst."

Abner raised the material that covered most of his face, but Asaph sensed that he was smiling behind the cloth.

"What about you?" Asaph said. "How did you hear about Jesus?"

"Who hasn't heard about him? Word about this prophet is being carried as far and wide as the dust you see carried in the wind. When we heard he had healed lepers, the ten of us decided we had to find him."

The wind picked up even more, and the sky became hazy with airborne earth. Asaph put a hand to his head to keep the cloth covering in place. "I thank you for allowing me to travel with you."

"It wasn't my idea," grumbled one of the other lepers who had been eavesdropping on their conversation.

"That's enough, Jethro," Abner shot back. "Who are we to complain about someone who wants to travel with us? Most people run from us in terror. Be happy somebody wants to walk with us, no matter what his motivation might be."

Jethro grunted and picked up his pace, moving farther ahead.

Abner glanced at Asaph. "I apologize for my brother's words. He can't see beyond the fact that you are a Jew. We are Samaritans."

Asaph stopped. Stunned.

"What's wrong?" Abner asked. "Does the fact that we're Samaritans upset you more than the fact that we're lepers?"

Asaph resumed walking. "I'm sorry. It's just that the history of our people has not been good."

That was an understatement. Jews and Samaritans had a history of hatred. When the Assyrians conquered the Northern Kingdom of Israel so many years ago, foreigners poured into the area, and there was much intermarrying with Jews—as well as idol worship. These intermingled, contaminated Jews became the Samaritans.

Ever since, pure Jews looked upon the Samaritans as a tainted people, and Samaritans had similar disdain for Jews. Samaritans worshipped at the Temple at Mount Gerizim because they believed that Adam sacrificed there; it was the "naval of the earth." The Jewish people worshipped at the Temple in Jerusalem.

There were many reasons for the animosity. But none of this seemed to matter to Abner.

"You do not mind that I am a Jew?" Asaph asked.

"We may have our disagreements. But that doesn't mean we should have our hatred."

Asaph nodded. This Abner was an extraordinary man.

Abner picked up a stone and flung it aside. "But my brothers in leprosy are learning. Some of them were initially opposed to seeking healing from a Jew . . . from Jesus. But I convinced them to welcome healing from whatever the source. So, they are coming around."

"How do you know where to find Jesus?"

"We have people who are our eyes and ears and report to us," Abner said. He suddenly seemed amused by his own comment. "Someone has to be our eyes and ears because we're losing ours."

Abner laughed, but Asaph could only give him an awkward grin. This man was joking about his disease! It didn't seem right, but neither did a Jew and Samaritan walking together amicably.

Soon, they approached a small village, visible through the brown haze. Asaph didn't know exactly where they were, but he guessed they were somewhere close to the border between Samaria and Galilee.

"One thing I'll say about Jesus," Abner said. "He doesn't avoid Samaria in his travels."

That was true. When traveling from Galilee to Judea, most Jews will not take the short path because it leads through Samaria. They take the long way through Perea to the east. But not Jesus. For him, it seems all ground is holy.

## Eliana

The night was lit by a hundred bobbing balls of fire as a mass of people carrying torches flowed to the center of the village. Bathed in the yellow glow, people found spots on the ground while Jesus prepared to speak. Several Pharisees stood to the side, arms crossed, as if putting up a physical barrier to Jesus's ideas.

Chaim sat down on a rock next to Eliana but not so close as to raise eyebrows. "Shalom, Eliana."

"Shalom, Chaim."

She could see that Chaim was fishing for something to say, but he just gave her an awkward grin. When he finally started to squeeze out a few words, one of the Pharisees near Jesus spoke up, and Eliana's attention flew elsewhere.

"When will the Kingdom of God come to us?" asked the Pharisee.

Torchlight flickered on Jesus's face. "The Kingdom of God is not something that can be observed, nor will people say, 'Here it is,' or 'There it is,' because the Kingdom of God is in your midst."

These words agitated the Pharisees, and even Chaim reacted with a sudden intake of air when Jesus made this declaration. But for Eliana, it made complete sense. The Kingdom of God had already arrived. It's here. Right now.

"Do you really believe this?" came a whisper from over her shoulder—a familiar voice. Her father had returned! He sat on the ground, placing himself between her and Chaim. She hadn't seen her father since their last encounter when he had left in a huff. For all she knew, he had gone back to Magdala.

"I do believe it," Eliana said.

"The Kingdom of God is here now?"

"Yes. I believe it."

Jesus looked down at his disciples who were gathered at his feet. "The time is coming when you will long to see one of the days of the Son of Man, but you will not see it. People will tell you, 'There he is!' or 'Here he is!' Do not go running off after them. For the Son of Man in his day will be like the lightning, which flashes and lights up the sky from one end to the other. But first he must suffer many things and be rejected by this generation."

"Did you hear that?" Eliana's father leaned over to her and whispered again. "Jesus said not to run off after people claiming to be the Son of Man. That's what I have been telling you all along."

"Jesus is not talking about himself."

"How do you know?"

"Sshhh." Eliana put a finger to her lips.

Jesus moved among the people. "Just as it was in the days of Noah, so also will it be in the days of the Son of Man. People were eating, drinking, marrying, and being given in marriage up to the day Noah entered the ark. Then the flood came and destroyed them all."

"But this . . ." began Eliana's father.

"Sshhh."

"It will be just like this on the day the Son of Man is revealed," Jesus continued. "On that day no one who is on the housetop, with possessions inside, should go down to get them. Likewise, no one in the field should go back for anything. Remember Lot's wife! Whoever tries to keep their life will lose it, and whoever loses their life will preserve it."

"That doesn't make sense." This time, Eliana's father spoke loudly enough for others to hear, including Chaim.

"SSHHH!"

Jesus went on to speak more about the Son of Man, and he followed with parables, as usual. Finally, when he had finished and retired for the night, Eliana's father was just getting started.

"Jesus said the Son of Man is to suffer and be rejected by this generation," he said. "But I believe the Son of Man, the Messiah, will be strong, not weak. He will conquer, not suffer."

"Since when does conquering not include suffering?" asked Chaim, interjecting his opinion with boldness.

"I'll grant you that, but do you really think the Kingdom of God is here, right here, right now?"

"Jesus is here, so the Kingdom is here," said Eliana.

"But when I look around, all I see is Roman power, Roman swords. I see the kingdom of pagan gods, not the Kingdom of God." Eliana's father turned and looked at Chaim. "Do you think Jesus is the Messiah?"

Chaim hesitated before stammering, "I think so. I think . . . Jesus will shatter the unrighteous rulers."

Judah lowered his voice. "And will he conquer the Romans?"

Chaim would not answer that question in public, so Eliana did it for him. "Yes, he will conquer Rome, but he won't need swords."

"He's going to conquer Rome without swords?" Her father cracked a smile. "I will have to see how this is done, so I suppose I should remain among his followers for a spell. I want to see how all of this plays out. And if Jesus needs someone with a sword, I will be ready."

"Jesus will have my sword too," Chaim said.

"You don't have a sword," Eliana pointed out.

"I will get one."

Eliana turned to face her father squarely. "Does that mean you will be staying with me?"

"I will."

"And will you follow Jesus?"

"I didn't say that. I will be observing Jesus, not following him."

Eliana was astounded—and pleased. Her father may not be a follower of Jesus, but at least he will be by her side, listening to Jesus's words and, as he said, observing. Some of it was bound to soak in. Two weeks ago, she never would have imagined this turn of events.

"You make me so happy, Abba." Eliana wrapped her arms around him.

"That's what fathers do." When he gave her a squeeze, suddenly she was ten years old all over again.

## **Nekoda**

Nekoda wore his purple once more. He was planning to talk with Rufus, and he needed to impress the man. He had been shocked to receive a message commanding him to appear before the captain of the guard. He had no idea Rufus was even in the area.

A servant, an elderly man, escorted Nekoda into the courtyard of a lavish home, which Rufus and his men had commandeered. Rufus lay on his side by a small fire, holding a cup of wine in his right hand and lounging like a tetrarch.

"Shalom," Nekoda said, lowering himself into a strange little chair, almost too small and too short for Nekoda. A child's chair. He must've looked like a fool, but that was probably what Rufus intended.

Rufus didn't respond with "Shalom." He said nothing, while a servant appeared at Nekoda's side with a bowl of water and a towel. The servant proceeded to wash the dust from Nekoda's feet. The water was refreshing, and the air felt good on his toes.

"I did not know you were in the region," Nekoda said, intimidated by Rufus's silence.

Rufus lowered his cup of wine. "Herod decided that if anyone was going to find Sveshtari, it would be me. Have you had any success tracking him down?"

Nekoda paused. He didn't want to admit the truth—he hadn't the slightest idea where to find Sveshtari amidst Jesus's followers. "I have some leads."

"You have been with Jesus's followers all this time, and all you have are leads? I have been among the Galileans for only two days, and I have more than leads."

"You found him?" Nekoda was astonished.

"I spotted him near the synagogue."

"And you captured him?"

In the low glow of the fire, Nekoda spotted a flicker of discomfort cross Rufus's face. Rufus took his time in answering.

"We came very close."

Nekoda smiled inside. The great Rufus found Sveshtari, but he failed to apprehend him. "I am sorry to hear that." He wasn't sorry in the least.

"I confirmed that Sveshtari is traveling with a woman we've also been hunting—the woman named Keturah, who once worked in Herod's palace. She has a baby, so that should narrow it down. There may be a thousand or two thousand following Jesus, but there can't be many women with a baby under the age of three months."

Nekoda was stunned. He had recently seen a woman with an infant, but where?

"If you find Keturah, you find Sveshtari."

"Excellent news," Nekoda said.

"We are approaching Jericho, and we intend to trap Sveshtari and Keturah within the city walls."

"Yes, yes. That makes sense. There are only two gates in and out of the city. Do you have enough men to guard both gates?"

"Easily."

Nekoda leaned forward, but it felt like the small chair was about to tumble from under him. He leaned back and steadied it.

"I will find this woman. I have a lead," Nekoda said.

"You do?"

"I saw a woman just recently holding a very young child." He recalled seeing this woman with Eliana, Chaim's friend.

"Can you find her again?"

"I know I can."

Nekoda needed only to find Chaim. His brother would lead him to Eliana, and Eliana would lead him to the woman with the baby. Then the woman with the baby would lead him to Sveshtari—a chain of opportunity and incrimination.

He was relieved. He had thought that if he didn't find Sveshtari, he was going to have to deliver his brother to Herod as the sacrificial lamb. But why kill a lamb when you can bring down a lion?

Sveshtari would not make it out of Jericho alive.

# 6.
## Luke, Chapter 18

### Eliana

Eliana hurried back to her tent in the dark, oil lamp in hand. Jesus and his followers were about a day's walk from Jericho, passing through a land of bandits. Sveshtari insisted on standing guard in front of the tent she shared with Keturah, although she thought the sheer numbers of people provided ample protection.

Still, it made her nervous being out and about, so she moved rapidly amidst the tents, and the back of her neck tingled with a strange sense that someone might come up from behind. She wasn't prepared when a man suddenly emerged out of the darkness from her right. For a moment, she thought that a demon had taken physical shape. The man looked to be a monster. He was covered in dirt, and his torn robe was caked with dried blood. His mouth was distorted by swelling, and he staggered like a living corpse. His clothes reeked.

It was Asaph.

"What happened?" She rushed beside him and put an arm around his waist.

"Snake." That's all he muttered as she helped him struggle to their tent, where Sveshtari stood guard.

"What do you mean by that?" Eliana asked.

Asaph tapped his swollen lip. "Snake bite."

"I'll tend to him," said Sveshtari because, obviously, Asaph would need a change of clothes. "It's good to see you again, Asaph, although it looks like you've done more than tangle with a snake. Let's fix you up," he said, leading Asaph into his tent.

By the time that Eliana saw Asaph again, he was a new man. He was dressed in a fresh robe, and the mud had been washed from his face, arms, and feet. He smelled much better too, thanks to the oils mixed with wine that Sveshtari had rubbed onto his wounds.

"I brought honey." Eliana handed the jar to Sveshtari, who used a sponge to apply the honey to an open cut on Asaph's left forearm.

"Thank you, Eliana." His words slurred, thanks to his swollen lip.

"So—what happened?" She hoped to get more than a single-word answer.

"I smashed into a rock while swimming away from Barabbas." He winced when Sveshtari dabbed a cut on his shoulder.

"Why would you be swimming away from Barabbas? Was he chasing you?"

"He wants to kill me."

"But why?"

"We ambushed a Roman contingent guarding the tax money. But there was a family in the wagon—and a boy. Barabbas ordered me to kill him."

Eliana took the jar of honey back from Sveshtari. "You disobeyed his order?"

"I did."

"I am very proud of you."

"Who is this Barabbas?" asked Sveshtari. "Killing children . . . The man deserves to be handed over to lions."

"Barabbas now leads the Zealot squad once led by . . ." Asaph glanced at Eliana, allowing her to finish his thought.

"Once led by my father," she said. "When my father left in search of me, Barabbas became the leader."

"So, you ran—and swam?" Sveshtari said to Asaph.

Asaph nodded. He appeared to be still terribly shaken—much more shaken than in the aftermath of the battle on the Cliffs of Arbel. Eliana had a nudging sense that she should ask him another question. A thought sparked in her mind, urging her to ask this question, but it wasn't the same as when Cavel—the demon—used to command her. Cavel's voice had been loud, clear, and menacing. This thought was her own. It was soft, a whisper floating through her mind.

"Where is Gershom?" she asked.

Asaph snapped his head in her direction; the look on his face spooked her. "Why do you ask? Why do you care? Am I in charge of Gershom's whereabouts?"

"I was worried that he, too, is being hunted by Barabbas," she said, honestly. "Is Gershom safe?"

"I don't know what happened to Gershom! I am the one who is being hunted like an animal!"

Eliana looked away, angry and embarrassed. She tried to tell herself that Asaph's defensiveness was just a reaction to fear. But something told her it was more than that.

She broke the uncomfortable silence, steering the conversation away from Gershom. "I never liked that man Barabbas. He says he is fighting for the Jewish people. But I think he fights because he savors it more than anything in life. Every time he is in Jerusalem, he stirs violence."

On the Cliffs of Arbel, Eliana had seen the look in Barabbas's eyes when he slit a Roman throat. His eyes glowed. She wished he had never joined her father's band of Zealots. Barabbas had a zeal for blood, not a zeal for the Lord.

"I am sorry, Eliana," Asaph mumbled as he dabbed more honey on his swollen, cut lip.

At first, she assumed he was saying "I am sorry" for snapping at her. But then came another whisper in her mind, telling her that Asaph was sorry about something much worse than that.

But now was not the time to probe. She noticed he still had a dab of blood under his right ear, and she used the honey-soaked sponge to wipe it away.

## Keturah

It took much of the morning to pack their belongings onto the donkey and for Keturah and Eliana to bake bread, the stock and store of life. The bread took the shape of disks, a cubit in diameter. Keturah created a hole in the center of each disk because Sveshtari liked to carry his bread on a pole as they traveled. She also put out dishes of figs and dried apricots.

Word got around that Jesus would be on the move today, heading west to Jericho. From there, they'd begin the grueling uphill climb to Jerusalem along a ridge road. People called the road "the way of blood" because robbers along the path were eager to harm you and pilfer your goods. But Keturah was confident that she would be more than safe in a crowd this size—especially with Sveshtari's protection.

Babette had been in a pleasant mood all morning—no screaming for food, mostly burbling smiles and happy, flailing arms. With Babette perched on her hip in a sling devised by Sveshtari, Keturah wandered into a small village. When she entered the central courtyard, she was shocked to find Jesus playing a game with some of the children. They were playing tag, and Jesus chased about ten children, who scattered like sheep in his path. Several times he reached out to tag a child but pretended that he couldn't quite make contact. After pausing to laugh and shake his head in wonder, it was off again in wild pursuit. Eventually, he tagged one of the children, and then Jesus switched from being the pursuer to the pursued.

Several adults stood to the side, some with scowls but most with expressions of bewilderment. Rabbis don't run, especially with children.

Finally, Jesus dropped onto a large stone and said he was too tired to play any longer. One of the older girls brought him a cup of water, while a small boy climbed onto his back. A little girl tugged on his hand, trying to yank him back into action.

After drinking deeply, Jesus put his left hand on the head of one child after another. He appeared to be blessing them. Keturah had a sudden inspiration to bring Babette to Jesus for his blessing, but as soon as she began to move in his direction, her child began to cry. Babette's wails became the breaking point for Jesus's disciples.

"Do not bother the master with your crying child!" exclaimed one of the disciples—she was not sure which one. He swooped down on her, blocking her way to Jesus.

Then Jesus's voice resounded, with more than a hint of rebuke.

"Let the little children come to me and do not hinder them!" The teacher looked directly at Keturah and Babette. He motioned her forward, even though Babette continued to squall. But as Keturah came within a few cubits of Jesus, Babette finally calmed, and the master motioned her even closer.

"The Kingdom of God belongs to such as these," he said, looking around at the adults who stood to the side, observing—with scowls still planted on some of their faces. Jesus reached out and lifted Babette gently from Keturah's arms. Several of the little girls crowded around, running their hands across Babette's peach-fuzz head.

Keturah glanced to her right and saw four of the disciples standing in a cluster with perplexed frowns. Jesus looked up from Babette to his disciples. "I tell you the truth, anyone who will not receive the Kingdom of God like a little child will never enter it."

At these words, one of the disciples turned on his heels and stormed away. It was Judas, the man who had hired Sveshtari to guard the money.

Looking back at Jesus, she saw that the rabbi had begun to pray silently over Babette, just as she had hoped. Then he kissed Babette on the forehead and handed her back to Keturah.

"Shalom," Jesus said, looking directly into Keturah's eyes.

In that moment, Keturah felt completely exposed. She had a sudden and shocking sense that Jesus knew everything about her. He knew she wasn't really a Jew. He knew she had been a slave in Herod's palace and that she wanted to murder the man she loved because he had killed her father. Most of all, she was certain that Jesus knew she felt alone in the world and could trust no one.

Then Jesus looked at her forehead, where her tattoo had once announced to the world that she was a runaway slave. "If you hold to my teaching, you are my disciple," he said to her. "Then you will know the truth, and the truth will set you free."

Keturah left the village, feeling so terrified that she almost burst out crying. Jesus said the truth will set her free, but she didn't feel free. She would always feel like a slave. Her identity had deep roots, and no words from a Jewish rabbi could change that. Her tattoo had been removed, but she still felt its presence itching her forehead—a declaration of her true status. Jesus could not set her free. The truth could not set her free. Nothing could set her free.

That was the hardest truth of all. She felt as helpless as the child in her arms.

## Nekoda

Nekoda couldn't believe his good fortune. It didn't take long for him to track down the woman with the baby because there she was, asking Jesus to bless her child.

Jesus rebuked his disciples for complaining about all the children clustering around him, but Nekoda could sympathize with them. It wasn't the job of rabbis like Jesus to teach children, and frolicking with them was demeaning for a teacher who took his job seriously.

Nekoda chose not to wear his purple robe this day because he didn't want to stand out as he followed Keturah to the edge of the village. When he spotted Eliana and Chaim greeting the woman with the infant, he banished any doubt that this was Keturah—the woman he hunted. Soon, a strong-looking man with soldier-like bearing arrived; Nekoda was also certain he was finally looking at the mysterious and elusive Sveshtari.

Nekoda couldn't do anything about Sveshtari now, of course. He wouldn't stand a chance if he tried to apprehend him alone. But at least he could confront his brother—which was what he did when he spotted Chaim heading for the center of the village a short time later.

"You told me you didn't know Sveshtari." Nekoda walked in stride beside his brother.

Chaim flinched at his words, stumbled, then caught himself. "Shalom to you too, brother," he said, obviously irritated by Nekoda's sneak attack. "What are you talking about?"

"I just saw you speaking with Sveshtari and the woman with the baby. Keturah."

Chaim didn't respond, probably wondering if he should keep stringing out his lies by claiming he didn't know Sveshtari. Fortunately, he decided it was fruitless to keep lying.

"What are you going to do about it?"

"That is not up to me. Sveshtari and Keturah are both wanted by Herod's guards."

"But they're my friends."

"Because I am a member of the Sanhedrin, I can cause problems for you and your dearest friend of all—Eliana. But if we can arrest Sveshtari and Keturah, then you and Eliana will be spared."

"You want me to lead your soldiers to them?"

"That is the plan."

Chaim came to a standstill and stared. He looked terrified by the choice, but that's just what Nekoda intended. Fear works wonders.

## Sveshtari

Sveshtari watched as a young boy led a donkey in circles around the massive millstone. The donkey was hitched to the stone so that as the animal walked in a circle, the massive stone wheel rolled around and around the vat of olives, crushing them beneath its weight. After the crushing came the pressing of the olives, and then the finest oil was given as first fruits to the priests. Some was used for cooking and medicine, while the poorest quality oil was saved for lamps.

As the boy began to fill a basket with the crushed mash of olives, Sveshtari suddenly heard his name being shouted. He slipped away from the olive press and turned in the direction of the clamor. A commotion stirred down the street—three men shoving someone in their midst.

He couldn't see who it was, but he heard the voice call out once again: "Sveshtari, where in the world are you?"

The voice belonged to Abel, the little thief.

"Sveshtari!"

Sveshtari strode toward the three men, who were oblivious to his approach. One of them reached for a knife attached to his waist.

"I wouldn't touch that if I were you," Sveshtari said. The three men pivoted to face him. The one man's hand remained poised over his knife's handle. As Sveshtari took three more steps forward, the man whipped the knife out of its sheath.

"Come no closer. Who are you?"

"A friend of the man you torment."

This made the men skittery. The other two men produced knives, and they tried to form a circle around Sveshtari. He didn't give them the chance. Snatching a piece of wood from a nearby pile, he hurled it point-blank into the face of one of the men, probably breaking his nose from the sound of it. Then he pivoted toward the second man, who tried to stab him. Sveshtari latched onto his wrist and drove the flat of his right hand into the man's face. Then he lifted the man from the ground and hurled him at the third attacker, sending them both sprawling to the ground.

It all happened in the time it took a person to breathe in and out.

Abel stood there staring with an enormous grin on his face. "You are astonishing!"

"And you were being attacked. What for? What have you done now?"

"Why do you assume that I have done anything? I was the victim here."

"That criminal owes us money," said one of the men, rising from the ground and sliding his knife back into its sheath. He obviously wanted no more of Sveshtari.

"Is that true?" Sveshtari asked.

"It might be. But they need to give me time to gather the money. It hasn't been that long since I decided to walk the straight and narrow path, and it's difficult getting money the honest way."

"The only straight and narrow thing that you need is the blade of a sword," mumbled the one with the mashed nose.

"Give him time," Sveshtari commanded.

"But we've already given him plenty of time. He—"

"Then give him *more* time to get the money."

By this point, the three men were all back on their feet, taking slow steps away from Sveshtari.

"But—"

"Give him time. I will make sure he pays you back."

"Do so," commanded the third man, trying to act more confident than he looked. When Sveshtari made a motion in his direction, the man backed up into one of the others, and they nearly tumbled to the dust together.

"I knew I came to the right person when I asked you to protect me," Abel said. "That was incredible!"

Sveshtari turned and began to make his way back to the oil press. Abel ran after him, trying to catch his eye.

"I meant it when I told them I want to pay them back the money I owe—and then some." He backpedaled so he could face Sveshtari.

"I sure hope so. For your sake."

"I also want you to know that I've done work on your behalf. I was just on my way to tell you that someone else is tracking your whereabouts."

This stopped Sveshtari in his tracks. "What are you talking about?"

"It's a Sadducee named Nekoda. He's been following you and Keturah. He's also been talking with the captain of Herod's guard."

"Rufus? Nekoda is talking with Rufus? You're sure about this?"

"Without a doubt. I'm good at what I do," Abel said, reminding Sveshtari of his abilities for the hundredth time. "Nekoda is the priest who struts around in his purple robe."

"I know who he is. He is the brother of Chaim."

"That's right, and he's been keeping an eye on all of you—even Keturah and Eliana. How do you plan to deal with it? If you're going to break his nose, promise you'll let me know. I'd love to watch."

"I'm not going to attack a priest—for now. But if he comes anywhere near Keturah, I'll kill him. Thank you for letting me know."

"No, I must thank *you*. I think we make a good team, don't you?"

"I am not on your team. I'm not on any team."

"All right, all right, look at it any way you want, Sveshtari. You keep protecting me, and I'll keep you informed. You scratch my back, and I'll scratch yours—and then you'll *break* the backs of our enemies."

Sveshtari shrugged and returned to the oil press, where he watched the millstone grind up more olives like an army crushing everything in its path.

## Asaph

Asaph had not been back to Jericho since the day, so long ago, when he fled in the night, afraid of being arrested for a crime he did not commit. But now he found himself trudging alongside Eliana on the dusty road leading west toward Jericho. The sky was clear, and the sun beat down on the string of pilgrims winding their way past the rolling brown hills flanking them on either side.

He hoped that by now the crime he had been accused of—stealing the vase—would be long forgotten. But stealing a vase was one thing; murdering Gershom was something entirely different. That crime would never be erased, which was why he chose to remain lost and anonymous within the multitude. There was safety in numbers, but he kept expecting to see Barabbas and the other Zealots show up in force to drag him off to some scrubland and stone him to death.

"How do you feel today, Asaph?"

Eliana constantly inquired about his state of mind, even more than his physical condition. He told no one about what had happened with Gershom, but Eliana seemed to know instinctively that something terrible had occurred.

"I'm feeling good." He tried to inject a bounce into his voice, but he wasn't known for his acting abilities.

"Mmmm." Eliana looked at him sideways.

Asaph dreamt about Gershom's death for two straight nights. The dream seemed so real as he watched himself hurl the rock at Gershom's face. In his dream, he saw the blood begin to flow, trickling down from Gershom's temple to his jaw. Then his dream slid into bizarre images as he saw himself fleeing toward the Jordan River, only to discover, to his horror, that the river had turned to blood.

Then a voice asked, "What have you done? Listen! Gershom's blood cries out to you from the ground, which opened its mouth to receive his blood from your hand."

When Asaph wheeled around and tried to run in the opposite direction from the river, his feet became mired. And when he looked down at his feet, he saw himself sinking into the soil, with blood bubbling up like hot tar.

He tried to put away all thoughts of Gershom as they approached Jericho, an oasis amid the brown barrenness. Plants flourished there, and so did people. Asaph once flourished in Jericho as well, but now he was as dried out as a broken clay pot.

Eliana broke the silence. "When you want to tell me the full story of what happened to you with the Zealots, I will listen."

Asaph grunted and shot a look at Eliana's dog, Lavi. The dog stared back, its tongue dangling from its dry mouth. Sometimes, he wished he could be as happy and naïve as a dog.

As they continued trudging along, Asaph soon spotted the figure of a beggar crouched by the side of the road, calling out to people. It was obvious the man was blind.

The beggar had found a pretty good spot—on the edge of the old city of Jericho, but before you reached the newer city. A short stretch connected the old and the new Jericho's, and the man had chosen this road to beg from passing crowds.

"What is happening? Why so many people?" the blind beggar shouted, for he could obviously hear the shuffling of many feet.

"Jesus of Nazareth is passing by," said one of the people in the crowd. The beggar appeared stunned, and then he broke into a smile.

Asaph sensed something coming toward him from behind—something powerful that raised the hairs on his neck. He wheeled around, expecting to see Barabbas descend on him with a raised sword. But it was not Barabbas, thank God. It was Jesus, surrounded by his twelve disciples and many women as well. The rabbi took long strides, and his open coat fluttered outward in the breeze, like wings. Normally, Jesus marched at the front of this parade of misfits, but on this day many people had rushed ahead of him so they could get to Jericho and be the first to claim lodging.

"Jesus, Son of David, have mercy on me!" the blind man shouted.

*Jesus. Son of David.*

It was a shocking title. Everyone knew that the Son of David referred to the Messiah, the Branch of Jesse, who would sit on the throne of David once again. But how did this blind beggar know any of that applied to

Jesus? There had been much talk about Jesus as Messiah, of course, but this was the first time that Asaph had heard anyone declare it out loud in a crowd. He had not even heard Jesus's disciples say any such thing in public.

For a blind man, this fellow sure saw a lot.

"Son of David, have mercy on me!" he exclaimed again.

"Quiet! You don't know what you're saying," said one of the men in the crowd, holding back the beggar.

But the beggar tried to press forward, reaching out his hand. "Have mercy!"

As Jesus stopped and found a seat on a nearby stone, the crowd came to a standstill, thronging on all sides, blocking his path to the blind beggar.

"Bring the man to me," he asked a pair of his disciples, James and John. The two Sons of Thunder did as he bid, fighting their way through the crowd. Taking the blind beggar by the hand, they led him to the teacher. The crowd parted.

"Are you bringing me to Jesus?" the beggar kept asking. "Are you taking me to the Son of David?"

"Yes, yes, he asked to see you," said John.

"The Son of David was sent to proclaim recovery of sight for the blind, to set the oppressed free, to proclaim the year of the Lord's favor!" the blind beggar exclaimed, barely able to contain himself.

Finally, the two disciples positioned the blind man directly in front of Jesus. The beggar extended his hand, like the branch of a thirsty tree, and he pawed at the air to determine if Jesus was standing right in front of him.

Jesus rose to his feet and moved within an arm's length of the beggar, whose hands finally found the teacher's robe. Jesus grasped the man's hand. "What do you want me to do for you?"

"Lord, I want to see." The beggar sounded shocked that Jesus would even ask a question with such an obvious answer. What else would he want? But Asaph had a sneaking suspicion that Jesus wanted to hear it from the man's lips. Was there power in speaking your petition out loud?

Then Jesus said: "Receive your sight; your faith has healed you."

The blind beggar took one step back and blinked—exaggerated blinks. He squeezed his eyes shut tightly, kept them shut for a few seconds, and opened them again. Then he squinted, as if the light overpowered his eyes. He rubbed them with his fingers and opened his eyes again. He looked around at the crowd, his eyes finally stopping on Jesus. Out of all the people, he seemed to know immediately which one had given him sight.

Then he hurled himself into Jesus's arms and began to cry out, "I see you! I can see you, Lord! Thank you! Thank you, Jesus! Thank you, my Lord!"

The crowd, which had been hushed by suspense, broke out cheering, and many ululated, creating a high-pitched trill with their tongues. One of the Pharisees even started to cheer until the look from a superior stopped him mid-clap.

Eliana latched onto Asaph's left arm. "Do you see? Do you see? I told you there is healing in Jesus's hands."

Asaph saw. But he wasn't sure if he believed. He had other things to occupy his mind, like whether he would be arrested in Jericho—or murdered by Barabbas.

When they arrived in Jericho, the city was just as Asaph remembered—a lush oasis in a rough land. It was warm, prosperous, and bustling—a city of palm trees with many springs to bring it to life. Combine that with the magnificence of Herod's winter palace in Jericho, and it seemed like paradise.

Nevertheless, Asaph knew he was anything but safe in Paradise City as he fought his way through the marketplace crowd, heading for his old home. Barabbas had taken away his sword, but he had another one that had been given to him by Judah. Sveshtari had closely guarded this second sword, and now it was securely strapped to his waist; but it wasn't enough to give him complete security. Not in this city, where he had once been declared an outlaw.

Ignoring the hawkers who stuck food and pottery in his face, he eventually wound up at the peaceful street passing by the wall that fronted his property. Like many homes of wealth, the wall was plain and unassuming. The beauty lay beyond the wall—inside the compound.

Asaph found the exterior door in the wall to be open, so he stepped into the familiarity of his former courtyard. He had been told that Malachi, his old tax-gathering assistant, was living big in his old house, and from the looks of the courtyard, that was true. He noticed several statues along the colonnade to his right—two of them pagan. Malachi must have tossed aside the final shred of Jewish faith that he had been clutching. The courtyard also displayed a greater abundance of greenery than he remembered, so someone was working hard to keep the plants thriving.

The main living quarters lay ahead, with an exterior staircase leading to a second floor—but so far, no sign of Malachi or Asaph's former slave, Calliste. Technically, Calliste still belonged to Asaph, but he doubted she or Malachi saw it that way now.

He was about to ascend the staircase when he heard laughter coming from one of the side rooms, and he wondered if he should leave or hide. He wasn't sure he had the strength for another confrontation. But indecision kept him rooted, and before he knew it, familiar faces emerged from the room. First came Calliste and then Malachi. When Calliste's eyes met his, she gasped and pedaled backward three steps, bumping into Malachi, who put his arms around her, demonstrating his possession of her.

Then Malachi broke into a grin, stepped around Calliste, and planted a kiss on each of Asaph's cheeks. His breath smelled of spirits. Malachi hadn't changed old habits.

"Asaph, my friend! I thought you were living in Galilee."

"I was."

Malachi's eyes sized him up from his feet to his head, pausing at his waist, where Asaph carried his sword and sling.

"You look well." Malachi spoke with a hint of fear. Asaph hadn't thought about it, but he probably struck a much more menacing figure than his old self. Living and training with the Zealots had strengthened him; it had worked away the softness of his easy life as a tax collector, like a snake shedding its skin. His body was as solid as bronze—and tanned to the color of bronze, too, by the sun.

Asaph said nothing about Malachi "looking well" because, to be honest, his old assistant had added considerable weight. The extra bulk made him look wealthy, as Malachi probably desired, but it wasn't very imposing.

Asaph enjoyed the awkward silence as he let his eyes drift around the courtyard once again. "I see you have made some changes to my home."

Casting a nervous glance at both men, Calliste excused herself and scurried off.

"I am afraid to speak the obvious," began Malachi, "but this house belongs to me. You were wanted by the authorities and didn't return to Jericho, so I was given ownership."

Asaph smiled. "But I *have* returned."

"Yes, but . . ."

Malachi took two steps closer, deciding it was time to exercise his territorial rights. "Yes, but it is no longer your home."

"And Calliste?"

"She is no longer your slave."

"She is yours to use—as you please?"

"I please her well. She is much happier than she was before."

Which was Malachi's way of saying that Asaph never really pleased her.

"The courtyard seems a little overdone." Asaph put his hands on his hips, his right hand's fingers nearly touching the hilt of his sword. "Too many naked pagan gods for my taste. Whatever happened to the vase that Zuriel planted in my house?"

"It was found near a well on the other side of the city."

"Where Calliste hid it?"

"The authorities assumed you left it there so you wouldn't have the burden of carrying it when you fled."

Asaph laughed. "And you? Have you also stolen my job as tax collector?"

"I was your assistant. It only made sense for me to take over your duties, and Zaccheus says I am his best man." Again, there was the insinuation that Malachi pleased the chief tax collector, Zaccheus, far more than Asaph ever did. "Listen to me, Asaph . . . It is still not safe for you to be in this city. Zuriel lives here. When he discovers you have returned, he will have you arrested."

Asaph had to smile at this, for Malachi was lying. Zuriel had been following Barabbas and the Zealots for several months now and hadn't lived in Jericho for at least that long.

"So, you would like me to leave you alone with my house and my slave and my job?" Asaph asked.

"They are no longer yours." Malachi took a step backward as he spoke these words. The man was afraid.

Again, Asaph laughed. "You always had a way of falling into prosperity—like the time you decided to sleep off your drunkenness in an open burial plot, and thieves just happened to use that hole to hide their stolen wine. You drank it all down before they could return and retrieve it." Asaph paused to take in his house. "And it looks like you stumbled into my property and drank all of my wine."

"I tell you. This property is not yours. If you want me to retrieve the authorities and have them make it clear for you, I can."

Asaph pulled out his sword just to draw a reaction from Malachi. It worked. The man's mouth and eyes went wide. But Asaph knew he wouldn't kill Malachi. In fact, he didn't know if he could ever kill another person, even in self-defense. Not after Gershom.

"Do not worry, Asaph. I will tell no one that you have returned. Believe me when I say that you are not safe in Jericho."

"That's what you told me the first time I fled from Jericho. You were so concerned for my safety. But have no fear. I am not staying in Jericho, and I have no plans to slit your throat." Asaph stared at his blade and noticed the tiniest fleck of red along the edge. Dried blood from the battle on Mount Arbel. He used his fingernail to scrape it away, making sure that Malachi saw the blood as well.

"But if you report me to Zuriel—to *anyone*—I cannot promise I won't come back for you."

"I told you. I won't report you."

Asaph had seen enough, so he yanked open the exterior door, letting it bang against the stone wall. Then he plunged back into the city and marched toward the sound of a commotion. Jesus and his followers were in the city, and no doubt, the sound was being stirred by his presence.

He decided to investigate, so he strode toward the center of the sound—a large, old sycamore tree.

# 7.
## Luke, Chapter 19

### Sveshtari: Jericho

Sveshtari, always alert for trouble, noticed a commotion stirring amid the people gathering around Jesus. A small man fought his way through the crowd, but people intentionally blocked his path, laughing in his face.

"Let me pass!" the slight man barked. But when he tried to plow his way through, several large men shoved him backward. For every three steps that the man moved forward, someone forced him back four steps. He was a small fry fighting against the currents of hostility. "You will pay for this!" He leveled a finger at one of his tormenters.

"What's going on with him?" Sveshtari asked a stranger, nodding in the direction of the small man.

"Him? That's the chief tax collector. Zacchaeus."

Sveshtari nodded. Zacchaeus should be glad that getting blocked by people was the worst of his problems. He knew many who would pay dearly for the privilege of driving a sword through the chest of a tax collector. A Roman collaborator.

Soon, the little man gave up on reaching the front of the crowd. Instead, he hopped up and down at the back of the gathering, trying desperately to catch a glimpse of Jesus. That just made him look even more foolish, and people began to laugh.

"Maybe my five-year-old son can lift you on his shoulders!" guffawed one observer.

"I want to see!" Zacchaeus shouted. Sveshtari couldn't help but think of the blind man who had just been healed by Jesus. He, too, wanted to see.

Zacchaeus eventually stormed off, probably to devise new ways to extract money from his tormentors. Maybe he could tax people according to their height. More height, more taxes.

Then a flash of purple caught Sveshtari's attention, and he remembered what Abel had told him about the wealthy Sadducee who was keeping an eye on him—the man named Nekoda. Chaim's brother. Sveshtari decided to follow the Sadducee at a safe distance. He circled around the back of the crowd as people continued to press close to Jesus, who spoke in a loud, commanding voice.

Reaching an old sycamore tree, Sveshtari stopped and peered out from behind its thick base. Nekoda headed for the main gate of Jericho, where he stopped to talk to several soldiers. One of them was his old nemesis, Rufus. Abel was right. This Sadducee was tracking him.

The man in purple pointed to the crowd, in the direction where Sveshtari had been standing only moments before. Then Rufus and three soldiers took up positions at the main gate. They were probably on high alert to make sure he didn't escape Jericho. Meanwhile, Nekoda motioned for three other soldiers to follow him, and they marched past the crowd toward the other end of the city. Most likely, they were going to station themselves at the opposite gate. The soldiers appeared to be sealing him inside the walls of Jericho.

Sveshtari was afraid something like this might happen if he entered the city, but he couldn't do anything about it. It would have been even more dangerous to remain outside the city walls—at the mercy of murderers and thieves.

"Would you mind giving me a boost?" came a voice from behind, triggering Sveshtari's bodyguard instincts. He whirled around, while his right hand went to the sword at his waist.

It was Zacchaeus, the small tax collector, who put up both hands in surrender. "Wait! I mean no harm."

Tension released from Sveshtari's muscles, and he took a deep breath. "What did you ask?"

Zacchaeus motioned toward the tree branches above. "I want to see Jesus. Would you mind giving me a boost?"

Sveshtari scowled. He would much prefer to toss the tax collector over the nearest wall than help him climb a tree.

"I am sorry I asked." Zacchaeus spoke with such sadness that it surprisingly stirred up pity in Sveshtari. Pity was a feeling of weakness, and Sveshtari had worked most of his career to keep it at bay. But he had spent far too much time in the company of women and Jesus. It was making him weak. He felt a little sorry for this little man, who had been so abused by the crowd.

"Why do you want to listen to Jesus?" Sveshtari asked before Zacchaeus could hurry away.

Zacchaeus turned and stared—then answered. "Haven't you ever heard Jesus speak? He said to love our enemies. Even tax collectors. That's a message I like to hear."

Sveshtari grunted. Loving others went both ways, he thought. Didn't it also mean that tax collectors should stop stealing from people?

Zacchaeus continued as if reading his thoughts. "Jesus inspired me to give back what I have taken. He said to give, and it will be given to you. It will be a good measure, pressed down, shaken together and running over, and it will be poured into your lap."

Sveshtari had heard those exact words from Jesus—many times. It conjured up the image of grain being poured into a container, then shaken to let it settle, creating space for even more grain to be added until it overflowed and spilled into the folds of your robe. An image of abundance.

Zacchaeus pointed at the branches of the sycamore tree. "No good tree bears bad fruit, and a bad tree does not bear good fruit. People do not pick figs from thornbushes, and I am sick and tired of being a thornbush."

Sveshtari folded his arms across his chest. "A good man brings good things out of the good in his heart." He, too, could recite the words of Jesus. "An evil man brings evil things out of the evil stored up in his heart. The mouth speaks what the heart is full of."

Zacchaeus beamed. "So, you *have* heard him speak before! Have you ever felt that he was speaking directly to you? He talks to thousands, but sometimes I feel like he's talking to me alone."

Sveshtari shrugged. He had to admit that he also felt a singular connection to Jesus at times, but he wasn't about to admit it.

"I know you don't believe it, but I truly want to be the good tree that bears good fruit," the tax collector said.

Sveshtari stared into Zacchaeus's eyes with an intensity that made the man blush. To his surprise, he believed Zacchaeus. Another sign of weakness. Bodyguards should be suspicious of everyone, especially tax collectors.

Sveshtari leaned over and laced his fingers together to form a stirrup. "Climb."

Bounding forward, Zacchaeus stepped into his hands, and Sveshtari raised him high, shocked at how little the man weighed. He wasn't exaggerating when he thought he could toss Zacchaeus over the wall. Sveshtari raised him high into a tree and thought, *What's wrong with me? I am doing a favor for a tax collector!*

Had he become too soft?

"Thank you, my friend!" Zacchaeus called out. To Sveshtari's amazement, the man began to shimmy out onto a large branch until he was directly over the crowd, looking down on Jesus.

When the people noticed what was happening, many began to laugh at the comical sight of a tax collector caught in a tree like some foolish cat. Jesus looked up, and he smiled as well. But his smile was that of a friend, not a mocker.

"Zacchaeus!" Jesus called out.

Sveshtari could see the shock in Zacchaeus's eyes. Was the man surprised that Jesus knew his name? Or because he had become the center of attention? What did he expect after climbing a tree in the eyes of an unfriendly crowd?

"Yes, Rabbouni?" Zacchaeus finally answered, his voice cracking like an adolescent boy. Again, some in the crowd snickered.

"Zacchaeus, come down!" Jesus motioned with his hand. "I must stay in your house today!"

The crowd was stunned into sudden silence as Zacchaeus stared down from the branch.

"Excuse me, Rabbouni, but what did you just say to me?"

"You heard me, Zacchaeus! Come down. I must stay in your house!"

Sveshtari had to fight away a tear when he saw the light in Zacchaeus's eyes. *A tear!* He was ashamed. He hadn't shed a tear since . . . well, he couldn't remember when. His father would beat him whenever he cried, so he never even shed tears in his youth. What was wrong with him today?

Sveshtari blinked away the tears pooling in his eyes, and he looked up as the little tax collector inched his way backward along the thick branch, an awkward maneuver that caused him to lose his balance. Suddenly, Zacchaeus lost his hold and slid over the edge, hanging on to the thick branch with both arms. Sveshtari rushed directly below and was there when the man lost his grip and tumbled from the tree. The drop was a good fifteen feet, but Sveshtari caught him and kept his balance while buffering the fall.

"You saved me again, my friend!" Zacchaeus grinned from ear to ear.

Sveshtari heard someone snipe at him, saying he should have let the tax collector land on his head. Someone else said they were surprised the tax collector's pockets hadn't spilled gold coins when he tumbled from the tree. But the greatest surprise—and anger—was directed toward Jesus, who had just announced for all to hear that he was going to spend the day in the home of the most hated man in Jericho.

Zacchaeus made a beeline for Jesus, and this time the people let him pass. They continued to stare daggers at the tax collector, but Zacchaeus did not even seem to notice the hatred being poured on him from both sides. He rushed up to Jesus and bowed before him. Then he stood tall—as tall as he could manage—and he threw his arms out wide.

"Look, Lord! Here and now, I give *half of my possessions* to the poor, and if I have cheated anybody out of anything, I will pay back four times the amount."

"Then there is going to be a long line at your house today!" shouted someone from the back of the crowd.

"I mean what I say!" Zacchaeus turned to address the people. "Four times the amount!"

Jesus stood up and placed both hands on Zacchaeus's shoulders. Smiling like a pleased father, he looked at the crowd and declared, "Today, salvation has come to this house, because this man, too, is a son of Abraham. For the Son of Man came to seek and to save what was lost."

Again, Jesus had given himself the title of "Son of Man," something that Sveshtari still did not understand. Eliana had tried to explain that it meant Jesus was the Christ and that he would come from above, unexpected and sudden like lightning. He would sit on the throne and judge all the earth.

Like a judge, Jesus had declared his verdict on this tax collector. He had announced salvation on the most despised man in Jericho. If Zacchaeus truly did give back four times what he had taken, then Jesus's actions today would probably be seen as yet another miracle, on par with opening the eyes of a blind man. But if the little man reneged on his promise, Sveshtari was afraid that Jesus would become the second most hated man in Jericho. He wondered if it was wise for Jesus to proclaim a miracle that depended on the actions of a repentant tax collector.

The crowd began to move again, following in Jesus's wake. Only this time Zacchaeus was nearly dancing at his side.

"Maybe I, too, need to give back four times what I stole," came a voice at Sveshtari's side. He turned to find Abel standing next to him, looking at Jesus and Zacchaeus. "If a tax collector can do it, shouldn't a repentant thief?"

"Is there really a difference?"

"My point exactly."

## Eliana

Eliana gathered up the bread remaining from the meal and placed it in a sack to carry on the road to Jerusalem. She and Keturah had just finished serving Asaph and Chaim, but both men seemed subdued. For Asaph, that had been the case since he returned from his mission with the Zealots. Something terrible had happened to him—something beyond what he had already disclosed. She also had no idea what was bothering Chaim, who was normally so bright and talkative, especially at meals.

Eliana hoped to find a moment to talk to each of them about what was eating at them. She secured the sack of bread to the donkey that Keturah and the baby would ride when they made the final steep climb from Jericho to Jerusalem. Word had gone out that Jesus would be leaving Jericho the next morning, and they would depart with the crowd. You never want to travel the dangerous road from Jericho to Jerusalem alone.

When she turned away from the donkey, she saw her father walking in her direction, his head lowered. All the men in her life seemed to be carrying heavy burdens this day.

"Daughter, can we talk somewhere private?"

"Of course, Abba."

After Eliana finished tying the food sack to the donkey, she and her father left the courtyard of the inn where the women—Eliana, Joanna, and Keturah—had stayed the night in Jericho. Joanna, an infinite well of resources, paid for their lodging.

Eliana followed her father along the *cardo*—the main north-south road running through the city. They walked in silence because idle talk did not seem appropriate at this time. She could tell that her father had something important to say. Finding a place close to Herod's winter palace, they sat by a public fountain—a very Roman feature in this palatial city.

Abba took Eliana by the hand. "I witnessed the healing of that blind man."

Eliana knew. She had seen her father mixed in with the crowd.

Her father reached into the fountain, scooped up some water, and splashed it on his dusty face. "I was sure the miracle had been staged."

Eliana started to jump to Jesus's defense, but Abba held up his hand to stop her. "Let me have my say, Daughter. I was suspicious, so I talked to the blind man at length, and if he was part of a ruse, then he is a very good actor. He seemed very confused by the things he was seeing for the first time, and he kept asking me questions about what he saw."

"Had he been blind since birth?"

"That is what he told me. He would look at something and ask me, 'Is that a rock?' Or 'Is that a basket?' About half of the time, he was wrong. But if he picked up the object, like the rock, and rolled it around in his hands, he knew immediately what it was. It was like he was learning a new language."

"I never thought about how confusing it might be to see for the first time. Everything must look very foreign."

"My point is . . . I believe the man. I truly believe he had been blind from birth—and that your Jesus has healed him."

Eliana's heart sped up. She squeezed her father's hand, and her eyes stung with tears. "He has healed many people. I was one of them."

"Until I talked with the blind man, I suppose I must have doubted that his disciples had truly healed you."

"You thought I too might have been putting on an act?"

"No, no, no, not you," her father said. "But I did think maybe you might have been deceiving yourself. Maybe you really weren't . . ."

Her father couldn't seem to say the words.

"But I was. I was possessed by a demon."

Her father waved his hands at her, signaling her to say no more. He clearly couldn't bear to hear those words. What father would want to hear such a thing? She respected his reluctance and said no more about demons.

"My point is . . ." Her father would not look her in the eyes. "I have decided that maybe there is more to this Jesus than I thought."

She kissed his hand three times. "Thank you, Abba."

"I will do more than reluctantly join you on this journey. I will give you my blessing to follow this Jesus."

*His blessing?*

Eliana could hold it in no more. She burst into tears. As Abba wrapped his arms around her, she could feel his body shake with emotion. She buried her face in his shoulder, and he held her like she remembered when she was only ten years old, whenever she was sad about being rejected by other children. He also held her this way when they were fleeing from the Romans, as they huddled terrified in a cave. He stroked her hair and squeezed her tightly.

Eliana had been reunited with her father for months now, but she knew that in a deeper sense this was the true reunion. She felt like the Children of Israel must have felt when they returned from exile in Babylon. *When the Lord restored the fortunes of Zion, we were like those who dreamed. Our mouths were filled with laughter, our tongues with songs of joy.*

After embracing each other for a happy eternity, her father pulled back and used his thumbs to wipe away the tears at the corners of her eyes. Eliana laughed at how childlike she felt, even at such an age.

"I want to learn more about Jesus," he said.

Eliana grinned and leaned back, looking straight up into the Nehemiah sky. "Restore our fortunes, Lord, like streams in the Negev. Those who sow with tears will reap with songs of joy."

Her father finished her thought. "Those who go out weeping, carrying seed to sow, will return with songs of joy, carrying sheaves with them."

They returned to the courtyard, and Eliana skipped almost the entire way there.

## Sveshtari

"The exits from Jericho are blocked."

Abel's voice came from directly behind Sveshtari who never even heard the man's footfall. Sveshtari was busily securing supplies to their donkey in the courtyard of the inn where they were staying in Jericho.

"For just once, can you not sneak up on me?" Sveshtari asked.

"It's what I do."

"Besides, I already know the gates are blocked by Rufus and his men. Tell me something I don't know."

"I know a tunnel that leads under the city walls."

"Are you serious?"

Sveshtari was beginning to appreciate his alliance with Abel. Ever since he spotted Rufus positioning his men at the city gates, he had been fretting about how he could possibly get out of the city alive. But Abel had just offered him the answer on a silver platter.

"I know nothing of this tunnel," Sveshtari said. "Can you show me?"

"Follow me."

Without another word, Sveshtari set aside his work and followed.

## Asaph

Asaph was shocked to see Eliana's father stride into the courtyard side by side with his daughter. Eliana was beaming, but she did that often. The surprising sight was the obvious joy on Judah's face.

Eliana slipped her arm around her father's waist. "My father and I are reconciled. Completely."

"Praise God," said Chaim. Not to be outdone, Asaph quickly added his own, "Thank God."

Asaph shot up from his seat on the ground to clasp hands with Judah, who couldn't stop grinning.

"I saw the blind man healed at the side of the road," Judah said. "Did you witness it?"

"I did. Do you think the man had really been blind since birth?"

The moment that Asaph asked the question, he realized his stupidity. It was obvious that Eliana's father had been thrilled by the healing, so why would Asaph question it?

But Judah didn't seem to mind the question. "I doubted too!" he said. And then he became uncharacteristically talkative. He took Asaph and Chaim aside to tell them all about his conversation with the blind man and how and why he was convinced of the man's truthfulness.

Asaph had never seen Judah this way—so buoyant. He could tell that Chaim noticed the change as well, and suddenly Asaph feared that Chaim might ask Judah to bless a marriage with his daughter before he had a chance to do the same.

With Judah feeling so good about his daughter—and about life—Asaph realized that now would be the best possible time to approach him about Eliana. That is, assuming Asaph could find time with him alone. They talked throughout the afternoon, but Chaim was always there.

As evening fell and darkness blanketed Jericho, they had their meal, and Judah insisted on a long and fervent prayer. Without a doubt, the man had changed. Asaph decided he had to ask Judah for his blessing while the time was ripe. So, when Chaim excused himself to retire for the night, Asaph saw his opportunity. He asked Judah if they could talk in private, so they stepped outside the courtyard and into the street, rounding the corner where the darkness was not so thick. Glimmers of fire lit up the windows of many houses, casting a net of light on the two men.

"I am very pleased to see you and Eliana reconciled and so happy together," Asaph began.

Judah smiled. "This is one of the finest days of my life. I do not want it to end."

"I hope for this to also be one of my finest days."

Judah continued to grin, oblivious to what Asaph was preparing to ask. "How so?"

"Judah, I would like to ask your blessing upon the union of Eliana and myself."

Judah's grin was gone in an instant. He did not look angry. Just confused. He bit his lip and furrowed his brow.

"Eliana has mentioned nothing to me of this."

"We have not discussed it. I would not dare to talk with her of my intentions without your blessing." Asaph hoped that Judah would go beyond a blessing and announce to Eliana that he had made the match, and all had been decided.

"Thank you for coming to me, Asaph." Judah rubbed his chin and sighed. "I give you my blessing if this marriage suits Eliana as well."

It was Asaph's turn to furrow his brow. "You intend to place this decision in her hands?"

"I just surrendered in my battle over her desire to follow Jesus. I certainly have no intention of starting another battle that I cannot win."

"But you are her father. A father is entitled to win all battles."

"I am beginning to wonder if you really know my daughter, Asaph. She has a mind of her own, and I do not intend to do as many fathers do, using any means possible to bend her to my will. I already tried that once when I locked her in that room. But someone left her door unlocked if you recall."

A hint of anger seeped into Judah's tone. This conversation was beginning to unravel. Asaph had been given Judah's blessing, contingent on Eliana's agreement of marriage, and he should have left it at that. But now he feared he was about to lose even this guarded approval.

"You are right, Judah. I apologize. I certainly know that Eliana can be willful . . ."

Immediately, he regretted using the word "willful." Did it sound too much like a criticism of his daughter? But Judah burst into a smile and slapped Asaph on the back.

"That is exactly the word! Perhaps you know my daughter after all."

Relief washed over Asaph. He smiled—awkwardly.

"Talk to Eliana," Judah said. "Pray with her on this matter."

The old Judah would not have been so quick to suggest prayer.

"I will."

"If she agrees to a marriage, then we will celebrate."

Judah planted a kiss on both sides of Asaph's face. But as he did, several men, all of them holding torches, emerged from a nearby alleyway. Cloaked in darkness except for his face, the leader looked directly at them and smiled.

It was Barabbas.

Flanking Barabbas were about a dozen other men—Zealots all of them. Asaph's skin tingled with tension. Barabbas had tracked him down. As Asaph pulled out his sword, he could see the shock in Judah's eyes. Judah looked confused because he had no idea about the bad blood between him and Barabbas. The question now was whose bad blood was going to be spilled?

## Keturah

"This is Abel," Sveshtari told Keturah, who shielded her baby, Babette, from the night breeze coming from the west and the Great Sea. Earlier in the evening, he had told her all about his encounter with Abel, and how the repentant thief offered to help them safely slip out of the city.

"He showed me the tunnel beneath the walls," Sveshtari said. "He's telling the truth. There is an escape route."

But Keturah thought the risk was too great. How could they trust a thief? Just because he showed Sveshtari a tunnel doesn't mean there won't be soldiers waiting for them when they get there.

With her face partly lit by the cooking fire, she nodded at the young man. Abel looked to be in his twenties—thin, somewhat short, with dark eyes and a mischievous grin. "Sveshtari told me all about you," Keturah said.

"Good things, I pray."

"He told me how he caught you attempting to thieve from the disciples."

"I am no longer that man." Abel maintained his silly grin.

"Sveshtari also told me you claimed that you stole to feed your family. So, where are your wife and children now? Remember, you just told me that you are no longer a man who steals. Does that mean you also no longer lie?"

Abel grinned, pausing before answering. "I said I am no longer that man, and that is the truth. So, I will tell no lies. I do not have a wife and child. I told the disciples that I stole to feed my family because I knew they prefer to hear that."

Keturah turned to face Sveshtari squarely. "See? You're relying on the help of a liar."

Sveshtari shrugged. "I knew he didn't have a family. I figured that out from the very beginning. But who am I to blame him for lying?"

"Yes, you, too, are a practiced liar," Keturah said.

"Listen," said Abel, "if you don't want to use the tunnel . . ."

"I didn't say that!" Keturah turned her fury on Abel.

Abel backpedaled, but he continued to grin. "Your woman has fire, Sveshtari."

"And I'm not *his woman*." Keturah turned to Sveshtari and caught him making faces at Abel and signaling for him to shut up.

Ignoring Sveshtari, Abel kept talking. "Listen, I lied to the disciples, but since that time they have showered me with affection so much greater than riches. I have had a new birth."

"A new birth?" Keturah jostled the child in her arms. "What in the world does that mean?"

"It means I've changed completely. I'm a new person. That's why I'm doing this as a favor to you."

Sveshtari laid a hand on his shoulder. "It's not entirely a favor. Remember, you asked me to protect you in return."

"True. But I have not asked for money."

Keturah pursed her lips and stared at Abel. Should they put their lives in the hands of a liar and a thief—even a repentant one? Abel hadn't asked

Sveshtari for money, but what if he had been paid by the Romans to lead them into the hands of the soldiers?

On the other hand, if they stayed in Jericho until the morning light, Rufus and his soldiers would surely track them down. Sveshtari reported that the number of guards at each gate had doubled since the afternoon.

Abel spread his arms wide. "If I had wanted to betray you for money, don't you think I would have already come to this courtyard with a half dozen soldiers at my side?"

*He makes another strong point.*

"All right then. We are ready to leave," Sveshtari said, making the final decision. He turned to Keturah and asked, "Have you told Eliana of our plans?"

"Have you told me what?" Eliana emerged from the inn and stepped into the light of the courtyard fire.

"About our departure," said Keturah, motioning toward Abel. "This is the man who will lead us out of the city. He has a secret way." She had already told Eliana about the guards at the gates—and how they had been sealed inside the walls of Jericho.

Eliana turned to Abel. "Thank you for helping my friends." Her approval made Keturah feel more secure in their decision.

Just then, they heard a commotion in the street on the other side of the high courtyard wall—raised voices that soon became shouts. One of the voices was Eliana's father, and Keturah's first fear was that Roman soldiers had descended on them. She was suddenly certain that they had been betrayed by this thief after all.

"If you brought the Romans here . . ." Sveshtari drew his sword.

"I tell you! I did not," said Abel. "Let us leave by the back way."

Hearing her father's voice, Eliana made for the courtyard door, but Sveshtari took her by the arm. "I will check it out. It may not be safe."

"You are going out there?" said Abel. "But what if there are soldiers? We need to flee."

"Not until I make sure my friends are safe."

"I know you are a protector at heart," said Abel, "but you carry your role too far. The purpose of this night is to escape, not fight."

But Keturah knew Sveshtari, and she knew he would not leave his friends when they might be in trouble, no matter what the risk. Sveshtari banged open the courtyard door, leaving Abel, Keturah, and Eliana standing in the fire's glow, unsure what to do next.

## Sveshtari

*They aren't Romans. Thank Mars.*

When Sveshtari exited the courtyard, he followed the voices to the street, where he found Judah and Asaph confronting a group of familiar faces. They faced the very same Zealots that Sveshtari had fought alongside on the Cliffs of Arbel.

Although these were supposed allies, hot words were being hurled, and the Zealot leader, Barabbas, was menacing, his face twisted in anger. Barabbas always had a volcanic manner, so Sveshtari approached cautiously, with his sword in hand. "What is going on? Your voices are going to attract Romans."

Barabbas pointed his sword at Sveshtari. "Stay out of this. We have no fight with you."

"But you do have a fight with Judah and Asaph? Why?"

"Only with Asaph. We have come to take him with us so we can administer justice," said Barabbas.

"For what?"

"For killing Gershom."

"You killed Gershom?" Eliana's pained voice rose from behind.

Sveshtari spun around. "I told you to stay in the courtyard!"

Eliana paid him no attention. She rushed toward Asaph, but her father intercepted her. "You murdered Gershom?" she asked again, her eyes wide with disbelief.

Asaph looked away, his gaze going to his feet. "I struck him with a rock in self-defense."

"And then you left him to die," said Barabbas.

"I did not intend to kill him—only to get away. He and Barabbas wanted to execute me because I would not kill a child."

Barabbas flung out a hand. "He's lying. I would never kill a child, even a Roman child."

Asaph jabbed a finger at Barabbas. "Liar! You killed the mother and father driving the wagon, and you ordered me to slay their boy!"

Sveshtari believed him. That sounded exactly like something Barabbas would do—although who was he to judge? In his former life, Sveshtari would have killed a child if Herod Antipas had ordered him to. Antipas's father, Herod the Great, had slaughtered an entire village of children; and if Sveshtari had been one of the king's soldiers at the time, he probably would have followed orders.

Judah turned to Asaph. "Are you saying that Gershom also wanted you to slay this boy? Is that why you killed him?"

"I cannot say what was in Gershom's heart," Asaph said. "I only know that I had escaped from Barabbas, and Gershom captured me, and . . . and I tell you . . . it was self-defense."

Barabbas spit at Asaph and made a move to grab him, but both Judah and Sveshtari blocked his way. Barabbas gripped his sword in one hand, and he used his other to unsheathe his knife—a curved Sicarii blade often wielded by assassins. Sveshtari's weapon was a *gladius*, a short sword used by Roman soldiers. Both the Sicarii knife and *gladius* were ideal for stabbing in close quarters.

Sveshtari kept an eye on Barabbas's blades, and if the Zealot made the slightest move to use them, the man would be dead in an instant. Barabbas was fierce, but he was not a disciplined fighter. Sveshtari had no fear of him.

"Soldiers coming!" one of the Zealots suddenly shouted, and Sveshtari glanced down the street to see approaching torches reflecting off golden armor. Roman soldiers approached from two directions, and they were caught in the middle. Zealots scattered like rats, most of them heading down an alleyway outlet.

"This way!" Sveshtari took Eliana by the hand and pulled her back toward the courtyard.

"What are you doing?" Judah asked. "Don't go into the courtyard! We will be trapped there!"

"Trust me!" Sveshtari barged into the courtyard with Eliana screaming at him to let go. Asaph and Judah were close behind.

"Romans are coming," Sveshtari said to Keturah and Abel, who had been waiting just inside the courtyard walls.

Abel took command with an authority well beyond his years. "Follow me."

"Who is this man?" asked Judah.

"No time to explain," Sveshtari said. "Just trust him. Trust me."

"You keep saying that."

Sveshtari secured the courtyard gate, knowing full well that it would slow down the Romans for only a short time. But every second counted as they followed Abel around the back of the inn to a second gate. He prayed to Zeus that most of the soldiers had taken off in pursuit of the Zealots and not them, but as they exited through the back gate, he could already hear the front gate being splintered by soldiers. The crack of wood sounded like Olympian thunder.

## **Eliana**

In the chaos, Eliana looked down to make sure her dog was running alongside. She worried about Chaim, who was back at the inn, probably sound asleep. The Romans weren't after him, so she prayed he would be fine.

They hurried along pitch-dark alleyways, but they could not move fast or they would trip over broken pottery and other debris in their path. Any sound would lead the Romans directly to them.

Elaina could hear the Roman soldiers shouting, but the commotion did not seem to be coming any closer.

"How much farther?" Sveshtari hissed at Abel.

"Patience."

Eliana didn't realize that Jericho had so many narrow, twisting alleyways. Most of the city had gone quiet for the night, but as soon as they entered the most disreputable section of the city, noise erupted on all sides, and watered-down wine flowed while women leaned out from lamp-lit doorways. Eliana had once spent her days and nights in such a place, and she silently prayed for the souls of every single person they passed. She was tempted to latch on to one of the women and drag her with them, yanking her to freedom. But they were moving too swiftly. There was no time to stop.

"What's the hurry, Abel?" asked one woman of the night. It seemed Abel had many friends in low places.

When they heard the marching of feet coming from their right, Abel made a sharp left turn and led them into an alleyway where he motioned for them to halt—and listen. Voices carried through the darkness—orders and shouts and the sounds of scrambling feet.

Soldiers were close.

Eliana glanced around the alleyway. It led to a dead-end wall much too high to climb. Abel had chosen their hiding place poorly because there was nowhere to go. But they couldn't risk leaving the alley because it sounded like soldiers swarmed everywhere. It would be only a matter of time before the soldiers checked this small alley and trapped them.

Abel motioned toward a wall. "Here. Through this opening."

"Is this the tunnel?" Eliana asked.

"No, but it's a good hiding place until we can get to the tunnel."

Although Eliana's eyes had adjusted to the dark, she could barely make out a hole at the base of one of the buildings. Abel lowered himself into the hole, and then his whisper came back to them from the darkness.

"It's safe. Follow me down. But leave the dog."

"I'm not leaving the dog. He saved my life."

"He saved mine too," said Keturah.

"He'll bark," said Abel.

"He won't."

"It's bad enough we have a baby, but a—"

Sveshtari crouched at the opening. "We don't have time to argue. The dog comes with us."

With Sveshtari's help, Eliana sat down, stuck her feet through the dark hole, and probed until she found a series of stone steps. She slid down five steps before landing with a thump on the cold ground; then she turned and took the baby from Keturah, who followed.

"What is this place?" asked Eliana.

"A Mithraic temple," whispered Keturah.

"Oh." Eliana had met people who worshipped in such a temple, which were usually built in caves or underground rooms of any sort. The subterranean room had a low ceiling, making it impossible to fully stand.

Eliana scooted deeper into the temple as the others climbed in. She felt her way along one wall, with Lavi panting by her side, and she made out the eerie stone image of the god Mithras straddling a bull and cutting its throat. A raven was perched on the bull's back, while a dog and scorpion attacked the dying animal. Ears of wheat rose from the bull's bleeding wound.

Eliana closed her eyes and prayed. She could sense the demons close, but she knew that evil entities were subject to the power of Jesus, so she said his name over and over again.

"Jesus, Jesus, Jesus . . ."

"Ssh," said Abel.

It sounded like soldiers had entered the alley. They heard footsteps shuffling outside, and the flicker of torchlight seeped into their hiding place. When Eliana opened her eyes, she saw, on the opposite side of the room, the carving of a creature with a man's body and a lion's head who was wrapped up in the coils of a snake. She began to panic. This felt too much like when her family had been on the run from the Romans, hiding in caves.

"Jesus, Jesus, Jesus . . ." She whispered because she sensed she had to say the name out loud. If she didn't speak it aloud, Eliana wasn't sure she could stop herself from bolting from this subterranean temple into the arms of a Roman soldier.

Keturah put an arm around Eliana and leaned her head against hers. "Jesus, Jesus, Jesus," Keturah whispered in unison. Eliana wondered if Keturah really believed there was power in that name. Or was it just a way to comfort her? Whatever Keturah's motive, it helped.

Outside, in the alley, came voices. Latin words. Romans.

Eliana nearly went faint. One moment, she was in the cramped underground temple, reciting Jesus's name, and the next moment she felt herself being transported in the spirit to what appeared to be an enormous temple of God Almighty. She stood high on a balcony, looking down on thousands upon thousands of people, each of them carrying a lamb to be sacrificed. They moved in a long procession on the floor far below, weaving from one side of the Temple to the other, but always progressing upward. Then she sensed herself turning and walking upward, higher and higher up a long staircase, like Jacob's ladder, and she realized that she, too, carried a lamb in her arms. She felt an overwhelming wave of peace and safety, and she heard the music of a ram's horn filling the space like a living sound.

She wanted to stay in this space forever, but she felt herself being shaken. Suddenly, she was back in the underground temple, where Keturah was nudging her and whispering her name. Lavi licked her face.

Asaph loomed over her. "Are you alright?"

She answered with a smile.

"You went quiet for a long time," said Keturah, "and I couldn't rouse you. I was scared."

"I'm fine."

"The soldiers are gone," Abel said. "We need to move. Now."

Back outside, Eliana basked in the fresh night air, and the feeling of safety remained with her. She wanted to shout her praises to the stars, but she knew better.

Abel moved to the end of the alley to make sure all was clear before he motioned them forward. "Not far now. We are almost to the tunnel."

"You scared me back there." Eliana's father took her right hand and ran his fingers over her palm.

"Jesus brought me to safety."

"He what?"

"Sshhh," said Abel.

"Halt!" came a voice from behind, and Eliana's peace shattered. She looked behind and saw faces in the dark—and spear points and flashes of swords. Then all became madness and darkness and unfiltered fear, mixed with shouts and commands.

The soldiers had found them.

"Take the women and baby with you!" Sveshtari shouted to Abel.

"But—"

"We'll meet up with you after we deal with these soldiers."

Abel pointed down the street. "Do you remember the way to the tunnel?"

"I do," said Sveshtari. "We'll be there soon! Now go! Quickly!"

Then Eliana felt her father's calloused hands release hers, while Abel pushed her forward.

As Abel led the way, Sveshtari, Asaph, and her father stayed back to hold off the soldiers, giving them precious time. There were only two soldiers, she noticed. Good odds. But she was still terrified by the thought of being separated from her father.

"No, Abba!"

"Go!"

"Hurry!" yelled Abel.

"Abba!"

"Go!"

"Move!"

Eliana took off running through an alley that squeezed in tightly from both sides. Then she followed Abel through a door and into a small room, where another man waited for them. Initially, she thought they had run directly into a net of hostile soldiers. But Abel knew the man, who held a small oil lamp.

The man motioned toward a gaping hole dug into the floor of the room. "Hurry, hurry, very little time." He shoved her in the direction of the tunnel, which Abel had already entered.

Eliana put up a fight. "I can't leave without my father!"

The man, stinking of fish and sweat, caught her mid-flight and lifted her from her feet, triggering a burst of barking from Lavi. Eliana was tempted to bite the man's hand, but that was something the old Eliana would have done.

Keturah took Eliana gently by the shoulders when the man had put her down. "Jesus is with you. Please, I need you to go down into the tunnel, so you can take Babette from my arms. Trust in Jesus."

Keturah was telling her to trust Jesus? A pagan was saying that?

She had no choice but to obey. Abel reached up from inside the tunnel, like a corpse reaching out of a grave, and he helped her down into the earth. Once Eliana and Lavi were inside the tunnel, she reached back and took Babette from Keturah's outstretched arms. Then, after Keturah had climbed inside the tunnel, the man above slid something over the hole. The lamplight vanished, plunging them into darkness once again.

"Follow me. Not far, and we'll be beyond the walls of Jericho."

Eliana handed Babette back to Keturah and was forced to crawl on her hands and knees through the cramped, narrow space. The earth around her smelled moist and rich, and small showers of soil occasionally rained down on them. The tunnel was mercifully short, so she was soon touched by a cool breeze. She spotted an opening ahead—and moments later, she was looking up at a circle of night sky. Abel climbed from the hole, then reached back and pulled her out of the ground. She rose to see a sky wild with stars. She stared in wonder.

"No stopping." Abel tugged on her sleeve.

Eliana looked back and saw Keturah and Babette rising from the ground. But no Sveshtari, no Asaph, and no father.

"Let's go!"

She obeyed and began running, with Lavi panting by her side. She felt like her entire life was nothing but running.

## Asaph

Asaph placed a stone in his sling. As the two Roman soldiers closed in, he let loose, and the missile raced through the dark, catching one of the soldiers squarely in the neck. The soldier let out a gurgling grunt, stumbling backward.

"Nice shot," said Sveshtari as he quickly advanced on the remaining soldier. The second soldier rushed forward, *gladius* in hand, but Sveshtari was faster, and his blade sliced the soldier's hand cleanly off at the wrist. One moment later, Sveshtari finished him; then he dealt a fatal blow to the soldier who was still leaning over, gagging and holding his neck.

It was all over in moments.

Sveshtari surveyed their handiwork. "That was easier than I thought. Let's move."

Only it wasn't all over.

Several more Romans poured out of another alleyway. Before Asaph or Sveshtari could react, the soldiers had disarmed Judah and nabbed him. Sveshtari rushed to his aid, but he ran into a wall of shields. Asaph released another rock, but it clanged feebly against one of the shields. Sveshtari was a man on fire, hacking and slicing, but the four Romans, with their shields leading the charge, forced him back.

Meanwhile, Judah disappeared, dragged away by his captors and vanishing into the darkness, swallowed whole by the night.

Seeing the futility of the fight, Sveshtari retreated and Asaph followed, with three soldiers at their backs. A spear whistled over Asaph's right shoulder. A little lower, and he would have been pinned to a wall. Asaph kept moving, his legs flying at a speed he didn't think he was capable of any longer. It seemed as if he was always running out of Jericho.

## Nekoda: Three days later, sunday morning, nisan 9, AD 33, jerusalem

Nekoda strode across the Temple grounds, his purple robe standing out in a sea of white clothing. He noticed the eyes of the people drawn to his glory. Normally, he would savor the gazes, but there was no time for that luxury today. He marched toward the Eastern Gate of Jerusalem with fury in his steps. He had heard that Jesus was approaching the gate, making his foul mood even worse.

Nekoda was angry about so many things that he had lost count of them. To begin with, he was furious that Rufus's men had failed to capture Sveshtari in Jericho—the top prize in Nekoda's mind. Rufus's men had hauled in a handful of Zealots, including Barabbas, and they were rotting in a filthy prison, awaiting execution. But Nekoda wanted Sveshtari most of all, and he had escaped.

Jerusalem overflowed with pilgrims, flocking to the city for Passover, and he despaired of ever finding Sveshtari in such a crowd. The soldiers had Sveshtari trapped in Jericho, and yet the man managed to slip away like a slick fish wriggling out of their hands.

But Sveshtari was not the only worry. There was also Jesus, who continued to stir up crowds with outrageous claims. Word even spread that he had raised a man from the dead in nearby Bethany. Nekoda had hired several more spies for the Passover celebration to help him monitor this false teacher and his followers, and they said he was continuing to make wild claims of being the Messiah.

And now this . . . Jesus was entering the Eastern Gate. The Golden Gate. The Mercy Gate. Jesus knew what he was doing, for the expected Messiah had been prophesied to enter Jerusalem by the Eastern Gate.

*"Then the man brought me to the gate facing east, and I saw the glory of the God of Israel coming from the east,"* the prophet Ezekiel proclaimed. *"His voice was like the roar of rushing waters, and the land was radiant with his glory. The glory of the Lord entered the temple through the gate facing east."*

Jesus knew those words—and the rabble knew those words. This false Messiah was playing with prophecy, molding it to fit his story. Nekoda would not allow such blasphemy.

The Sanhedrin had ordered Nekoda to sow discord among the followers of Jesus, but all his attempts had failed. He released rumor after rumor about Jesus, like releasing wolves into a pack of sheep. But they did nothing to stop Jesus's momentum. For every rumor that his spies spread, Jesus responded with yet another miracle—or alleged miracle.

Word must have spread that Jesus was coming because many pilgrims flocked to the Eastern Gate to meet this man. The day was warm and bright, bustling with animal life—sheep and doves everywhere. The city smelled of animals—a rustic odor, the incense of the countryside.

Most of the rabble stepped aside when they saw Nekoda's purple robes, although a few gave him an eye of bitter judgment because he wore the color of Roman royalty. But he had more serious matters to worry about than disapproving peasants.

Nekoda passed through the Golden Gate and stared across the Kidron Valley from the eastern wall of the city. Just beyond, the slope dipped down into the valley and then climbed back up steeply to the Mount of Olives.

The last time he had been on the Mount of Olives was to witness the sacrifice of the Red Heifer, whose ashes would be collected and placed in a container of water, then sprinkled on those who needed purification.

He stared at the river of pilgrims, marching on the road that led directly to the Golden Gate. Although the day was dusty, he could make out a man seated on a donkey in a sea of people.

*It can't be. He wouldn't dare.*

It appeared that Jesus was the one seated on that donkey. Yes, the man certainly knew what he was doing. This imposter had chosen the donkey to fulfill the prophecy of Zechariah, who said, *"Rejoice greatly, Daughter Zion! Shout, Daughter Jerusalem! See, your king comes to you, righteous and victorious, lowly and riding on a donkey, on a colt, the foal of a donkey . . . He will proclaim peace to the nations. His rule will extend from sea to sea and from the River to the ends of the earth."*

Jesus could not proclaim his intentions any clearer, even if he carried a sign above his head announcing himself to be King of the Jews. By entering the Golden Gate on a donkey, he was declaring himself Messiah.

Then the rabble began to chant.

"Blessed is the king who comes in the name of the Lord!"

"Peace in heaven and glory in the highest!"

People waved palm branches, some laying down their branches and coats for him to pass over. These were ways to treat an approaching king. Nekoda wondered if Jesus's disciples had chosen palm branches because of their connection to the Festival of Booths when people waved palms to celebrate their delivery out of slavery in Egypt. He wouldn't put it past them. If Jesus was willing to call himself Messiah, he would not hesitate to put himself on par with Moses, the deliverer.

It wasn't long before most of the crowd was rejoicing, jumping up and down, waving palms, shouting, and singing. The women began ululating, and the sound nearly drove Nekoda mad. Some of those fools probably had no idea who Jesus was, but they got caught up in the insanity.

Nekoda's day was getting worse. He had seen enough, so he turned on his heels and stormed back into the city, slamming his shoulder against any person who would not clear out of his path.

By now, he was certain. Jesus was too dangerous to live. Jesus had to die.

## Eliana: monday, nisan 10, AD 33

The Temple was mobbed. Eliana tried to keep her eyes locked on Jesus and his disciples as they jostled through the packed Court of Gentiles—the outer ring of the Temple Mount, the only space where non-Jews could be present. Signs warned Gentiles that if they progressed any closer to the heart of the Temple, if they dared to set foot in the next ring, the Court of Women, they could be killed.

The Court of Gentiles was also where the doves, sheep, and oxen were sold for sacrifice, so it teemed with animal life. The smells of animal sweat and dung were pungent, and the air was filled with the sound of birds cooing and wings flapping and sheep bleating and oxen bellowing.

Eliana's mind was as noisy as the courtyard, buzzing with angry thoughts. She was furious that her father had been captured and imprisoned. How could Sveshtari and Asaph allow such a thing to happen? She had trusted them. And now she was separated from her abba once again. She felt like lashing out at somebody. Anybody.

With her mind churning, Eliana lost sight of Jesus; her vision was suddenly crowded by strange men and women passing in front of her, exchanging foreign coins for the Tyrian shekel used to purchase animals. This only angered her even more. She heard a cacophony of foreign tongues being spoken as some of the moneychangers got into arguments with Passover pilgrims. Twice, Eliana was nearly knocked to the ground by big, burly men, one of them leading an ox by a rope. She didn't recall the Court of the Gentiles ever being this chaotic, this loud, this smelly.

At last, she caught sight of Jesus again. He had his eyes closed and seemed to be praying, although how he could concentrate in the chaos was beyond her. Several disciples stood nearby, also straining to pray, but it had to be difficult in this environment. People pressed in on her until she could barely move, but then the crowd expanded, like a chest breathing in and out.

With his eyes still closed, Jesus raised his hands with upturned palms. She could sense his pent-up power. It was like viewing an approaching storm cloud, filled with wind and rain and strained to the bursting point. Suddenly, he opened his eyes and moved swiftly toward the nearest moneychanger who was placing coins in the hands of a pilgrim and arguing about the exchange rate.

Jesus latched onto the moneychanger's table with both hands and heaved it onto its side. As money showered onto the stone floor, the table struck the ground sideways with a crack. Heads turned and eyes locked on the rapidly unfolding scene. Then Jesus overturned some of the benches used by people selling doves, and several birds flew out of the men's hands. One flew directly over Eliana's head. Eliana laughed, channeling her anger into the unexpected intensity of the moment.

Jesus whirled around to face the stunned crowd. "It is written . . . My house will be a house of prayer, but you have made it a den of robbers!"

"How dare you call us robbers?" one of the moneychangers shouted back. "Without us, there would be chaos in the Temple! How would people be able to buy their sacrificial animals, if not for us?"

When Jesus spoke those words—"a den of robbers"—Eliana's mind flew to her past. She saw herself back in the cave, the den where brigands hid her away after abducting her in Bethlehem. Caves were everywhere in her life. Only days before she was captured, she had seen the baby Jesus, who was born in a cave of a much different sort because there was no room in the inn.

When Eliana's family fled from the Romans, they found refuge in caves, and she was reunited with her father in a cave on the Cliffs of Arbel. Most recently, she hid in the pagan cave of Mithras. But, most painfully, the brigands imprisoned her in caves for an entire year before moving her to more permanent slave quarters. So, she knew exactly what it was like to be trapped in a den of thieves.

*Will you steal and murder, commit adultery and perjury, burn incense to Baal and follow other gods you have not known, and then come and stand before me in this house, which bears my Name, and say, "We are safe"—safe to do all these detestable things? Has this house, which bears my Name, become a den of robbers to you? But I have been watching! declares the Lord.*

With these words, the prophet Jeremiah once rebuked people who live their lives immersed in sin and then come to God's house, His holy Temple, to declare refuge from judgment. They seek the safety to keep sinning! They are like brigands who drag all their loot to a cave, where they find safety from judgment and punishment, only to rob again.

Is that what Jesus meant by his reprimand?

Eliana's mind returned to the present moment, watching as Jesus swept through the Temple like a river roaring, a swirling stream of Living Water, cleansing the Court of Gentiles. He declared judgment on the people's feeble attempts to make blood sacrifices, to make themselves right before God, only to return to the world to sin again. The Temple was a house of prayer—not a cave of robbers, eager to steal again!

Without the Temple, however, they were lost, Eliana thought. Without this cave of safety, where would they find redemption? Will Jesus provide a different cave of safety? A new Temple?

Eliana lost sight of Jesus, who moved on like a force of nature, disappearing into the mob. As she rushed around, trying to find any sign of her Lord, her foot slipped on some of the coins that had spilled to the ground. A man cursed her for stepping on his money, but Eliana paid him no heed.

She scoured the crowd for Jesus, her Shiloh, her place of peace. Without him, she was lost.

# 8

## LUKE, CHAPTER 20

### ASAPH: TUESDAY, NISAN 11, AD 33, JERUSALEM

ASAPH LET OUT a groan as he lifted his right foot and saw that he had stepped in dung—compliments of the many animals brought into the Court of Gentiles for sale as Passover sacrifices.

Normally, Eliana would have laughed, but she hadn't even smiled since the night they fled Jericho. When Asaph and Sveshtari eventually reunited with Eliana, Keturah, and Abel on the road between Jericho and Jerusalem, he had the unpleasant job of giving her the news that her father had been captured.

For two days, she didn't talk to either him or Sveshtari, blaming them for not keeping her father out of the hands of the Romans. Asaph absorbed her anger in silence. He knew it would be useless to defend their actions.

"You should have at least tried to rescue my abba," Eliana said, finally breaking the silence as they made their way through the Court of Gentiles. Chaim and Asaph flanked her on either side.

Eliana had already thrown those words at him in the immediate aftermath of the incident—and he still had no answer. They probably would have died trying to save Judah, but maybe that would have been the better alternative. At least there was honor in trying.

"Sveshtari said it was better to retreat, regroup, and find a way to rescue your father from the Jerusalem prison," Asaph answered, hearing the hollowness of his words even as he delivered them. "We will find a way to rescue him."

"I spent most of my life without my father! It isn't fair that now he is abducted and taken away from me!"

"I agree," Asaph said softly. "It isn't fair."

"Yes, it isn't fair," echoed Chaim. He had taken advantage of Eliana's anger at Asaph to make inroads on her affection. Chaim had been safely asleep in bed on the night they escaped, so she didn't blame him for her father's abduction. That, too, wasn't fair, but such was life.

Asaph scraped the dung from his sandal on a stone step. When one of the vendors saw what he was doing, the middle-aged man charged at him with a stick, and Asaph slipped into the crowd, catching up with Eliana and Chaim.

The Court of Gentiles was wild and noisy, especially as they passed the moneychangers. Twice, Asaph had to slap away a moneychanger tugging on his sleeve. With so many people and so much money flowing into the Court of the Gentiles, the moneychangers fought over customers like dogs on a bone.

"It's Jesus!" Eliana suddenly made a beeline for the Royal Stoa—the line of colonnades along the southern side of the Court of Gentiles, where rabbis taught. Eliana almost smiled—*almost*. Only Jesus seemed to have that power over her.

Asaph, Chaim, and Lavi followed in her wake. Asaph couldn't help but notice the irony that he and Chaim were no different than dogs, tagging along like companion animals, eager to please.

Eliana shoved through the crowd to get near Jesus as he spoke. Asaph and Chaim followed close behind, trying to be more tactful as they squeezed their way through the people.

When they finally reached her, Asaph saw Chaim's face go white. Chaim's brother, Nekoda, stood about five cubits in front of Jesus, part of a pack of about a dozen Pharisees and Sadducees. You couldn't miss the purple robe that advertised Nekoda's importance.

When Asaph turned to say something to Chaim, the man had fled. Chaim wanted no part of his brother, and Asaph couldn't blame him.

Nekoda glared at Jesus and spit out his words like nails. "Tell us by what authority you are doing these things. Who gave you this authority?"

Asaph knew what Nekoda was trying to do. He was trying to shame Jesus, trying to prove to the crowd that this teacher had no true authority. Jesus was not a priest. He was not a legal expert. He was not a member of the Sanhedrin. And he was definitely not the king he made himself out to be.

But Jesus did not seem flustered by the question.

"I will also ask you a question," Jesus finally said, leveling his gaze at Nekoda. "Tell me: John's baptism—was it from heaven, or of human origin?"

The question slapped away Nekoda's haughty look. Nekoda turned and began to converse with the other priests. Asaph almost laughed out loud because he was astounded by how quickly Jesus had turned the tables. If the priests answered that John's baptism came from heaven, Jesus could ask them why they didn't believe the words of John. After all, hadn't John baptized Jesus and proclaimed him as the coming king?

But if they said that John's baptism came from human origins, not heaven, the Pharisees and Sadducees risked the wrath of the crowd. John still had a strong following, and any word against the prophet could put the priests in danger.

Finally, after a long discussion, one of the other priests stepped away from the pack to declare their answer—or non-answer. "We don't know where John's baptism was from." It was the only response he could give.

Jesus extended his arms to his sides and shrugged. "Neither will I tell you by what authority I am doing these things."

Just like that, Jesus had humiliated his enemies. Turning back to the people, he continued to teach. Nekoda and the other priests looked like foolish schoolchildren, staring in disbelief at what Jesus had done. People in the crowd laughed, and when Asaph turned to face Eliana, he saw that a miracle had occurred.

Eliana was smiling again.

## Sveshtari

Not much in the world frightened Sveshtari. But this did.

It seemed as if he were staring into the mouth of Hades itself—a yawning black opening. Abel, the little thief, suggested that they enter this foul underworld to rescue Eliana's father. The palace, built by Herod the Great, was a massive enclosure along the northwest corner of the city's wall; the sewer pipe stretched from the palace to the west, draining into the Hinnom Valley, which wrapped around the western side of the city.

Abel motioned toward the blackness. "It's the only way you're going to get inside Herod's palace. You can't just knock on the front door and ask to enter."

"Perhaps I could disguise myself as a common laborer and enter the palace that way." Sveshtari wracked his brain for any other option than clambering through a drainage pipe. He preferred to fight in wide, open spaces. Battlefields were his home. Dark, smelly, enclosed spaces were not. Just thinking about it made his guts turn.

Abel shrugged. "We would never be able to reach the prison disguised as laborers. Even if you got onto the palace grounds, you, of all people, should know they wouldn't let us anywhere near the prison cells."

Abel was right.

"The drainage pipe it is." Sveshtari sighed, knowing he had no other choice if he wanted to get inside the palace fortress where Eliana's father was imprisoned. "But I am going to need a guard's uniform."

"That's the easy part." Abel grinned like an imp. "I can get those for us on the black market."

"*Us?* You're going too?"

"Of course! You think Asaph will also want to join us?"

"I'm sure he will. He wants to make amends to Eliana, so find a uniform for him—and one for Chaim while you're at it. How narrow does it get in there?"

"I've traveled this sewer one other time and there are some tight places, but you will be fine."

"I was talking about Chaim, not me," Sveshtari said. "He's lost a fair amount of weight in recent months, but he's still not a small man."

"I'll see what I can do. It's a fairly straight shot to the palace. No branches to the right or left. We can't go wrong."

Still, there was no telling what they might encounter in the darkness of the sewer. As a boy, Sveshtari was terrified of darkness—and especially of the god of deep darkness, Scotus. This son of chaos was the father of Thanatos, god of death.

Sveshtari's father once forced him to conquer this fear by taking him to a deep wood and leaving him there in the dark to find his way home. The trial worked, and he learned to feel comfortable in the shadows. But his father took his lessons one step too far by leading him into the twisting tunnels of a dark cave and leaving him there to find his way out.

Sveshtari was eight at the time, and he never found his way out. He wandered for what seemed like days until a search party, led by his disapproving and disappointed father, eventually discovered him.

Since then, the combination of darkness and narrow spaces triggered his deepest fears.

"So, it's settled," said Abel. "We move in two days."

"Why not tomorrow night?" Sveshtari wanted to get this over with as soon as possible.

"I said I can get Temple guard uniforms, but not overnight."

Sveshtari grunted as they climbed out of the Hinnom Valley and entered Jerusalem through the Garden Gate, not far from Golgotha, the Place of the Skull.

Abel pointed at Sveshtari's beard. "You will have to shave. Herod likes his soldiers Roman style. Smooth chins."

"You don't have to tell me," Sveshtari snapped. "I was a guard once."

"Just a reminder. No need to get angry."

Sveshtari grunted as they moved through the morning bustle. The streets of Jerusalem were packed with vendors and saturated by the smells of spices and animals. Abel had a bouncing gait and persistent smile, both of which got on Sveshtari's nerves. Despite it all, however, he was starting to like this audacious little thief.

"Why haven't you taken Keturah as your wife?" Abel blurted, bouncing in front of Sveshtari and backpedaling as he talked. He also had a habit of asking intrusive questions.

"None of your business."

"She is smitten by you. You know that, don't you?"

"You don't hear very well, do you? It's none of your business."

"I know you have a history together . . ."

"And how do you know that?"

"I'm good at what I do."

"So you keep telling me."

Abel laughed boisterously, slapping Sveshtari on the back. Abel was the only one who could get away with backslapping.

Time to change the subject. "I still don't know why you are doing this for us," Sveshtari said. "What's in it for you? You don't need my protection any longer, now that we're out of Jericho, where your creditors live."

Abel's smile vanished, and he seemed genuinely hurt by the question. "I don't just do things when there are rewards for me."

"Sorry."

Abel's smile returned just as quickly. "The disciples took me in, even when there was nothing in it for them. And Jesus said we should do for others what we'd like them to do for us. So those are my reasons."

"You're a follower of Jesus now?"

"Of course! Why haven't you decided to follow the Messiah?"

"Because, for one, I don't believe in a messiah," Sveshtari said. "And I am not really Jewish, if you haven't noticed."

"Jesus has a way of reaching out to Jews and non-Jews alike."

Abel was right. Not only did the rabbi consort with women followers, but he also had a soft spot for Gentiles . . . and tax collectors . . . and prostitutes . . . and Samaritans . . . and pagans. He had never seen anyone quite like him. But that didn't mean he was about to follow him.

"People walking in darkness have seen a great light!" Abel exclaimed.

"What's that supposed to mean?"

"It's from the prophet Isaiah! We all need a great light, don't we, especially when we have to walk through drainage pipes."

"Don't remind me."

Sveshtari quickened his pace, but Abel kept up with him, still bouncing as he went along.

"If I were you, I would become betrothed to Keturah as soon as you can." He was not letting go of that topic. "You'd be a fool not to."

Not many people could call Sveshtari a fool without paying the price. But Sveshtari found himself laughing at this man's brazenness.

"If you don't want to marry her, would you let me have her?" Abel added. "Agreed?"

Sveshtari laughed even louder at the very idea as the two of them worked their way back to the lower city.

## Keturah

Keturah stirred the pot of boiling water, which contained a bubbling mixture of pomegranate skin and wool. In this soup, the red of the pomegranate skin transferred to the wool, transforming the white puff to red. In another pot of boiling water, saffron had been mixed with wool, turning it orange.

Keturah and Eliana were being put up in the home of an older couple who lived in Bethany, a small town located a short walk from Jerusalem. Jesus was staying in Bethany, where people claimed he had raised a man named Lazarus from the dead. Eliana witnessed this astounding miracle, but Keturah did not, and frankly, she found it hard to believe.

Over the past few months, as Keturah traveled with the Jews, some of their ways transferred to her, seeping into her spirit like pomegranate red leaching into white wool. She found herself strangely drawn to Jesus, a rabbi, and she was beginning to question the fickleness of the gods. She had grown up thinking that humans were created as playthings of the gods—as slaves catering to the whims of volatile deities. But Jesus talked about God as a Father—Abba, he said. She ached for her own father, and she was driven by the notion that God could be her Father—a Father who could not be killed by a bodyguard's knife.

Sighing, she switched the stirring from her right hand to her left. Keturah was constantly on edge, wondering when Rufus would step in front of her and either slash her throat or take her by the hair and sell her back into slavery. She also feared for Sveshtari, who was being hunted by Rufus as well, and she feared for Eliana, whose father was sitting in prison, if he was even alive.

Strangely enough, she was also afraid for Jesus. Yesterday, he had several confrontations with the Pharisees and Sadducees in Jerusalem, including Chaim's brother, Nekoda. Adding to the tension, he had overturned the tables of the moneychangers in the Temple, condemning them for turning his house of prayer into a den of thieves. Jesus had entered Jerusalem like a peaceful king, but she was afraid he would be carried out in a dead man's shroud.

"Keturah? Keturah, are you even listening?" Eliana's voice broke her out of her trance.

She looked up to see Eliana standing with a water jar perched on her hip. She had gone for water quite a while ago, and Keturah had not seen her standing there.

"I'm sorry, Eliana. Just lost in thought."

Eliana knelt beside Keturah, picked up a large spoon, and began to stir the pot of saffron orange while Keturah kept on with the pomegranate red.

"Sveshtari has a plan," she said.

"A plan?"

"To free my father."

Keturah had a sinking sensation, taking her even lower than she already felt. She knew Sveshtari wouldn't let Eliana's father sit in prison without attempting a rescue, but it was painful to hear someone say it was really happening. He was putting his life on the line. He might not survive the week.

"How will they do it?"

"Through the sewers."

"Sewers?" That was a strange choice. The only thing in life that scared Sveshtari was dark, enclosed spaces. "And he agreed to this? Who will be with him?"

"Abel will guide them. But Asaph and Chaim will also be with them—assuming Abel can find uniforms for them to wear. If they don't find enough uniforms, I'm afraid Chaim and Asaph will come to blows over who will get to join the rescue."

Keturah scooped up some of the wool to check its color. The wool was stained blood-red. "I wonder if the first thing Chaim and Asaph will do after rescuing your father is ask for permission to marry you."

Eliana bit her lip and kept stirring. "I am afraid you might be right."

"Why are you afraid of having a wealth of suitors?"

"Because I do not know if I want to marry at such an age—and I do not like the idea of being forced to choose between them."

"You could let your father choose. Isn't that the way?"

"No. That will not do."

"Who do you love more?" Keturah asked.

"At first, I was drawn to Asaph—until I discovered that he killed Gershom. He also allowed my father to be captured."

"Sveshtari could not stop the soldiers from taking your father—and if he could not do it, then it must have been impossible."

Eliana shook her head. "I know you are probably right. But still... I am beginning to be drawn to Chaim. But more than anything, I am confused. I think you are fortunate in having only one man—a strong man. One who protects."

"*One who killed my father.*" Keturah stared daggers at Eliana, who turned away. It wasn't often that Eliana couldn't meet her gaze.

"I am sorry." Eliana spoke softly, almost a whisper.

"Jesus says we should forgive, and Sveshtari has begged my forgiveness again and again and again. But I still cannot give it to him. I want to hold on to my anger, but it's like holding on to a wildcat as it shreds you."

Keturah was afraid that Eliana was going to tell her what people keep reminding her. They say that if Sveshtari had not killed her father, others would have done it—and they probably would have tortured him before killing him. That may be true, but she wished her father could have at least accomplished his mission before he died. Why couldn't Sveshtari have hesitated just long enough for her father to kill Herod Antipas? Sveshtari prevented her father from avenging her mother's death.

"Forgiveness is hard," Eliana said. "I still haven't forgiven Asaph for letting my father be captured."

Keturah took odd comfort in Eliana's admission of weakness. Ever since her healing, Eliana had become almost saintly in her devotion to Jesus. Her inability to forgive Asaph made her a little more human. And Asaph's sin was nothing compared to what Sveshtari had done.

"Keturah, may we talk?" This time, the voice belonged to Sveshtari. Keturah craned her neck to see him approaching.

"What you have to say to me can be spoken in front of Eliana." Keturah reveled in her obstinacy.

"This cannot be spoken in front of others." He glanced over at Eliana. "I am sorry."

"Don't be," said Eliana. "I will leave you two alone."

Eliana set aside the stirring spoon, brushed the dust from her robe, and hurried away from the house, leaving Sveshtari and Keturah alone beneath the overhang of the courtyard.

Sveshtari crouched to Keturah's level, but she would not look him in the eyes. He was probably going to ask for her forgiveness for the millionth time, but she was determined not to give it to him. She would not even give him her gaze.

She felt Sveshtari's fingers touch her chin and raise her face. She considered resisting this gentle move, but she did not. His fingers were calloused and smelled of earth. She felt tears coming, but she would not cry. She would not let it happen.

She braced herself for his request to forgive him. She was determined to say no with a firmness that would hurt.

"Keturah," he said, pausing to moisten his lips. "Keturah, I think we should marry."

Keturah dropped her stirring spoon. When she reached for it, she burned her fingers on the pot of boiling water, let out a shout, and began to cry. Why couldn't Sveshtari just leave her alone?

## Eliana

Jesus was at it again, and Eliana couldn't resist. She followed him throughout the Court of Gentiles, where he had been in a running battle with the scribes, Pharisees, and Sadducees. She was thrilled with his wordplay.

The Court of Gentiles was even more packed as Passover approached, so Eliana had to keep Lavi on a leash; if she didn't, her dog surely would get lost amid the million ankles rushing this way and that. She made sure she had a front-row seat for Jesus's teaching.

Once again, Jesus squared off with a group of Pharisees and Sadducees that included Chaim's brother, Nekoda. After Nekoda's earlier rebuff, he hung back and let others speak.

"Teacher, we know that you speak and teach what is right, and that you do not show partiality but teach the way of God in accordance with the truth," sneered one of the men, a Pharisee. Was he being sarcastic? Probably. "Is it right for us to pay taxes to Caesar or not?"

The man couldn't hide his motives any more than he could hide his smirk. It was obvious that the teachers of the Law were still trying to trap Jesus. They hoped his answer would make him sound like either a Roman appeaser or a rebel.

Jesus simply smiled back. "Show me a denarius."

This caught the teacher off guard. He blinked but made no move.

"Please. Show me a denarius." Jesus held out his hand.

With grudging slowness, the Pharisee dug out a denarius coin and placed it in Jesus's palm. The rabbi held it up, flashing in the sunlight. "Whose image and inscription are on it?"

"Caesar's," the man muttered.

Everyone knew that the image of Tiberius Caesar was emblazoned on the coin, along with the words: "Tiberius Caesar son of the divine Augustus."

"Then give back to Caesar what is Caesar's, and to God what is God's." Jesus flipped the coin in the air and then tossed it back to the man. The Pharisee caught it with a scowl.

Eliana laughed quietly. The teachers of the Law were testing Jesus's loyalty, but the Nazarene danced out of their trap. The coin carried Caesar's image, so give the coin to him. But each person carries the image of God, so we should give ourselves to Him.

Still, Jesus's enemies didn't give up. It was the Sadducees' turn to trip him up.

"Teacher," said one of the Sadducees in the crowd, "Moses wrote for us that if a man's brother dies and leaves a wife but no children, the man must marry the widow and have children for his brother."

No controversy there, Eliana thought. Everyone knew that the goal of a levirate marriage was to extend the name of a man who died with no children. Your name was your immortality, especially to Sadducees who did not believe in the resurrection. So, if a man without children died, his brother would step in, marry the man's wife, and have children with her to carry on the deceased's legacy.

"Now there were seven brothers," the Sadducee continued. "The first one married a woman and died childless. The second and then the third married her, and in the same way the seven died, leaving no children. Finally, the woman died too. Now then, at the resurrection, whose wife will she be since the seven were married to her?"

*What an absurd example*, Eliana thought. What were the chances that seven brothers would die childless and marry the same woman? They were trying to make belief in the afterlife look ridiculous, especially since it was forbidden for a woman to have more than one husband. More importantly, they were trying to make Jesus look ridiculous. But no matter how preposterous the premise, Eliana had no idea how Jesus was going to get out of this one.

"The people of this age marry and are given in marriage," Jesus began. "But those who are considered worthy of taking part in that age and in the resurrection of the dead will neither marry nor be given in marriage, and they can no longer die; for they are like the angels. They are God's children since they are children of the resurrection."

*There will be no marriage in the resurrection of the dead?* This caught Eliana by surprise, especially since she knew that two men—Asaph and Chaim—still sought marriage with her in this present age. The idea of being like the angels, who do not marry, filled Eliana with an unknown glow. But Jesus was speaking of the age to come, with the resurrection of the dead. What about *now*? Should she still marry in this age?

Jesus continued. "But in the account of the bush, even Moses showed that the dead rise, for he calls the Lord 'the God of Abraham, and the God of Isaac, and the God of Jacob.' He is not the God of the dead, but of the living, for to him all are alive."

This time, Eliana laughed out loud, and Nekoda snapped his head around and glared at her. Jesus's answer was brilliant! When Moses talked to God in the burning bush, Yahweh announced that He was the God of Abraham, Isaac, and Jacob. And since Yahweh was not the God of the dead, these prophets of old must still be alive! So, how could the Sadducees deny the resurrection?

Even some of the teachers of the law in the crowd appreciated what Jesus had done. "Well said, teacher!"

But Jesus received no such admiration from the Sadducees, who didn't know how to respond. One of them tried to ask a follow-up question, but Eliana couldn't hear what he said in the commotion. Then she noticed that the purple robe was on the move, flowing in her direction. Nekoda had his eyes on her and was coming straight for her. If he tried to harm her, she had her dog as protection.

Nekoda stepped before her, and he looked ready to breathe fire. His face had almost gone as purple as his robe.

"I know your father is in prison, and I know your father is a Zealot criminal," the priest snapped. "And yet you have the nerve to laugh at the very people who hold the fate of your father in their hands?"

Eliana's heart raced. She held tightly to Lavi's leash as her dog barked at Nekoda.

"Dogs are not the only ones who bite." Nekoda leaned in closer. "I could have you arrested too. You are the daughter of a Zealot criminal, and I can have you hurled into prison."

Would he dare? Eliana looked around for any sign of the Temple guards.

"I am a friend of your brother's," she said. Surely that meant something to this man.

"You think I wouldn't harm you just because of my brother?" Nekoda grinned maliciously. "My brother is dead to me. You have no protection."

Eliana was ashamed of how fearful she had suddenly become. She looked around for any sign of Jesus. Maybe he would see what was happening and come to her rescue. He had saved her from one demon before. Perhaps he could save her from another.

But she saw no sign of Jesus. He had moved on, taking much of the crowd with him.

"Jesus can't help you," Nekoda said.

"Your brother cares for me." Eliana glanced away, praying that Chaim's devotion would protect her. "Your friends were just talking to Jesus about the importance of family and marriage and blood and names. Chaim is blood."

"Chaim has betrayed me, just as he betrayed you," Nekoda said.

"What do you mean? Chaim hasn't betrayed me!"

"Of course, he has. He and I have been the ears and eyes for Herod Antipas for a long time now."

"I don't believe you. It was Chaim who alerted us to the attack on Mount Arbel."

The moment those words left her mouth, Eliana knew she had fallen into Nekoda's trap, like some dumb animal tumbling into a pit.

Nekoda grinned. "Thank you for confirming what I already suspected."

"You wouldn't hurt your brother."

"I won't hurt him if he does as I ask."

"And what do you ask?"

"Not for much. Just for the heads of Sveshtari and Keturah."

For a moment, she seriously considered releasing Lavi with the word *kill*. Although he was only a moderate-sized dog, he had killed a man before. But Jesus was still close by, and she couldn't bear for him to know that she had taken revenge in his very presence. She couldn't bear another humiliation. She couldn't bear to disappoint him.

She turned and ran before she did something she regretted. She wouldn't let a demon take control of her again.

# 9
## Luke, Chapter 21

### Eliana: Wednesday, Nisan 12, AD 33, Jerusalem

A RICH BLUE SKY hung over the glimmering gold and white of the Temple as Jesus crossed the crowded Court of Women—the only part of the Temple, besides the Court of Gentiles, where women could gather. Eliana, following in the crowd, reveled in Jesus's righteous anger. She simmered with the same level of anger, but hers was directed at Nekoda for his threats.

She was also tormented by his claim that Chaim had betrayed their people. That wasn't the Chaim she knew. But was it the old Chaim that she never knew?

Chaim, who was at her side, couldn't help but notice. "You are unusually quiet."

"I have my reasons."

She knew she should ask him directly about his brother's accusations, but she didn't want to start an argument when she preferred to listen to Jesus. She remained quiet, but questions buzzed in her head. Had Chaim truly been a spy for Herod, along with his brother? Was he still reporting on their activities, even now? Where was his loyalty? With her? With Herod? With Nekoda?

Jesus motioned toward the pack of Sadducees and Pharisees, who followed in his wake. Eliana's fury flared when she spotted Nekoda in his purple robes. She wanted to tear those robes to shreds.

"Beware of the teachers of the law!" Jesus shouted as the crowd pressed around him. "They like to walk around in flowing robes and love to be greeted with respect in the marketplaces and have the most important seats in the synagogues and the places of honor at banquets. They devour widows' houses and, for show, make lengthy prayers. These men will be punished most severely."

When people turned to stare at Nekoda and his purple robes, he looked like a trapped animal. Served him right. She also noticed Chaim grinning at his brother's embarrassment, and she was tempted, once again, to ask him point blank: "Did you betray us?"

Next, Jesus's gaze was drawn to the thirteen chests lined up near the massive, bronze Nicanor Gate leading into the Court of the Israelites. The chests were narrow at the top and wide at the base, making them look like trumpets; that was why they were called *shophars*. Each trumpet, from one to thirteen, was used to collect money for specific purposes; at this moment, a wealthy man was pouring his coins into one of the trumpets, making a big show of it—trumpeting his riches.

When the man turned around, he appeared shocked to see Jesus and the crowd staring at him. He gave them an awkward smile before marching off.

Then a most curious thing happened. An old woman—she had to be at least eighty—hobbled up to one of the trumpets, oblivious to her surroundings. Perhaps her vision was nearly gone, so she didn't notice the people staring at her. The woman, dressed in the tattered mourning clothes that singled her out as a widow, dug around in her pouch for money, and Eliana could see her pull out two small copper coins. Two lepta, the smallest coin in circulation.

With a shaking hand, the old widow had to concentrate mightily to get her aim right and drop the two lepta into the narrow neck of the treasury trumpet. Then she shuffled off, still oblivious to her audience. It took sixty-four lepta to equal one denarius, one day's wages. But based on how hard this woman had to dig through her pouch to pull out the two copper coins, it was obvious she had very few of them to her name.

Jesus spun around to face his followers. "Truly I tell you, this poor widow has put in more than all the others." He extended his arms to the side, as if measuring the woman's generosity. "All these people gave their gifts out of their wealth; but she, out of her poverty, put in all she had to live on."

Eliana hurried off in the direction of the widow, digging out her own modest collection of coins. As she pushed through the crowd, she noticed—in her peripheral vision—Jesus's head turning to follow her. Jesus smiled as if he knew exactly what she was doing. Eliana rushed forward, stopping the old woman and pressing the coins into her palm.

Carrying out this act of kindness worked a wonder on Eliana. It drained the anger poisoning her blood.

"That was a great kindness," said Chaim, the irritating man still at her side.

"Maybe you should try it yourself," Eliana snarled before storming off.

Just like that, her anger had returned. She didn't look back, but she was certain that Chaim was probably standing there, looking mystified by her mounting rage.

## Nekoda

Nekoda watched as several of Jesus's disciples hustled their teacher out of the Temple Mount—probably because they knew he had gone too far with his accusations against the priests. As they passed by, Nekoda heard one of the disciples marvel at the beauty of the stones that made up the Temple. Nekoda followed close behind, furious. After all, hadn't this beauty been bought through the offerings given by the wealthy men whom Jesus so recently disparaged?

"As for what you see here," he heard Jesus say, "the time will come when not one stone will be left on another; every one of them will be thrown down."

The words brought Nekoda to a standstill. These were words of treason, words about tearing down the Temple. When the first Temple, the Temple of Solomon, had been destroyed by the Babylonian Nebuchadnezzar, it had been one of the greatest tragedies in the history of the Jewish people. And now this so-called messiah spoke of tearing it down again? Who did he think he was? The Messiah was destined to destroy Roman oppressors, not tear down the holy Temple.

Nekoda decided he would bring these words to the attention of Caiaphas, the high priest, as further evidence that the Jesus movement had to be crushed in its infancy, and the false prophet must die. Caiaphas's house was located near Herod's palace in the upper city, where Nekoda and other wealthy men resided. But as he turned and made his way in that direction, he spotted Rufus. Nekoda also needed to talk with Rufus, so he pushed through the crowd, knocking aside a man who did not clear his path in time.

Nekoda fell into step with Rufus. "I have information on Sveshtari. But this time, you must capture Sveshtari. You cannot fail us again."

After what had happened in Jericho, Nekoda now had the upper hand. In Jericho, Nekoda delivered Sveshtari into Rufus's hands, and Herod's captain had failed to snare him.

"Don't soil your robes," Rufus snarled. "He will not get away from us. Just tell me where we can find him."

"That is exactly what you told me in Jericho. But Sveshtari still escaped."

"We succeeded in capturing a dozen Zealots, including Barabbas and Judah."

"That was not enough, and you know it." Nekoda took extra pleasure in humiliating Rufus. "I want Sveshtari's head on a platter, and so does Herod Antipas."

"So, where is he? Or do you plan to gloat all day?" Rufus picked up the pace, and his long legs and long strides made it hard for Nekoda to keep up. That was probably the idea, Nekoda thought. A man hustling to keep pace with another man looked like a fool.

"One of my spies tells me that Sveshtari is planning to free Judah," Nekoda said, out of breath. "He overheard him making plans to use the drainage pipe to gain access into the palace."

Rufus came to an abrupt halt and turned to face Nekoda. "When will this happen?"

Nekoda tried to hide the fact that he was breathing hard, but it was difficult to disguise his heaving chest. "Tomorrow evening. This time, any failure on your part will not be tolerated."

Nekoda couldn't disguise his pleasure in making the threat. But what he said was true. Herod would not allow Rufus to fail a second time in capturing Sveshtari. In fact, Nekoda was actually surprised that Rufus had not already been punished severely for letting Sveshtari slip away in Jericho; but Herod had taken so much pleasure in the capture of the dozen Zealots that he overlooked it—for now.

Rufus glowered. "My men will be there. Sveshtari will be dead by Friday."

"You had better be telling . . ." Nekoda started to say, eager for more taunts, but Rufus was having nothing of it. The captain strode off in the direction of the palace, nearly doubling his pace, and this time Nekoda wasn't going to attempt to stay with him. He had made his point, delivered his taunts, and given Rufus the information he needed to finish off Sveshtari.

Now, he had to ensure that Caiaphas would agree to finish off Jesus as well. He strolled toward the upper city, carrying information that would convince Caiaphas, once and for all, that Jesus must die. *Every stone of the Temple will be thrown down, indeed!* No one makes such a threat and lives. When Caiaphas was done with him, Jesus would become the stone that was thrown down from on high.

## Sveshtari

The palace guard's uniform was worn out by neglect and battle, but it would have to do. Abel had acquired a Celtic-style helmet made of iron with large pieces to protect Sveshtari's cheeks and a gold torque to fit around his neck. The ring mail lorica was missing certain pieces, but it was adequate to provide some protection to his chest. And the leather waistbelt fit surprisingly well. Somehow, Abel had come up with uniforms that fit both Sveshtari and Asaph. He had even found a uniform for himself, and he scrounged up a parchment-covered wooden shield sporting an iron boss planted in the very center to help deflect weapons. While Abel ran off to hunt down a uniform for Chaim, Sveshtari and Asaph admired what he had found for them.

Sveshtari turned his helmet over in his hands. "Abel did well. It fits almost perfectly. He has a good eye for measurements."

"It probably comes from years of thievery—sizing up the things he steals." Asaph tried on the woolen cloak, which was secured by a golden brooch. "Can he be trusted?"

"He got us out of Jericho, didn't he?" Sveshtari said.

"Barely. But I still think someone tipped off Rufus and his soldiers. They knew exactly where to find us. How do we know it wasn't Abel?"

Sveshtari grunted in response. He too thought someone tipped off the guards. The soldiers had come directly for them; they did not conduct a house-to-house search. They knew. But he sensed that Abel was not their informant.

"Chaim was safely asleep when the soldiers came," he observed.

Asaph's eyes lit up in the meager light of the oil lamp. He leaned closer to Sveshtari. "I have thought of him as well."

*Of course, you thought of Chaim,* Sveshtari thought. Chaim was Asaph's rival for the heart of Eliana. If Chaim turned out to be the traitor in their midst, Eliana would give all her affections to Asaph.

"But would Chaim really do anything to threaten his relationship with Eliana?" Sveshtari asked.

"Nekoda still has a lot of control over him."

Fear of his brother could drive Chaim to do just about anything. Sveshtari understood that. But would it drive him to put Eliana's life in danger by bringing the soldiers down upon them?

If it turned out to be true, Eliana would never forgive Chaim. Sveshtari had learned the hard way that seeking forgiveness is a long and difficult march. When he had asked Keturah to marry him, she did not answer for the longest time. He sat next to her, not saying anything, waiting calmly for her to respond. At one point, he took her hand, causing her to coil and tense, but she didn't pull her hand away. That was something, wasn't it? Still, Keturah never answered him.

On the other hand, Keturah did not say no, so maybe there was still hope. But it felt as if he had been pursuing her forgiveness for half a lifetime already! Couldn't Keturah see that he had been powerless to save her father's life? Couldn't she appreciate that he put his own life at risk by saving her? He wondered if he should just give up this useless pursuit. He could find plenty of other women who would be attracted to someone like him. Maybe his devotion to one woman was as futile as pursuing one God. There is just too much heartbreak. At least with many women and many gods, if one of them displeases you, you can move on to the next one.

Besides, right now he should be thinking about breaking into the palace, not worrying about whether Keturah will ever give him an answer.

"Do you know anything about the other Zealots surrounding Barabbas?" Sveshtari asked Asaph, trying to shake loose from his sense of despair. "Could any of them have been feeding information to Herod's men—or the Romans?"

Asaph shook his head. "I would be shocked. I rode with them for much of the year. For any of them to betray Barabbas . . . I don't see it. It had to be either Abel or Chaim."

Sveshtari mulled it over. "Abel is still seeking a uniform that will fit Chaim," he noted. "But he is not sure he can find one in time."

Asaph looked down and stared at the flickering oil lamp. "Do we dare go through with this, knowing we could be betrayed again?"

Sveshtari shrugged. After the frustrations with Keturah, he was feeling particularly futile about life. "I have made a promise to save Judah. It's up to you whether you want to join me."

"I too have made a promise," Asaph said defensively.

Asaph had a good reason to pursue this suicide mission. If they rescued Judah, he would reap the benefits of Eliana's devotion. But what would Sveshtari reap? Does Keturah even care whether he lived or died?

More to the point, Sveshtari thought, does *he* even care if he lived or died?

## Keturah

"I am sorry, Eliana." Keturah drew her knees to her chest as she sat on her mat. She had awakened from a nightmare and lit a small oil lamp; the glow from the meager light was enough to wake Eliana. Fortunately, she did not wake the wet nurse, Ruth, nor Babette, both of whom shared the room in the guest house in the southwest corner of Jerusalem. The house was adjacent to the Essene quarter, where the "devout men" lived a life of aesthetic discipline.

"You could not sleep?" whispered Eliana, remaining stretched out on her mat, propping her head in her right hand.

"Bad dream."

"Would you like to talk about it?"

"I dreamt that all of Jerusalem was rocked by a terrible earthquake. The Temple collapsed to ruins, and I saw foxes tied together in pairs, tail to tail, with a firebrand attached to their tails."

"Like the story of Samson taking vengeance on the Philistines?"

"Yes. The foxes were running through Jerusalem setting fires wherever they went."

Eliana sat up. "But who are the little foxes in your dream? Jesus called Herod a fox many times."

Keturah shrugged. "All I know is that it seemed so real. It was so real that when I awoke, I had to look out the window to make sure Jerusalem hadn't been set on fire by foxes—or destroyed by an earthquake."

"The words of Joanna must have sunk in deep."

Keturah nodded. Joanna had told them all about the things that Jesus said to his disciples on the Mount of Olives. Jesus pronounced that nation will rise up against nation, and kingdom against kingdom. There will be great earthquakes, famines, pestilences, and great signs from heaven. He also said the authorities will seize them and put them in prison, all on account of him. Then Jerusalem will be surrounded by armies, and they will know its desolation was near.

It was not the best story to hear before retiring for the night.

"I do not think Jesus was speaking of this happening next week," Eliana said.

"How do you know? You must have felt the tension in the city today. Jerusalem is like a dry cornfield, waiting for a spark. Jesus also told his disciples that they will be betrayed by parents, brothers, sisters, relatives, and friends, and they will even be put to death. I fear for Sveshtari, Asaph, Chaim, and Abel. Will they be betrayed when they break into the palace?"

"Are you saying it's too risky for them to rescue my father?" Eliana asked with an accusatory tone.

"No, no, not at all. I am just afraid. I want them to free your father, but I'm afraid our men are walking into a trap."

Eliana did not answer immediately. She stared across the darkness at Keturah, who averted her eyes and studied the oil lamp.

Then Eliana took Keturah's hand. "I am sorry. You are right. It will do my father no good if they walk into a trap. But I truly believe that Jesus speaks of the future, not of this week."

"I hope you are right. But the risk of violence is growing, and it's not just our men I am afraid for." Keturah paused. "I am also afraid something is about to happen to Jesus. The way he has been teaching at the Temple . . . The priests will tolerate only so much. Maybe the priests are the little foxes."

"They certainly seem afraid—like foxes with their tails tied together."

"When people are afraid, they injure—they kill."

Eliana scooted closer and placed a second hand over Keturah's. "Is Sveshtari your man? You described Sveshtari and Asaph as *our men*."

Keturah shrugged. "I am so confused." She sighed heavily. "Sveshtari asked me to become his wife."

Eliana squeezed her hand. "Did you agree?"

"I said nothing."

"Nothing?"

"Nothing."

"Not yes or no?"

"Nothing."

"Didn't you at least tell him you would think about it?"

"I just walked away. I love him, but I think I also still hate him."

Keturah was afraid that Eliana was going to quote the words of Jesus about loving others. But her friend said nothing. Instead, Eliana rubbed Keturah's hand, as if she were trying to bring warmth to a frozen body. Keturah wanted to tell Eliana that she felt guilty about loving Sveshtari; she felt like she was betraying her father by wanting to be with the man who killed him. It wasn't right.

Keturah sensed that Eliana was praying, and she wondered if she too should pray. But she still didn't know who to pray to. Ishtar? Venus? Yahweh?

So, in her confusion, Keturah remained silent. Just as she had done when Sveshtari asked her to marry him, she said nothing.

# 10

## Luke, Chapter 22

### Nekoda

Nekoda felt the envy working on him, poking and prodding. It happened every time he approached the magnificent house of Caiaphas, the high priest, because this was the type of mansion that he aspired to occupy someday. Upon entering, he was immediately ushered inside a large reception hall, adjacent to a lavish courtyard and a maze of storerooms, side rooms, a fresco room, and a *mikveh* for ritual cleansing.

He also dreamed of someday becoming high priest, but he was realistic. The family of Annas had a tight grip on the office, and the Romans had enough of a leash on this family to keep them in power. Annas's son-in-law, Caiaphas, had been high priest for over ten years now, but most people knew the real power behind the office was still Annas.

The Sanhedrin was comprised of three groups—scribes, elders, and priests such as Nekoda. Over a dozen had gathered in a dimly lit side room of Caiaphas's lofty home on Jerusalem's western hill.

"We believe we will have the Thracian bodyguard by the name of Sveshtari in custody by tomorrow evening," Nekoda reported.

"You told me much the same when you had this man trapped in Jericho," said Caiaphas.

"Our guards gathered many fish in their nets that night, including Barabbas." Nekoda tried not to sound too defensive.

"But you let a big fish slip away. How can you be so confident you will catch him tomorrow evening?"

"The same spy who supplied accurate information about his whereabouts in Jericho now tells me that he will be attempting to enter Herod's palace through the drainage pipes."

"Like a sewer rat?"

Nekoda nodded. "We will wait until Sveshtari and his fellow rebels are inside the pipe, and then we will position guards at both ends. This time there is no way out."

As Caiaphas moved a few steps closer, the golden bells lining the fringes of his robe jangled. "I want him taken alive."

"We will take him alive," said Nekoda, knowing that if the guards deemed it necessary, they would kill Sveshtari. Personally, Nekoda would prefer Sveshtari dead because he didn't want to take a chance that he might escape again.

Caiaphas glared at Nekoda, a pitiful attempt at fierceness. Nevertheless, Nekoda averted his gaze because he knew that was what the high priest wanted.

"Because of what happened on the Cliffs of Arbel, I am sure the Romans will want him crucified. I, too, want him to die a gruesome death as an example for others." Caiaphas waved his hand. "But we have spent too many words on this one. Our chief business is an even larger fish—Jesus. We must hook him and gut him."

"Since we cannot condemn a person to death, we must find a way to get the Romans to do it for us," said one of the scribes, a man named Eli.

Caiaphas nodded and stroked his beard. "Jesus cannot be arrested in broad daylight. It would cause a mob action. He is too popular."

"Then we should arrest him and try him at night," said Eli, as if that would be the simplest thing.

"Eli, you know we cannot condemn a man without the testimony of witnesses." All eyes turned to the man who spoke those words. Nekoda wasn't surprised. It was Nicodemus, a member of the Sanhedrin who took far too much pleasure in his independent thinking. His tone bordered on defiance. "There must be witnesses for the defense, as well as witnesses for the prosecution," Nicodemus said.

Nekoda rolled his eyes. It was not the first time that Nicodemus had spoken up for Jesus.

Caiaphas waved off Nicodemus's comment. "We do not have the luxury of time to go through such an elaborate trial."

"Justice is not a luxury." Nicodemus, self-righteous to the core, stared up and down at Caiaphas in his regal priestly garments and the breast piece with chains of braided gold.

Caiaphas shrugged. "A drawn-out trial will only incite violence and rebellion. Eli is correct. We must act quickly and in darkness."

The conversation continued, but it did not seem to go anywhere as various priests simply parroted what the high priest wanted to hear—that Jesus must die, that it must be approved by the Roman authorities, and that it must be done quickly. Nekoda's mind began to drift until he felt a touch on his shoulder. He turned to see Rufus, grinning. Rufus had slipped into the room silently.

"You have news about Sveshtari?" Nekoda asked.

"Even better." Rufus looked over his shoulder and nodded. A man scurried from the shadows—a common man, dressed in plain attire. He carried the smell of sheep on his clothes. As the man took another step closer, the light of a nearby torch brought his face into sharper relief.

Nekoda knew he had seen the man's face before, but he had a difficult time placing it.

"This is one of Jesus's followers," said Rufus, still grinning.

*Of course, that's it*! Nekoda thought. Nekoda's spies regularly reported back on all of Jesus's disciples, so he knew them by name, but he didn't always have a face to go with each one.

"This is Judas," said Rufus. "He has a proposition for the high priest."

## Eliana: Thursday, Nisan 14, AD 33, Jerusalem

Eliana drew a wooden bucket of water from the well and poured it into a jar. She aimed with precision so that not a single precious drop would be lost. Morning had broken across Jerusalem, and several women were lined up at the well. Eliana had awakened extra early to reach the well before the line became long.

The city was crowded and noisy as worshippers streamed past, carrying their Passover lambs to the Temple Mount to be sacrificed. It was Nisan 14, which was also the day that Abraham was willing to sacrifice his only son, Isaac. But God had stopped Abraham's hand from shedding blood because the Lord had provided the sacrifice—a ram caught in a thicket. Each of these Passover lambs was an echo of that sacrificial ram.

For Galileans and Pharisees, their calendar day began at sunrise, so they considered Thursday to be Nisan 14—the day to sacrifice the immaculate lambs from 3 to 5 p.m., followed by the Passover meal in the evening. This was the plan for Jesus and his disciples. Sadducees, however, used a different reckoning. For them, Nisan 14 did not begin until sunset, so they would not sacrifice their lambs until the following afternoon on Friday.

This difference of opinion was a good thing, Eliana thought, because it alleviated some of the crowding on the Temple Mount. She couldn't imagine the madhouse if everyone sacrificed their lambs on the same afternoon.

"Can I help you?" Asaph said, appearing suddenly at her side.

Startled, some of the water sloshed out, splattering on the ground. "Asaph!"

"I'm sorry. I'm sorry."

After she finished pouring the bucket into her jar, she moved aside to let the next woman dip from the well. Asaph followed, but not too closely, because he could tell she was agitated. Eliana headed back toward the guesthouse, where Keturah busily prepared food.

"I'm sorry about the water," he said, keeping his distance.

"It's not spilled water that angers me."

She paused, crouched on the ground, and set down her heavy jar.

Asaph crouched next to her. "What is it?"

"I need to tell you something, but I'm afraid you won't try to rescue my father when you hear it."

"Nothing you say could stop me from rescuing your father. I give you my promise."

Eliana sighed. Asaph will regret that promise the moment she tells him what's on her mind. "Chaim has been spying for Herod. I fear he has revealed your plans. I will not hold you to your promise if you think it is unwise to rescue my father."

Asaph stared back at her. She could see the surprise in his raised eyebrows and wide-open eyes. He didn't say anything for several heartbeats. Then he licked his lips and started to speak, but nothing came out. After that false start, he straightened his spine—and he also seemed to *strengthen* his spine in the process.

"My word is a firm foundation, so our plans will not change. But you said Chaim has been spying for Herod. Does that mean he is no longer doing so?"

"I don't know. Nekoda came to me . . ."

"Nekoda! You listened to that man?"

"He told me that he and his brother had been the eyes and ears for Herod."

"But Chaim has changed," Asaph said.

"I know, but . . ."

"You, of all people, should know what it's like to change."

"But what if Chaim *hasn't* changed?" Eliana didn't want Asaph to glibly ignore her warning. She didn't want him throwing his life away for her.

Asaph sat on the ground and wiped the dust from his hands. "Chaim was the one who saved us on Mount Arbel by warning us. Does that sound like the actions of a traitor?"

"No, but Chaim's brother wields a power over him. What if Chaim is not strong? Should you try another way into the palace to rescue my father?"

"There is no other way."

Eliana's eyes brimmed. She didn't want to influence Asaph with her tears. She wanted him to feel the freedom to change his mind about the rescue mission. But she couldn't stop the flow.

Asaph wiped away her tears with the corner of his sleeve. "I will not call off the rescue mission."

"But what if you have been betrayed?"

"We have to try, no matter what. I have faith in Chaim. I have faith in Yahweh. We will be victorious." And then Asaph prayed. "Rescue me from my enemies, Lord, for I hide myself in you. Teach me to do your will, for you are my God; may your good Spirit lead me on level ground."

"Lead him on level ground," Eliana repeated. But she knew the mission ahead would be anything but level ground. It would be an uphill battle every bloody step of the way.

### Asaph

Asaph walked away from the well, wondering if he had disguised his fears adequately. When Eliana said that Chaim had been spying for Herod, he had the sudden sense that he was standing on a precipice, like a Temple wall, looking down from a dizzying height. Everything was a balancing act. One false step, and he plunges to his death. He had to balance his devotion to Eliana, his commitment to rescue her father, and his fear of dying.

He told Eliana that he trusted Chaim, but was he deceiving himself? He still found it hard to believe that Chaim had betrayed them. Chaim must've changed, or he was the greatest actor Asaph had ever met.

Even more surprising was that he found himself defending Chaim, his rival for Eliana's affections. The old Asaph would not have done that. The new Asaph not only defended Chaim, but he assured Eliana that the rescue mission would not be scrapped. This elevated him in her eyes, but would it cost him his life?

As Asaph mulled this over, he became aware that someone was running down the street in his direction, weaving around shopkeepers and animals. Squinting, he saw that it was a man named Jacob—one of the Zealots under Barabbas.

As Asaph turned to run, Jacob called out. "Asaph, wait! I come as a friend!"

*A friend?* Asaph doubted that. He began running, making a left turn onto a narrow street winding its way through a market area, where men sold baskets, pots, and wooden planks. Turning right, Asaph came upon an unexpected obstacle. A shopkeeper had spread his baskets across the entire narrow street—something the city tries to discourage. People clogged the pathway on both sides of the baskets. There was only one route open for Asaph—straight across the display. If he stepped on a basket, it was the fool's own fault, so he plunged forward.

"Stop! Stop!" The shopkeeper waved his arms when he saw Asaph barreling his way.

"Stop, Asaph, stop!" came Jacob's cry from behind.

Asaph was not about to stop. As he reached the man's display, he leaped, legs outstretched like an Olympic long jumper. He soared. He thought he might just make it. And he almost did. Almost.

His right foot landed squarely on top of a basket, crushing it, and causing him to stumble.

The shopkeeper threw up his arms, his face flaming red. "What do you think you're doing? You owe me for that basket!"

Asaph maintained his footing, barely, and he stumbled forward—only to trip on a steppingstone, a raised rock that people used to get from one side of the street to the other during heavy rains. Asaph hit the ground hard.

The shopkeeper was on in him in a heartbeat, screaming in his ear—and Jacob was on him in two heartbeats. Jacob helped Asaph to his feet. Asaph tried to break away, but Jacob kept a firm grip on his arm. He drew Asaph around the corner, but the shopkeeper pursued them, still shouting. The shopkeeper didn't back away until Jacob drew his knife.

Seeing the blade flash in the morning light, Asaph tried once again to break free, but Jacob was strong. He held him firm with one hand, while he used the other to wave his knife.

When the shopkeeper retreated, Jacob put away his knife and laid both hands on Asaph's shoulders, giving him a teeth-rattling shake. "Will you stop and listen? I've been looking for you! *I know you didn't kill Gershom!*"

Asaph stopped resisting. "What?"

Jacob removed one of his hands from Asaph's shoulders as if gauging whether he would try to escape. But Asaph wasn't going anywhere. He wanted to hear what this Zealot had to say.

"Zuriel has been telling everyone that you killed Gershom. But it isn't true. Zuriel killed him."

"How do you know this?"

"I saw Zuriel do it."

"But I struck Gershom with a rock. I thought I had murdered him."

"He wasn't dead. While I was hunting for the little boy, I saw Zuriel come across Gershom, who was bleeding from the head but very much alive. Gershom was sitting on the ground, dazed, when Zuriel came up from behind and finished him off."

Asaph took hold of Jacob's robes. "Did you tell this to Barabbas?"

"As soon as Zuriel left our camp to track you down, I told Barabbas what I had seen. But he didn't believe me. He said Zuriel and Gershom were friends."

"If they're friends, why do you think Zuriel did it?" Asaph asked.

"Because they weren't friends any longer. Gershom had grown to hate Zuriel, who had become as bloodthirsty as Barabbas. Zuriel saw his chance to finish off Gershom and blame you for the murder. He never passes up a good opportunity."

Asaph was baptized by this news. He bowed his head and tried to fight back his tears. It would be embarrassing to break down in front of this man. "Thank you for telling me this."

"I thought you needed to know . . . in case something happens to me."

Asaph looked back up. "In case something happens to you?"

"By now, Zuriel surely found out what I saw—and what I said to Barabbas. If he finds me, he'll try to kill me."

Asaph put an arm around his shoulder. "Then come with me. We can offer you protection."

"No. Zuriel is hunting you, too. Better if we split up."

Asaph was about to mention that Sveshtari could protect Jacob when the seller of baskets came barging back up. With Jacob's knife sheathed, the shopkeeper had another burst of courage.

The seller grabbed Asaph by the shoulder. "You must pay me for this damaged basket!"

"And *you* must not place your wares in the middle of the road!"

"You crushed the basket! You buy it!"

"I will not!"

Asaph tore away from the shopkeeper, looking for Jacob, but the Zealot was gone. Asaph searched the crowded marketplace, but he was nowhere in sight. Asaph began to wonder if Jacob was a real person, delivering real news, or whether he had imagined him. Or was Jacob an angel, delivering news as sweet as honey? Whoever Jacob might be, it was as if someone had come by and lifted a huge beam from his shoulders.

He rushed through the multitude with a lightness of foot, hoping to find Eliana and tell her the good news. *He was not a murderer. His hands were cleansed of blood.*

## Keturah

Keturah sat with Sveshtari in a courtyard as evening descended. She was agitated and confused, for Sveshtari and Asaph were preparing to leave for what could be a suicide mission.

"You never answered me," Sveshtari said.

Keturah looked away. "I don't have an answer." This was true. When Sveshtari asked her to become betrothed, she didn't have a "yes" or a "no." She still didn't.

"You could have told me that. But you just walked away."

"I couldn't talk about it."

"But—"

Sveshtari stopped mid-sentence. Keturah realized she was being unfair by not speaking to him after he had asked her to become betrothed. But losing her mother and father in the same year was also unfair. Who was he to complain?

Sveshtari scratched at the back of his hand. "How long will it take for you to decide?"

Keturah didn't have an answer for that either, but she felt she should. Sveshtari might not live through the night, so didn't he deserve to know if he had something to live for? She was tempted to tell him "yes," so he would fight all that much harder to survive. If he left without hope, he might be killed, but she could change it all with one simple word.

She could always change her mind later, couldn't she?

Keturah moved in closer and wrapped her arms around him, pulling him in so he could kiss the top of her head—just as he used to do. His embrace felt safe, and she wondered if she was a fool not to give in and agree to become his wife. Few women are even given a choice. When a king conquers a land, he takes whatever woman he wants. And when a woman comes of age, her mother and father bargain for a husband. He was giving her a *choice*!

But she had spent most of her life as a servant or slave. She enjoyed the slice of freedom she had recently been given, and she wondered if she would betray that freedom if she agreed to marry this man just to give him hope to stay alive. The sacrifice seemed too steep.

Sveshtari didn't let go, and she didn't try to break the embrace. She stalled for time.

Still, he clutched her. Maybe he, too, was afraid to let go because she might give him an answer that he didn't want to hear. Keturah buried her face in his chest, and she heard someone clear his throat in the background.

"It is time," said Asaph.

Finally releasing his hold on Keturah, Sveshtari looked down at her, locking eyes. He waited for her to answer.

"We need to be going." Asaph beckoned from the shadows.

Sveshtari ran his hands up and down Keturah's shoulders. "I pray to the gods that I will see you again."

"You *will* see me again." And then before she had time to think, she added, "You have to come back. We must marry."

Sveshtari broke into the biggest of grins, and then he hugged her again, this time lifting her off the ground. She could sense the energy flow through his arms and legs; she prayed to Yahweh that this strength would keep him alive.

He kissed her on the lips and gave her another long look, and she tried to work up a smile. She succeeded, mostly. Then Sveshtari, Abel, and Asaph marched into the darkness. Keturah let out her breath and sat down, still not believing what she had said.

How could she lie so boldly? But, more importantly, was she lying to him or to herself?

## Asaph

Asaph prayed. If he had learned anything since joining the Zealots, it was that prayer lifted him up whenever he found himself sliding into the pit.

"Now this I know: The Lord gives victory to his anointed," Asaph said aloud, while Abel grinned and Sveshtari stared at him with a perplexed look. "He answers him from his heavenly sanctuary with the victorious power of his right hand. Some trust in chariots and some in horses, but we trust in the name of the Lord our God. Lord, give victory! Answer us when we call!"

When Asaph had finished, Sveshtari continued to stare. "You were praying to Yahweh?"

"It was a Psalm of David, our great king."

"Does it guarantee victory?"

"There are no guarantees except that Yahweh is with us always."

Asaph found it strange to hear himself talking this way. He had soaked up the faith of his fathers for the past year, and now he was speaking this faith in the boldest possible way. It felt odd but deeply satisfying.

"So, you mean that Yahweh is fickle—like my gods?" Sveshtari asked.

"Not fickle. But He cannot be controlled by our words and our desires. We are the fickle ones. His word stands firm in the heavens."

Sveshtari grunted. "That is very strange."

"To all perfection, I see a limit. But God's commands are boundless. His word is a lamp unto my feet."

Abel handed a lit torch to Asaph. "His word may be a lamp unto our feet, but I suggest we still use these. It's as dark as Hades in there." Swinging his torch, Abel motioned toward the opening of the sewer, tossing light into the dark hole. The cloths wrapped around the end of each torch had been dipped in sulfur and lime, so they wouldn't extinguish when they got wet—important when you're moving through a drainage tunnel.

All three of them were equipped with spears, swords, and daggers. But Chaim was not with them because Abel could not find a fourth uniform. This worried Asaph, who feared that Chaim was the informant. It seemed risky being bottled up inside this sewer, trapped like voles beneath the ground—but this was the only way to infiltrate the palace. The drainage pipe emptied into the Hinnom Valley on the western side of Jerusalem, its opening barely visible unless you knew exactly where to find it.

"Onward." Sveshtari led the way, crouching and stepping sideways into the sewer. Asaph could see the gleam of fear in Sveshtari's eyes—perhaps the only time he had ever seen trepidation in his friend.

Asaph ducked, but at least the pipe was large enough to walk through in a monkey-like crouch.

"Does it ever get extremely narrow?" Asaph asked.

"In a few places," Abel said. "But you can squeeze through—if you hold your breath."

Asaph hoped he was joking, but it didn't sound like it.

Abel held a finger to his lips. "Our voices carry, though. Silence from this point on."

Darkness. Confinement. And now silence. Asaph prayed. Silently.

*Deliver me from my enemies, O my God. Save me from men of bloodshed, for they have set an ambush for my life. They return at night, they howl like a dog and go around the city. They belch forth with their mouth; swords are in their lips. But you, O Lord, laugh at them. Awake to punish them. Do not be gracious to any who are treacherous in iniquity.*

## Keturah

The hour had come.

Keturah helped Eliana set the table for the Passover meal; the table was long and rectangular, raised slightly from the floor. They also scattered pillows around the table, where Jesus and the disciples would recline. They were expecting all twelve of Jesus's disciples, so they set out thirteen wooden plates with high rims. Also . . . four clay cups at each place. Eliana told Keturah that the tradition was to partake of four cups of wine during the Passover meal.

It seemed so foreign and strange.

Earlier, Eliana had guided her through the preparation of the Passover lamb, which was roasted in a special rounded oven. They inserted two skewers into the lamb. One skewer rose vertically from the bottom of the lamb to the top, while the other was horizontal, penetrating the forelegs. That way, the lamb could be roasted standing straight up with its forelegs spread to each side.

The Passover meal was being held in a large upper room in John Mark's house—the same home where Eliana and Keturah were staying. Eliana and Keturah were given the job of table servers for the men. They lit the oil lamps as the sun began to set, casting a reddish glow through the windows of the house.

Voices erupted from below. The first disciples had arrived.

"You smell like fish, James!" It was the boisterous voice of Thomas.

Four men appeared in the doorway. Nathanael burst into a smile. "He and his brother always smell like fish, even when they haven't been fishing for weeks."

James and John, the Zebedee brothers, seemed to take the ribbing in stride. John laughed. "Perhaps after so much fishing, we have become part fish ourselves."

"We are fishers of men," added James. "And who knows more about catching fish than a man who is part fish?"

More voices rose from the flight of stairs, filling the house. When Jesus arrived, he sat at the head of the table as more disciples filed into the upper room, sometimes in pairs. Keturah and Eliana stood silently to the side, prepared to replenish food and wine.

When everyone was present, silence descended. The light sent shadows dancing on the walls. All eyes turned to Jesus.

"I have eagerly desired to eat this Passover with you before I suffer," he said.

Keturah shot a look at Eliana, who stared at Jesus, looking utterly confused. Keturah leaned over and whispered. "What does he mean—'before I suffer'? Is this a normal part of the Passover?"

Retaining her gaze on Jesus, Eliana shook her head slowly.

"For I tell you," Jesus continued, "I will not eat it again until it finds fulfillment in the kingdom of God."

Keturah wanted to whisper more questions, but she was afraid of disrupting the ceremony. Besides, Eliana's eyes remained riveted to Jesus. She paid no attention to Keturah.

After Jesus prayed over the first cup of wine, he dipped the bitter herbs in salt water, representing the bitterness that the Jewish people experienced while enslaved in Egypt. This was something Keturah could understand. She knew the bitterness of slavery first-hand—the powerlessness, the humiliation, the pain. It seemed strange for these men to be remembering such a terrible time. Keturah had been trying to erase it from her mind.

Then the disciples began to sing, proclaiming these words:

"The Lord is exalted over all the nations, his glory above the heavens. Who is like the Lord our God, the One who sits enthroned on high, who stoops down to look on the heavens and the earth?

"He raises the poor from the dust and lifts the needy from the ash heap; he seats them with princes, with the princes of his people. He settles the childless woman in her home as a happy mother of children."

Keturah's heart leaped when they sang about lifting the needy from the ash heap. Her thoughts immediately flew to her daughter, Babette, whom she had lifted from the ash heap. She was childless, but after rescuing Babette, she had become a "mother of children." The "happy" part remained to be seen.

Next came the drinking of the second cup of wine. Jesus gave thanks and said, "Take this and divide it among you. For I tell you I will not drink again from the fruit of the vine until the kingdom of God comes."

*The Kingdom of God*? Eliana spoke many times of this kingdom, but Keturah still didn't know how this handful of rustic men were going to tear down Rome and replace it with a new kingdom. It would surely take an entire army of gods to do such a thing.

Then Jesus broke a piece of bread, gave thanks, and said, "This is my body given for you; do this in remembrance of me."

"What's he trying to say?" Keturah whispered to Eliana.

## Eliana

"I have no idea." This was not part of a normal Passover meal.

But as Jesus broke the bread and passed it around the table, Eliana remembered. Her mind sailed off into a vision. She saw herself standing in the field near Bethsaida when the people were hungry. Jesus was there, just as she remembered, feeding the people with bread and fish, given to him by a little boy. He kept breaking the bread and breaking it again, and it never ran out. He fed a multitude.

In this vision, she saw herself standing up and singing praises:

*"Therefore let all the faithful pray to you*
*while you may be found;*
*surely the rising of the mighty waters*
*will not reach them.*

*"You are my hiding place;*
*you will protect me from trouble*
*and surround me with songs of deliverance."*

*Deliverance.* That word captured it all—Eliana's deliverance from darkness and Israel's deliverance from Egyptian slavery, celebrated at Passover. The angel of Death had passed over the Israelite houses, where the blood of the Passover lamb had been smeared. Eliana felt as if the angel of Death had also passed over her, preserving her life and surrounding her with songs of deliverance. She was safe in her hiding place. She was safe beneath the wings of her Protector.

Eliana then saw herself rising into the air and flying over the city of Jerusalem, a jumble of white stone houses. It was evening, and lights sparkled in every window like terrestrial stars. She flew lower and saw a canopy—a wedding canopy, a protective canopy raised above the heads of the bride and groom. She swooped down to see a wedding in progress, the bride and groom standing beneath the canopy of protection, the *chuppah*, which represents their house. The house, this canopy, is open on all four sides to welcome others, just as the tent of Abraham was open to welcome three heavenly strangers.

"Eliana." Keturah hissed in her ear, shattering the vision. Keturah gave her a gentle nudge, bringing Eliana back to earth.

It was time for Jesus and the disciples to eat their Passover meal, so the two women sprang into action; they filled the cups, which were not to be confused with the four Passover cups of wine. Buoyed by what she had experienced in her vision, Eliana felt inexpressible joy as she removed plates and scurried from disciple to disciple. Nothing could darken her mood. She was safe in this house, this room, with Jesus.

When the meal was over, Jesus lifted the third cup of wine and said, "This cup is the new covenant in my blood, which is poured out for you."

But then Jesus spoke a shocking sentence, like the sudden shattering of a clay jar. "But the hand of him who is going to betray me is with mine on the table."

Eliana nearly dropped the pitcher of wine from her right hand. The entire room went quiet. It seemed as if another power had entered the house. Was it an Angel of Death, with darkness streaming from its presence like a leviathan shedding black water?

Closing her eyes, Eliana prayed. Softly. "Help us, Jesus."

When she opened them again, she saw Jesus look around the table and say, "The Son of Man will go as it has been decreed. But woe to that man who betrays him!"

*Betrayal? Where did this come from?*

The disciples, equally perplexed, began to ask each other who would dare betray Jesus. A couple of disciples claimed they would never consider betraying their Lord. Why would they turn on the person who was going to put them on a throne? This, strangely enough, led to an argument about who was the greatest in this new kingdom. Didn't they realize that arguing about who was the greatest was a betrayal in itself—a betrayal of Jesus's message? Haven't they been listening to a word he's been speaking? Eliana wanted to scream, but she just stood there, rooted in fear.

Jesus cut through the arguing with a voice of authority. "The kings of the Gentiles lord it over them; and those who exercise authority over them call themselves Benefactors. But you are not to be like that. Instead, the greatest among you should be like the youngest, and the one who rules like the one who serves."

As Jesus said this, his eyes turned to Eliana. The disciples turned and looked at her as well, and she nearly fled in panic.

"For who is greater, the one who is at the table or the one who serves?" Jesus asked. "Is it not the one who is at the table? But I am among you as one who serves."

Eliana felt as if Jesus had turned things upside down; he was overturning the Passover table, just as he had overturned the moneychangers' table in the Temple. He seemed to be declaring that servanthood makes for greatness.

Jesus looked around the table once again, with tenderness. "You are those who have stood by me in my trials. And I confer on you a kingdom, just as my Father conferred one on me, so that you may eat and drink at my table in my kingdom and sit on thrones, judging the twelve tribes of Israel."

*So, there would be thrones after all. But they would sit in those thrones as servants, not tyrants*, Eliana thought.

Then Jesus looked at Peter, singling him out. "Simon, Simon, Satan has asked to sift all of you as wheat. But I have prayed for you, Simon, that your faith may not fail. And when you have turned back, strengthen your brothers."

Peter leaped to his feet as if to demonstrate his readiness for action. "Lord, I am ready to go with you to prison and to death!"

If Peter was expecting applause, he didn't get it. Instead, Jesus looked suddenly sad. He stared down at the cup of wine before him, not saying a word, his hand around the base. Then he raised his head and looked the big fisherman directly in the eyes.

"I tell you, Peter, before the rooster crows today, you will deny three times that you know me."

Eliana wanted to stay and hear more, witness it all, but Keturah kept tugging on her robe. "Eliana, the mistress wants us to wash the dishes. We must leave the men alone to speak of these matters. This is beyond our need to hear."

Eliana nearly snapped back at Keturah. How could she say these matters were beyond them? They involved her as directly as anything in her life! She had given her life to Jesus. She deserved to know what was going to happen, with all this talk about death and betrayal and denials!

It reminded her of when her family fled from the Romans and were on the run. Her father wouldn't speak openly about the danger they faced, not wanting to stir up fears. But his silence raised even greater terror. And now Keturah said she didn't need to hear what was happening?

"*Eliana.*" Her friend tugged even harder on her sleeve.

Picking up an oil lamp, Eliana followed Keturah down the stairs, the light bouncing on white walls. As much as she wanted to stay and hear more, she had work to do. Such is life when you're serving at the Passover table.

## Nekoda

Nekoda's legs burned and his heart pounded after the climb from the Kidron Valley up the slope of the Mount of Olives on the eastern side of Jerusalem. In the rapidly falling darkness, he followed in the wake of the other priests and a large pack of Temple guards. They were on the way to arrest Jesus, who was reported to be in the Garden of Gethsemane with his disciples. Easy pickings.

The Sanhedrin was looking for a way to arrest Jesus when he was far from the crowds. Judas had served him up on a platter, telling them that Jesus and the disciples had left a house in Jerusalem and were making their way to the Mount of Olives, just east of the Jerusalem walls. Nekoda worried that the Temple police hadn't left enough soldiers back at the palace to capture Sveshtari. But that decision was out of his control.

They entered Gethsemane, the "place of the oil press," so named because of the olive trees that grow in abundance here. Nearby was an olive press, equipped with a massive millstone weighing over eleven and a half talents. Nekoda's family once operated an olive press, and as a boy, he would hitch a donkey to the millstone; the animal would pull the stone in a circle, crushing the olives beneath its massive, rolling bulk. Their millstone had a beveled edge, which pushed the olive seeds off to each side, rather than crushing the entire olive, seeds and all. The result was the finest oil.

Nekoda smiled at the thought that they were about to crush a man beneath the weight of their authority. They were about to erase Jesus's name from history.

With Judas leading the way, their contingent carried torches that cast a dancing light among the twisted branches of the ancient olive trees in the Garden of Gethsemane. Thirty pieces of silver was all that Judas had asked for—a bargain price to rid Jerusalem of the latest and most dangerous Messiah.

Judas told them he would identify Jesus with a kiss because, in the darkness, they had to be certain to snag the right man. Jesus was surrounded by his followers, all of them bearded and rough-looking men of the land. Even though Nekoda had witnessed Jesus preaching in the Temple many times, it would be easy to grab the wrong bearded Jew. Nekoda's chief worry was that if Jesus and the disciples decided to flee, they might not be able to catch the Nazarene in the chaos of the darkness.

In addition to spears and swords, many carried clubs—effective weapons to lay a man flat without killing him. They wanted Jesus alive. They wanted him tried in public. They wanted his blood to flow before the eyes of his followers.

The soldiers streamed past a wide-based olive tree, with branches twisting into all sorts of shapes, like a deformed beggar along the roadside. On the other side of this tree, they spotted a mass of moving shadows.

"What is the meaning of this?" shouted one of the disciples as the soldiers marched before them, bristling with weaponry.

Judas stepped out from their contingent, and Nekoda watched as the traitor scanned the disciples for the face he sought to betray.

A voice spoke calmly from the darkness. "Judas, are you betraying the Son of Man with a kiss?"

It was Jesus.

*Strange*, thought Nekoda. Had someone tipped off Jesus to their plan? How on earth did he know that Judas was going to identify him in the darkness by planting a kiss on both cheeks?

After a moment's hesitation, Judas did as planned. He stepped toward the sound of the voice, placed his hands on Jesus's shoulders, and greeted him with an unholy kiss.

The soldiers surged forward to make the arrest.

Meanwhile, the disciples milled about like confused sheep; this was the most dangerous point. If the disciples were going to physically resist, this was the time.

"Lord, shall we strike with our swords?" one of the disciples shouted.

*Swords?* Nekoda hadn't counted on the disciples being armed. This could get out of hand.

Suddenly, off to his right, a burly man rushed forward, raising his blade and slicing downward toward the exposed head of Caiaphas's servant. The servant screamed, dropped to his knees, and clamped a hand to the side of his head, his wound bleeding black in the shadows. Nekoda backpedaled because the guards might start swinging clubs and swords with little care about which Jews they were striking.

"No more of this!" Jesus shouted, stretching out a hand and placing it in the path of the disciple's sword. The disciple held back, for fear of cutting off his teacher's hand at the wrist. In the torchlight, Nekoda could see the disciple's confusion; it appeared to be the one they called Peter.

Looking ashamed and shocked by his sudden outburst of violence, Peter stared sheepishly at the ground and slid his sword back into its sheath. Nekoda laughed under his breath. It was fine wine to see Peter disgraced.

Then Jesus turned his attention to the high priest's servant, who was still on his knees, gripping the side of his head and trying to suppress a groan. The Nazarene crouched and drew the servant's hand away from his head, studying the wound like a physician might. In the dark and from this distance, Nekoda couldn't see exactly what had happened, but there was blood on the servant's hand, and it matted the man's hair around his ear.

Reaching out, Jesus touched the servant's ear, held his hand in place for a few moments, and then drew it back. Immediately, the servant began to probe the side of his head, like a blind man feeling a face, and his eyes lit up. Nekoda groaned. What kind of magic trick had Jesus done now?

It was obvious that the high priest's injured servant thought something remarkable had happened—the fool. He was playing directly into Jesus's hands. Nekoda was tempted to box that man's ears for making Jesus look both compassionate and powerful at the same time. He hoped the high priest would have his servant suitably punished.

Then Jesus stood and gazed around at the weapons amassed against him. "Am I leading a rebellion, that you come with swords and clubs?"

*Well, yes*, thought Nekoda, *you are leading a rebellion. Not a very good one. But you are rebelling against the authority of the Law.*

"Every day I was with you in the Temple courts, and you did not lay a hand on me. But this is your hour—when darkness reigns."

*When darkness reigns.* At those words, Nekoda was tempted to snatch a club from the hands of one of the soldiers and smash it against the Nazarene's jaw. The implication of his words was obvious. He was calling them cowards, coming in the darkness to make this arrest, rather than doing it by day. But Nekoda called it common sense. If they did it by day, they could have a real rebellion on their hands.

Nekoda and the others knew that arresting a man at night and taking him to the high priest's house violated Jewish legal procedure. But Nekoda was never one to stick to legal niceties, and neither was Caiaphas.

Then, in the background, Nekoda noticed one of the disciples run off into the darkness, his clothing catching on an olive branch and being yanked off as he ran. The disciple kept on running, as naked as the day he was born. This broke some of the tension, and Nekoda laughed aloud at the bizarre scene. Then he crossed his arms across his chest and watched with satisfaction as Jesus was led away to be crushed and then pressed until his blood flowed like oil.

## Sveshtari

As the tunnel narrowed, Sveshtari's panic expanded.

By this time, he, Asaph, and Abel were on their hands and knees, crawling through the cold, wet tunnel. Sveshtari was in the lead, with a sword at his side, a shield strapped to his back, and a torch in his right hand. The walls were so tightly constricted that, at one point, he thought he might have to remove his breastplate to squeeze through.

"This is narrower than I bargained for," he whispered to Abel.

"Don't worry, it'll widen out soon."

Sveshtari had become accustomed to the smell. There wasn't much water moving through the pipe, and while most of it seemed relatively clean—devoid of human filth—the stagnant smell was pervasive, although not overwhelming. Herod Antipas, like his father, loved all things Roman, and he had established baths in his palace. Most of the water flowing through the drainage pipes came from the baths.

Still, Sveshtari vowed he would head straight for the Hebrew *mikveh* when he made it out of this tunnel and palace alive—assuming he survived. He never felt a greater appreciation for this Jewish ritual, which preceded entry into the Temple. He wanted badly to be cleansed.

Abel was right that they had just squeezed through the tunnel's narrowest point because it steadily widened, and Sveshtari's panic began to settle. His breathing steadied, and his heart rate slowed to a simple, steady clip. It seemed as if they had been inside this pipe forever, so they should be reaching the palace grounds soon. The tunnel made a slight turn to the right, and the water in the sewer began to deepen, just slightly, coming a little past Sveshtari's wrist as he continued along on hands and knees.

Finally... a glimmer of light. Far ahead, he spotted light pouring down from a shaft opening into the drainage system. He twisted around to look at Asaph and Abel, and he motioned ahead at the light. They both nodded.

Sveshtari tried not to slosh the water or clink his shield against the stone walls. They were not sure where this entry shaft would bring them inside Herod's palace, but it would probably not be a heavily trafficked area. Nevertheless, they needed to be as quiet as possible. He paused to listen. Was that a scuff of feet on stone?

Sveshtari began moving again, slowly, and the pipe continued to widen and rise in height. In fact, soon he was able to move into a squatting position. From the squat, he waddled forward—an awkward way of moving but a better defensive position than crawling on hands and feet.

Then: the sound of something clattering. He stopped. Listened. It sounded like a shaft of wood falling against a stone floor. A spear? Next: a hushed voice. A scolding voice.

Twisting around, Sveshtari motioned for Abel and Asaph to halt. Without a doubt, he had heard the noise coming from the opening into the sewer. There was an unfriendly welcome party waiting above. *They had been betrayed.*

"Should we abort the mission?" Asaph whispered, barely audible.

Sveshtari shook his head. If they had a waiting party above, chances were good that they also had enemies at the opposite end of the tunnel in the Hinnom Valley. They were trapped, surrounded by a shroud of stone, with death at either end.

## Eliana

Someone came to them in the night, tapping on the door rapidly, urgently. The frantic knocking pulled Eliana back to her childhood memory of the night she slept on the roof when their neighbor came to the house carrying news that the Romans were coming for her father. Any time she heard rapid pounding on a door, her heart caved in.

Eliana opened the door tentatively and found Joanna on the threshold, holding an oil lamp. Eliana expected the worst. She was certain that Joanna had come to report that Asaph and Sveshtari were dead. Their men had been betrayed and killed. She was sure of it. Everyone in her life was being blown away, like a tent in a dust storm.

"It's Jesus," Joanna said.

Although it wasn't Asaph or Sveshtari, this still had to be bad news. She saw it in Joanna's eyes.

Keturah came up behind Eliana and asked, "What happened?"

"Jesus has been betrayed. Arrested. Please hurry! We must go to him!"

"Go?" asked Keturah. "What can we possibly do? We can't stop the Romans."

Eliana wheeled around and nearly shouted. "But we can be witnesses!"

"Eliana's right. Please, Keturah . . ."

Eliana twinged with guilt for snapping at her friend, but Keturah didn't seem phased.

"Let me first make sure that Ruth will watch Babette." After vanishing into the next room to speak with the wet nurse, Keturah reappeared wearing a cloak. Eliana also threw on a cloak and picked up an oil lamp before plunging into the pitch dark. Lavi remained behind to guard the house. The night was brisk, with a whipping west breeze as they moved through the narrow streets of the lower city and uphill toward the heart of power—Herod's palace and the high priest's home. The upper city.

The home of Caiaphas was a sprawling gem located not far from Herod's palace, which Sveshtari and Asaph were infiltrating at this very moment. The only good that could possibly come from Jesus's arrest was that all the attention would be drawn to the high priest's home, so maybe that would clear the way for Sveshtari and Asaph to break into the palace. But Eliana rebuked herself for even allowing such a thought. The arrest of Jesus was a terrible twist of events, no matter how much it might help Sveshtari and Asaph's mission.

When the three women reached the high priest's home, they found shadows moving everywhere, slipping in and out of the flickering torchlight. It was like she had been cast into the netherworld of Hades. A woman, flanked by a guard, stood at the entrance to the high priest's house, screening the people who sought to enter.

"You may not pass," said the woman when Eliana tried to stroll in. A guard stepped into her path, and Eliana decided diplomacy was the wisest approach.

"May we enter? We have business with the high priest." She was not about to tell the woman or guard that they were friends of Jesus.

"What kind of business would you have with the high priest?"

"Important business. Can we pass?"

"No."

Eliana craned her neck, trying to catch a glimpse of the courtyard beyond the slightly ajar door. "What is happening inside?"

"That is none of your business," said the woman. "This is a matter for the Sanhedrin."

Eliana wanted to remind the woman that a trial could not take place in front of the entire Sanhedrin during the night; they had to wait for daylight, so the trial could be public and fair. It was the Jewish way. But she didn't want to antagonize this lady any more than she already had, so she bit her tongue.

"Please," said Joanna. "We promise to remain in the courtyard. We have no plans to cause a disturbance. My husband is Chuza."

At the mention of Chuza, the woman stared at Joanna with suspicion obvious in her eyes.

"You cannot pass." The woman—and the guard—stood firm.

"Do not worry, Sarah, they are with me," came a voice from the dark.

Eliana spun around to see one of the Sons of Thunder—John, the son of Zebedee. He approached carrying a load of salted fish, and striding next to him was another disciple—Peter, the man who had pulled Eliana from the sea on the day she nearly drowned.

The woman stared in disbelief. "They are with you?"

"That's what I said," answered John.

Eliana beamed. "It's true. We are with them."

"And we have a delivery to make." John strained under the heavy basket. The Zebedee family had a large and prosperous fishing enterprise that stretched from Galilee to Jerusalem, and they were famous for their salted fish. The Zebedees supplied the choicest fish to Caiaphas's household, so they had special access to the compound.

The woman gave them a final stare-down before stepping aside. Then they entered the courtyard—John, Peter, Eliana, Joanna, and Keturah. A fire blazed in the center of the courtyard, where several servants of the high priest warmed their hands. But no sign of Jesus.

"Stay by the fire and do not cause a scene," John told the women. "I must deliver this fish. I'll see what I can find out about what is happening."

But as soon as John was gone, Eliana began to edge away from the fire.

"Where do you think you are going?" asked Peter, who remained at the fire, warming his hands.

"Just looking."

"You can look from here."

Eliana ignored the command, knowing that Peter would not force her back to the fire. He wouldn't cause a scene. Several priests soon arrived, and she watched them cross the courtyard and enter a room on the far side. That must be where they were holding Jesus. She caught a glimpse of the room's lighted interior, certain she saw Jesus with his back to the door, facing a line of priests.

"Please, Eliana, back to the fire." Joanna placed her hands gently on her shoulders. "You are attracting attention."

Eliana did not care about the danger. Whatever they were going to do to Jesus, let them do it to her as well! But for Joanna's sake, she slunk back to the fire, where a servant girl stared intently at Peter.

"This man was with him," the servant girl blurted, pointing at Peter and glancing at Keturah. "He was with Jesus."

Keturah did not answer. She looked horror-stricken.

"Woman, I don't know him," Peter said.

"We came to deliver fish," Eliana explained.

The servant girl then stared at Eliana. "I have never seen you here before."

"That is because I have never been here before." Eliana smiled, but the girl did not smile back. Then the girl just shrugged and ambled off, returning to her work.

Soon after, John came back, having made his delivery, but he had no news to report. The household servants knew nothing of what was happening to Jesus.

"I'll continue to ask questions," said John, who had free range of the house, and off he went again.

The night crawled along, cold and breezy—boredom punctuated by moments of terror. One of those moments came in the form of a man from Caiaphas's household, who stopped at the fire when he caught sight of Peter's face.

The man stared directly at Peter. "You are also one of them."

"Man, I am not!" Peter was large, and his size could be intimidating. It also made him stand out, which was why people noticed him. He used his powerful presence against this accuser, and the man slunk off, without any further trouble.

Eliana stared at Peter, remembering that Jesus said he would deny him. But Peter insisted that he would be willing to die for Jesus! Where was his honor? Wasn't it bad enough that Judas had betrayed Jesus? Peter was the *leader* of the Twelve, and what kind of leader would melt under the slightest heat of questioning? His name meant "rock." Where was the strength of his convictions?

Peter did not meet her eyes. She could see the shame weighing on him like a heavy yoke on a tired animal.

Finally, as the night stretched on interminably, something began to happen in the room where they were keeping Jesus. Several guards took Jesus to a balcony above the courtyard—probably to get him out of the room while the priests conferred about what they should do next.

Eliana had the urge to call out to Jesus, to tell him she loved him, but she held back. Perhaps she was as much of a coward as Peter. Jesus looked down at her over his shoulder, holding the gaze for a long time, and he smiled. Eliana smiled back through her tears. She felt terror for Jesus—and for herself.

Then another man, who had been at the fire numerous times throughout the night, wandered up and fixed a hard gaze at Peter. The big fisherman stared down at the fire, trying to hide his face.

The man nodded toward Peter. "Certainly, this fellow was with him, for he is a Galilean."

Eliana had wondered whether Peter's Galilean accent would give him away. Maybe that was why Peter hardly spoke a word around the fire.

"Man, I don't know what you're talking about!" Peter bellowed like a wounded animal.

Then Peter's eyes shot upward, and Eliana followed the gaze to the balcony, where Jesus turned around at Peter's words. This time, Jesus was not smiling. He wasn't angry either. He looked incredibly sad as if he had just been given the news that someone close to him had died.

When Eliana's gaze moved back to Peter, she saw the shame tattooed on his face, like the words once emblazoned across Keturah's forehead. As a cock crowed in the distance, Peter's eyes went wide and glistened in the firelight. Eliana had never seen him weep, but he looked to be on the verge of losing all control. She also noticed that he had his hands much too close to the fire, but he didn't seem to care.

Eventually, the bite of the flames caused Peter to yank his hands back. Then he turned and strode from the courtyard and into the darkness, wiping his eyes with his sleeve.

Initially, Eliana had been disappointed by Peter's persistent denials of Jesus; then she felt angry; now she had only pity.

Looking back up at the balcony, she was shocked to see that the Temple guards had placed a blindfold over Jesus's eyes. Then one of the guards—a large one—hauled off and slapped Jesus so hard on the left cheek that he nearly knocked him over.

"Prophesy!" the guard shouted. "Who hit you?"

Jesus didn't answer.

The guard on the other side of Jesus slapped him across the right cheek, but this time the teacher remained sure-footed. The slap cracked across the entire courtyard, and everyone looked up at the sound.

"Tell us! Who hit you this time? Surely, you know. You are the Son of God!"

Eliana wanted to look away, but she forced herself to stare. She was determined to be a witness to all that happened to Jesus. She had to be near him, to remember the words, the actions, the suffering.

Another crack across Jesus's face. This was followed by a closed-fist strike, knocking him to the ground. This was not in the Jewish law! This was not how you treated a prisoner! She wanted to scream, and she began to pace, keeping her eyes fixed on the balcony.

Her stomach was stricken with a twist of pain, and she nearly crumpled to the ground. Keturah and Joanna wrapped their arms around her as she gasped for air. For the first time since she had been healed, she felt the presence of Cavel.

"Away, Satan!" she screamed.

She sensed Cavel trying to fight his way back into her life, trying to climb back onto his former throne. But she was not going to let that happen. There was no way Cavel was going to stop her from being a witness to the devil's work.

## Sveshtari

There was no doubt about it. Temple guards were just above them, waiting for them to climb out of the sewer like foxes from their hole, directly into the decapitating swings of their swords. Sveshtari motioned for Asaph and Abel to stay back while he ventured forward. He wasn't stupid enough to blindly climb out of the tunnel and into the ambush, but if he could pull one of them inside the sewer, he stood a fighting chance.

This final stretch of the tunnel widened a little, allowing Sveshtari to stand with room above his head. As he neared the opening above, he intentionally made noise and kept his torch lit because he wanted the guards to believe he was oblivious to their trap.

Only a few cubits from the edge of the shaft, Sveshtari paused. A short ladder stretched upward to the room above. It was going to be difficult attacking while perched on the rungs of a ladder, so he was at a distinct disadvantage. His only hope was the element of surprise. He sheathed his sword, carefully set aside his torch, and positioned his shield above his head as he approached the ladder.

Putting his hand firmly on a rung, he took a deep breath. Then he exploded, rushing upward through the opening as swords crashed down against his shield. Rising from the tunnel, he saw the feet of two men on the right side of the hole, and one of them was within reach—as he hoped. He latched onto the man's ankle and yanked the soldier from his feet, dragging him back into the sewer screaming. The man's head banged against the rungs of the ladder before slamming against the floor of the sewer. Quickly and efficiently, Sveshtari finished him off.

He wasn't exactly sure how many other men waited in ambush above, but it was far fewer than he expected. Guessing that the other soldiers had temporarily stepped away from the sewer opening to avoid the same fate as their comrade, Sveshtari rushed back up the ladder while he still had the chance to exit the sewer unscathed. As he appeared in the room above, he found three remaining soldiers who had instinctively retreated from the hole. He charged the man to his right, skewered him on his *gladius* sword, and then spun around, using the man as a human shield against the other two attackers. Their blades struck home but on the wrong target. They stabbed their own man. Shoving the bleeding man at the other two soldiers, Sveshtari now had room to move.

The two soldiers tried to come at him from both sides. He knew the dangers of fighting in a triangle, with an attacker coming from either side, so Sveshtari kept moving, forcing the guards to come at him in a single line—a much more manageable position. But he hadn't bargained on one thing. The bleeding man on the ground was still alive, and he latched onto Sveshtari's ankle, preventing him from maneuvering.

As the other two guards closed in, Asaph rose from the tunnel. The guards were so intent on finishing off Sveshtari that they had no time to react when Asaph drove his sword into one man's side. As the second guard turned toward this new threat, Sveshtari pounced, finishing him off, along with the man still clutching his ankle. Just like that, it was over. Three dead men lay at their feet, with the fourth corpse below in the sewer.

Sveshtari grabbed hold of the ankles of one corpse. "Quickly, Asaph, help me drag these bodies into the sewer. Before anyone else arrives."

"What would you have me do?" asked Abel, who had climbed out of the hole after the violence had subsided.

Sveshtari ripped the cloak from the back of one of the dead guards. "Mop up the blood. No time to waste."

Fortunately, the sewer entry point was out of the way, far from palace traffic. Dragging the other three bodies into the tunnel was quick, but it took a long time to clean the blood from the floor, even with all three men mopping side by side.

"You and Abel stay here," Sveshtari said. "You can pass yourselves off as guards. I will locate and free Judah."

"Let me go with you," said Asaph.

Sveshtari knew Asaph wanted to be able to tell Eliana that he was the one who delivered her father from prison, but that was not a good enough reason to join him. "You stay here with Abel. We need two of you guarding the tunnel. And we can't leave Abel here alone."

"I will second that," said Abel.

Asaph pointed at Sveshtari. "Then you stay here. I'll free Judah."

"No." Sveshtari was adamant. "I know the palace better than you."

"He's right, you know," said Abel. "You should stay with me."

"But—"

Sveshtari wheeled away from Asaph. "We're wasting time arguing. I will be back soon—with Judah. Eliana will still be impressed by what you did."

Sveshtari probably shouldn't have added that jab. The last thing he needed was to irritate Asaph because they had to stand united. But what was said was said. He couldn't take it back any more than he could give life back to the men he killed.

"The Lord protect you," Sveshtari said, exiting the room before Asaph had a chance to squawk anymore. As he moved swiftly though the underground passages of Herod's palace, it dawned on him that this was the first time he had ever invoked the name of Yahweh.

## Nekoda: Daybreak on Friday, Nisan 15, AD 33, Jerusalem

Morning light crept across Jerusalem from the east, filtering through the Eastern Gate, crawling across the Temple Mount, and slipping in through cracks and crevices in the high priest's house. With daylight, the rest of the Sanhedrin had also crept from their homes—the rich from the upper city and the men of modest means from the lower city near the Pool of Siloam.

Jesus stood silently before the assembly. Nekoda wasn't comfortable with the taunting of Jesus, and the bruise above the Galilean's right eye was a badge of abuse. This was not the way to hand down convictions in Nekoda's mind.

Caiaphas, in full priestly regalia, sat at the core of the assembly, and he leaned forward toward Jesus. "If you are the Messiah, tell us."

That was one way to do it—simply ask Jesus to blurt out his crime. In Jewish Law, you cannot force someone to convict themselves with their own words, so Nekoda thought this was a clumsy approach. But Caiaphas could be that way—not as polished as his politically skilled father-in-law, Annas.

"If I tell you, you will not believe me," Jesus said, "and if I asked you, you would not answer."

Just as Nekoda expected, Jesus was being his usual cagey self. He wasn't going to say anything that would be cause for condemnation.

"But from now on," Jesus continued, "the Son of Man will be seated at the right hand of the mighty God."

*Hold on.*

Nekoda scooted forward on his chair. Maybe Jesus was going to convict himself after all. Was Jesus claiming to be the Son of Man foretold by the prophet Daniel? Was he claiming to be the one "like a son of man, coming with the clouds of heaven"—the one who approached the throne of the Ancient of Days? Was Jesus claiming to have been given all authority, glory, and sovereign power, sitting at the right hand of God?

One of the Pharisees shouted, "Are you then the Son of God?"

Another blunt-force question. But Jesus was groggy from the long night. Maybe he would slip up and confess. "You say that I am."

Nekoda sat up straight. Was that an admission of guilt? Jesus didn't say he was God, but he also didn't deny it.

Some of Nekoda's colleagues in the Sanhedrin concluded that this was all the evidence they needed.

"Why do we need any more testimony?" said one of the elders. "We have heard it from his own lips."

Not technically—but close.

Suddenly, Caiaphas shot to his feet, took hold of his garment, and tore his blue robe. "Blasphemy!"

Nekoda winced at this shocking move. A high priest is forbidden to tear his robe, even in a moment of sorrow or anger. The blue of his garment is the symbol of the sky, so the high priest was essentially ripping the very heavens wide open.

"Take him before Pilate," Caiaphas quietly announced when the enormity of the moment had passed like a storm.

The punishment for claiming to be the Son of God was death, but for a sentence of death they needed the Romans to pass judgment. They needed Pilate.

Oddly, Nekoda thought about his old friend, Jeremiel, who once craved to be on the Sanhedrin. If Jeremiel had gotten his wish and were here today, what would he think of this? Nekoda suspected he would be wary of working with the Romans to convict this Jesus.

But Caiaphas and his father-in-law, Annas, had found ways to work with the Romans before. Besides, why should people worry about a little cooperation with the empire? Roman roads crisscrossed the land, and Jews and others gladly walked their highways. Why should this road be any different? This path led to crucifixion, a fitting destination for someone like Jesus who claimed to sit on a cosmic throne.

# II
## Luke, Chapter 23

### Sveshtari

Sveshtari moved swiftly through the dark underground labyrinth beneath Herod's palace, finally with space to breathe. He was in his element, striding with authority. If he encountered any other guards, he wanted them to know that he owned this environment.

He marched by one guard, who was positioned at a door, but it was not a familiar face—no one who would recognize him. He added an extra swagger as he strode past, and the guard instinctively took one step backward. Sveshtari hadn't forgotten how to stir dread in subordinates.

The air was wet with underground moisture, and trickles of water streaked the chipped, rocky walls. Torches lit the way, along with oil lamps tucked into niches, taking him in and out of shadows. It was early morning by now, but no light could reach the subterranean world.

Finally, he came to a door that would lead him into a room facing three dingy prison cells. There were no long-term prisoners in these cells. These were temporary holding pens, where some awaited their banishment to a slave ship—and some awaited execution.

There was little doubt which destiny faced Judah and his men.

As Sveshtari barged into the room, two guards looked up from their game of dice. He was pleased there were only two. This should be easy.

"Which cell contains the Zealots?" he demanded, glancing around at his three choices of doors. Several dirty faces peered from behind the bars, and he noticed that one of the faces belonged to Barabbas.

"What do you want with the Zealots?" One of the guards rose from his dice. "Say, aren't you . . . ?"

The guard had recognized him, but Sveshtari didn't let him finish his sentence before drawing his short sword and burying it in his stomach. The second guard was faster than he bargained for, however. The man nearly took off his head with a cat-fast swipe of his sword. Sveshtari felt the breeze of the blade as he danced out of its path while extracting his sword from the other guard's stomach. The prisoners that filled the three cells began to shout, egging him on, calling for bloodshed.

From the corner of his eye, Sveshtari tried to figure out which prison cell contained Judah, but he forced himself to focus on his opponent. This guard was quick, strong, and talented—a cut above most young soldiers—and demanded his full attention. As they circled each other, Sveshtari brought out his shield, which had been strapped to his back. The guard had a shield as well, so this was not going to be easy. Sveshtari was beginning to realize how out of shape he had become. He had hoped to finish off the two guards quickly, before any others blundered by. As their swords banged against shields, the noise carried, and he feared it would bring other soldiers running.

He had to finish this quickly, but the guard kept deflecting his attacks, seemingly without effort, and Sveshtari felt himself breathing hard—much harder than he remembered from other fights in his life. But he was determined to stay alive. He used the knowledge that Keturah had finally agreed to be his wife to enflame his survival instincts.

Sparks flew as blades connected, and Sveshtari tried to pin the guard to the wall with his shield, but his opponent slipped free and sliced his right shoulder. The cut wasn't deep and didn't impede Sveshtari's ability to attack. If he had lost the full movement of his right arm, he would have been a dead man.

His opponent was too quick. Sveshtari tried to drive him close to one of the prison windows, where the prisoners reached their arms through, trying to snag the guard. But the guard cut off two fingers from one of the prisoner's hands, and no one tried that again. All arms drew back into their cells in unison, and the man howled from inside the prison cell.

Sveshstari felt a burning in his chest, while the guard taunted him with a grin.

"You have tired legs."

Sveshtari was furious, but the guard was right. He had become soft during his time with the followers of Jesus. He should have kept training in secret, away from Hebrew eyes, but it had seemed too much of a bother.

As the young man rained blows on him, his bleeding right shoulder began to ache. Maybe the cut was worse than he thought. His shield shuddered under every blow as he backpedaled, losing ground, giving way. This tired lion was about to be put down.

The stone wall was just behind his back. Nowhere to go. He tried to slide sideways, into open space, but the young guard wouldn't give him that luxury. The guard moved in for the kill.

Spotting an oil lamp flickering just over his left shoulder in a niche in the wall, Sveshtari saw redemption. Dropping his shield, he reached back, grabbed the oil lamp, and hurled it at his opponent, hot liquid splashing the man's face. Then he charged forward, driving his sword into the neck of his startled and scorched opponent.

Moments later, the guard was down.

Sveshtari regretted killing such a skilled opponent. What a waste of life and talent. He snatched the prison key hanging on the wall.

"Judah!" he shouted.

One of the Zealots answered back, "He's in here."

Sveshtari started with that cell, unlocking the door and throwing it open. Five men tumbled out, one of them Eliana's father.

"Now for the others," said Judah. But before Sveshtari could make a move toward the second prison door, three more guards charged into the room. The freed prisoners, without weapons, were as helpless as Temple lambs. Two of them tried to overpower the guards, but fists didn't stand much of a chance against sharpened steel.

"This way!" Sveshtari grabbed Judah by the back of the collar before he could become the next sacrificial lamb. He was determined to get out of the room with Judah alive. They had only moments to act. The Temple guards took one look at Sveshtari's sword and decided to concentrate on the unarmed prisoners before they tried to go after someone with a blade.

There was a second exit from the room, and Sveshtari barreled through it, plunging into another labyrinth. Judah followed, tentatively, looking back in despair as his fellow prisoners were cut down. Then he followed Sveshtari into the dungeon hallways. Sveshtari slammed the door shut behind them, slipping a nearby torch through the door handle to secure it long enough to make their escape.

They could hear the screaming and slaughter on the other side of the door, and he was afraid that Judah would be tempted to go back and throw away his life. But those men were beyond saving.

Sveshtari and Judah took off running, following an alternate route back to the sewers. With their plan unraveling, he wouldn't be surprised if they found Asaph and Abel dead when they got there.

## Nekoda

Jerusalem was awake, and word about Jesus's arrest spread rapidly up and down the streets and alleys. The priests had to act fast before things spun out of control.

The Temple guard was out in full force, and they hustled Jesus from the home of Caiaphas up the sloping streets to Herod's palace where Pontius Pilate was staying.

Pilate, who made his headquarters at Caesarea Maritima on the coast of the Great Sea, was in Jerusalem for Passover to make sure the crowds did not get out of hand. His presence in the city was convenient for the Sanhedrin because they needed Pilate's approval to execute Jesus. Pilate was a weak and pliable prefect, so if they could play up Jesus's threat to the peace of the city during Passover, they should have no trouble getting him to agree.

They hustled Jesus into the praetorium, where Pilate had established his temporary headquarters. But the priests went no farther, not daring to enter the praetorium or else they would be considered unclean on the Passover and unable to participate in ceremonies. As a result, they lost control over their prisoner. Jesus was passed on to Pilate's soldiers who dragged him before the Roman prefect.

Nekoda and the other priests amassed as a body outside the gate, shouting "Blasphemy!" loud enough for Pilate to get the message. But they were left helpless, unable to witness Pilate's questioning of Jesus. They could not hear or see what was taking place on the other side of the wall.

Nekoda was tempted to enter the praetorium anyway because Pilate could not be trusted to do the right thing. This was the man who brought the image of Caesar, borne on military insignia, into the walls of Jerusalem in open defiance of Jewish law. Pilate had eventually backed down under pressure and removed the insignia, so Nekoda hoped they could bend his will again by applying the right kind of pressure.

"Blasphemy!" Nekoda shouted even louder. He wasn't one to normally participate in unbecoming outbursts in public, but he found himself strangely excited by the slowly building fury of the crowd.

Finally, Pilate came out from the praetorium to speak with them. Roman soldiers hauled Jesus out as well, his hands bound. Pilate was a tall, lean man with a narrow face and slightly sunken cheeks. Creases crossed his forehead like furrows in a field, and he stared at the crowd with clear disdain.

Before Pilate could even open his mouth, the priests began to shout. "We have found this man subverting our nation!"

That was a good argument, Nekoda thought, but not convincing enough. They needed to make it clear that *Rome* was being subverted, not the Jewish people.

"He opposes payment of taxes to Caesar and claims to be Messiah, a king!" Nekoda shouted.

By adding the word "king," Nekoda made it clear that this was not just a problem for the Jews. Pilate might not care about another Messiah, but telling the prefect that Jesus was a rival king meant so much more. And, of course, declaring that Jesus opposed paying taxes to Caesar . . . that was hitting Pilate where it hurts. Any threat to his coffers was a capital offense.

Finally, Pilate quieted the crowd so he could speak to Jesus. Nekoda folded his arms and calmly waited for the prefect to do his job. This time, the questioning would be in front of the priests rather than behind Pilate's walls.

"Are you the king of the Jews?" the prefect asked Jesus.

Jesus stared with eyes aflame. "You have said so."

Nekoda rolled his eyes. There were those evasive words again: *You have said so.* Was he admitting to being king of the Jews or not?

Then Pilate, that spineless toad, announced, "I find no basis for a charge against this man."

The crowd exploded. Shaking fists, one Pharisee bellowed, "He stirs up the people all over Judea by his teaching!"

Nekoda could do even better than that argument. "He started in Galilee and has come all the way here!"

Nekoda knew that the mention of "Galilee" could work wonders. Twenty-some years ago, a Galilean had led a tax revolt. Pilate needed to be reminded that Galileans were backward country dwellers who bristled at Rome and their puppet prefects.

"You are a Galilean?" Pilate asked Jesus, but the teacher would not respond.

"Yes, he came down here from Capernaum!" one priest shouted.

This gave Pilate pause. The prefect had killed many Galileans in the Temple during the Day of Atonement because he knew the trouble they caused. Nekoda congratulated himself on bringing up Jesus's place of origins.

"If this man is from Galilee, then take him to Herod!" Pilate decided. Herod Antipas was the tetrarch in charge of Galilee, so Pilate was pushing the problem of Jesus into someone else's hands. That was not what the priests wanted. They wanted Rome to rule.

Once again, the priests erupted as one, voicing their anger at Pilate for evading his duty to judge the guilty.

"Crucify him!" someone shouted—the first time Nekoda heard those words shouted on this day. Pilate turned around at the sound of the word "crucify" and scanned the crowd. Then he turned away from the mob and disappeared into the praetorium, knowing full well that the priests could not follow.

So, Jesus was dragged off again, this time to see Herod Antipas. Another disagreeable vermin. "Antipas" meant "one who is against everyone," and there couldn't be a more fitting name. He may not have been as blatantly evil as his father, Herod the Great, or even as one of his brothers, Herod Archelaus, but he was still a decadent fool.

Nekoda and other members of the Sanhedrin followed the soldiers to Herod's palace where they clustered closely around the tetrarch's extravagant throne. Herod Antipas looked amused as Jesus was dragged before him, and Nekoda wondered if he was taking any of this seriously. The tetrarch propped up his head with one hand, his body tilted to the side, the grin of a schoolboy plastered on his silly face.

"So, this is Jesus!" He sat up straight and clapped his hands. "I have been wanting to see him for a long time!"

Herod rose from his throne and stepped down to inspect Jesus from close range. But as soon as he realized that he was slightly shorter than Jesus, he hopped back on his platform where he could look down on the prisoner. The grin never left his face.

The tetrarch put both hands on his hips and stood with legs apart like some Herculean hero. "I hear you can perform miracles! Show me!"

*Herod Antipas wants Jesus to perform a miracle?* Nekoda was astounded and a little afraid. What if Jesus performed a miracle right here, right now? If Herod witnessed such a thing, Nekoda had no doubt that the tetrarch would be afraid to see him executed. He would release him in an instant.

But Jesus did not perform like a trained animal, and Nekoda thanked God for that. In fact, Jesus did not even speak. Herod tried pelting Jesus with question after question, but the false Messiah had gone as dumb as Zechariah on the day that that priest burned incense so long ago.

Nekoda could see that Jesus's silence unnerved Herod, but the tetrarch tried to cover up his uneasiness with frivolity. He unleashed his soldiers, allowing them to circle Jesus like bullies in a courtyard, a pack of them, mocking Jesus and spitting in his face. Jesus did not even raise a hand to wipe the spittle from his cheek.

Herod wasn't just making a mockery of Jesus. He was making a mockery of their system of justice.

"He deserves to be killed!"

"He claims to be the Son of Man!"

"He wants to take your throne!"

That last line was the most potent. Herod Antipas sat back down on his throne as if to show that no one could push him out of his seat. Then he put on the pose of amused indifference once again and commanded one of his soldiers to dress Jesus in an elegant, white robe—the dazzling white of a ruler.

"Take him back to Pilate!" he said, flicking his hand at Jesus and still grinning, always grinning.

This was getting ridiculous, Nekoda thought. First Pilate. Then Herod. Now Pilate again! Herod was not taking the charges against Jesus seriously. They didn't bring Jesus before him just so the tetrarch could taunt him and ask for a performance, a children's magic show.

The priests wanted a spectacle, not a show. They wanted Jesus to become a living spectacle—a warning to anyone else who was tempted to call themselves the Son of God.

They wanted Jesus dead and buried.

## Asaph

Asaph spotted a dab of blood that they had missed on the stone floor. Retrieving the cloth that they had ripped off one of the dead bodies, he sopped up the blood and tossed the rag inside the drainage tunnel.

He and Abel stood on opposite sides of the drainage opening, pretending to stand guard. Asaph didn't feel much like talking, but it was obvious that Abel preferred to fill the silence with babble.

"I watch you with Eliana," Abel said. "Do you plan to become betrothed?"

"I am not sure that is something you need to know."

Abel grinned. "I don't *need* to know. But I am curious to know. That other man—Chaim . . . He seems fixed on her as well. Is that true?"

Abel was quickly becoming an irritant.

Asaph shifted the weight on his feet. "Did you even try to find a uniform to fit Chaim?"

"These uniforms are not easy to come by. And I couldn't find one his size."

Asaph grunted. There were many reasons to resent Chaim, and the idea that he was safely outside the palace walls, probably with Eliana, was one of them.

Asaph looked up at the ceiling, hoping Abel would realize he did not want to talk. Abel did not get the hint. "Chaim's brother is on the Sanhedrin, is he not?"

Asaph sighed. He did not want to spend the last morning of his life thinking about Chaim and chatting with a reformed thief. "Yes, his brother is a Sadducee on the Sanhedrin."

"Do you think it might have been Chaim who betrayed us to his brother?"

Asaph couldn't resist this question. "It is highly probable."

"At least you can die knowing you will rest in the bosom of Abraham."

"True. Death does not carry the same sting."

One year ago, the thought of dying struck Asaph with the darkest terror. Now, he can sing with the Psalmist. *You will not fear the terror of night, nor the arrow that flies by day, nor the pestilence that stalks in the darkness, nor the plague that destroys at midday.*

Abel started to ask another question when sounds erupted from behind the door to Asaph's left. Footsteps. Clanking. Asaph stiffened and stood up straight, drawing his sword. Abel did the same.

"Lord, help us," Abel said.

"Amen."

"Just act like we belong here."

Spoken like a former swindler.

The door swung open, and Asaph let out a soft sigh of thanks as Sveshtari rushed into the room with Judah steps behind. Judah stopped in his tracks when he laid eyes on Asaph. "You came on this mission too?"

"I am doing this for Eliana."

"No time for marriage negotiations. How do we get out of here?" Abel said. "They are waiting for us on the other end of the drainage pipe."

Sveshtari motioned toward another door. "I know a way out. But remember, Judah, you are my prisoner. I am taking you to meet your fate, so act like a prisoner."

"Then why aren't my hands tied?"

"Good point."

Abel cut a leather cord from his uniform. "This will work."

"Quickly, quickly," Sveshtari said as Abel bound Judah's hands in front. Then they moved out as a group into the tunnel, praying they could reach the light of day.

## Keturah

Keturah was sick and tired of it all. She wanted to run away, find a quiet corner outside of Jerusalem's walls, and just curl up with her child. But instead, she was caught in a cauldron of hatred and anger. She also knew she could not desert her friends at a time like this. Eliana wanted her at her side. What's more, Eliana's father was in prison, awaiting execution. And the man she had just agreed to become betrothed to was putting his life at risk to free him.

Strange. In the middle of it all, she also had a sense that she shouldn't desert Jesus. She kept thinking of the woman who had poured expensive perfume on his feet and washed them with her hair. She felt a kinship with that woman. When Keturah was forced into slavery and carried that tattoo on her forehead, she had been defiled, just like the woman with the perfume. But she sensed that Jesus still called to her as if he wanted to pour perfume on her head and anoint her with a new life.

So, Keturah would not desert him. She accompanied Eliana to Herod's palace where the crowd grew in both size and anger.

"They're allowing only certain people in," Eliana said.

She was right. Priests were handpicking the people who could enter the courtyard—and she was certain they were choosing only enemies of Jesus.

"They cannot stop us," Keturah said, surprising herself with her boldness. Those were the kinds of words that she might expect from Eliana. Not from her mouth. Eliana stared at her in disbelief.

Before she could change her mind, Keturah fought her way forward. Others were trying to shove their way in—mostly men. Not too many women dared make the attempt.

"Head toward that priest," Eliana shouted in her ear, pointing at one of the priests blocking the way. "He is observant of *negiah*. He will not touch a woman."

Keturah strode toward this priest, shouting, "Away! I am a *niddah*!"

Keturah knew that no sane woman would announce to a crowd that she was experiencing her time of bleeding, but she did not feel particularly sane today. Besides, it worked. Men scrambled out of her path as if she were a leper, and the priest that Eliana had targeted backpedaled as fast as he could. He had been in the process of handing coins to a man and then sending him into the courtyard. But when he saw Keturah bolt toward him, he moved away quickly, clearing an opening for the two women to slip through, untouched.

"You are as crazy as me," Eliana said, once they were inside the palace grounds.

## Sveshtari

Fresh air and freedom. Sveshtari savored the pleasure of open air as they emerged from the bowels of the palace. He was surprised that they encountered no resistance along the way, and now he understood why. Most of the Temple guard was being used to maintain order outside the palace—if you could call it order. Chaos was the order of the day.

People flocked from all points in the city, many trying to get into the palace grounds to see what was happening. He was tempted to ask, but such a question would seem odd coming from a person wearing a Temple guard uniform. If anyone knew what was going on, a guard should.

Feeling suddenly conspicuous in his uniform, he turned to the others. "We need to split up and ditch these uniforms. We will meet tonight at the home of John Mark."

"Agreed," said Abel. "I feel more exposed in this uniform than if I were naked."

The four of them moved off in different directions. It was easy to get lost in a crowd this size, so Sveshtari decided to make his way toward the shops lining the street near the Temple Mount on the eastern side of Jerusalem. There, he could purchase some clothing and find a secluded place to get out of this uniform.

The streets became increasingly crowded as he approached the Temple, where preparations were being made for the afternoon sacrifices. Sveshtari ducked down a narrow alleyway, encountering a couple of men leading their donkeys. Sveshtari squeezed past one of the donkeys, which turned toward him and shook its head, hooves clattering against stone.

Sveshtari angled right, onto a street lined with shops. He purchased a simple tunic and robe, which would allow him to blend back in with the Hebrew masses. Then he would slip away to John Mark's house, where he hoped he could catch up on lost sleep.

Maybe then he would finally find some peace. He had enough excitement for one day.

## Eliana

Eliana and Keturah linked arms as they awaited the verdict. They both stared toward the balcony before them, where the authorities had brought Jesus, who now wore a dazzling white robe. Very strange. But even more perplexing, standing on the opposite side of Pilate was Barabbas, the very man who had been thrown into prison with her father! She scanned the balcony for any sign of her father or other Zealots. But it was only Jesus, Pilate, and Barabbas, plus some Roman guards with their red crests flashing brilliantly in the Jerusalem light, like birds of prey.

Pilate leaned his right hand on a railing and extended his left hand in the direction of Jesus. "You brought me this man as one who was inciting the people to rebellion!"

Eliana held her breath as the prefect leaned over the railing, looking down on the crowd. "I have examined him in your presence, and I have found no basis for your charges against him!"

Eliana felt Keturah tighten the lock on her arm in joyous solidarity. Jesus was going to be freed! But immediately the crowd became agitated on all sides. The courtyard was packed with paid enemies of Jesus. She sensed it. She knew it.

"Neither has Herod, for he sent him back to us!" Pilate continued, shouting over the rumble of discontent. "As you can see, he has done nothing to deserve death. Therefore, I will punish him and then release him."

The crowd let loose like a sudden storm.

"Away with this man!"

"Crucify him! Crucify him!"

"No! Free him!" Eliana screamed, and so did Keturah, but what were the voices of two women?

"Release Barabbas to us!" many shouted.

"Free Barabbas!"

Eliana now understood why Barabbas stood on the balcony alongside Jesus. It was a tradition to release a prisoner for Passover.

Amazingly, Pilate persisted on Jesus's behalf, appealing to the people again. "Jesus has done nothing to deserve death!"

"Free Jesus!" Eliana shouted, drawing glares from several men around her.

"Be quiet, or we will silence you," one of them snapped.

Eliana shouted even louder. "Free Jesus! Free Jesus!"

But it was like screaming into a tempest. People all around her kept bellowing, "Crucify him! Crucify him!"

For a third time, Pilate pleaded with the crowd. "Why? What crime has this man committed? I have found in him no grounds for the death penalty. Therefore, I will have him punished and then release him."

Surely, Pilate preferred to convict Barabbas, who had murdered Roman soldiers and tried to ignite a rebellion. These types of men are swiftly crushed by the Roman justice system. Pilate had to feel sick at the prospect of freeing Barabbas instead of a man whose only crime was blaspheming in the eyes of these hard-headed subjects.

"Give us Barabbas!"

"Barabbas!"

Eliana and Keturah continued to scream Jesus's name over and over and over, but no one heard. She felt all hope sliding away, like a rockslide beneath her feet. Pilate stared from the balcony, scanning the throng, aware that he faced a riot if he didn't do what the crowd demanded.

He held the life of two men in his hands, so he chose to release one—Barabbas—and he washed his hands of the other. Eliana nearly fainted, but Keturah caught her, and they wrapped their arms around each other, sobbing and wailing.

Pilate had surrendered. The mob's will be done.

## Keturah: The Third Hour (9 a.m.)

It was unbearable.

Keturah kept her eyes closed throughout the scourging, but the sound was bad enough. She heard the whip, with pieces of bone and metal dancing on the tips of three snake-like tendrils, as it struck Jesus's back again and again. Thirty-nine times. She was tempted to put her hands over her ears, to cut off both sound and images, but she thought Eliana would bite her head off if she did. Eliana was determined to watch it all. Something about wanting to be a witness.

When Keturah finally looked up, she caught a glimpse of Jesus—just the flash of an image—and she nearly vomited. She had heard about scourgings but never imagined them like this. She didn't understand how one body could endure so much brutality and keep breathing. But the Romans were experts at knowing just how far they could go without killing Jesus. The crucifixion still lay ahead; killing him before he could endure the ultimate humiliation would be too merciful.

The soldiers forced Jesus to wear a purple robe—purple! The robe of royalty. The most expensive of garments. They put a fake scepter in his hand and then, most awful, they formed a circle of thorns into a crown and jammed it onto his head. The thorns sank into his scalp like the teeth of wild dogs. Again, Keturah turned away when she realized what they were about to do. Several women screamed. One of them was Jesus's mother. Was she, too, trying to be a witness? Why else would a mother keep her eyes open for this?

When the soldiers encircled Jesus and mocked him, Eliana leaped to her feet and tried to attack them. But one of the soldiers wheeled around before she reached them and sent her sprawling with the back of his hand.

One of the Roman soldiers, a young man who had been standing in the background, rushed over and tried to help Eliana back to her feet. But Eliana nearly bit him.

Keturah kept her eye on that one young Roman soldier, and she noticed that he did not participate in the mocking. He stood firmly at attention, but he would not look at what was being done to Jesus. Once, her eyes met with his, and they looked at each other, holding the gaze. There was nothing romantic in the shared stare. They knew that each one of them was just trying to avert their gaze, unwilling to look at what unfolded so close by.

When the soldiers were done with their mocking, Pilate washed his hands, as if a small bowl of water could cleanse his sins. Pilate could jump into a *mikveh* and fully immerse himself thirty-nine times over, and it still would not wash away the guilt of what he was allowing to happen.

But it got even worse. When they laid a plank of wood on Jesus's bloody shoulders, it all came rushing back to Keturah. Rufus had done the same to her—had forced her to carry a piece of wood strapped to her back. She remembered the feeling in her upper back as her muscles spasmed with inconceivable pain. She remembered tumbling to the ground with men on all sides spitting on her. Kicking her. The wood she had carried was a sliver compared to what had been placed on Jesus's ragged back, now exposed to the unmerciful air after the purple robe was ripped off, taking skin with it.

Hanging around Jesus's neck was a wooden sign, the *titulus*, which carried the words, "Jesus of Nazareth, the king of the Jews." Once again, Keturah understood. She knew the pain of carrying a statement of shame on your body because her forehead had been stained with the words declaring to all that she was an escaped slave. The *titulus* declared Jesus to be a king, not a slave, but it was a mockery of his kingship—and a mockery of the Jews. This sign was a necklace of humiliation.

Jesus moved slowly, like a broken animal that had been run over by a chariot. Keturah trudged alongside Joanna and Eliana, who continued to keep their eyes fixed on every step that Jesus took. Eliana made a move to try to help Jesus, but once again the soldiers kept her at a distance.

"Do you need a woman to help you carry your load?" a soldier taunted.

One of the Roman soldiers—the one who tried to help Eliana back to her feet—yanked a good-sized man from the crowd and forced him to help Jesus carry the cross. The sun was merciless, heating up the cobblestone streets. Both sides of the road were lined with people, many who looked like they were watching a parade, a Roman triumph. But some were weeping, wailing. One man ripped his clothes. Keturah thought it might have been one of the disciples. She didn't know. It was all a blur.

Once, when Jesus fell and Keturah cried out, Jesus looked over at her and the other women and spoke. How he found the strength to talk, she didn't know. But he said, "Daughters of Jerusalem, do not weep for me; weep for yourselves and your children."

*Weep for ourselves?* Keturah had no idea what he was talking about.

"For the time will come when you will say, 'Blessed are the childless women, the wombs that never bore and the breasts that never nursed!' Then they will say to the mountains, 'Fall on us!' and to the hills, 'Cover us!'"

Keturah had no idea what Jesus was trying to tell them. Was something even worse approaching? How could things get any worse? And why would any woman wish she were barren?

As Jesus staggered through the city gate, Keturah saw the small hill just ahead—Golgotha. It was called the Place of the Skull because it looked as if two eye sockets and the nose socket of a skull had been carved into the side of the hill. The Jews believed that Adam, the first man, was buried at Golgotha. So, it was a fitting place to die.

"Why won't Jesus put an end to this?" Keturah asked Eliana as they trudged toward the hill. "If he can perform miracles, why can't he stop this madness?"

Eliana wouldn't answer. She wouldn't take her eyes away from Jesus, who was now stretched out on the cross. Keturah saw the soldiers grab large mallets and long spikes, and she looked down, covering her face, but she didn't cover her ears.

She heard the nails being driven through his wrists, and her imagination provided the rest.

## Eliana

Eliana watched with fury as the soldiers cast lots, tossing flat stones to determine who would walk away with Jesus's clothes. As she watched, contemplating whether she should hurl curses at them or try to steal back Jesus's clothes, she remembered a Psalm that she once recited during the darkest moments of her own captivity: *Do not be far from me, for trouble is near and there is no one to help.*

Those words were a great comfort to a young girl who had been snatched from her family and thrown into the hands of villains. *Do not be far from me.*

The next words of the Psalm were also etched in her heart.

*A pack of villains encircles me; they pierce my hands and my feet. All my bones are on display; people stare and gloat over me. They divide my clothes among them and cast lots for my garment.*

*They pierce my hands and feet. They divide my clothes.*

She had recited those words almost every day of her captivity. The words spoke of David, but they became her words too. Were they pointing toward this moment as well? Did these words, ultimately, belong to Jesus?

*Roaring lions that tear their prey open their mouths wide against me. I am poured out like water, and all my bones are out of joint. My heart has turned to wax; it has melted within me. My mouth is dried up like a potsherd, and my tongue sticks to the roof of my mouth; you lay me in the dust of death.*

Asaph used to speak of the Roman soldiers as lions, and he once used the term in awe. But now, she saw what these lions were capable of as they gathered around Jesus's clothes, dividing them up like the flesh of a fresh kill.

"You were there from the beginning, Eliana," came a voice next to her. Turning, she was stunned to see Jesus's mother.

Mary's eyes were transfixed on her son who hung before her on a cross, his throne of pain. Was she just as determined to see this through to the end? It had been agony for Eliana; she couldn't imagine what it must be like for Mary.

"Yes, I was there." That was all that Eliana could think of saying. The image of the newborn baby Jesus in Bethlehem was a memory set in stone.

"I held him in my arms," Mary said, turning to look at Eliana. "But you held him in your arms too."

Eliana's eyes stung with tears. "He was so small."

When Mary began to sob quietly, Eliana wrapped her in an embrace, holding her close. As Mary's body shook, Eliana glanced at Keturah, who stared at them helplessly.

"You once told me my son was the protector of your heart," Mary whispered, barely getting out the words. "Then why did he allow the sword to pierce *my* heart? Why can he not protect my heart too?"

What could Eliana say? Nothing. So, she held on to Mary, and Mary clung to her, like survivors of a shipwreck holding on to pieces of a once mighty ship. Eliana was trying to be strong throughout this ordeal, trying to be a good and faithful witness. But she lost all control and began crying as hard as Mary. Keturah, standing only a few feet away, slumped to the ground and began to weep as well, burying her face in her sleeve.

"He saved others!" one of the soldiers shouted to the people gathered. "Let him save himself if he is the Christ of God, the Chosen One!"

*Yes, let him save himself*, Eliana thought. *Why won't he save himself? Why won't he guard our hearts?*

One of the soldiers put a rag soaked in wine vinegar on the end of a pole and held it up to Jesus's mouth, just out of reach. When one of the soldiers snapped at him, ordering him to give Jesus the wine vinegar, the other soldier cursed and shoved the rag angrily into Jesus's face.

Eliana almost looked away. Almost. After staring at so many horrors over the past hour, she was tempted to turn away at this point. In comparison to the earlier taunts and tortures, shoving a rag in her Lord's face seemed so tame. But she had reached a breaking point and wondered if she could watch much more.

Nevertheless, she did not turn away. She continued to stare until this moment—and every painful image that came before—was burned into her memory. The sky began to darken. It was the sixth hour. Noon.

## Asaph

Asaph stared at the darkening sky, which looked as if a burial shroud was being lowered over the entire city of Jerusalem. Was a tempest approaching? Or a dust storm? Or something more ominous?

The wind snapped at the sleeves of his robe. He was glad to be out of the guard's uniform, but he continued to carry his sling in his belt, as well as a sack of stones draped over his shoulder. He rarely parted with his sling.

Now that he was no longer dressed in authority, he felt the freedom to ask questions.

"What is happening outside the gate?" he asked a shopkeeper, who came into the narrow street to stare up at the sky.

"What?" the shopkeeper said, distracted.

"What is happening?"

"In the sky? I wish I knew."

"No. Outside the city walls."

The shopkeeper scowled. "Where have you been all morning? They are crucifying three men. Go see for yourself. They will not die for many hours yet."

"What are the names of the men?"

The shopkeeper shrugged. "One of them is the Galilean. The one who entered the city like a king. He's going out like a criminal."

"Jesus?"

"That's the one. He claims he is the Son of God." The shopkeeper looked back up at the growing gloom. "Do you think this black sky has anything to do with Jesus?"

Asaph left that question hanging in the air and hurried toward the city gate. If Jesus was being executed, then Eliana must be with him at Golgotha. She would not desert Jesus. She would be with him every step of the way. As he hurried along, he prayed she hadn't done anything foolish like attack a Roman soldier.

But as he turned away from the shops at the foot of the Temple Mount, he spotted soldiers advancing. Instinctively, he ducked into a woodshop, where a carpenter was fashioning a yoke. The soldiers were Herod's guards, not Romans, and they were probably looking for them. But it was even worse than that. The guard leading the pack was Rufus, and just a few steps behind him were Nekoda, his brother Chaim, and a man whose face was concealed by a hood.

So, his suspicions were true. Chaim *had* betrayed them. Chaim deserved to die.

## Eliana

The air became gray, drained of all light, when Eliana suddenly took her eyes off Jesus. She had vowed to focus all her attention on the cross, but she looked away when she suddenly caught a glimpse of someone climbing up the side of the Skull.

Her father approached. He was free! Somehow, Sveshtari, Asaph, and Abel had successfully freed her abba from prison.

Eliana didn't wait for her father to climb all the way up the side of the hill. She bounded down to him. It reminded her of the day she bounded down the hill after seeing the newborn baby in Bethlehem—although running down a hill when you were ten was much easier than doing it in your forties. And this skull-like mountain of horror was a far cry from the lush green grass of Bethlehem's hills.

"Take it easy." Abba held up his hand. "I don't want you to break a leg."

But Eliana didn't slow down, even when she almost tripped on a jagged rock. Father and daughter melted together in their second miraculous reunion. Every time that she did not think she would ever see her father again, Yahweh protected her heart.

"How are Sveshtari, Asaph, and Abel?" she asked.

"All well. But Sveshtari says that someone betrayed them. Soldiers were waiting for them at the end of the sewer pipe."

"And yet they made it?"

"There were only four guards waiting for them inside the palace. Not nearly enough to handle Sveshtari."

"So Sveshtari is alive?" asked Keturah, who had climbed down the slope, trailing after Eliana.

"Very much alive. He is finding a way to exchange his uniform for ordinary clothing."

"Then will he come here?"

"As soon as he learns what is happening, I am sure he will come. He will know to find you here."

Eliana's abba stared up the hill at the three battered figures hanging from the crosses. The crucified men followed a gruesome rhythm. Unable to exhale, they were forced to push up with their feet, raising themselves on the cross so they could breathe out. But they couldn't hold that position for long, and they would slump again and begin to choke, slowly suffocating.

Strangely, Eliana noticed that Jesus and the two criminals seemed to be in conversation. What could three men be discussing when they were in agony and so close to death? But if she knew Jesus, he would be ministering to others to the very end.

She still could not absorb that this was the end. Jesus had been so alive and vibrant only one day earlier. The teachings, the excitement, the hope, the promise, the people shouting "Hosanna!" How could it go so wrong so quickly?

"How did this come to be?" her father asked, still staring at the crosses.

"They tried him in the night for blasphemy—for claiming to be the Son of God," Keturah said because Eliana was too overwhelmed to speak.

"And the Romans agreed to crucifixion for blasphemy?"

"Pilate wanted to free Jesus, but the people—followers of the Sanhedrin—wanted him to free Barabbas instead."

"*Barabbas* is free?" Judah rubbed the temple of his head as if his mind couldn't take in all that had happened while he was in prison.

Eliana took her father by the arm. "There are too many soldiers here. You must go back, hide yourself in the crowds."

"These soldiers do not know my face," he said as they turned to make their way back up the bones of the hill. "Especially in the darkness. What is happening in the heavens?"

"It's Jesus," Eliana said. The darkness must be falling because of her Lord.

With her father on one side and Keturah on the other, their arms entangled, they returned to the killing ground.

## Sveshtari

Sveshtari gave thanks to Yahweh, for the Jewish God must have sent the darkness as a special gift to him. Sveshtari had just spotted Rufus, Nekoda, Chaim, and a man with a hood moving swiftly in his direction when the darkness suddenly descended like the wings of a bird, giving him extra cover to hide in the crowd.

He sprinted down one of the streets running south from the Temple Mount, only to see more soldiers advancing north in his direction. Backtracking, he ran to the southern side of the Temple Mount, taking three steps at a time up the Monumental staircase. Reaching the Temple Mount, he raced through the Huldah Gate, into the Court of the Gentiles. This was the most crowded place on the Mount, providing the most protection.

As people stopped to stare at the darkened sky, Sveshtari found protection in the colonnade running along the western side of the Temple Mount. He paused and took refuge behind one of the massive pillars, staring back to see if Rufus, Nekoda, Chaim, and the hooded man had followed him.

No sign of his pursuers. The colonnade was packed, so he decided to remain on the Temple Mount rather than slip out another gate and return to the main city. He also prayed they might be less likely to create a scene so close to the Temple—the throne room of their God. Yesterday, thousands of Passover lambs had been killed in the Court of Priests outside the Temple doors, and the priests would soon be killing another lamb at the ninth hour, followed by thousands more Paschal lambs. But they would be less likely to shed human blood there.

The location of the Temple, Mount Moriah, was where the Hebrew God had commanded Abraham to kill his son Isaac. But at the last moment, an angel stayed Abraham's hand. Sveshtari didn't know his Jewish theology, but he hoped that meant Yahweh disapproved of killing humans in this sacred place.

Sveshtari backpedaled deeper into the shadows of the colonnade, but not so far back as the wall. He wanted to maintain four directions of movement. No walls at your back. He needed all possible escape routes.

## Asaph

Asaph lost sight of Sveshtari, which was a good thing. If he couldn't see him, perhaps his pursuers had lost sight of him as well. It was easy to do in the strange and singular darkness that had fallen on the city. This had to be the Hand of God. It was God's judgment for the crime taking place on Golgotha at this very moment.

Sensing the coming judgment, Asaph followed Rufus, Nekoda, Chaim, and the hooded man up the Monumental Stairs to the Temple Mount. The Temple was built on a threshing floor that King David had purchased so long ago—and a threshing floor is both a place of blessing and a place of judgment.

Asaph had worked a threshing sledge when he was young, hooking it to a donkey that pulled it across the wheat, crushing the heads and separating the grain seeds from the plant stalks. Then he would use the winnowing fork to toss the chopped-up wheat stalks into the air. The wind would carry the lightweight chaff the farthest, while the straw would fall a bit closer to the harvester. The heavy grain would land the closest of all.

The threshing floor was a place of blessing because it was where the grain was separated from the stalks and the chaff. But it was also the metaphorical seat of judgment, separating the sinners from the redeemed, like chaff blowing away in the wind.

Today, there would be a winnowing. The chaff would be hit by a mountaintop wind and carried into oblivion, while the good grain would fill the baskets to overflowing. Nekoda, Rufus, and Chaim would all be destroyed. He sensed it. Judgment was coming with the darkness.

To save himself, Asaph knew he should turn around and head back into the city and lose himself in the twisted alleyways. But he would not desert Sveshtari. He would fight to the bloody finish.

He moved into the Court of Gentiles, the outermost court encircling the Temple. Nekoda, Rufus, Chaim, and the hooded man headed for the eastern side of the Temple Mount, moving alongside Solomon's Porch. Rufus led the way, while Nekoda followed behind and seemed to be arguing with Chaim like only brothers could do.

Finally throwing up his hands, Nekoda parted ways with the group, heading deeper into the Temple grounds, deeper toward God's presence. Asaph assumed Nekoda must be leaving to serve at the second sacrifice of the day when the lamb would be killed at the ninth hour.

Minus Nekoda, the group moved on, and Asaph followed. But he kept his distance, watching and waiting and praying for Yahweh to crush them like sheaves beneath a sledge.

## Nekoda

Nekoda tried to put his meddling brother out of his mind and focus on the second of the perpetual sacrifices that took place every day in the Temple. Ever since they were young, Chaim had a soft heart—too soft. Chaim would even feel sorry for the lambs—the unblemished lambs—brought to be sacrificed twice per day in the Temple.

On Passover, the number of animals sacrificed was multiplied by the thousands. That's why Chaim had little desire to carry on their family's glory and become a priest; he couldn't even slit a lamb's throat. For the past year, Chaim had been living like a nomad with that band of Messiah misfits, wandering from Galilee to Jerusalem. It made Nekoda spitting mad just thinking about it.

But he also had another nagging thought. Sveshtari and Asaph had somehow escaped from the palace prison, along with one of the Zealots, leaving a trail of slaughter in their wake.

They must atone. They must pay. A life for a life.

As if that wasn't enough worry to pile on his shoulders, he kept glancing at the sky. It had a greenish-black look, with clouds swirling like smoke from a sacrificial fire. The heat of the morning had been replaced by a cool breeze, which sent the altar flames dancing in all directions.

He prayed to get his mind back in order as preparations were made for the sacrifice. One of the priests had gone to the Chamber of the Lambs to select one of the six blemish-free young sheep being kept there. After a final inspection, the lamb was given water from a golden vessel to make the animal's skin easier to remove. Then the lamb was tied to the altar in preparation for the sacrifice at the ninth hour. The lamb, perfect in form, bleated and tugged at the chain.

In disgust, Nekoda thought about how Chaim didn't have the stomach for sacrifice. He was a disgrace to their family, and sometimes Nekoda wondered whether they were really related at all.

## Sveshtari

He had been spotted! Rufus, Chaim, and the hooded man saw him as they approached from the northern end of the Temple Mount. Sveshtari shoved a man out of his path and sprinted through the colonnade on the western side of the Mount, looking for the most crowded sections where he could lose himself.

As he raced past a large table where moneychangers were hard at work, Sveshtari heaved one of the tables on its side, blocking the path of his pursuers and creating chaos in his wake. Pandemonium erupted as the moneychangers, cursing and screaming, dove for the coins, which cascaded on the ground like a waterfall of Mammon.

He scrambled for the exit at the southwestern corner of the Temple, bounding down the enormous staircase that was packed with people, most of them moving in the opposite direction, flowing up to the Temple Mount.

"Stop him!" shouted Rufus.

Most people did nothing. They took one look at Sveshtari and realized how foolhardy it would be to try to stop such a man, barreling down the long stairway at breakneck speed. They would have more success trying to stop a runaway chariot. But one man, a good-sized fellow, decided to be a hero. He stepped from the crowd and extended his hands, trying to catch Sveshtari in a bear hug, but Sveshtari put his head down like a ram and knocked him flying backward. He hoped the man didn't break any bones, but he didn't have time to care.

At the foot of the staircase, Sveshtari found himself at the beginning of the stepped street stretching downward to the Pool of Siloam at the southern end of the city. There, he could slip out through the city's Water Gate and be done with Jerusalem. But he spotted a contingent of Temple guards hustling up the street from the south, so he wheeled around—and saw Rufus, Chaim, and the hooded man coming at him from the north.

Nimbly, he ducked left into a shop where a man was spinning a vase. Sveshtari grabbed a finished vase, spun around, and hurled it at Rufus, who rushed at him with his sword drawn. Rufus tried to duck, but the vase cracked him in the shoulder, while Sveshtari vaulted through an open window on the opposite side of the shop, only to encounter more soldiers. The net was closing in. He realized he had no choice.

Once again, he had to go underground.

## Asaph

Asaph followed the trail of chaos out of the Temple Mount and onto the main street leading south, downhill to the Pool of Siloam. Soldiers seemed to be emerging from the streets on all sides, and he thought for sure that Sveshtari was doomed—until the man just disappeared. One second, he was there, and the next moment, he was gone. Sveshtari had slipped down the narrow staircase leading beneath the street to a major drainage passageway. The drainage system ran directly beneath the stepped street going south through the city.

Asaph also spotted Rufus close behind Sveshtari, flying down the stairway leading underground. When the third man—the one in the hood—tried to follow, Chaim stepped in front of him, blocking the path to the drainage system. Chaim extended his arms to the sides and seemed to be arguing, screaming at the man. And then, without missing a beat, this hooded man sank his sword in Chaim's mid-section and gave it a twist before yanking it free.

Chaim tumbled sideways onto the street, while the hooded man stepped over him and plunged into the drainage system. Shocked, Asaph rushed to Chaim's side; he was still conscious, clutching his stomach, trying to raise himself from the ground.

"Chaim! Chaim! Look at me!"

Strangely, Chaim smiled. He blinked and stared up at Asaph as if trying to focus his eyes. "Asaph? I'm so sorry."

Sorry? Was he sorry for betraying them? Asaph could never forgive that.

"I am sorry that I failed to protect you from my brother." A trickle of blood slid down his chin.

"What are you talking about?"

"I failed you twice! Twice! I am so sorry!"

Asaph supported his head as Chaim winced from a spasm of pain.

"I don't understand. What do you mean?"

"That man . . . that man told Nekoda you were sneaking into the palace through the sewers. He betrayed you!"

"That man? What man?"

"The man . . . I tried to convince Nekoda that the man was lying; I said you wouldn't be so foolish as to come through the sewers. But Nekoda didn't believe me, and it was too late to warn you. I am so sorry. I failed you."

"What man?"

"The man who betrayed you . . ."

"You mean the man who stabbed you? Who is he?"

"I tried to stop him, but . . . they . . . they . . . am I going to die, Asaph?"

Asaph looked at the wound, where blood continued to stream. Chaim's face had gone as white as a senator's bleached robe. Asaph ripped off the bottom of his own robe and pressed the cloth against the wound.

Chaim began to tremble. "I am sorry for my brother's actions. I tried to stop him. I tried to be a friend."

"I know, I know, Chaim. You were a good friend."

"I am going to die, aren't I?"

"Only God knows."

"Yes. God knows." Chaim's eyes began to glaze over. "Many bulls surround me." Leaning his head back, he stared up at the dark sky. "Strong bulls of Bashan encircle me. But you, Lord, do not be far from me. You are my strength; come quickly, come quickly."

A crowd had gathered around Chaim and Asaph, but no one stepped forward to help. None of them were doctors, but even if there were a physician nearby, nothing could be done for this man.

"Deliver me from the sword." Chaim mumbled, barely audible. "Deliver my precious life from the power of the dogs."

Asaph leaned close to Chaim's mouth, taking in the words, and he, too, began to pray. Chaim's voice was faint, like someone sliding deeper and deeper down a sloping tunnel. "Rescue me from the mouth of the lion, Asaph. Save me from the horns of the wild oxen. Many bulls surround me. Many, many strong bulls of Bashan."

Then Chaim was gone, slipping into a tunnel from which there was no return.

## Keturah

The darkness continued into the eighth hour and closed in on the ninth hour. Jesus was still alive, but barely. By this time, the soldiers had become bored with their mockery of him—and some looked unnerved by the darkness that had deepened all around them as if the world had fallen into a deep well.

Keturah moved closer to the cross, unsure why she was drawn there. She didn't want to look upon Jesus. She couldn't. He continued to raise himself up on the cross, pushing with his feet to exhale. Then he slumped back down, and the suffocation would begin all over again.

Jesus hadn't spoken for a while now, but Keturah could still not get his earlier words out of her mind. "Father, forgive them, for they do not know what they are doing."

When he spoke those words, he had been looking at the soldiers as they divided up his clothes. Keturah could not understand Jesus. Who could forgive something like this?

The first time she heard Jesus exhort people to forgive their enemies, he had been standing on a beautiful mountainside, surrounded by flowers. Back then, Keturah thought it was easy for him to say we should forgive our enemies when he's standing amidst flowers; try doing it when you're surrounded by evil.

Now, he was doing it. He was on another mountainside, only this one was a skull, without a flower in sight. And he was truly doing it, forgiving his enemies. So why couldn't she forgive?

Keturah beat her chest and tossed dirt on her head, as the Jews did. At one time, she never understood why Jews did such things, but now it was clear. She wanted to bury herself. She wanted to go down into a grave because the misery above ground was too much. She had to go deep, go down, go underground.

Slowly, methodically, she picked up handfuls of earth and poured it on her head, feeling it trickle down her face. Again and again, she did this, and she thought about Sveshtari. He was alive. He had survived the rescue mission, and this reality began to set in. She had promised to be betrothed to him. She had given her word, but she had only done so to give him courage and hope in his fight. Could she really follow through on her promise; could she really forgive him?

Scooping up another handful of dirt, she poured it on her head and rubbed it into her face. She was a daughter of the dust, covering herself in a shroud of dirt. She never realized how grief could feel so much like dying.

The ninth hour neared.

## Sveshtari

For the second time this day, Sveshtari was running through a drainage tunnel, only this time he was trying to escape a city, rather than break into a palace. The water in the tunnel was up to his knees as he sloshed along the pitch-black path. Fortunately, he could stand upright in the tunnel, but it seemed as if it went on forever, taking him slowly, steadily downhill toward the southern end of Jerusalem.

He never paused, never let up, but he heard the sloshing sound of his pursuers not far behind. Or was that just an echo of his own movements? He wasn't about to pause to listen and find out. He pressed forward.

Finally, he emerged aboveground, exhausted, legs burning from the exertion of pushing through so much water. He fell to all fours, panting like an animal, and then he forced himself back to standing. But in that moment of rest, he heard the sounds of pursuit coming from behind, back in the tunnel. They were close.

He sprinted toward the Pool of Siloam where a crowd had gathered. Not far away was the Water Gate, his escape from the city.

"Stop him!" came the voice of Rufus from behind.

Sveshtari displayed his short sword, daring anyone to try. Then he was hit by a moving wall. His senses had been deadened by exhaustion, and he didn't see the man coming—a huge monster of a man slamming into him from the right side.

They both tumbled into the pool. The man was enormous and strong, but the water neutralized some of his power, and Sveshtari arose from the water first. He lost his sword in the tumble, but he drove his elbow into the man's face, cracking the nose with an audible snap. Blood gushed, contaminating the pool.

Sveshtari spotted his sword and dove beneath the water to retrieve it. But as he did, Rufus pounced, and he felt the man's hand clamp down on his head, forcing it to remain beneath the water.

He was drowning.

## Asaph

When it was clear that Chaim was dead, far beyond any help in this life, Asaph sprinted down the stepped road leading to the southern part of the city. Reaching the Pool of Siloam, he spotted Rufus holding a man's head beneath the water. The man was thrashing but unable to rise. A second man—the one in the hood—began to help Rufus as they struggled to drown the man, like a stray cat.

The man beneath the water had to be Sveshtari.

Asaph didn't know if he had time to reach the Pool of Siloam before Sveshtari drowned, so he pulled out a stone from his pouch. He had only three, and he loaded his sling and fired. The shot missed, but it plunked in the water only one cubit from Rufus. The guard didn't even flinch, but the man in the hood did. He turned, but in the gloom and from this distance, Asaph could not make out his face.

Quickly, Asaph reloaded, and this time the rock hit Rufus squarely between the shoulder blades. Rufus let out a shout and stood up straight, giving Sveshtari a fighting chance. Sveshtari rose from the water like some behemoth from the deep, and he struck Rufus in the throat with a sweeping arm movement, sending the soldier tumbling backward. Then Sveshtari plunged back into the pool, but why?

One moment later, he emerged with his sword in hand. But he was surrounded, three against one, because a large man had come to the aid of Rufus and the hooded man. As Asaph sprinted toward them, he drew out his dagger. He wished he had a sword, but this would have to do.

## NEKODA

The unblemished lamb was brought forth to the Place of Slaughtering for the second *tamid* sacrifice of the day. Nearby was the square stone altar, with a ramp leading up to it.

The priest making the sacrifice stood on the east side of the lamb and held the animal's head down, its face turned to the west, as he tied it to a ring in the Place of Slaughter. Nekoda stood next to this priest, holding a golden bowl in his hands.

Then the Temple gates were opened, and three blasts were blown on three trumpets, announcing the imminent sacrifice. The priest thrust his knife upwards into the lamb's windpipe, and blood gushed into the golden bowl in Nekoda's hands. The blood was rich and red and bountiful.

Taking the cup, rounded on the bottom so it could not be set down, Nekoda approached the altar and sprinkled blood on it, covering two sides. He poured the remainder of the blood at the base of the altar and watched as the red river drained into a hole that carried away this thread of life.

It was then that even stranger things began to happen.

## Asaph

Asaph let loose with a war cry as he charged down the stairs toward the Pool of Siloam. All three of the men turned to look, giving Sveshtari the chance to act, and he hacked the big man with his sword across the exposed flesh on the back of his neck. The big man crumpled into the water face first. He was still alive, but not for long. He would not rise from the waters.

Rufus wheeled back around just in time to fend off Sveshtari's next attack, while the third man—the one in the hood—glared at Asaph. At last, Asaph could see his face, for the man had lowered his hood as he turned.

It was Zuriel. He was the one who betrayed them! He was the one who had killed Chaim!

The shock brought Asaph to a standstill. But only briefly. He climbed into the Pool of Siloam and hurled himself on his enemy, dagger slicing down, but Zuriel danced out of the path. He was surprisingly quick.

"You're not going to leave Jerusalem alive," Zuriel said. "You know that, don't you?"

"The Lord is my fortress." Asaph moved in with his dagger poised. In the corner of his eye, he could see Sveshtari and Rufus in a furious fight. "He is my shield, the horn of my salvation."

"Pray all you want, Asaph. God will not hear you."

"The Lord has transformed me, but I see you are the same old Zuriel. Have you stoned any women lately?"

Screaming, Zuriel attacked with his short sword, and Asaph backpedaled in the water. Asaph had only a dagger and was panicked by the futility of fighting a man with a sword.

"After your precious Messiah is dead, we will gather up what's left of his pitiful followers, including your beloved Eliana, and we will slaughter them all."

Asaph tried to slice Zuriel's right arm—his sword arm—but he nearly lost a hand trying. Zuriel's blade trimmed off Asaph's little finger.

He didn't feel the pain immediately, but he soon would.

Asaph prayed for Sveshtari to finish off Rufus because he needed his friend's help. He could not win this battle with Zuriel alone. But Sveshtari was having a tough time with Rufus, a younger, taller man.

Then, to Asaph's horror, he saw Sveshtari lose his footing in the water and fall backward. Rufus moved in for the kill.

## Eliana

Eliana approached Keturah, who was tossing dust on her head. Letting out a low moan, Eliana knelt beside her friend.

One of the centurions came close to the cross, and Eliana noticed that it was the same young soldier who had tried to help her back to her feet when she was knocked down by one of the soldiers. She felt guilty about snapping at him with such venom. He was the only soldier who had behaved like a human. She should have seen that.

Then . . . something started to happen. Jesus had been constantly pushing himself up, trying to get into a position to exhale, but he hadn't spoken for a long time. Now, she heard him struggling to talk, fighting for the words.

Eliana rose to her feet, and so did Keturah. They looked up as Jesus put enormous effort into raising himself as high as possible on the cross. For a moment, Eliana almost wondered if he was going to push himself up so strongly that he might lift himself off the cross.

At the highest point on the cross, Jesus looked up at the dark sky and shouted, "Father, into your hands I commend my spirit!"

Jesus let out a long breath as if blowing on embers to bring flames to life. Then his body sagged, slumping back onto the cross, and Eliana knew it was over.

"Surely this was a righteous man," the centurion said.

And then it happened.

## Nekoda

The Temple Mount began shaking as if the entire structure was being tilted to one side and then yanked back by tremendous opposing forces, fighting over holy ground. Nekoda was thrown sideways against the altar. He banged his head against the stone and was temporarily dazed. Blood trickled down the side of his head.

Then came another jolt as an earthquake threw him in the opposite direction, and he fell onto his back. From this position, he could see bits and pieces of stone breaking away from the beautiful Temple. One of the pieces crashed only a few cubits from his head. If it had landed on him, it would have killed him instantly.

Then he heard a rip as if the very earth beneath his back was being torn apart like fabric—as if God was ripping His own robe as a sign of mourning. People screamed, and some knelt and prayed that the earth wouldn't open beneath them and swallow them up.

Several priests ran into the Temple through the double-folding doors and the outer veil. They wouldn't dare go any farther. They wouldn't enter the Holy of Holies, which could only be breached by the high priest one day a year.

Scrambling back to his feet, Nekoda ran for the door of the Temple and another jolt sent him staggering to the right like a sailor on a ship in a storm. This time he maintained his footing and ran into the Temple, coming to a stop in the Holy Place. Directly ahead of him was the entrance to the Holy of Holies, which was screened by the Inner Veil. To his horror, the curtain had been torn from top to bottom, exposing the Holy of Holies to all eyes.

Nekoda covered his face, but he had already seen what he was not allowed to look upon. The veil—a curtain the thickness of a man's hand—had cherubim woven into it. These were images of angels guarding the path to God's throne with fiery swords in their hands. But when the curtain tore, the path to the throne had been opened, ripping the swords in half. Nekoda had seen it with his own eyes, or he never would have believed it. It was as if the universe, the garment of God, had been torn open.

With his eyes covered, he backed out of the Temple. When he was finally outside, he turned and ran. He thought, for the first time in his life, that the world was coming to an end.

## Asaph

Before Rufus could strike the fallen Sveshtari, the world started shaking like a cast lot. Rufus fell. Sveshtari fell. Then Asaph staggered sideways, tumbling into the water. People on all sides were hurled to the ground as if they were being cut down by some enormous scythe. In this fight among four men, whoever got to their feet first might very well decide who would live and who would die.

Rufus got to his feet first, while Sveshtari still struggled to stand. Asaph, dagger drawn, was the next to rise, and he hurled himself on Rufus's back, driving his blade into his shoulder. He aimed for the back of his neck, but with the world shaking and Rufus moving, the knife misdirected and sank into his shoulder. But it was enough to give Sveshtari a fighting chance to stand.

Another jolt sent them staggering again, and all the water in the pool shifted to one side like a tipped vessel. But Sveshtari kept his balance, kept his head, and struck. He sank his sword into Rufus's side, bypassing his breastplate and cutting him to his heart.

Asaph stepped backward, incredulous that it was finished. Rufus fell to his knees, dying before his eyes. Asaph shouldn't have stopped to stare, however. He should have remembered that Zuriel was still behind him.

He felt the hot sting of Zuriel's blade entering his back as another quake shook all of Jerusalem. He shouted Sveshtari's name and staggered forward, feeling the blade still in his back. As he dropped his sling, he turned and saw Zuriel fleeing, running hard through the water and starting to climb out of the pool.

Asaph felt the power draining from his body, but he pushed through the pain and drew out a stone—a heavy rock with jagged edges. Asaph didn't have the time to retrieve his sling, which had fallen into the water, so he hurled the rock by hand.

The rock struck Zuriel in the back of his head. He watched as Zuriel stopped dead in his tracks and tumbled backward into the water. At the same time, Asaph found that he, too, was falling backward. He toppled into the bloody water, and the cords of the grave coiled around him.

## Eliana: Friday Afternoon

Eliana washed Chaim's body, removing the dust of the city and the crusted blood surrounding his wound. He had been stabbed in the side, just as the soldiers had driven a spear into Jesus's side to make sure he was dead.

She couldn't help but think of Adam, who was put into a deep sleep so God could create Eve from his side. That incision had brought new life—a bride for Adam. But what possible good could come from a knife being sunk into Chaim's side or a spear into Jesus's side? Where were their brides? Chaim had wanted Eliana to be his betrothed, and she had let him down.

Now, Chaim was dead, Jesus was dead, and Asaph was dying. Eliana had taken too many blows to keep going. She felt like one of those women pushed into a pit while people stood all around, pelting her with rocks until she died.

Eliana would have liked to help prepare Jesus's body, but many other women were already busy handling that job, including Joanna and another wealthy woman named Susanna. But poor Chaim had no one to tend to him. His family had turned their backs on him, so all he had left were followers of Jesus. Jesus would've been pleased that Chaim was not overlooked.

Shockingly, the dry spices to anoint Jesus's body—the myrrh and aloes—had been donated by Nicodemus, a member of the Sanhedrin. But as she learned, Nicodemus was a sympathetic soul. Jesus's teachings had pierced his heart.

The place where Jesus's body was placed that day was a newly cut tomb not far from the site of the crucifixion. The tomb had been donated by Joseph of Arimathea—another member of the Sanhedrin! Joanna told her that Joseph had always loved Jesus and had been a disciple. She wondered why both men, Nicodemus and Joseph, remained secret disciples rather than stepping boldly into the light and proclaiming their allegiance to Jesus. Could they have made more of a difference? Could they have saved Jesus's life? Wouldn't it have been better for them to prevent Jesus's death rather than providing a tomb and spices after he was killed?

Such cowardice angered her, but Joanna calmed her spirit. She said Joseph had fought a losing battle on Jesus's behalf.

Before Sabbath fell on the Friday of Jesus's death, before the sun set, the women wrapped his body in linen packed with dry spices—a temporary measure to preserve the body until the Sabbath was over. The women planned to return to the grave on Sunday morning with spices to finish the task.

Eliana did the same for Chaim. But she felt like she was sleepwalking through it all. Jesus had died, and she was furious at him.

# 12
## Luke, Chapter 24

### Keturah

Keturah and Sveshtari decided to marry, but this was not the time to announce joyous news. They kept it a secret.

On Friday afternoon, Keturah helped Eliana prepare Chaim's body, while Eliana's father found an acceptable tomb in which to place him. When they weren't preparing Chaim's body for burial, they were at Asaph's bedside praying. Joanna had hired a physician, but the doctor did not think Asaph was going to make it, at least not without prayer.

Saturday was the Sabbath, so all day was spent praying and sleeping, off and on. Sleep was healing but fitful and sometimes frightening. Keturah kept dreaming that she was carrying the wooden beam on her back, trudging to Golgotha on the cobblestone road right behind Jesus who also carried his cross. Although it was nightmarish, there were moments in her dream when Jesus would turn, look at her, and smile. Those moments were strange but healing.

Keturah and Eliana stayed in a home in the lower city, next door to where Asaph was lying—alive, but just barely. They nursed him all day, but death approached. Then would come a third burial. The Jews believed that three was a number of perfection, but three burials in one week was not her idea of perfection.

Sveshtari helped in any way he could. He told Keturah that he was thinking of becoming a God-fearer—a Jew, but only to a certain point. God-fearers were not circumcised, and they didn't abide by the myriad of laws. But they were disciples of Yahweh.

It seemed so strange. They had been pretending to be Jews for more than a year, and now, suddenly, it was no longer an act for Sveshtari. It was as if he had been wearing a mask for so long that when he finally removed it, he discovered that his face had conformed to the mold.

Come Sunday, it was back to keeping watch at the house where Asaph continued to sleep. Keturah prayed that his sleep was more peaceful than hers. Eliana had set a meal on a small table by Asaph's bedside as if she were expecting him to wake up fully healed and ready to devour several rounds of bread and a bowl overloaded with fruit.

Keturah was staring at this cluster of grapes, daydreaming, when Joanna rushed into the house. She'll never forget the image of those purple grapes because that was the very last thing she saw before her world changed, and nothing looked the same again.

"His body is gone!" Joanna shouted.

## Eliana: Sunday Morning

Eliana's legs were moving faster than they did when she was a young girl, racing Asaph through the winding streets of their hometown. She even ran faster than on the morning she held the baby Jesus in her arms in the hills of Bethlehem.

Today, if what Joanna told her was true, she was running toward an empty cave—a startling contrast to the cave where Jesus had been born amid the stench of donkeys and sheep. The Bethlehem cave had echoed to the cries of newborn life, while this cave glowed with the radiance of risen life.

According to Joanna, the first women to discover the empty tomb were Mary Magdalene, Mary the wife of Clopas, and Salome, who had all brought spices to the tomb in the early morning to finish anointing the body. Joanna met them on the way, and when they reached the tomb, they found the stone rolled away and Jesus's body gone. The tomb was empty!

In place of Jesus's body, Joanna said they encountered two men in dazzling apparel. Terrified, the women fell to the ground, and the men said to them, "Why do you seek the living among the dead? Remember how he told you, while he was still in Galilee, that the Son of Man must be delivered into the hands of sinful men, and be crucified, and on the third day rise."

*He has risen indeed*! Eliana was certain of it. She took off running an instant later.

"Wait for me!" Joanna called from behind, but Eliana didn't slow down until she reached the garden.

With her legs shaking and her heart still racing, she cautiously entered the garden, where she came to the tomb cut into the soft limestone of the hill. The massive round stone lay on its back a short distance away. Who could have moved such a weight? Certainly not the women. It would have taken several men to roll it aside—or perhaps a single angel.

"See," said Joanna when she finally caught up to her.

Eliana nodded. Then she ducked and stepped into the chamber, which was sunk just below ground level. She spotted the grave clothes, laid out on the shelf of stone where the body had been placed. Eliana raised the clothes to her nose and inhaled the spices that had been placed on Jesus's body to keep away the foul odor.

But there was no stench of decay—just the sweet scent of new life, like the fragrant powder on a newborn's skin. There had been a birth in this cave. A rebirth. And like all births, women were the ones in attendance. Women were the first to witness that Jesus had risen to new life.

Dropping to her knees, Eliana buried her face in the grave clothes and sobbed. Jesus hadn't deserted her after all. He was alive. He was still the protector of her heart.

Joanna knelt beside her and wrapped an arm around her shoulder.

"We have eaten the bitter herbs," said Joanna, raising the image of the Passover dinner when Jews swallowed the bitterness that reminded them of their bondage as slaves.

"But God provided the lamb," Eliana said, wiping away her tears. "God provided the spotless lamb."

"And we have escaped like birds from the fowler's snare," Joanna whispered, echoing the song of ascents.

"The snare has been broken, and we have escaped," Eliana continued.

Death, the ultimate trap, had been shattered, and a thousand birds rose up from a thousand hearts.

## Asaph

When Asaph opened his eyes, he was shocked to see a little boy and girl standing by his bedside. For a moment, he wondered if they were angels. Or perhaps he was looking at himself when he was young, standing side by side with Eliana when they were children. He felt groggy and disoriented, so he couldn't be sure of anything.

"You aren't dead," the girl said as if accusing him of a crime.

"I'm not?" Asaph was a little disappointed. He didn't mind the idea that he had made it to the other side with a table loaded with bread and fruit waiting for him. The sun was shining strong, and the last thing he remembered, the sky had been as black as the back of a cobra. When he raised himself a little in bed, a bolt of pain shot down his back. If this was the afterlife, there shouldn't be pain.

The little boy poked him in the shoulder. "You don't feel dead."

"Mama, the dead man's talking!" shouted the girl. Then a middle-aged woman came running into the room with a cloth in her hands.

"Praise God! Hannah, go find Eliana and Keturah!"

*Eliana and Keturah*. Finally, something familiar—two names he could hold on to. Then he laid his head back down and lost consciousness instantly.

When he opened his eyes again, he found himself staring up at familiar faces—Eliana and Keturah. It was dark, and their faces were partially veiled in shadow.

"It's about time." Eliana beamed. "We sat by your bedside in perpetual prayer for over a day, and when we leave for a moment, you decide to wake up. Then, when we hear that you're awake, we come running to your side, only to find you sleeping again."

"Sorry?"

Eliana poked him playfully, just like she had done when they were children. "Don't be sorry. I think Jesus healed you."

"Jesus? But Jesus was crucified." As the fog began to lift, confusion set in.

Eliana's grin grew bigger. Either she was holding in some good news, or she had gone crazy.

"Jesus did die, didn't he?" Asaph asked. "Or did I imagine that he was being crucified?"

"He died and was buried on Friday, the same day we almost lost you," chimed in Keturah.

Eliana leaped to her feet. "But today he was seen again! Alive!"

"Alive? Stop teasing me." Asaph winced when he laughed.

"I'm not teasing you! Jesus is alive."

Asaph stared at Eliana, looking for any sign of joking. He saw not a hint.

"You really believe your words, don't you?"

"*I know it.* Jesus is alive, and he healed you! Two miracles!"

"He came here to heal me?" Asaph began to think he was the crazy one, and all of this was a strange vision in his head.

"He didn't come here," Eliana said, "but we prayed in his name all the same."

Asaph started at those words. Had she spoken blasphemy? She said she prayed in his name!

"Did you see Jesus?"

"We didn't," said Keturah. "But Mary his mother, the other two Mary's, and Salome did when they brought the spices to the tomb this morning."

"And the disciples saw him soon after!" Eliana added.

Asaph groaned as he lay back down, then let out a big breath.

"I think we're overwhelming you," Eliana said, still giving him that big grin of hers. It had been a long time since he had seen her this happy. He liked it. Even if she was acting like a crazy woman, he liked her when she was happy.

## Nekoda

Nekoda sat in his courtyard in the dark, with a small fire burning to keep him warm and provide some light. He clutched a goblet of wine in his right hand—his third cup of the evening. His grown sons were asleep, so he sat alone. He had barely slept at all since Friday.

Nekoda had a beautiful home—two stories, a lush courtyard overflowing with flowers, a fountain, and many servants. But it seemed so trivial after all that had happened. His brother was dead, Rufus was found floating face down in the Pool of Siloam, and Zuriel had barely survived with a bloody skull before fleeing Jerusalem. The events of the weekend had shaken him as severely as the earthquake had shaken the Temple. He felt as if the core of his soul had been torn down the middle like the Inner Veil.

How did the Psalmist put it? *The earth trembled and quaked, and the foundations of the mountains shook; they trembled because he was angry. Smoke rose from his nostrils; consuming fire came from his mouth, burning coals blazed out of it. He parted the heavens and came down; dark clouds were under his feet.*

The darkened sky, the earthquake, and now these wild stories about Jesus . . . It sent Nekoda's head spinning. Herod and Pilate were both furious about the stories whipping through the city like wildfire—how some women had visited Jesus's tomb and found it empty. They said Jesus was alive!

Sadducees like himself do not believe in life after death, so this was all a bit disturbing. He tried to dismiss it, but after what he witnessed this weekend, he didn't think he would ever be able to dismiss anything concerning Jesus. Even if Jesus wasn't alive, Nekoda would like to know how a tomb came to be empty, and how the stone was rolled away when Pilate had set up a guard to watch over it. Those soldiers faced the penalty of death if they let someone steal the body, so how did the body disappear? The empty tomb was the only undeniable fact in this strange story. His spies had reported back that, yes, Jesus's body had disappeared.

When Nekoda heard that Chaim had been killed, he wept like he hadn't in years. As much as his little brother annoyed him, he loved Chaim.

Yes, his brother had a soft heart and could weep over a sacrificial lamb. But Nekoda had to admit . . . that was also why he loved Chaim.

He had also once loved Jeremiel, and his friend was gone too. Jeremiel had grown to despise him, which made Nekoda incredibly sad. He worried that his brother had grown to despise him as well.

Sighing, he rose to his feet—a little unsteady from so much wine. He hadn't watered it down, so it was potent. He walked over to an olive tree, where he had draped his purple robe over a branch. His precious purple robe. Like his house, the robe seemed so trivial now.

Setting his goblet on the ground, he draped the robe over his arm, walked slowly across his courtyard, and paused before his fire. Then he did what he had been contemplating all evening. He tossed the purple robe onto the flames and watched it burn.

After it had turned to ashes, Nekoda staggered to his bedroom, climbed beneath his thick blanket, and fell fast asleep.

## Keturah

"I love you, Eliana," said Keturah, wrapping her in a warm, sisterly embrace. "I will miss . . ." Her final words were swallowed up in tears. She didn't think she would be able to get through this without weeping.

"We will see each other again, Keturah." Eliana barely completed her sentence before breaking down.

Keturah could not believe the path they had followed. Who would have imagined that the woman who growled at her and spit at her like an irritable camel so long ago would become her dearest friend in the world?

They held each other and didn't let go until Sveshtari finally cleared his throat. He stood to the side with Babette cradled in his arms—a remarkable sight.

Keturah released Eliana from her embrace, but the two women continued to remain linked by their hands. "Do you really think we will see each other again?" Keturah asked. "Do you think you will come to us in Galilee?"

Eliana grinned. "I have become Galilean at heart. When Asaph fully recovers, we too may not be able to stay in Jerusalem."

"But I feel guilty about leaving you here in danger." Keturah had tried to talk Sveshtari into delaying their departure, but he and Abel both said they needed to go now—before the authorities tracked them down.

"Rufus may be dead, but you and Sveshtari are still being hunted, so you must go," Eliana told her. "We are not in danger—at least not yet. So, when Asaph fully recovers . . . you may be seeing us sooner than you think."

Keturah kissed her hand. "You *must* come to us."

"I am Jewish, and we Jews are wayfarers. So be confident. We will see you again."

"I pray for it!" Keturah said, and the two women embraced again. Sveshtari rolled his eyes at Abel, who stood nearby with the two donkeys—one for Keturah and the other on which the wet nurse, Ruth, was already mounted. Abel just shrugged.

Then Eliana placed her hands on Keturah's bowed head and said, "May it be Your will, Lord, our God and the God of our ancestors, that You lead us toward peace, guide our footsteps toward peace, and make us reach our desired destination for life, gladness, and peace. May You rescue us from the hand of every foe, ambush along the way, and from all manner of punishments that assemble to come to earth. May You send blessing in our handiwork, and grant us grace, kindness, and mercy in Your eyes and in the eyes of all who see us. May You hear the sound of our humble request because You are God Who hears prayer requests. Blessed are You, Lord, who hears prayer."

For a third time, the women embraced, and Sveshtari finally spoke up. "We really must go, Keturah. Abel has a man at the gate who is expecting us."

"I love you, Eliana! I will pray for you and Asaph every step of the way to Galilee!"

Sveshtari handed the baby off to Abel so he could help Keturah onto the back of the donkey. Then Abel passed the baby to her and led the animal into the darkness. Keturah looked back until Eliana disappeared and all that she could see were the oil lamps flickering through the windows.

## Sveshtari

"Thank you for helping us once again," Sveshtari said to Abel as they headed toward the Essene gate in the southwest corner of the city, where it emptied into the Hinnom Valley. "We make a good team."

"I am honored to help," said Abel. "I have seen you in action the past week, and I am in awe."

"All honor goes to the Lord on High—and to His son, Jesus."

"So, you believe Jesus is the Messiah?"

"I am still learning. Only a month ago, I was worshipping Mars."

"But you and Keturah have become God-fearers?"

"We are learning to be."

Abel laughed. Then he spoke in a whisper so Keturah could not hear. "So, you believe in the one God, Sveshtari, but not in the one *circumcision*?"

God-fearers were Gentile converts, but not full Jews. Sveshtari felt comfortable with this first step into the ancient waters. Becoming a God-fearer meant no circumcision, which Abel found perpetually amusing.

"I find it funny that you can take any wound in battle—but circumcision is a wound too far." Abel burst out laughing.

"You were circumcised at eight days old and have no memory of it." Sveshtari had an edge of irritation to his voice. "Try it at your age now."

"If I did, I wouldn't be leading you out of the city. You would be carrying me out of the city in the back of a wagon." Abel started laughing again.

"I do not know what you two find so funny, but I suggest we be quieter," Keturah called from the back of the donkey. "The gate approaches."

Abel had a friend who kept watch at the Essene Gate; it seemed as if he had friends and contacts everywhere. This friend let them pass, and the group moved out into the Jerusalem night. The sky was clear and filled with stars, as numerous as the children of Abraham.

"When you reach Galilee, will you have a betrothal ceremony?" Abel asked.

"Did anyone ever tell you that you talk too much, Abel?" said Sveshtari.

"All the time. But seriously, how does it work for a God-fearer? Will a rabbi marry you?"

To be honest, Sveshtari did not know the answer. But he and Keturah would marry when they reached Galilee, one way or another. Neither of them had parents alive to seal the contract, so he was not sure how it worked. But they would make it happen.

"The *erusin*, or sanctification of your marriage, must be done in the presence of two male witnesses not related to either of you. Could I be one of those witnesses?"

"Do we have a choice?" Keturah said, laughing.

"Good point," said Abel. "You do not."

They moved slowly through the darkness, turning north and passing along the western edge of Jerusalem, its massive walls to their right, looming over them in the dark. The stars were thick against the black curtain of sky.

"Will you name your first-born son Abel?"

"If it will keep you quiet, we will," said Sveshtari. Abel, Keturah, and the wet nurse all broke into laughter, and the sound carried through the night, echoing against the hills on their left.

## Eliana: Monday

Eliana sat in the corner of Asaph's room, spinning wool, while a physician checked Asaph's wound. It was morning, a sunny day. It would be hot by mid-day, but right now it was the temperature of paradise, and the scent of flowers and fruit trees was strong, drifting in through the window.

"Your husband is healing," said the physician. "Two days ago, I did not think it was possible."

Eliana did not correct the man about their marital status and neither did Asaph. He just smiled at her, as if hearing the word "husband" was the greatest sound.

"Two days ago, the world was very different." Eliana paused in her work and set the small spindle in her lap.

"You are right. Stories about Jesus have been spreading throughout the city."

"And I think they'll keep spreading beyond Jerusalem."

"I think so, too," said the physician. "That is why I have been talking to Jesus's disciples, asking questions about what happened on Friday—and yesterday at the tomb. I want to know how it all unfolded."

"Were you in Jerusalem on Friday, when Jesus was crucified?" Asaph asked the physician.

"No, I was in Jericho. But as soon as I arrived in the city, Joanna told me about Jesus—and about your condition. Did you witness any of what happened?"

"I was in a sewer tunnel."

"A sewer?"

Before the physician could ask any questions about why in the world Asaph was in a sewer tunnel, Eliana blurted out, "I witnessed it all."

The man turned and stared at her, cocking his head. He scratched his beard and bit his lip. "You witnessed it *all*?"

Eliana nodded. "I was there for the trial, the scourging, the crucifixion . . . I saw it all. I would not look away. I forced myself to see everything, to *remember* everything."

The physician glanced at Asaph, as if to ask, "Is your wife telling the truth?"

"She is a determined woman," Asaph said.

"I can see that." The physician looked at Eliana for a few moments before turning back to Asaph. "I am also a historian in addition to a physician. That is why I have been speaking to as many witnesses as I can find before the people scatter. Would it be permissible for me to speak with your wife?"

There was that word: *wife*. Asaph glanced at Eliana, trying to contain his smile. "Yes, Luke. You have my permission."

"Very good!" The physician clapped his hand before saying a final prayer over Asaph. Then Luke stood to leave, shaking the dust from his robe. At the door, he stopped and looked at Eliana. "And you didn't turn away once during the scourging?"

"I did not turn away. Not for a single one of the thirty-nine lashes." Eliana could feel a wave of emotion threatening to break her down, but she held back her feelings.

"Your wife is a remarkable woman," Luke said, and once again Asaph did not correct his use of the word "wife." Neither did Eliana. She liked the sound of it.

Asaph and Eliana shared a smile as she returned to her work. She raised the spindle in the air, connected the new wool to the wool already wrapped around the wooden tool, and began to spin the two pieces. Taking hold of the pointed bottom, she spun the spindle, and it twirled around and around, uniting the two pieces of wool until they became a single, unified piece. Together, the two strands became very strong.

# AUTHOR'S NOTES

I have spent the past few months immersed in the stories of Jesus—specifically, Jesus movies. I've been taking a seminary course about "Jesus at the Movies," and I learned that my novels *Thrones in the Desert* and *Swords in the Desert* are a blend of the two primary approaches in retelling the Greatest Story Ever Told.

The traditional approach has been to harmonize the four Gospels or to tell the story from the viewpoint of one Gospel. This approach goes back to cinema's earliest days, including Cecil B. DeMille's silent movie, *The King of Kings*, in 1927 (which I found surprisingly compelling).

The second approach to telling Jesus's story is best represented by *Ben-Hur*, the blockbuster that won 11 Academy Awards in 1959, including Best Picture. This alternative approach, sometimes called "sword and sandals" stories, does not directly retell the story of Jesus but instead focuses on periphery fictional heroes such as Ben-Hur or on minor Gospel characters such as Barabbas. Other books and films that take this approach include *Quo Vadis* (1951), *The Robe* (1953), and *Barabbas* (1961).

My novels are a blend because they do focus on a single Gospel—Luke. This is the traditional approach. But I also view the Gospel of Luke through the eyes of fictional characters—the sword and sandals approach.

In writing my novels, I have been especially inspired by *Ben-Hur*, although Jesus is much more prominent in my stories. In *Ben-Hur*, Jesus is never directly shown. Instead, we see Jesus's arm as He gives water to an imprisoned Ben-Hur, and sometimes we see Him from behind or from a great distance.

Ironically, even though we don't see much of Jesus in *Ben-Hur*, I found the few scenes of Him more moving than the direct portrayal of Jesus in movies from the same period, such as *The Greatest Story Ever Told* (1965). Part of the problem with many depictions of Jesus is that showing the full humanity and divinity of Christ is a tremendous challenge for any actor or filmmaker—although the more recent movies and series, such as *The Passion of the Christ* (2004) and *The Chosen* (2017), have done a much better job.

However, I didn't choose my approach because of the difficulty of presenting Jesus. For one, it's easier to present Jesus in print than on screen. I chose to tell the Gospel story through the eyes of fictional characters because I didn't think I could put myself in the shoes of Biblical characters, such as the disciples or Mary Magdalene.

I also wanted to avoid fictionalizing any Biblical characters, even though I did a little bit of that when Eliana interacts with Mary and Joanna. But those scenes are few and far between. Almost all the dialogue from Biblical characters in the novel are direct quotes from the Bible.

My goal, Lord willing, is to continue to follow these fictional characters into the Book of Acts, which Luke also authored. Perhaps these characters and their descendants can even progress into the early history of the Church.

I used many sources for both novels. In addition to the *NIV Bible*, here are some of the key resources I used:

*Chronological Aspects of the Life of Christ,* by Harold W. Hoehner. Academic Books, 1977.

*The City in Roman Palestine,* by Daniel Sperber. Oxford University Press, 1998.

*The Crucifixion of the King of Glory,* by Eugenia Scarvelis Constantinou. Ancient Faith Publishing, 2022.

*Daily Life in the Time of Jesus,* by Henri Daniel-Rops. Servant Books, 1961.

*Every Living Thing: Daily Use of Animals in Ancient Israel,* by Oded Borowski. Altimira Press, 1998.

*Herod Antipas: A Contemporary of Jesus Christ,* by Harold W. Hoehner. Zondervan Publishing House, 1972.

*Holman Bible Atlas,* by Thomas V. Brisco. Holman Reference, 1998.

*The Life and Times of Jesus the Messiah,* by Alfred Edersheim. Hendrickson Publishers, 1993.

*Lexham Geographic Commentary on the Gospels,* edited by Barry J. Beitzel and Kristopher A. Lyle. Lexham Press, 2017.

*The New International Commentary on the New Testament: The Gospel of Luke,* by Joel B. Green. William B. Eerdmans Publishing Company, 1997.

*New Testament History,* by F.F. Bruce. Doubleday, 1969.

*Policing the Roman Empire: Soldiers, Administration, and Public Order,* by Christopher J. Fuhrmann. Oxford University Press, 2012.

*The Slave in Greece and Rome,* by Jean Andreau and Raymond Descat. The University of Wisconsin Press, 2006.

*Slavery in the Roman World,* by Sandra R. Joshel. Cambridge University Press, 2010.

*The Wars of the Jews,* by Flavius Josephus, translated by William Whiston. Thomas Nelson, 1998.

*The World Jesus Knew,* by Anne Punton. Monarch Books, 1996.

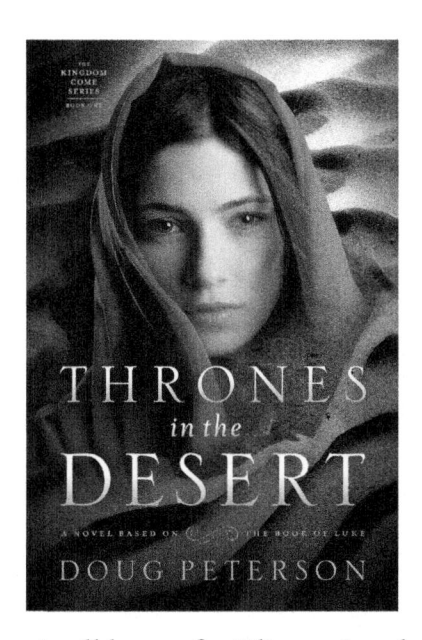

To discover how it all began for Eliana, Asaph, Keturah, and Sveshtari, check out *Thrones in the Desert*.

# ACKNOWLEDGMENTS

Most of my books are dedicated to individuals—beloved friends and family who've shaped my journey. But for *Swords in the Desert*, I'm honoring two institutions that have deeply impacted both this book and its predecessor, *Thrones in the Desert*: Urbana Theological Seminary and Cornerstone Fellowship in Urbana, Illinois.

Behind these institutions are people whose influence runs through every chapter. My journey into the Gospel of Luke began when my pastor at Cornerstone, Seth Kerlin, spent an entire year walking us through it. (Yes, a full year—and I loved every minute of it.)

At Urbana Theological Seminary, I've been auditing classes for over eight years. In that time, I've learned more about Scripture and theology than I did in the previous six decades. Dr. Ken Cuffey's Old and New Testament survey courses opened my eyes in ways I'll always be grateful for. Ken also led a life-changing trip to Israel, where I experienced unforgettable baptisms in the Sea of Galilee beneath a sunset that looked like fireworks.

I'm deeply grateful to those who read early drafts of this manuscript, especially my wife, Nancy, who read it multiple times. My thanks also go to: Heath and Cavan Morber; Vern Fein; my brother, Ric; and my late sister, Kathy.

A special thanks to Alyssa Durst for her thoughtful and thorough editing—and a shout-out to her husband, Pearce, whose "Jesus at the Movies" class gets a mention in the Author's Notes.

Kirk DouPonce, thank you for yet another stunning cover. *Thrones in the Desert* received more compliments for its cover than any of my previous 93 books—no small feat! And to Vincent Davis II, thank you for your guidance through the publishing and promotional process.

Dave and Leanne Lucas—thank you for your enduring friendship and support. And to Scott Irwin, you're not just a trusted friend and prayer partner—you've been an invaluable help every step of the way.

I hope this isn't the final chapter for Eliana, Keturah, Asaph, Sveshtari, and Nekoda. Maybe we'll reunite in the Book of Acts. Can you thank fictional characters? I think you can—and I will. Thank you for letting me tell your stories.

May His Kingdom come.

—Doug Peterson

# ABOUT THE AUTHOR

Doug Peterson is the award-winning author of 94 books, including 8 historical novels, 21 comic books (and counting), and over 40 children's books for the best-selling VeggieTales series.

Doug's passion for writing can be traced to grade school, when he ran his own media empire, publishing the monthly *Peterson Popper* magazine and *The Weekly Waste* newspaper (with a circulation of three). By the time he was in fourth grade, he had written and bound dozens of his own books, including such classics as *20,000 Leagues Under a Swimming Pool* and *In Cold Ketchup* (real titles).

Doug graduated with a journalism degree from the University of Illinois in 1977 and did a short stint as the editor of a small, weekly Wisconsin newspaper. (Their motto: "This is Wisconsin, so we pay you in cheese.") Fearing that he might be forced to root for the Packers, Doug and his wife returned to the University of Illinois in 1979, where he began work as a science writer and half-time freelance writer and has remained for over 40 years.

Doug's VeggieTales book *The Slobfather* won the 2004 Gold Medallion Award for preschool books, and he was co-storywriter for the best-selling video *Larry-Boy and the Rumor Weed*. His popular short story, "The

Career of Horville Sash," was made into a music video featuring Grammy-winner Jennifer Warnes, and he co-wrote "Roman Ruins," an episode in the bestselling line of How to Host a Murder party games.

Doug has a love for history, so he made the transition to historical novels with *The Disappearing Man*, published by Bay Forest Books in 2011 and chosen by Canton, Ohio, for its One Book, One Community program. His first Civil War book, *The Lincoln League*, is scheduled to go into film production in 2026.

A versatile writer, Doug co-authored two stage plays—one based on Dietrich Bonhoeffer, the Church's voice of resistance in Germany during World War II, and the other about the improbable friendship between Benjamin Franklin and evangelist George Whitefield.

Most recently, he was hired to write an extensive series of comic books on American history, illustrated by Marvel and DC artists. His non-fiction work includes the popular book *Of Moose and Men*, co-written with Tennessee comedian Torry Martin, and *Back to the Futures*, co-written with ag economist Scott Irwin.

Doug has been married for 49 years and has two sons and four grandchildren. He and his wife live in Champaign, Illinois.

# OTHER TITLES

DOUG PETERSON
A BERLIN MYSTERY
THE PUZZLE PEOPLE

Printed in Great Britain
by Amazon